W9-AKH-221

Dante's Divine Comedy

HELL ≈ PURGATORY ≈ PARADISE

DANTE ALIGHIERI

Dante Alighieri

Dante's DIVINE COMEDY
HELL ~ PURGATORY ~ PARADISE

by Dante Alighieri

With illustrations by
Gustave Doré

Edited and with introductory text by
Anna Amari-Parker

CHARTWELL
BOOKS, INC.

This edition printed in 2010 by
CHARTWELL BOOKS, INC.
A Division of **BOOK SALES, INC.**
276 Fifth Avenue Suite 206
New York, New York 10001 USA

Copyright © 2006 Arcturus Publishing Limited
26/27 Bickels Yard, 151–153 Bermondsey Street,
London SE1 3HA

All rights reserved. No part of this publication may be reproduced,
stored in a retrieval system, or transmitted, in any form or by
any means, electronic, mechanical, photocopying, recording or
otherwise, without written permission in accordance with the
provisions of the Copyright Act 1956 (as amended). Any person or
persons who do any unauthorised act in relation to this publication
may be liable to criminal prosecution and civil claims for damages.

ISBN-13: 978-0-7858-2120-5
ISBN-10: 0-7858-2120-1
AD000153EN

Printed in China

Contents & List Of Plates

Purgatorio 164

Paradiso 286

Introduction

DANTE ALIGHIERI (1265–1321) was born into a noble Florentine family in a city torn apart by rival clans. While feudal aristocracy backed imperial authority (Ghibellines), the Alighieri family supported the pope (Guelphs). Their party eventually splintered into hostile White and Black factions. Offended by Pope Boniface VIII's interference in secular affairs, Dante, too, became embroiled in this sectarianism and joined the White Guelphs. He was banished following the Black Guelph victory of 1302. Although he enjoyed the patronage of powerful northern Italian princes, his future political allegiances were misguided. He died in exile in Ravenna in 1321.

The Divine Comedy, the first book to be written in the Italian *vulgare* instead of Latin, was begun in 1308 and contains three *cantiche* – *Inferno* (Hell), *Purgatorio* (Purgatory) and *Paradiso* (Paradise) – written in *terza rima*, a verse scheme of three-line stanzas with interlocking rhyme patterns (aba, bcb, cdc, and so on). Dante's influences included the classics, the neo-Platonists, Aristotle, natural philosophy and theology. The *Inferno's* opening canto is a microcosm of the entire work and its topography prefigures the three realms of the soul's afterlife: the dark wood (Hell), the barren slope (Mount Purgatory) and the blissful mountain (Paradise).

The epic poem juxtaposes human privation, injustice and imperfection with divine freedom, justice and perfection. Dante's allegorical theme of God's gradual revelation to an unsuspecting, unprepared pilgrim beautifully illustrates the concept of the rational human soul choosing salvation of its own free will. The use of real-life characters, autobiographical detail, personal failures and triumphs, sophisticated eschatological discourse and the denunciation of contemporary politics renders the poem unique. The images remain unsurpassed – galloping centaurs, devils, chained giants, cannibalism, dazzling angels,

supernatural rivers and trees, configurations of lights and a heavenly stadium.

The symbolism of each realm with its various landscapes, rivers, guardians, inhabitants, pageants and dramas, combined with important number patterns (seven terraces, nymphs and capital sins; the Trinity; Lucifer's three faces; Cerberus' three heads; the heavenly trio (Mary, Lucy and Matilda); three theological virtues; the triune nature of Geryon; and three beasts and three Furies), gives the poem a tight complexity.

The technique of having two Dante characters, the Poet and the Pilgrim, allows the narrative to reach out to the universal reader whilst operating on a personal level. During his spiritual journey, the pilgrim participates in the sin of every sinner, the penance of every repentant soul and the bliss of the blessed – he is Everyman. Sometimes his pity is stirred by the damned – many sinners try to trick him (*Inf.* V) and each other (*Inf.* XXI–XXIII) – which threatens his safety. Exchanges in Hell are hurried, devious and insincere, in marked contrast with the stoical patience of Purgatory and Heaven's peaceful eternity.

Beatrice's intervention when the pilgrim is lost and contemplating suicide (*Inf.* I) reveals that benign forces have authorized the whole pilgrimage. God's supervision is also evident from the events paralleling the Advents of Christ: the arrival of the angel at the gates of Dis (*Inf.* IX) is like the First Coming or Christ's Harrowing of Hell; the pair of angels making their descent into the valley (*Purg.* VIII) is like the Second Coming or Christ entering Christian hearts; and Beatrice appears in the Earthly Paradise (*Purg.* XXX) like the Third Coming or Final Judgment.

Virgil and Beatrice embody qualities that change with major shifts in the narrative. Where logic is required over faith (Hell), Virgil is a wonderful personification of reason or human wisdom: he wards off danger and shows the way in spite of his pre-Christian limitations (*Inf.* IX). Where faith supersedes reason, he fades into the background (*Purg.* III) and feels self-conscious (*Purg.* VII, XXI), his answers limited by a lack of Christian knowledge (*Purg.* VI). Stepping in to pass judgment on the pilgrim after he has been crowned and mitred by Virgil is Beatrice (*Purg.* XXVII). She appears on the pageant's chariot as the Sacrament of the Body of Christ in the Church. No longer just an earthly model of beauty and courtesy, she now embodies divine wisdom, revelation and grace (*Purg.* XXX) and in her eyes is reflected the dual nature of Christ in the Griffin (*Purg.* XXXI).

Hell (*Inferno*)

Dante categorizes sin as being without malice (Incontinence) or with malicious intent (Violence or Fraud). Cowardice and indecisiveness escape this dichotomy and are marginalized within Limbo. Heresy is in a kind of no-man's land as it refutes Christian reality and the soul's immortality yet does not involve sinful action. Hell, under the city of Jerusalem in the Northern Hemisphere, extends funnel-like into the earth's core. Dante and Virgil are forced to climb down Lucifer's body because Mount Purgatory lies in the opposite (Southern) Hemisphere.

The pilgrim's behaviour sometimes mirrors that of the damned – for example, he chooses not to interact with the Indecisives (*Inf.* III); he compares his excusable vandalism of church property with Boniface's inexcusable destruction of the Church's foundations (*Inf.* XIX); and the language he uses when conversing with the Thieves suggests that he is contributing to the transformations themselves (*Inf.* XXIV).

Here are a few examples of *contrapasso* (the logical relationship between punishment and offence). The Suicides severed ties with their body so they will be denied human form on Judgment Day (*Inf.* XIII). The Profligates, who were violently wasteful, are chased and torn by dogs through trees because property was seen as an extension of the body and this kind of violence was tantamount to suicide (*Inf.* XIII). The Flatterers are immersed in their verbal diarrhoea (*Inf.* XVIII). The Simonists are given inverted baptisms with fire to illustrate their ecclesiastical perversion (*Inf.* XIX). The Benedictine garb of the Hypocrites condemns their false piety (*Inf.* XXIII) whilst the Thieves' multiple transformations parody reincarnation and reflect their inability to separate 'mine' from 'thine' (*Inf.* XXV). Fraudulent, silver-tongued rhetoric is condemned by the flaming tongues that consume the evil counsellors (*Inf.* XXVI–XXVII) while those who divided institutions, communities and families are ripped open (*Inf.* XXVIII). The corrosive influence of falsification on metals (Alchemists), money (Counterfeiters), identity (Imposters) and truth (Liars) is fittingly expressed through the diseased state of their bodies and minds (*Inf.* XIX–XXX).

Church doctrine unfolds within a dark, noisy, smelly and antagonistic panorama where teachings are witnessed through the actions of sinners. As the pilgrim progresses through Purgatory on his way to Paradise, learning more and more by example, he hears long discourses about philosophical and theological doctrine from his teachers (Virgil, Beatrice, Statius, Lucy, Saint Bernard) until his faith comes to be examined by three of the Apostles (Peter, James and John).

Purgatory (*Purgatorio*)

Hell and Heaven are eternal states. Purgatory is a place of transition where souls do penance and are in contact with the living (*Purg.* XXXIII). Death's second kingdom is courteous yet disciplined with a gatekeeper at Peter's Gate, the Rule of the Mountain and angel guardians stationed all the way up the terraces to the

Earthly Paradise. It is fitting that the journey from Ante-Purgatory to the First Cornice should be the most arduous.

The mood is one of joy – lovers are reunited and all souls are bound for Heaven – but there is melancholy and austerity here as well because acute contrition is required to purge the stain of capital sin. Rituals to eradicate its root include penitence (*Purg.* IX, XXXI), a seven-fold pardon and two baptisms – one by water (*Purg.* XXXIII), the other by fire (*Purg.* XXVII). In a reversal of *Inf.* XVI, when Virgil cast off his pupil's cord (foolish self-confidence) before entering Lower Hell, the pilgrim girds himself with a reed (*Purg.* I) to clothe his spirit in humility.

Everywhere there is the promise of God's love: in visions of the Host (the Sun, Beatrice riding the chariot), Cato's face (*Purg.* I), the ship of souls (*Purg.* II), the murmur of prayer and angelic voices, the pageants (*Purg.* XXIX, XXX, XXXII) and the seven terrace warders. Punishment is borne willingly. On every cornice, penitence comprises the penance itself followed by a meditation made up of the Whip (examples of the opposing virtue) and the Bridle (deterrent examples of the sin), plus a prayer, a benediction and the pardon of the angel.

Paradise (*Paradiso*)

The structure of the heavenly ascent is based on the accepted Ptolemaic model – seven concentric planetary spheres revolving around the Earth. Beyond Saturn, the planets are enclosed in the Starry Heaven, where changeless angelic intelligences control the motion and order of the visible universe circling around the Primum Mobile, which is motionless. The abode of God, the Empyrean or Tenth Heaven, lies beyond time, space and movement.

Dante places different groups of souls on each level to represent the stages of spiritual advancement that are possible through the active and the contemplative life. This arrangement does not physically exist of course – all souls share one God and one Heaven and are not

attached to a particular sphere (*Par.* IV) – but it is part of God's plan to provide some sort of sequence so that the pilgrim may be able to grasp a fragment of the ultimate reality of it all.

The tone of Paradise is at once liturgical, lyrical and scientific, dominated by the presence of light, song, discourse, visions and revelations. A sense of harmony, of spirits united in love and will, is reflected in the encounters and conversations with the souls (manifested as light forms) who speak, sing or blush in anger at humanity's earthly wrongdoings. The blessedness of unity with God is conveyed in those cantos where souls are not presented individually but as part of a symbolic figure or a larger whole: the double configuration of lights (*Par.* XII–XIII), the ruby-studded Cross (*Par.* XIV–XV), the eagle of justice (*Par.* XIX–XX), the ladder (*Par.* XXI), the lit-up message (*Par.* XVIII) and, finally, the mystic rose (*Par.* XXX–XXXII).

Paradise is a blinding vision beyond human comprehension where words fall short yet astounding lucidity prevails: the indescribable beauty of Beatrice's face when the Empyrean momentarily shines through her (*Par.* III); the radiance of the blessed wearing their body of glory (*Par.* XXXII); Dante gazing into the divine light and seeing the created universe in its entirety (*Par.* XXXIII); the mystery of the Holy Trinity expressed through geometric perfection (*Par.* XXXIII).

Anna Amari-Parker, 2006

Inferno

At the age of thirty-five Dante is lost in a dark forest, having missed the 'straightforward way'. The way to salvation is symbolized by the sun behind the mountain but it is barred by a Leopard, a Lion and a She-Wolf. The beasts represent different sins. After Dante's love, Beatrice, intercedes on his behalf he is joined by the poet Virgil, who becomes his guide through the underworld. They cross the Acheron, on Charon's ferry, and reach the Gate of Hell. From there they descend through the nine Circles of Hell, each circle representing a different sin. The punishments are chillingly appropriate. They finally reach the lake of ice where the three-headed Lucifer resides. Each head is chewing a sinner (Judas, Brutus and Cassius). The pair escape by climbing down Lucifer's furry legs. After passing through the centre of the Earth, they emerge to 'rebehold the stars'.

Contents

Canto I

In the middle of his life, Dante has left the 'straightforward pathway' and is lost in a dark forest. He tries to regain the path by climbing a mountain but his way is barred by a Leopard, a Lion and a She-Wolf. Each creature represents a different sin. Virgil appears and offers to show him another way, one that leads through Hell and Purgatory. After that, a 'more worthy' guide (Beatrice) will lead him to Paradise: Virgil, as a Pagan, is not allowed to go there. Dante gladly adopts Virgil as his leader.

Midway upon the journey of our life
  I found myself within a forest dark,
  For the straightforward pathway had been lost.

Ah me! how hard a thing it is to say
  What was this forest savage, rough, and stern,
  Which in the very thought renews the fear.

So bitter is it, death is little more;
  But of the good to treat, which there I found,
  Speak will I of the other things I saw there.

I cannot well repeat how there I entered,
  So full was I of slumber at the moment
  In which I had abandoned the true way.

But after I had reached a mountain's foot,
  At that point where the valley terminated,
  Which had with consternation pierced my heart,

Upward I looked, and I beheld its shoulders,
  Vested already with that planet's rays
  Which leadeth others right by every road.

Then was the fear a little quieted
  That in my heart's lake had endured throughout
  The night, which I had passed so piteously.

And even as he, who, with distressful breath,
  Forth issued from the sea upon the shore,
  Turns to the water perilous and gazes;

So did my soul, that still was fleeing onward,
  Turn itself back to re-behold the pass
  Which never yet a living person left.

After my weary body I had rested,
  The way resumed I on the desert slope,
  So that the firm foot ever was the lower.

And lo! almost where the ascent began,
  A panther light and swift exceedingly,
  Which with a spotted skin was covered o'er!

And never moved she from before my face,
  Nay, rather did impede so much my way,
  That many times I to return had turned.

The time was the beginning of the morning,
  And up the sun was mounting with those stars
  That with him were, what time the Love Divine

At first in motion set those beauteous things;
  So were to me occasion of good hope,
  The variegated skin of that wild beast,

The hour of time, and the delicious season;
  But not so much, that did not give me fear
  A lion's aspect which appeared to me.

He seemed as if against me he were coming
  With head uplifted, and with ravenous hunger,
  So that it seemed the air was afraid of him;

And a she-wolf, that with all hungerings
  Seemed to be laden in her meagreness,
  And many folk has caused to live forlorn!

She brought upon me so much heaviness,
  With the affright that from her aspect came,
  That I the hope relinquished of the height.

And as he is who willingly acquires,
  And the time comes that causes him to lose,
  Who weeps in all his thoughts and is despondent,

E'en such made me that beast withouten peace,
  Which, coming on against me by degrees
  Thrust me back thither where the sun is silent.

Midway upon the journey of our life / I found myself within a forest dark, /
For the straightforward pathway had been lost.

Inf. I, lines 1–3

And lo! almost where the ascent began, / A panther light and swift exceedingly, /
Which with a spotted skin was covered o'er!

Inf. I, lines 31-33

He seemed as if against me he were coming / With head uplifted, and with ravenous hunger,

Inf. I, lines 46-47

While I was rushing downward to the lowland,
  Before mine eyes did one present himself,
  Who seemed from long-continued silence hoarse.

When I beheld him in the desert vast,
  "Have pity on me," unto him I cried,
  "Whiche'er thou art, or shade or real man!"

He answered me: "Not man; man once I was,
  And both my parents were of Lombardy,
  And Mantuans by country both of them.

'Sub Julio' was I born, though it was late,
  And lived at Rome under the good Augustus,
  During the time of false and lying gods.

A poet was I, and I sang that just
  Son of Anchises, who came forth from Troy,
  After that Ilion the superb was burned.

But thou, why goest thou back to such annoyance?
  Why climb'st thou not the Mount Delectable,
  Which is the source and cause of every joy?"

"Now, art thou that Virgilius and that fountain
  Which spreads abroad so wide a river of speech?"
  I made response to him with bashful forehead.

"O, of the other poets honour and light,
  Avail me the long study and great love
  That have impelled me to explore thy volume!

Thou art my master, and my author thou,
  Thou art alone the one from whom I took
  The beautiful style that has done honour to me.

Behold the beast, for which I have turned back;
  Do thou protect me from her, famous Sage,
  For she doth make my veins and pulses tremble."

"Thee it behoves to take another road,"
  Responded he, when he beheld me weeping,
  "If from this savage place thou wouldst escape;

Because this beast, at which thou criest out,
  Suffers not any one to pass her way,
  But so doth harass him, that she destroys him;

And has a nature so malign and ruthless,
  That never doth she glut her greedy will,
  And after food is hungrier than before.

Many the animals with whom she weds,
  And more they shall be still, until the Greyhound
  Comes, who shall make her perish in her pain.

He shall not feed on either earth or pelf,
  But upon wisdom, and on love and virtue;
  'Twixt Feltro and Feltro shall his nation be;

Of that low Italy shall he be the saviour,
  On whose account the maid Camilla died,
  Euryalus, Turnus, Nisus, of their wounds;

Through every city shall he hunt her down,
  Until he shall have driven her back to Hell,
  There from whence envy first did let her loose.

Therefore I think and judge it for thy best
  Thou follow me, and I will be thy guide,
  And lead thee hence through the eternal place,

Where thou shalt hear the desperate lamentations,
  Shalt see the ancient spirits disconsolate,
  Who cry out each one for the second death;

And thou shalt see those who contented are
  Within the fire, because they hope to come,
  Whene'er it may be, to the blessed people;

To whom, then, if thou wishest to ascend,
  A soul shall be for that than I more worthy;
  With her at my departure I will leave thee;

Because that Emperor, who reigns above,
  In that I was rebellious to his law,
  Wills that through me none come into his city.

He governs everywhere, and there he reigns;
  There is his city and his lofty throne;
  O happy he whom thereto he elects!"

And I to him: "Poet, I thee entreat,
  By that same God whom thou didst never know,
  So that I may escape this woe and worse,

Thou wouldst conduct me there where thou hast said,
  That I may see the portal of Saint Peter,
  And those thou makest so disconsolate."

Then he moved on, and I behind him followed.

"Behold the beast, for which I have turned back; / Do thou protect me from her, famous Sage,"

Inf. I, lines 88–89

Then he moved on, and I behind him followed.

Inf. I, line 136

Canto II

*The end of the day has come and Dante is having doubts. He does not feel
worthy enough to undertake his journey. Virgil accuses him of cowardice and
tells of how the Virgin Mary turned to Saint Lucia, who in turn asked for
Beatrice, Dante's love, to go down into Limbo, where Virgil resides. There
Beatrice, with 'voice angelical', asked Virgil to assist Dante, whose way was
impeded. At this, Dante is heartened, and declares to Virgil that 'one sole will
is in us both'.*

Day was departing, and the embrowned air
  Released the animals that are on Earth
  From their fatigues; and I the only one

Made myself ready to sustain the war,
  Both of the way and likewise of the woe,
  Which memory that errs not shall retrace.

O Muses, O high genius, now assist me!
  O memory, that didst write down what I saw,
  Here thy nobility shall be manifest!

And I began: "Poet, who guidest me,
  Regard my manhood, if it be sufficient,
  Ere to the arduous pass thou dost confide me.

Thou sayest, that of Silvius the parent,
  While yet corruptible, unto the world
  Immortal went, and was there bodily.

But if the adversary of all evil
  Was courteous, thinking of the high effect
  That issue would from him, and who, and what,

To men of intellect unmeet it seems not;
  For he was of great Rome, and of her empire
  In the empyreal heaven as father chosen;

The which and what, wishing to speak the truth,
  Were stablished as the holy place, wherein
  Sits the successor of the greatest Peter.

Upon this journey, whence thou givest him vaunt,
  Things did he hear, which the occasion were
  Both of his victory and the papal mantle.

Thither went afterwards the Chosen Vessel,
  To bring back comfort thence unto that Faith,
  Which of salvation's way is the beginning.

But I, why thither come, or who concedes it?
  I not Aeneas am, I am not Paul,
  Nor I, nor others, think me worthy of it.

Therefore, if I resign myself to come,
  I fear the coming may be ill-advised;
  Thou'rt wise, and knowest better than I speak."

And as he is, who unwills what he willed,
  And by new thoughts doth his intention change,
  So that from his design he quite withdraws,

Such I became, upon that dark hillside,
  Because, in thinking, I consumed the emprise,
  Which was so very prompt in the beginning.

"If I have well thy language understood,"
  Replied that shade of the Magnanimous,
  "Thy soul attainted is with cowardice,

Which many times a man encumbers so,
  It turns him back from honoured enterprise,
  As false sight doth a beast, when he is shy.

That thou mayst free thee from this apprehension,
  I'll tell thee why I came, and what I heard
  At the first moment when I grieved for thee.

Among those was I who are in suspense,
  And a fair, saintly Lady called to me
  In such wise, I besought her to command me.

Day was departing,

Her eyes were shining brighter than the Star;
  And she began to say, gentle and low,
  With voice angelical, in her own language:

'O spirit courteous of Mantua,
  Of whom the fame still in the world endures,
  And shall endure, long-lasting as the world;

A friend of mine, and not the friend of fortune,
  Upon the desert slope is so impeded
  Upon his way, that he has turned through terror,

And may, I fear, already be so lost,
  That I too late have risen to his succour,
  From that which I have heard of him in Heaven.

Bestir thee now, and with thy speech ornate,
  And with what needful is for his release,
  Assist him so, that I may be consoled.

Beatrice am I, who do bid thee go;
  I come from there, where I would fain return;
  Love moved me, which compelleth me to speak.

When I shall be in presence of my Lord,
  Full often will I praise thee unto him.'
  Then paused she, and thereafter I began:

'O Lady of virtue, thou alone through whom
  The human race exceedeth all contained
  Within the heaven that has the lesser circles,

So grateful unto me is thy commandment,
  To obey, if 'twere already done, were late;
  No farther need'st thou ope to me thy wish.

But the cause tell me why thou dost not shun
  The here descending down into this centre,
  From the vast place thou burnest to return to.'

'Since thou wouldst fain so inwardly discern,
  Briefly will I relate,' she answered me,
  'Why I am not afraid to enter here.

Of those things only should one be afraid
  Which have the power of doing others harm;
  Of the rest, no; because they are not fearful.

God in his mercy such created me
  That misery of yours attains me not,
  Nor any flame assails me of this burning.

A gentle Lady is in Heaven, who grieves
  At this impediment, to which I send thee,
  So that stern judgment there above is broken.

In her entreaty she besought Lucia,
  And said, "Thy faithful one now stands in need
  Of thee, and unto thee I recommend him."

Lucia, foe of all that cruel is,
  Hastened away, and came unto the place
  Where I was sitting with the ancient Rachel.

"Beatrice" said she, "the true praise of God,
  Why succourest thou not him, who loved thee so,
  For thee he issued from the vulgar herd?

Dost thou not hear the pity of his plaint?
  Dost thou not see the death that combats him
  Beside that flood, where ocean has no vaunt?"

Never were persons in the world so swift
  To work their weal and to escape their woe,
  As I, after such words as these were uttered,

Came hither downward from my blessed seat,
  Confiding in thy dignified discourse,
  Which honours thee, and those who've listened to it.'

After she thus had spoken unto me,
  Weeping, her shining eyes she turned away;
  Whereby she made me swifter in my coming;

And unto thee I came, as she desired;
  I have delivered thee from that wild beast,
  Which barred the beautiful mountain's short ascent.

What is it, then? Why, why dost thou delay?
  Why is such baseness bedded in thy heart?
  Daring and hardihood why hast thou not,

Seeing that three such Ladies benedight
  Are caring for thee in the court of Heaven,
  And so much good my speech doth promise thee?"

Even as the flowerets, by nocturnal chill,
  Bowed down and closed, when the sun whitens them,
  Uplift themselves all open on their stems;

Such I became with my exhausted strength,
  And such good courage to my heart there coursed,
  That I began, like an intrepid person:

"Beatrice am I, who do bid thee go;"

Inf. II, line 70

"O she compassionate, who succoured me,
 And courteous thou, who hast obeyed so soon
 The words of truth which she addressed to thee!

Thou hast my heart so with desire disposed
 To the adventure, with these words of thine,
 That to my first intent I have returned.

Now go, for one sole will is in us both,
 Thou Leader, and thou Lord, and Master thou."
 Thus said I to him; and when he had moved,

I entered on the deep and savage way.

Canto III

As Dante and Virgil enter Hell's ante-chamber, they see words inscribed above its gate and hear the cries of the Indecisive, the first group of damned souls. These moral 'cowards', rejected by Heaven yet ignored by Hell, have to chase a banner whilst being plagued by hornets and flies. Charon the Boatman refuses to carry Dante, a living soul, across the river Acheron on Hell's outer boundary, but Virgil declares that Heaven wills it. A fierce wind picks up and Dante swoons.

"Through me the way is to the city dolent;
 Through me the way is to eternal dole;
 Through me the way among the people lost.

Justice incited my sublime Creator;
 Created me divine Omnipotence,
 The highest Wisdom and the primal Love.

Before me there were no created things,
 Only eterne, and I eternal last.
 All hope abandon, ye who enter in!"

These words in sombre colour I beheld
 Written upon the summit of a gate;
 Whence I: "Their sense is, Master, hard to me!"

And he to me, as one experienced:
 "Here all suspicion needs must be abandoned,
 All cowardice must needs be here extinct.

We to the place have come, where I have told thee
 Thou shalt behold the people dolorous
 Who have foregone the good of intellect."

And after he had laid his hand on mine
 With joyful mien, whence I was comforted,
 He led me in among the secret things.

There sighs, complaints, and ululations loud
 Resounded through the air without a star,
 Whence I, at the beginning, wept thereat.

Languages diverse, horrible dialects,
 Accents of anger, words of agony,
 And voices high and hoarse, with sound of hands,

Made up a tumult that goes whirling on
 For ever in that air for ever black,
 Even as the sand doth, when the whirlwind breathes.

And I, who had my head with horror bound,
 Said: "Master, what is this which now I hear?
 What folk is this, which seems by pain so vanquished?"

And he to me: "This miserable mode
 Maintain the melancholy souls of those
 Who lived withouten infamy or praise.

Commingled are they with that caitiff choir
 Of Angels, who have not rebellious been,
 Nor faithful were to God, but were for self.

The heavens expelled them, not to be less fair;
 Nor them the nethermore abyss receives,
 For glory none the damned would have from them."

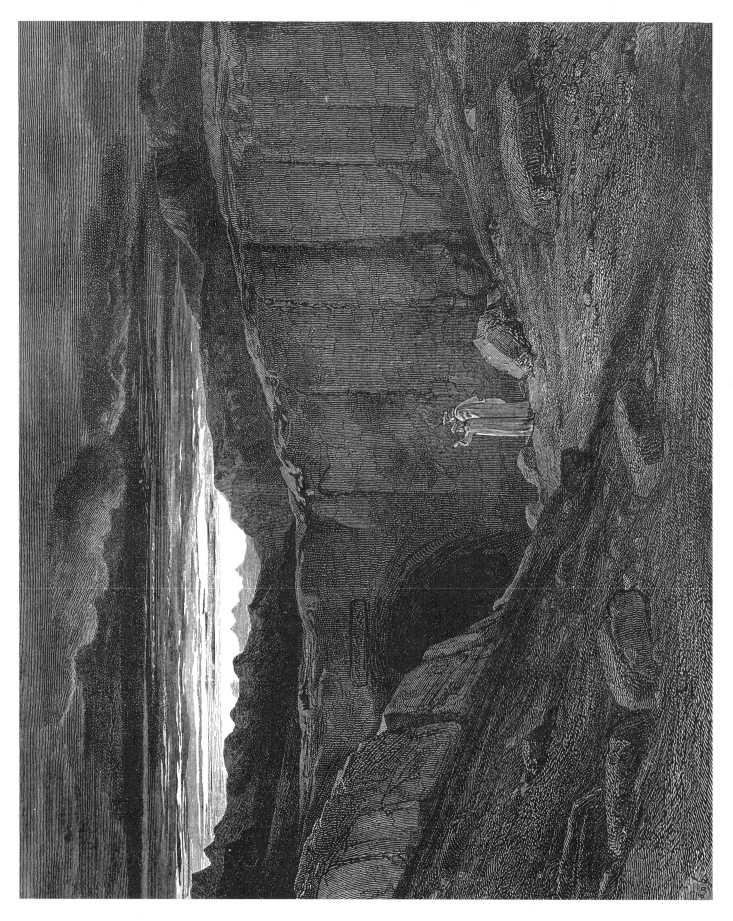

"All hope abandon, ye who enter in!"

Inf. III, line 9

And I: "O Master, what so grievous is
  To these, that maketh them lament so sore?"
  He answered: "I will tell thee very briefly.

These have no longer any hope of death;
  And this blind life of theirs is so debased,
  They envious are of every other fate.

No fame of them the world permits to be;
  Misericord and Justice both disdain them.
  Let us not speak of them, but look, and pass."

And I, who looked again, beheld a banner,
  Which, whirling round, ran on so rapidly,
  That of all pause it seemed to me indignant;

And after it there came so long a train
  Of people, that I ne'er would have believed
  That ever Death so many had undone.

When some among them I had recognised,
  I looked, and I beheld the shade of him
  Who made through cowardice the great refusal.

Forthwith I comprehended, and was certain,
  That this the sect was of the caitiff wretches
  Hateful to God and to his enemies.

These miscreants, who never were alive,
  Were naked, and were stung exceedingly
  By gadflies and by hornets that were there.

These did their faces irrigate with blood,
  Which, with their tears commingled, at their feet
  By the disgusting worms was gathered up.

And when to gazing farther I betook me,
  People I saw on a great river's bank;
  Whence said I: "Master, now vouchsafe to me,

That I may know who these are, and what law
  Makes them appear so ready to pass over,
  As I discern athwart the dusky light."

And he to me: "These things shall all be known
  To thee, as soon as we our footsteps stay
  Upon the dismal shore of Acheron."

Then with mine eyes ashamed and downward cast,
  Fearing my words might irksome be to him,
  From speech refrained I till we reached the river.

And lo! towards us coming in a boat
  An old man, hoary with the hair of eld,
  Crying: "Woe unto you, ye souls depraved!

Hope nevermore to look upon the heavens;
  I come to lead you to the other shore,
  To the eternal shades in heat and frost.

And thou, that yonder standest, living soul,
  Withdraw thee from these people, who are dead!"
  But when he saw that I did not withdraw,

He said: "By other ways, by other ports
  Thou to the shore shalt come, not here, for passage;
  A lighter vessel needs must carry thee."

And unto him the Guide: "Vex thee not, Charon;
  It is so willed there where is power to do
  That which is willed; and farther question not."

Thereat were quieted the fleecy cheeks
  Of him the ferryman of the livid fen,
  Who round about his eyes had wheels of flame.

But all those souls who weary were and naked
  Their colour changed and gnashed their teeth
                                        together,
  As soon as they had heard those cruel words.

God they blasphemed and their progenitors,
  The human race, the place, the time, the seed
  Of their engendering and of their birth!

Thereafter all together they drew back,
  Bitterly weeping, to the accursed shore,
  Which waiteth every man who fears not God.

Charon the demon, with the eyes of glede,
  Beckoning to them, collects them all together,
  Beats with his oar whoever lags behind.

As in the autumn-time the leaves fall off,
  First one and then another, till the branch
  Unto the earth surrenders all its spoils;

In similar wise the evil seed of Adam
  Throw themselves from that margin one by one,
  At signals, as a bird unto its lure.

So they depart across the dusky wave,
  And ere upon the other side they land,
  Again on this side a new troop assembles.

And lo! towards us coming in a boat / An old man, hoary with the hair of eld, /
Crying: "Woe unto you, ye souls depraved!"

Inf. III, lines 82–84

Charon the demon, with the eyes of glede, / Beckoning to them, collects them all together, /
Beats with his oar whoever lags behind.

Inf. III, lines 109–111

"My son," the courteous Master said to me,
  "All those who perish in the wrath of God
  Here meet together out of every land;

And ready are they to pass o'er the river,
  Because celestial Justice spurs them on,
  So that their fear is turned into desire.

This way there never passes a good soul;
  And hence if Charon doth complain of thee,
  Well mayst thou know now what his speech imports."

This being finished, all the dusk champaign
  Trembled so violently, that of that terror
  The recollection bathes me still with sweat.

The land of tears gave forth a blast of wind,
  And fulminated a vermilion light,
  Which overmastered in me every sense,

And as a man whom sleep hath seized I fell.

Canto IV

*Virgil shows Dante the mournful shadows of virtuous non-Christians like himself who
haunt Limbo, Hell's First Circle, and suffer the spiritual torment of forever seeking
God in vain. Virgil speaks about Christ's descent into Hell and his salvation of several
Old Testament patriarchs. A glowing light reveals four other great pagan figures –
Homer, Horace, Ovid and Lucan. The pilgrim perceives a splendid castle of light in the
distance, where the most renowned non-Christian philosophers, poets and warriors dwell.*

Broke the deep lethargy within my head
  A heavy thunder, so that I upstarted,
  Like to a person who by force is wakened;

And round about I moved my rested eyes,
  Uprisen erect, and steadfastly I gazed,
  To recognise the place wherein I was.

True is it, that upon the verge I found me
  Of the abysmal valley dolorous,
  That gathers thunder of infinite ululations.

Obscure, profound it was, and nebulous,
  So that by fixing on its depths my sight
  Nothing whatever I discerned therein.

"Let us descend now into the blind world,"
  Began the Poet, pallid utterly;
  "I will be first, and thou shalt second be."

And I, who of his colour was aware,
  Said: "How shall I come, if thou art afraid,
  Who'rt wont to be a comfort to my fears?"

And he to me: "The anguish of the people
  Who are below here in my face depicts
  That pity which for terror thou hast taken.

Let us go on, for the long way impels us."
  Thus he went in, and thus he made me enter
  The foremost circle that surrounds the abyss.

There, as it seemed to me from listening,
  Were lamentations none, but only sighs,
  That tremble made the everlasting air.

And this arose from sorrow without torment,
  Which the crowds had, that many were and great,
  Of infants and of women and of men.

To me the Master good: "Thou dost not ask
  What spirits these, which thou beholdest, are?
  Now will I have thee know, ere thou go farther,

That they sinned not; and if they merit had,
  'Tis not enough, because they had not baptism
  Which is the portal of the Faith thou holdest;

And if they were before Christianity,
  In the right manner they adored not God;
  And among such as these am I myself.

For such defects, and not for other guilt,
  Lost are we and are only so far punished,
  That without hope we live on in desire."

Great grief seized on my heart when this I heard,
  Because some people of much worthiness
  I knew, who in that Limbo were suspended.

"Tell me, my Master, tell me, thou my Lord,"
  Began I, with desire of being certain
  Of that Faith which o'ercometh every error,

"Came any one by his own merit hence,
  Or by another's, who was blessed thereafter?"
  And he, who understood my covert speech,

Replied: "I was a novice in this state,
  When I saw hither come a Mighty One,
  With sign of victory incoronate.

Hence he drew forth the shade of the First Parent,
  And that of his son Abel, and of Noah,
  Of Moses the lawgiver, and the obedient

Abraham, patriarch, and David, king,
  Israel with his father and his children,
  And Rachel, for whose sake he did so much,

And others many, and he made them blessed;
  And thou must know, that earlier than these
  Never were any human spirits saved."

We ceased not to advance because he spake,
  But still were passing onward through the forest,
  The forest, say I, of thick-crowded ghosts.

Not very far as yet our way had gone
  This side the summit, when I saw a fire
  That overcame a hemisphere of darkness.

We were a little distant from it still,
  But not so far that I in part discerned not
  That honourable people held that place.

"O thou who honourest every art and science,
  Who may these be, which such great honour have,
  That from the fashion of the rest it parts them?"

And he to me: "The honourable name,
  That sounds of them above there in thy life,
  Wins grace in Heaven, that so advances them."

In the mean time a voice was heard by me:
  "All honour be to the pre-eminent Poet;
  His shade returns again, that was departed."

After the voice had ceased and quiet was,
  Four mighty shades I saw approaching us;
  Semblance had they nor sorrowful nor glad.

To say to me began my gracious Master:
  "Him with that falchion in his hand behold,
  Who comes before the three, even as their lord.

That one is Homer, Poet sovereign;
  He who comes next is Horace, the satirist;
  The third is Ovid, and the last is Lucan.

Because to each of these with me applies
  The name that solitary voice proclaimed,
  They do me honour, and in that do well."

Thus I beheld assemble the fair school
  Of that lord of the song pre-eminent,
  Who o'er the others like an eagle soars.

When they together had discoursed somewhat,
  They turned to me with signs of salutation,
  And on beholding this, my Master smiled;

And more of honour still, much more, they did me,
  In that they made me one of their own band;
  So that the sixth was I, 'mid so much wit.

Thus we went on as far as to the light,
  Things saying 'tis becoming to keep silent,
  As was the saying of them where I was.

We came unto a noble castle's foot,
  Seven times encompassed with lofty walls,
  Defended round by a fair rivulet;

This we passed over even as firm ground;
  Through portals seven I entered with these Sages;
  We came into a meadow of fresh verdure.

People were there with solemn eyes and slow,
  Of great authority in their countenance;
  They spake but seldom, and with gentle voices.

Lost are we and are only so far punished, / That without hope we live on in desire."

Inf. IV, lines 41–42

Thus I beheld assemble the fair school / Of that lord of the song pre-eminent, /
Who o'er the others like an eagle soars.

Inf. IV, lines 94–96

Thus we withdrew ourselves upon one side
  Into an opening luminous and lofty,
  So that they all of them were visible.

There opposite, upon the green enamel,
  Were pointed out to me the mighty spirits,
  Whom to have seen I feel myself exalted.

I saw Electra with companions many,
  'Mongst whom I knew both Hector and Aeneas,
  Caesar in armour with gerfalcon eyes;

I saw Camilla and Penthesilea
  On the other side, and saw the King Latinus,
  Who with Lavinia his daughter sat;

I saw that Brutus who drove Tarquin forth,
  Lucretia, Julia, Marcia, and Cornelia,
  And saw alone, apart, the Saladin.

When I had lifted up my brows a little,
  The Master I beheld of those who know,
  Sit with his philosophic family.

All gaze upon him, and all do him honour.
  There I beheld both Socrates and Plato,
  Who nearer him before the others stand;

Democritus, who puts the world on chance,
  Diogenes, Anaxagoras, and Thales,
  Zeno, Empedocles, and Heraclitus;

Of qualities I saw the good collector,
  Hight Dioscorides; and Orpheus saw I,
  Tully and Livy, and moral Seneca,

Euclid, geometrician, and Ptolemy,
  Galen, Hippocrates, and Avicenna,
  Averroes, who the great Comment made.

I cannot all of them pourtray in full,
  Because so drives me onward the long theme,
  That many times the word comes short of fact.

The sixfold company in two divides;
  Another way my sapient Guide conducts me
  Forth from the quiet to the air that trembles;

And to a place I come where nothing shines.

Canto V

*Dante and Virgil descend from the First Circle to the Second. Minos stands at the
entrance, judging transgressors and selecting a place in Hell for each of them. The
Lustful are eternally tossed upon the 'infernal hurricane'. Virgil answers Dante's
question by describing the shades of famous lovers – Semiramis of Assyria, Dido of
Carthage, Helen of Troy, Achilles, Paris, Paolo Malatesta and Francesca Da Rimini.
Dante is saddened by the story of the last of these.*

Thus I descended out of the first circle
  Down to the second, that less space begirds,
  And so much greater dole, that goads to wailing.

There standeth Minos horribly, and snarls;
  Examines the transgressions at the entrance;
  Judges, and sends according as he girds him.

There standeth Minos horribly, and snarls; / Examines the transgressions at the entrance; /
Judges, and sends according as he girds him.

Inf. V, lines 4–6

I say, that when the spirit evil-born
  Cometh before him, wholly it confesses;
  And this discriminator of transgressions

Seeth what place in Hell is meet for it;
  Girds himself with his tail as many times
  As grades he wishes it should be thrust down.

Always before him many of them stand;
  They go by turns each one unto the judgment;
  They speak, and hear, and then are downward hurled.

"O thou, that to this dolorous hostelry
  Comest," said Minos to me, when he saw me,
  Leaving the practice of so great an office,

"Look how thou enterest, and in whom thou trustest;
  Let not the portal's amplitude deceive thee."
  And unto him my Guide: "Why criest thou too?

Do not impede his journey fate-ordained;
  It is so willed there where is power to do
  That which is willed; and ask no further question."

And now begin the dolesome notes to grow
  Audible unto me; now am I come
  There where much lamentation strikes upon me.

I came into a place mute of all light,
  Which bellows as the sea does in a tempest,
  If by opposing winds 'tis combated.

The infernal hurricane that never rests
  Hurtles the spirits onward in its rapine;
  Whirling them round, and smiting, it molests them.

When they arrive before the precipice,
  There are the shrieks, the plaints, and the laments,
  There they blaspheme the puissance divine.

I understood that unto such a torment
  The carnal malefactors were condemned,
  Who reason subjugate to appetite.

And as the wings of starlings bear them on
  In the cold season in large band and full,
  So doth that blast the spirits maledict;

It hither, thither, downward, upward, drives them;
  No hope doth comfort them for evermore,
  Not of repose, but even of lesser pain.

And as the cranes go chanting forth their lays,
  Making in air a long line of themselves,
  So saw I coming, uttering lamentations,

Shadows borne onward by the aforesaid stress.
  Whereupon said I: "Master, who are those
  People, whom the black air so castigates?"

"The first of those, of whom intelligence
  Thou fain wouldst have," then said he unto me,
  "The empress was of many languages.

To sensual vices she was so abandoned,
  That lustful she made licit in her law,
  To remove the blame to which she had been led.

She is Semiramis, of whom we read
  That she succeeded Ninus, and was his spouse;
  She held the land which now the Sultan rules.

The next is she who killed herself for love,
  And broke faith with the ashes of Sichaeus;
  Then Cleopatra the voluptuous."

Helen I saw, for whom so many ruthless
  Seasons revolved; and saw the great Achilles,
  Who at the last hour combated with Love.

Paris I saw, Tristan; and more than a thousand
  Shades did he name and point out with his finger,
  Whom Love had separated from our life.

After that I had listened to my Teacher,
  Naming the dames of eld and cavaliers,
  Pity prevailed, and I was nigh bewildered.

And I began: "O Poet, willingly
  Speak would I to those two, who go together,
  And seem upon the wind to be so light."

And, he to me: "Thou'lt mark, when they shall be
  Nearer to us; and then do thou implore them
  By love which leadeth them, and they will come."

The infernal hurricane that never rests / Hurtles the spirits onward in its rapine;

Inf. V, lines 31–32

"O Poet, willingly / Speak would I to those two, who go together, /
And seem upon the wind to be so light."

Inf. V, lines 73–75

Soon as the wind in our direction sways them,
  My voice uplift I: "O ye weary souls!
  Come speak to us, if no one interdicts it."

As turtle-doves, called onward by desire,
  With open and steady wings to the sweet nest
  Fly through the air by their volition borne,

So came they from the band where Dido is,
  Approaching us athwart the air malign,
  So strong was the affectionate appeal.

"O living creature gracious and benignant,
  Who visiting goest through the purple air
  Us, who have stained the world incarnadine,

If were the King of the Universe our friend,
  We would pray unto him to give thee peace,
  Since thou hast pity on our woe perverse.

Of what it pleases thee to hear and speak,
  That will we hear, and we will speak to you,
  While silent is the wind, as it is now.

Sitteth the city, wherein I was born,
  Upon the sea-shore where the Po descends
  To rest in peace with all his retinue.

Love, that on gentle heart doth swiftly seize,
  Seized this man for the person beautiful
  That was ta'en from me, and still the mode offends me.

Love, that exempts no one beloved from loving,
  Seized me with pleasure of this man so strongly,
  That, as thou seest, it doth not yet desert me;

Love has conducted us unto one death;
  Caina waiteth him who quenched our life!"
  These words were borne along from them to us.

As soon as I had heard those souls tormented,
  I bowed my face, and so long held it down
  Until the Poet said to me: "What thinkest?"

When I made answer, I began: "Alas!
  How many pleasant thoughts, how much desire,
  Conducted these unto the dolorous pass!"

Then unto them I turned me, and I spake,
  And I began: "Thine agonies, Francesca,
  Sad and compassionate to weeping make me.

But tell me, at the time of those sweet sighs,
  By what and in what manner Love conceded,
  That you should know your dubious desires?"

And she to me: "There is no greater sorrow
  Than to be mindful of the happy time
  In misery, and that thy Teacher knows.

But, if to recognise the earliest root
  Of love in us thou hast so great desire,
  I will do even as he who weeps and speaks.

One day we reading were for our delight
  Of Launcelot, how Love did him enthral.
  Alone we were and without any fear.

Full many a time our eyes together drew
  That reading, and drove the colour from our faces;
  But one point only was it that o'ercame us.

When as we read of the much-longed-for smile
  Being by such a noble lover kissed,
  This one, who ne'er from me shall be divided,

Kissed me upon the mouth all palpitating.
  Galeotto was the book and he who wrote it.
  That day no farther did we read therein."

And all the while one spirit uttered this,
  The other one did weep so, that, for pity,
  I swooned away as if I had been dying,

And fell, even as a dead body falls.

"Love has conducted us unto one death; / Caina waiteth him who quenched our life!" /
These words were borne along from them to us.

Inf. V, lines 106–108

"That day no farther did we read therein."

Inf. V, line 138

I swooned away as if I had been dying, / And fell, even as a dead body falls.

Inf. V, lines 141–142

Canto VI

The Gluttons, denizens of the Third Circle, are sunk in fetid mud and pelted by hail,
rain and snow. Virgil placates the three-headed Cerberus, their bellicose guardian, by
feeding his appetite with fistfuls of earth. Ciacco, a contemporary of Dante, approaches
the pair of travellers and makes a political prophecy about Florence. Dante asks Virgil
about the Last Judgement as the two poets approach the next circle.

At the return of consciousness, that closed
  Before the pity of those two relations,
  Which utterly with sadness had confused me,

New torments I behold, and new tormented
  Around me, whichsoever way I move,
  And whichsoever way I turn, and gaze.

In the third circle am I of the rain
  Eternal, maledict, and cold, and heavy;
  Its law and quality are never new.

Huge hail, and water sombre-hued, and snow,
  Athwart the tenebrous air pour down amain;
  Noisome the earth is, that receiveth this.

Cerberus, monster cruel and uncouth,
  With his three gullets like a dog is barking
  Over the people that are there submerged.

Red eyes he has, and unctuous beard and black,
  And belly large, and armed with claws his hands;
  He rends the spirits, flays, and quarters them.

Howl the rain maketh them like unto dogs;
  One side they make a shelter for the other;
  Oft turn themselves the wretched reprobates.

When Cerberus perceived us, the great worm!
  His mouths he opened, and displayed his tusks;
  Not a limb had he that was motionless.

And my Conductor, with his spans extended,
  Took of the earth, and with his fists well filled,
  He threw it into those rapacious gullets.

Such as that dog is, who by barking craves,
  And quiet grows soon as his food he gnaws,
  For to devour it he but thinks and struggles,

The like became those muzzles filth-begrimed
  Of Cerberus the demon, who so thunders
  Over the souls that they would fain be deaf.

We passed across the shadows, which subdues
  The heavy rain-storm, and we placed our feet
  Upon their vanity that person seems.

They all were lying prone upon the earth,
  Excepting one, who sat upright as soon
  As he beheld us passing on before him.

"O thou that art conducted through this Hell,"
  He said to me, "recall me, if thou canst;
  Thyself wast made before I was unmade."

And I to him: "The anguish which thou hast
  Perhaps doth draw thee out of my remembrance,
  So that it seems not I have ever seen thee.

But tell me who thou art, that in so doleful
  A place art put, and in such punishment,
  If some are greater, none is so displeasing."

And he to me: "Thy city, which is full
  Of envy so that now the sack runs over,
  Held me within it in the life serene.

You citizens were wont to call me Ciacco;
  For the pernicious sin of gluttony
  I, as thou seest, am battered by this rain.

And I, sad soul, am not the only one,
  For all these suffer the like penalty
  For the like sin;" and word no more spake he.

I answered him: "Ciacco, thy wretchedness
  Weighs on me so that it to weep invites me;
  But tell me, if thou knowest, to what shall come

And my Conductor, with his spans extended, / Took of the earth, and with his fists well filled, / He threw it into those rapacious gullets.

Inf. VI, lines 25–27

"For the pernicious sin of gluttony / I, as thou seest, am battered by this rain."

Inf. VI, lines 53–54

The citizens of the divided city;
  If any there be just; and the occasion
  Tell me why so much discord has assailed it."

And he to me: "They, after long contention,
  Will come to bloodshed; and the rustic party
  Will drive the other out with much offence.

Then afterwards behoves it this one fall
  Within three suns, and rise again the other
  By force of him who now is on the coast.

High will it hold its forehead a long while,
  Keeping the other under heavy burdens,
  Howe'er it weeps thereat and is indignant.

The just are two, and are not understood there;
  Envy and Arrogance and Avarice
  Are the three sparks that have all hearts enkindled."

Here ended he his tearful utterance;
  And I to him: "I wish thee still to teach me,
  And make a gift to me of further speech.

Farinata and Tegghiaio, once so worthy,
  Jacopo Rusticucci, Arrigo and Mosca,
  And others who on good deeds set their thoughts,

Say where they are, and cause that I may know them;
  For great desire constraineth me to learn
  If Heaven doth sweeten them, or Hell envenom."

And he: "They are among the blacker souls;
  A different sin downweighs them to the bottom;
  If thou so far descendest, thou canst see them.

But when thou art again in the sweet world,
  I pray thee to the mind of others bring me;
  No more I tell thee and no more I answer."

Then his straightforward eyes he turned askance,
  Eyed me a little, and then bowed his head;
  He fell therewith prone like the other blind.

And the Guide said to me: "He wakes no more
  This side the sound of the angelic trumpet;
  When shall approach the hostile Potentate,

Each one shall find again his dismal tomb,
  Shall reassume his flesh and his own figure,
  Shall hear what through eternity re-echoes."

So we passed onward o'er the filthy mixture
  Of shadows and of rain with footsteps slow,
  Touching a little on the future life.

Wherefore I said: "Master, these torments here,
  Will they increase after the mighty sentence,
  Or lesser be, or will they be as burning?"

And he to me: "Return unto thy science,
  Which wills, that as the thing more perfect is,
  The more it feels of pleasure and of pain.

Albeit that this people maledict
  To true perfection never can attain,
  Hereafter more than now they look to be."

Round in a circle by that road we went,
  Speaking much more, which I do not repeat;
  We came unto the point where the descent is;

There we found Plutus the great enemy.

Canto VII

*At Virgil's behest, Plutus, god of material wealth, dissipates into thin air between the
Third and Fourth Circles. The poets watch the noisy Hoarders and the Spendthrifts
rolling huge weights at one another. After discussing Fortune's distribution of temporal
riches, they reach the river Styx, the second of Hell's rivers, which is the Fifth Circle.
Here are mired the Wrathful, who tear at one another, and the Sluggish, who doze
beneath the slime. Dante and Virgil come to the foot of a high tower.*

"*Pape Satan, Pape Satan, Aleppe!*"
  Thus Plutus with his clucking voice began;
  And that benignant Sage, who all things knew,

Said, to encourage me: "Let not thy fear
  Harm thee; for any power that he may have
  Shall not prevent thy going down this crag."

Then he turned round unto that bloated lip,
  And said: "Be silent, thou accursed wolf;
  Consume within thyself with thine own rage.

Not causeless is this journey to the abyss;
  Thus is it willed on high, where Michael wrought
  Vengeance upon the proud adultery."

Even as the sails inflated by the wind
  Involved together fall when snaps the mast,
  So fell the cruel monster to the earth.

Thus we descended into the fourth chasm,
  Gaining still farther on the dolesome shore
  Which all the woe of the universe insacks.

Justice of God, ah! who heaps up so many
  New toils and sufferings as I beheld?
  And why doth our transgression waste us so?

As doth the billow there upon Charybdis,
  That breaks itself on that which it encounters,
  So here the folk must dance their roundelay.

Here saw I people, more than elsewhere, many,
  On one side and the other, with great howls,
  Rolling weights forward by main force of chest.

They clashed together, and then at that point
  Each one turned backward, rolling retrograde,
  Crying, "Why keepest?" and, "Why squanderest thou?"

Thus they returned along the lurid circle
  On either hand unto the opposite point,
  Shouting their shameful metre evermore.

Then each, when he arrived there, wheeled about
  Through his half-circle to another joust;
  And I, who had my heart pierced as it were,

Exclaimed: "My Master, now declare to me
  What people these are, and if all were clerks,
  These shaven crowns upon the left of us."

And he to me: "All of them were asquint
  In intellect in the first life, so much
  That there with measure they no spending made.

Clearly enough their voices bark it forth,
  Whene'er they reach the two points of the circle,
  Where sunders them the opposite defect.

Clerks those were who no hairy covering
  Have on the head, and Popes and Cardinals,
  In whom doth Avarice practise its excess."

And I: "My Master, among such as these
  I ought forsooth to recognise some few,
  Who were infected with these maladies."

And he to me: "Vain thought thou entertainest;
  The undiscerning life which made them sordid
  Now makes them unto all discernment dim.

"Be silent, thou accursed wolf; / Consume within thyself with thine own rage."

Inf. VII, lines 8–9

Forever shall they come to these two buttings;
  These from the sepulchre shall rise again
  With the fist closed, and these with tresses shorn.

Ill giving and ill keeping the fair world
  Have ta'en from them, and placed them in this scuffle;
  Whate'er it be, no words adorn I for it.

Now canst thou, Son, behold the transient farce
  Of goods that are committed unto Fortune,
  For which the human race each other buffet;

For all the gold that is beneath the moon,
  Or ever has been, of these weary souls
  Could never make a single one repose."

"Master," I said to him, "now tell me also
  What is this Fortune which thou speakest of,
  That has the world's goods so within its clutches?"

And he to me: "O creatures imbecile,
  What ignorance is this which doth beset you?
  Now will I have thee learn my judgment of her.

He whose omniscience everything transcends
  The heavens created, and gave who should guide them,
  That every part to every part may shine,

Distributing the light in equal measure;
  He in like manner to the mundane splendours
  Ordained a general ministress and guide,

That she might change at times the empty treasures
  From race to race, from one blood to another,
  Beyond resistance of all human wisdom.

Therefore one people triumphs, and another
  Languishes, in pursuance of her judgment,
  Which hidden is, as in the grass a serpent.

Your knowledge has no counterstand against her;
  She makes provision, judges, and pursues
  Her governance, as theirs the other gods.

Her permutations have not any truce;
  Necessity makes her precipitate,
  So often cometh who his turn obtains.

And this is she who is so crucified
  Even by those who ought to give her praise,
  Giving her blame amiss, and bad repute.

But she is blissful, and she hears it not;
  Among the other primal creatures gladsome
  She turns her sphere, and blissful she rejoices.

Let us descend now unto greater woe;
  Already sinks each star that was ascending
  When I set out, and loitering is forbidden."

We crossed the circle to the other bank,
  Near to a fount that boils, and pours itself
  Along a gully that runs out of it.

The water was more sombre far than perse;
  And we, in company with the dusky waves,
  Made entrance downward by a path uncouth.

A marsh it makes, which has the name of Styx,
  This tristful brooklet, when it has descended
  Down to the foot of the malign gray shores.

And I, who stood intent upon beholding,
  Saw people mud-besprent in that lagoon,
  All of them naked and with angry look.

They smote each other not alone with hands,
  But with the head and with the breast and feet,
  Tearing each other piecemeal with their teeth.

Said the good Master: "Son, thou now beholdest
  The souls of those whom anger overcame;
  And likewise I would have thee know for certain

Beneath the water people are who sigh
  And make this water bubble at the surface,
  As the eye tells thee wheresoe'er it turns.

Fixed in the mire they say, 'We sullen were
  In the sweet air, which by the sun is gladdened,
  Bearing within ourselves the sluggish reek;

Now we are sullen in this sable mire.'
  This hymn do they keep gurgling in their throats,
  For with unbroken words they cannot say it."

Thus we went circling round the filthy fen
  A great arc 'twixt the dry bank and the swamp,
  With eyes turned unto those who gorge the mire;

Unto the foot of a tower we came at last.

"For all the gold that is beneath the moon, / Or ever has been, of these weary souls /
Could never make a single one repose."

Inf. VII, lines 64–66

"Son, thou now beholdest / The souls of those whom anger overcame;"

Inf. VII, lines 115–116

Canto VIII

Dante realizes that the fires on top of the tower are a signal to the city of Dis. Phlegyas
quickly appears and the two poets are ferried across the Styx. An angry shadow,
Philippo Argenti, rises up from the mire and tries to attack the boat. Repelled by
Virgil, he is then viciously attacked by the other souls. The poets disembark at the gate
of Dis. They are denied access by the demonic angels within. Virgil goes alone to speak
with them, to no avail. The poets must wait for help from Heaven.

I say, continuing, that long before
  We to the foot of that high tower had come,
  Our eyes went upward to the summit of it,

By reason of two flamelets we saw placed there,
  And from afar another answer them,
  So far, that hardly could the eye attain it.

And, to the sea of all discernment turned,
  I said: "What sayeth this, and what respondeth
  That other fire? and who are they that made it?"

And he to me: "Across the turbid waves
  What is expected thou canst now discern,
  If reek of the morass conceal it not."

Cord never shot an arrow from itself
  That sped away athwart the air so swift,
  As I beheld a very little boat

Come o'er the water tow'rds us at that moment,
  Under the guidance of a single pilot,
  Who shouted, "Now art thou arrived, fell soul?"

"Phlegyas, Phlegyas, thou criest out in vain
  For this once," said my Lord; "thou shalt not have us
  Longer than in the passing of the slough."

As he who listens to some great deceit
  That has been done to him, and then resents it,
  Such became Phlegyas, in his gathered wrath.

My Guide descended down into the boat,
  And then he made me enter after him,
  And only when I entered seemed it laden.

Soon as the Guide and I were in the boat,
  The antique prow goes on its way, dividing
  More of the water than 'tis wont with others.

While we were running through the dead canal,
  Uprose in front of me one full of mire,
  And said, "Who'rt thou that comest ere the hour?"

And I to him: "Although I come, I stay not;
  But who art thou that hast become so squalid?"
  "Thou seest that I am one who weeps," he answered.

And I to him: "With weeping and with wailing,
  Thou spirit maledict, do thou remain;
  For thee I know, though thou art all defiled."

Then stretched he both his hands unto the boat;
  Whereat my wary Master thrust him back,
  Saying, "Away there with the other dogs!"

Thereafter with his arms he clasped my neck;
  He kissed my face, and said: "Disdainful soul,
  Blessed be she who bore thee in her bosom.

That was an arrogant person in the world;
  Goodness is none, that decks his memory;
  So likewise here his shade is furious.

How many are esteemed great kings up there,
  Who here shall be like unto swine in mire,
  Leaving behind them horrible dispraises!"

And I: "My Master, much should I be pleased,
  If I could see him soused into this broth,
  Before we issue forth out of the lake."

The antique prow goes on its way, dividing / More of the water than 'tis wont with others.

Inf. VIII, lines 29–30

Then stretched he both his hands unto the boat; / Whereat my wary Master thrust him back,

Inf. VIII, lines 40–41

And he to me: "Ere unto thee the shore
  Reveal itself, thou shalt be satisfied;
  Such a desire 'tis meet thou shouldst enjoy."

A little after that, I saw such havoc
  Made of him by the people of the mire,
  That still I praise and thank my God for it.

They all were shouting, "At Philippo Argenti!"
  And that exasperate spirit Florentine
  Turned round upon himself with his own teeth.

We left him there, and more of him I tell not;
  But on mine ears there smote a lamentation,
  Whence forward I intent unbar mine eyes.

And the good Master said: "Even now, my Son,
  The city draweth near whose name is Dis,
  With the grave citizens, with the great throng."

And I: "Its mosques already, Master, clearly
  Within there in the valley I discern
  Vermilion, as if issuing from the fire

They were." And he to me: "The fire eternal
  That kindles them within makes them look red,
  As thou beholdest in this nether Hell."

Then we arrived within the moats profound,
  That circumvallate that disconsolate city;
  The walls appeared to me to be of iron.

Not without making first a circuit wide,
  We came unto a place where loud the pilot
  Cried out to us, "Debark, here is the entrance."

More than a thousand at the gates I saw
  Out of the Heavens rained down, who angrily
  Were saying, "Who is this that without death

Goes through the kingdom of the people dead?"
  And my sagacious Master made a sign
  Of wishing secretly to speak with them.

A little then they quelled their great disdain,
  And said: "Come thou alone, and he begone
  Who has so boldly entered these dominions.

Let him return alone by his mad road;
  Try, if he can; for thou shalt here remain,
  Who hast escorted him through such dark regions."

Think, Reader, if I was discomforted
  At utterance of the accursed words;
  For never to return here I believed.

"O my dear Guide, who more than seven times
  Hast rendered me security, and drawn me
  From imminent peril that before me stood,

Do not desert me," said I, "thus undone;
  And if the going farther be denied us,
  Let us retrace our steps together swiftly."

And that Lord, who had led me thitherward,
  Said unto me: "Fear not; because our passage
  None can take from us, it by Such is given.

But here await me, and thy weary spirit
  Comfort and nourish with a better hope;
  For in this nether world I will not leave thee."

So onward goes and there abandons me
  My Father sweet, and I remain in doubt,
  For No and Yes within my head contend.

I could not hear what he proposed to them;
  But with them there he did not linger long,
  Ere each within in rivalry ran back.

They closed the portals, those our adversaries,
  On my Lord's breast, who had remained without
  And turned to me with footsteps far between.

His eyes cast down, his forehead shorn had he
  Of all its boldness, and he said, with sighs,
  "Who has denied to me the dolesome houses?"

And unto me: "Thou, because I am angry,
  Fear not, for I will conquer in the trial,
  Whatever for defence within be planned.

This arrogance of theirs is nothing new;
  For once they used it at less secret gate,
  Which finds itself without a fastening still.

O'er it didst thou behold the dead inscription;
  And now this side of it descends the steep,
  Passing across the circles without escort,

One by whose means the city shall be opened."

I could not hear what he proposed to them; / But with them there he did not linger long, /
Ere each within in rivalry ran back.

Inf. VIII, lines 112–114

Canto IX

The poets are waiting for Divine assistance at the gate of Dis. Unnerved by Virgil's anxiety, Dante asks him if he knows the way through Hell. Virgil reassures him. Three Furies appear at the tower, shrieking and tearing at their breasts and invoking Medusa. Dante shields his gaze to avoid being turned to stone. An angel makes a dramatic entrance before opening the gate. The sarcophagi of the groaning Heretics burn beyond.

That hue which cowardice brought out on me,
  Beholding my Conductor backward turn,
  Sooner repressed within him his new colour.

He stopped attentive, like a man who listens,
  Because the eye could not conduct him far
  Through the black air, and through the heavy fog.

"Still it behoveth us to win the fight,"
  Began he; "Else. . .Such offered us herself. . .
  O how I long that some one here arrive!"

Well I perceived, as soon as the beginning
  He covered up with what came afterward,
  That they were words quite different from the first;

But none the less his saying gave me fear,
  Because I carried out the broken phrase,
  Perhaps to a worse meaning than he had.

"Into this bottom of the doleful conch
  Doth any e'er descend from the first grade,
  Which for its pain has only hope cut off?"

This question put I; and he answered me:
  "Seldom it comes to pass that one of us
  Maketh the journey upon which I go.

True is it, once before I here below
  Was conjured by that pitiless Erictho,
  Who summoned back the shades unto their bodies.

Naked of me short while the flesh had been,
  Before within that wall she made me enter,
  To bring a spirit from the circle of Judas;

That is the lowest region and the darkest,
  And farthest from the heaven which circles all.
  Well know I the way; therefore be reassured.

This fen, which a prodigious stench exhales,
  Encompasses about the city dolent,
  Where now we cannot enter without anger."

And more he said, but not in mind I have it;
  Because mine eye had altogether drawn me
  Tow'rds the high tower with the red-flaming summit,

Where in a moment saw I swift uprisen
  The three infernal Furies stained with blood,
  Who had the limbs of women and their mien,

And with the greenest hydras were begirt;
  Small serpents and cerastes were their tresses,
  Wherewith their horrid temples were entwined.

And he who well the handmaids of the Queen
  Of everlasting lamentation knew,
  Said unto me: "Behold the fierce Erinnys.

This is Megaera, on the left-hand side;
  She who is weeping on the right, Alecto;
  Tisiphone is between;" and then was silent.

Each one her breast was rending with her nails;
  They beat them with their palms, and cried so loud,
  That I for dread pressed close unto the Poet.

"Medusa come, so we to stone will change him!"
  All shouted looking down; "in evil hour
  Avenged we not on Theseus his assault!"

"Turn thyself round, and keep thine eyes close shut,
  For if the Gorgon appear, and thou shouldst see it,
  No more returning upward would there be."

Thus said the Master; and he turned me round
  Himself, and trusted not unto my hands
  So far as not to blind me with his own.

"This is Megaera, on the left-hand side; / She who is weeping on the right, Alecto; /
Tisiphone is between;"

Inf. IX, lines 46–48

O ye who have undistempered intellects,
  Observe the doctrine that conceals itself
  Beneath the veil of the mysterious verses!

And now there came across the turbid waves
  The clangour of a sound with terror fraught,
  Because of which both of the margins trembled;

Not otherwise it was than of a wind
  Impetuous on account of adverse heats,
  That smites the forest, and, without restraint,

The branches rends, beats down, and bears away;
  Right onward, laden with dust, it goes superb,
  And puts to flight the wild beasts and the shepherds.

Mine eyes he loosed, and said: "Direct the nerve
  Of vision now along that ancient foam,
  There yonder where that smoke is most intense."

Even as the frogs before the hostile serpent
  Across the water scatter all abroad,
  Until each one is huddled in the earth.

More than a thousand ruined souls I saw,
  Thus fleeing from before one who on foot
  Was passing o'er the Styx with soles unwet.

From off his face he fanned that unctuous air,
  Waving his left hand oft in front of him,
  And only with that anguish seemed he weary.

Well I perceived one sent from Heaven was he,
  And to the Master turned; and he made sign
  That I should quiet stand, and bow before him.

Ah! how disdainful he appeared to me!
  He reached the gate, and with a little rod
  He opened it, for there was no resistance.

"O banished out of Heaven, people despised!"
  Thus he began upon the horrid threshold;
  "Whence is this arrogance within you couched?

Wherefore recalcitrate against that will,
  From which the end can never be cut off,
  And which has many times increased your pain?

What helpeth it to butt against the fates?
  Your Cerberus, if you remember well,
  For that still bears his chin and gullet peeled."

Then he returned along the miry road,
  And spake no word to us, but had the look
  Of one whom other care constrains and goads

Than that of him who in his presence is;
  And we our feet directed tow'rds the city,
  After those holy words all confident.

Within we entered without any contest;
  And I, who inclination had to see
  What the condition such a fortress holds,

Soon as I was within, cast round mine eye,
  And see on every hand an ample plain,
  Full of distress and torment terrible.

Even as at Arles, where stagnant grows the Rhone,
  Even as at Pola near to the Quarnaro,
  That shuts in Italy and bathes its borders,

The sepulchres make all the place uneven;
  So likewise did they there on every side,
  Saving that there the manner was more bitter;

For flames between the sepulchres were scattered,
  By which they so intensely heated were,
  That iron more so asks not any art.

All of their coverings uplifted were,
  And from them issued forth such dire laments,
  Sooth seemed they of the wretched and tormented.

And I: "My Master, what are all those people
  Who, having sepulture within those tombs,
  Make themselves audible by doleful sighs?"

And he to me: "Here are the Heresiarchs,
  With their disciples of all sects, and much
  More than thou thinkest laden are the tombs.

Here like together with its like is buried;
  And more and less the monuments are heated."
  And when he to the right had turned, we passed

Between the torments and high parapets.

He reached the gate, and with a little rod / He opened it, for there was no resistance.

Inf. IX, lines 89–90

"My Master, what are all those people / Who, having sepulture within those tombs, /
Make themselves audible by doleful sighs?"

Inf. IX, lines 124–126

Canto X

Dante and Virgil walk around the tombs of the Heretics who sought temporal bliss. This sin of the intellect, though not a source of sinful action, lies between Incontinence and Violence. Hearing a fellow Tuscan speak, Farinata rises up from one of the graves. Farinata's political tirade against Florence is interrupted by the appearance of Cavalcante De' Cavalcanti, who asks about his son Guido. Dante is intrigued to discover that the damned can foresee the future and recall the past but have no knowledge of the present.

Now onward goes, along a narrow path
  Between the torments and the city wall,
  My Master, and I follow at his back.

"O power supreme, that through these impious circles
  Turnest me," I began, "as pleases thee,
  Speak to me, and my longings satisfy;

The people who are lying in these tombs,
  Might they be seen? already are uplifted
  The covers all, and no one keepeth guard."

And he to me: "They all will be closed up
  When from Jehoshaphat they shall return
  Here with the bodies they have left above.

Their cemetery have upon this side
  With Epicurus all his followers,
  Who with the body mortal make the soul;

But in the question thou dost put to me,
  Within here shalt thou soon be satisfied,
  And likewise in the wish thou keepest silent."

And I: "Good Leader, I but keep concealed
  From thee my heart, that I may speak the less,
  Nor only now hast thou thereto disposed me."

"O Tuscan, thou who through the city of fire
  Goest alive, thus speaking modestly,
  Be pleased to stay thy footsteps in this place.

Thy mode of speaking makes thee manifest
  A native of that noble fatherland,
  To which perhaps I too molestful was."

Upon a sudden issued forth this sound
  From out one of the tombs; wherefore I pressed,
  Fearing, a little nearer to my Leader.

And unto me he said: "Turn thee; what dost thou?
  Behold there Farinata who has risen;
  From the waist upwards wholly shalt thou see him."

I had already fixed mine eyes on his,
  And he uprose erect with breast and front
  E'en as if Hell he had in great despite.

And with courageous hands and prompt my Leader
  Thrust me between the sepulchres towards him,
  Exclaiming, "Let thy words explicit be."

As soon as I was at the foot of his tomb
  Somewhat he eyed me, and, as if disdainful,
  Then asked of me, "Who were thine ancestors?"

I, who desirous of obeying was,
  Concealed it not, but all revealed to him;
  Whereat he raised his brows a little upward.

Then said he: "Fiercely adverse have they been
  To me, and to my fathers, and my party;
  So that two several times I scattered them."

"If they were banished, they returned on all sides,"
  I answered him, "the first time and the second;
  But yours have not acquired that art aright."

Then there uprose upon the sight, uncovered
  Down to the chin, a shadow at his side;
  I think that he had risen on his knees.

Round me he gazed, as if solicitude
  He had to see if some one else were with me,
  But after his suspicion was all spent,

Weeping, he said to me: "If through this blind
  Prison thou goest by loftiness of genius,
  Where is my son? and why is he not with thee?"

As soon as I was at the foot of his tomb / Somewhat he eyed me, and, as if disdainful, /
Then asked of me, "Who were thine ancestors?"

Inf. X, lines 40–42

And I to him: "I come not of myself;
  He who is waiting yonder leads me here,
  Whom in disdain perhaps your Guido had."

His language and the mode of punishment
  Already unto me had read his name;
  On that account my answer was so full.

Up starting suddenly, he cried out: "How
  Saidst thou,—he had? Is he not still alive?
  Does not the sweet light strike upon his eyes?"

When he became aware of some delay,
  Which I before my answer made, supine
  He fell again, and forth appeared no more.

But the other, magnanimous, at whose desire
  I had remained, did not his aspect change,
  Neither his neck he moved, nor bent his side.

"And if," continuing his first discourse,
  "They have that art," he said, "not learned aright,
  That more tormenteth me, than doth this bed.

But fifty times shall not rekindled be
  The countenance of the Lady who reigns here,
  Ere thou shalt know how heavy is that art;

And as thou wouldst to the sweet world return,
  Say why that people is so pitiless
  Against my race in each one of its laws?"

Whence I to him: "The slaughter and great carnage
  Which have with crimson stained the Arbia, cause
  Such orisons in our temple to be made."

After his head he with a sigh had shaken,
  "There I was not alone," he said, "nor surely
  Without a cause had with the others moved.

But there I was alone, where every one
  Consented to the laying waste of Florence,
  He who defended her with open face."

"Ah! so hereafter may your seed repose,"
  I him entreated, "solve for me that knot,
  Which has entangled my conceptions here.

It seems that you can see, if I hear rightly,
  Beforehand whatsoe'er time brings with it,
  And in the present have another mode."

"We see, like those who have imperfect sight,
  The things," he said, "that distant are from us;
  So much still shines on us the Sovereign Ruler.

When they draw near, or are, is wholly vain
  Our intellect, and if none brings it to us,
  Not anything know we of your human state.

Hence thou canst understand, that wholly dead
  Will be our knowledge from the moment when
  The portal of the future shall be closed."

Then I, as if compunctious for my fault,
  Said: "Now, then, you will tell that fallen one,
  That still his son is with the living joined.

And if just now, in answering, I was dumb,
  Tell him I did it because I was thinking
  Already of the error you have solved me."

And now my Master was recalling me,
  Wherefore more eagerly I prayed the spirit
  That he would tell me who was with him there.

He said: "With more than a thousand here I lie;
  Within here is the second Frederick,
  And the Cardinal, and of the rest I speak not."

Thereon he hid himself; and I towards
  The ancient poet turned my steps, reflecting
  Upon that saying, which seemed hostile to me.

He moved along; and afterward thus going,
  He said to me, "Why art thou so bewildered?"
  And I in his inquiry satisfied him.

"Let memory preserve what thou hast heard
  Against thyself," that Sage commanded me,
  "And now attend here;" and he raised his finger.

"When thou shalt be before the radiance sweet
  Of her whose beauteous eyes all things behold,
  From her thou'lt know the journey of thy life."

Unto the left hand then he turned his feet;
  We left the wall, and went towards the middle,
  Along a path that strikes into a valley,

Which even up there unpleasant made its stench.

Canto XI

Continuing their visit of the heretical Sixth Circle, poet and pilgrim are overcome by the foul stench wafting up from the abyss ahead. Both pause and read the inscription on the tomb of Pope Anastasius II. Seeing Dante's willingness to learn, Virgil instructs him further on the subtle classification of punishment in Hell before finally urging him on as it is nearly dawn.

Upon the margin of a lofty bank
  Which great rocks broken in a circle made,
  We came upon a still more cruel throng;

And there, by reason of the horrible
  Excess of stench the deep abyss throws out,
  We drew ourselves aside behind the cover

Of a great tomb, whereon I saw a writing,
  Which said: "Pope Anastasius I hold,
  Whom out of the right way Photinus drew."

"Slow it behoveth our descent to be,
  So that the sense be first a little used
  To the sad blast, and then we shall not heed it."

The Master thus; and unto him I said,
  "Some compensation find, that the time pass not
  Idly;" and he: "Thou seest I think of that.

My son, upon the inside of these rocks,"
  Began he then to say, "are three small circles,
  From grade to grade, like those which thou art leaving.

They all are full of spirits maledict;
  But that hereafter sight alone suffice thee,
  Hear how and wherefore they are in constraint.

Of every malice that wins hate in Heaven,
  Injury is the end; and all such end
  Either by force or fraud afflicteth others.

But because fraud is man's peculiar vice,
  More it displeases God; and so stand lowest
  The fraudulent, and greater dole assails them.

All the first circle of the Violent is;
  But since force may be used against three persons,
  In three rounds 'tis divided and constructed.

To God, to ourselves, and to our neighbour can we
  Use force; I say on them and on their things,
  As thou shalt hear with reason manifest.

A death by violence, and painful wounds,
  Are to our neighbour given; and in his substance
  Ruin, and arson, and injurious levies;

Whence homicides, and he who smites unjustly,
  Marauders, and freebooters, the first round
  Tormenteth all in companies diverse.

Man may lay violent hands upon himself
  And his own goods; and therefore in the second
  Round must perforce without avail repent

Whoever of your world deprives himself,
  Who games, and dissipates his property,
  And weepeth there, where he should jocund be.

Violence can be done the Deity,
  In heart denying and blaspheming Him,
  And by disdaining Nature and her bounty.

And for this reason doth the smallest round
  Seal with its signet Sodom and Cahors,
  And who, disdaining God, speaks from the heart.

Fraud, wherewithal is every conscience stung,
  A man may practise upon him who trusts,
  And him who doth no confidence imburse.

This latter mode, it would appear, dissevers
  Only the bond of love which Nature makes;
  Wherefore within the second circle nestle

Hypocrisy, flattery, and who deals in magic,
  Falsification, theft, and simony,
  Panders, and barrators, and the like filth.

We drew ourselves aside behind the cover / Of a great tomb, whereon I saw a writing, /
Which said: "Pope Anastasius I hold."

Inf. XI, lines 6–8

By the other mode, forgotten is that love
  Which Nature makes, and what is after added,
  From which there is a special faith engendered.

Hence in the smallest circle, where the point is
  Of the Universe, upon which Dis is seated,
  Whoe'er betrays for ever is consumed."

And I: "My Master, clear enough proceeds
  Thy reasoning, and full well distinguishes
  This cavern and the people who possess it.

But tell me, those within the fat lagoon,
  Whom the wind drives, and whom the rain doth beat,
  And who encounter with such bitter tongues,

Wherefore are they inside of the red city
  Not punished, if God has them in his wrath,
  And if he has not, wherefore in such fashion?"

And unto me he said: "Why wanders so
  Thine intellect from that which it is wont?
  Or, sooth, thy mind where is it elsewhere looking?

Hast thou no recollection of those words
  With which thine Ethics thoroughly discusses
  The dispositions three, that Heaven abides not,—

Incontinence, and Malice, and insane
  Bestiality? and how Incontinence
  Less God offendeth, and less blame attracts?

If thou regardest this conclusion well,
  And to thy mind recallest who they are
  That up outside are undergoing penance,

Clearly wilt thou perceive why from these felons
  They separated are, and why less wroth
  Justice divine doth smite them with its hammer."

"O Sun, that healest all distempered vision,
  Thou dost content me so, when thou resolvest,
  That doubting pleases me no less than knowing!

Once more a little backward turn thee," said I,
  "There where thou sayest that usury offends
  Goodness divine, and disengage the knot."

"Philosophy," he said, "to him who heeds it,
  Noteth, not only in one place alone,
  After what manner Nature takes her course

From Intellect Divine, and from its art;
  And if thy Physics carefully thou notest,
  After not many pages shalt thou find,

That this your art as far as possible
  Follows, as the disciple doth the master;
  So that your art is, as it were, God's grandchild.

From these two, if thou bringest to thy mind
  Genesis at the beginning, it behoves
  Mankind to gain their life and to advance;

And since the usurer takes another way,
  Nature herself and in her follower
  Disdains he, for elsewhere he puts his hope.

But follow, now, as I would fain go on,
  For quivering are the Fishes on the horizon,
  And the Wain wholly over Caurus lies,

And far beyond there we descend the crag."

Canto XII

Dante and Virgil enter the Seventh Circle by means of a landslide created by Christ when he harrowed Hell. The Minotaur, guardian of the Violent, breaks into a fit of rage on seeing the poets. Fleeing past him, the poets reach Phlegethon, a river of boiling blood that is filled with those that have inflicted violence on others. Three fierce Centaurs shoot arrows at souls attempting to rise above the level commensurate with their punishment. Virgil asks Chiron, their leader, to lend one of his band to them, so that they might ford the river. Nessus is chosen, who points out sinners along the way.

The place where to descend the bank we came
  Was alpine, and from what was there, moreover,
  Of such a kind that every eye would shun it.

Such as that ruin is which in the flank
  Smote, on this side of Trent, the Adige,
  Either by earthquake or by failing stay,

For from the mountain's top, from which it moved,
  Unto the plain the cliff is shattered so,
  Some path 'twould give to him who was above;

Even such was the descent of that ravine,
  And on the border of the broken chasm
  The infamy of Crete was stretched along,

Who was conceived in the fictitious cow;
  And when he us beheld, he bit himself,
  Even as one whom anger racks within.

My Sage towards him shouted: "Peradventure
  Thou think'st that here may be the Duke of Athens,
  Who in the world above brought death to thee?

Get thee gone, beast, for this one cometh not
  Instructed by thy sister, but he comes
  In order to behold your punishments."

As is that bull who breaks loose at the moment
  In which he has received the mortal blow,
  Who cannot walk, but staggers here and there,

The Minotaur beheld I do the like;
  And he, the wary, cried: "Run to the passage;
  While he wroth, 'tis well thou shouldst descend."

Thus down we took our way o'er that discharge
  Of stones, which oftentimes did move themselves
  Beneath my feet, from the unwonted burden.

Thoughtful I went; and he said: "Thou art thinking
  Perhaps upon this ruin, which is guarded
  By that brute anger which just now I quenched.

Now will I have thee know, the other time
  I here descended to the nether Hell,
  This precipice had not yet fallen down.

But truly, if I well discern, a little
  Before His coming who the mighty spoil
  Bore off from Dis, in the supernal circle,

Upon all sides the deep and loathsome valley
  Trembled so, that I thought the Universe
  Was thrilled with love, by which there are who think

The world ofttimes converted into chaos;
  And at that moment this primeval crag
  Both here and elsewhere made such overthrow.

But fix thine eyes below; for draweth near
  The river of blood, within which boiling is
  Whoe'er by violence doth injure others."

O blind cupidity, O wrath insane,
  That spurs us onward so in our short life,
  And in the eternal then so badly steeps us!

I saw an ample moat bent like a bow,
  As one which all the plain encompasses,
  Conformable to what my Guide had said.

And between this and the embankment's foot
  Centaurs in file were running, armed with arrows,
  As in the world they used the chase to follow.

Beholding us descend, each one stood still,
  And from the squadron three detached themselves,
  With bows and arrows in advance selected;

And from afar one cried: "Unto what torment
  Come ye, who down the hillside are descending?
  Tell us from there; if not, I draw the bow."

My Master said: "Our answer will we make
  To Chiron, near you there; in evil hour,
  That will of thine was evermore so hasty."

Then touched he me, and said: "This one is Nessus,
  Who perished for the lovely Dejanira,
  And for himself, himself did vengeance take.

And he in the midst, who at his breast is gazing,
  Is the great Chiron, who brought up Achilles;
  That other Pholus is, who was so wrathful.

Thousands and thousands go about the moat
  Shooting with shafts whatever soul emerges
  Out of the blood, more than his crime allots."

Near we approached unto those monsters fleet;
  Chiron an arrow took, and with the notch
  Backward upon his jaws he put his beard.

After he had uncovered his great mouth,
  He said to his companions: "Are you ware
  That he behind moveth whate'er he touches?

Thus are not wont to do the feet of dead men."
  And my good Guide, who now was at his breast,
  Where the two natures are together joined,

Replied: "Indeed he lives, and thus alone
  Me it behoves to show him the dark valley;
  Necessity, and not delight, impels us.

Some one withdrew from singing Halleluja,
  Who unto me committed this new office;
  No thief is he, nor I a thievish spirit.

But by that virtue through which I am moving
  My steps along this savage thoroughfare,
  Give us some one of thine, to be with us,

And who may show us where to pass the ford,
  And who may carry this one on his back;
  For 'tis no spirit that can walk the air."

Upon his right breast Chiron wheeled about,
  And said to Nessus: "Turn and do thou guide them,
  And warn aside, if other band may meet you."

We with our faithful escort onward moved
  Along the brink of the vermilion boiling,
  Wherein the boiled were uttering loud laments.

People I saw within up to the eyebrows,
  And the great Centaur said: "Tyrants are these,
  Who dealt in bloodshed and in pillaging.

Here they lament their pitiless mischiefs; here
  Is Alexander, and fierce Dionysius
  Who upon Sicily brought dolorous years.

That forehead there which has the hair so black
  Is Azzolin; and the other who is blond,
  Obizzo is of Esti, who, in truth,

Up in the world was by his stepson slain."
  Then turned I to the Poet; and he said,
  "Now he be first to thee, and second I."

A little farther on the Centaur stopped
  Above a folk, who far down as the throat
  Seemed from that boiling stream to issue forth.

A shade he showed us on one side alone,
  Saying: "He cleft asunder in God's bosom
  The heart that still upon the Thames is honoured."

Then people saw I, who from out the river
  Lifted their heads and also all the chest;
  And many among these I recognised.

Thus ever more and more grew shallower
  That blood, so that the feet alone it covered;
  And there across the moat our passage was.

"Even as thou here upon this side beholdest
  The boiling stream, that aye diminishes,"
  The Centaur said, "I wish thee to believe

That on this other more and more declines
  Its bed, until it reunites itself
  Where it behoveth tyranny to groan.

And on the border of the broken chasm / The infamy of Crete was stretched along, /
Who was conceived in the fictitious cow;

Inf. XII, lines 11–13

Beholding us descend, each one stood still, / And from the squadron three detached themselves, / With bows and arrows in advance selected;

Inf. XII, lines 58–60

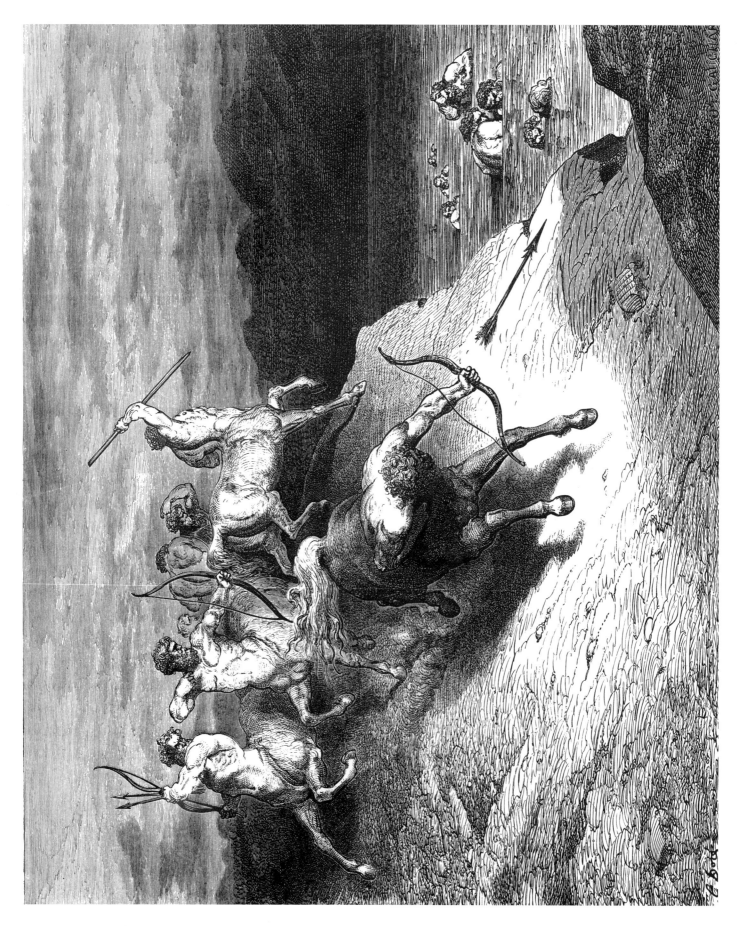

Chiron an arrow took, and with the notch / Backward upon his jaws he put his beard.

Inf. XII, lines 77–78

Justice divine, upon this side, is goading
  That Attila, who was a scourge on Earth,
  And Pyrrhus, and Sextus; and for ever milks

The tears which with the boiling it unseals
  In Rinier da Corneto and Rinier Pazzo,
  Who made upon the highways so much war."

Then back he turned, and passed again the ford.

Canto XIII

*The swift passage across the third river of Hell plunges the visitors into the thick
Wood of the Suicides who are denied bodily form. Dante breaks off a branch from
a nearby tree. It weeps blood and speaks. This wretch was once Pier delle Vigne,
chief adviser to Frederick II of Sicily, who explains that he and other sinners like
him suffer indescribable torment when the half-bird, half-beast harpies rend their
bark. This exchange is interrupted by two Profligates, Lano of Siena and Giacomo
da Sant'Andrea, who are being pursued by hounds. One of them gets torn to pieces
by the creatures. The poets speak to a Florentine, who is now a weeping bush.*

Not yet had Nessus reached the other side,
  When we had put ourselves within a wood,
  That was not marked by any path whatever.

Not foliage green, but of a dusky colour,
  Not branches smooth, but gnarled and intertangled,
  Not apple-trees were there, but thorns with poison.

Such tangled thickets have not, nor so dense,
  Those savage wild beasts, that in hatred hold
  'Twixt Cecina and Corneto the tilled places.

There do the hideous Harpies make their nests,
  Who chased the Trojans from the Strophades,
  With sad announcement of impending doom;

Broad wings have they, and necks and faces human,
  And feet with claws, and their great bellies fledged;
  They make laments upon the wondrous trees.

And the good Master: "Ere thou enter farther,
  Know that thou art within the second round,"
  Thus he began to say, "and shalt be, till

Thou comest out upon the horrible sand;
  Therefore look well around, and thou shalt see
  Things that will credence give unto my speech."

I heard on all sides lamentations uttered,
  And person none beheld I who might make them,
  Whence, utterly bewildered, I stood still.

I think he thought that I perhaps might think
  So many voices issued through those trunks
  From people who concealed themselves from us;

Therefore the Master said: "If thou break off
  Some little spray from any of these trees,
  The thoughts thou hast will wholly be made vain."

Then stretched I forth my hand a little forward,
  And plucked a branchlet off from a great thorn;
  And the trunk cried, "Why dost thou mangle me?"

After it had become embrowned with blood,
  It recommenced its cry: "Why dost thou rend me?
  Hast thou no spirit of pity whatsoever?

They make laments upon the wondrous trees.

Inf. XIII, line 15

Then stretched I forth my hand a little forward, / And plucked a branchlet off from a great thorn; / And the trunk cried, "Why dost thou mangle me?"

Inf. XIII, lines 31–33

Men once we were, and now are changed to trees;
  Indeed, thy hand should be more pitiful,
  Even if the souls of serpents we had been."

As out of a green brand, that is on fire
  At one of the ends, and from the other drips
  And hisses with the wind that is escaping;

So from that splinter issued forth together
  Both words and blood; whereat I let the tip
  Fall, and stood like a man who is afraid.

"Had he been able sooner to believe,"
  My Sage made answer, "O thou wounded soul,
  What only in my verses he has seen,

Not upon thee had he stretched forth his hand;
  Whereas the thing incredible has caused me
  To put him to an act which grieveth me.

But tell him who thou wast, so that by way
  Of some amends thy fame he may refresh
  Up in the world, to which he can return."

And the trunk said: "So thy sweet words allure me,
  I cannot silent be; and you be vexed not,
  That I a little to discourse am tempted.

I am the one who both keys had in keeping
  Of Frederick's heart, and turned them to and fro
  So softly in unlocking and in locking,

That from his secrets most men I withheld;
  Fidelity I bore the glorious office
  So great, I lost thereby my sleep and pulses.

The courtesan who never from the dwelling
  Of Caesar turned aside her strumpet eyes,
  Death universal and the vice of courts,

Inflamed against me all the other minds,
  And they, inflamed, did so inflame Augustus,
  That my glad honours turned to dismal mournings.

My spirit, in disdainful exultation,
  Thinking by dying to escape disdain,
  Made me unjust against myself, the just.

I, by the roots unwonted of this wood,
  Do swear to you that never broke I faith
  Unto my lord, who was so worthy of honour;

And to the world if one of you return,
  Let him my memory comfort, which is lying
  Still prostrate from the blow that envy dealt it."

Waited awhile, and then: "Since he is silent,"
  The Poet said to me, "lose not the time,
  But speak, and question him, if more may please thee."

Whence I to him: "Do thou again inquire
  Concerning what thou thinks't will satisfy me;
  For I cannot, such pity is in my heart."

Therefore he recommenced: "So may the man
  Do for thee freely what thy speech implores,
  Spirit incarcerate, again be pleased

To tell us in what way the soul is bound
  Within these knots; and tell us, if thou canst,
  If any from such members e'er is freed."

Then blew the trunk amain, and afterward
  The wind was into such a voice converted:
  "With brevity shall be replied to you.

When the exasperated soul abandons
  The body whence it rent itself away,
  Minos consigns it to the seventh abyss.

It falls into the forest, and no part
  Is chosen for it; but where Fortune hurls it,
  There like a grain of spelt it germinates.

It springs a sapling, and a forest tree;
  The Harpies, feeding then upon its leaves,
  Do pain create, and for the pain an outlet.

Like others for our spoils shall we return;
  But not that any one may them revest,
  For 'tis not just to have what one casts off.

Here we shall drag them, and along the dismal
  Forest our bodies shall suspended be,
  Each to the thorn of his molested shade."

We were attentive still unto the trunk,
  Thinking that more it yet might wish to tell us,
  When by a tumult we were overtaken,

In the same way as he is who perceives
  The boar and chase approaching to his stand,
  Who hears the crashing of the beasts and branches;

And two behold! upon our left-hand side,
  Naked and scratched, fleeing so furiously,
  That of the forest, every fan they broke.

He who was in advance: "Now help, Death, help!"
  And the other one, who seemed to lag too much,
  Was shouting: "Lano, were not so alert

Those legs of thine at joustings of the Toppo!"
  And then, perchance because his breath was failing,
  He grouped himself together with a bush.

Behind them was the forest full of black
  She-mastiffs, ravenous, and swift of foot
  As greyhounds, who are issuing from the chain.

On him who had crouched down they set their teeth,
  And him they lacerated piece by piece,
  Thereafter bore away those aching members.

Thereat my Escort took me by the hand,
  And led me to the bush, that all in vain
  Was weeping from its bloody lacerations.

"O Jacopo," it said, "of Sant' Andrea,
  What helped it thee of me to make a screen?
  What blame have I in thy nefarious life?"

When near him had the Master stayed his steps,
  He said: "Who wast thou, that through wounds so many
  Art blowing out with blood thy dolorous speech?"

And he to us: "O souls, that hither come
  To look upon the shameful massacre
  That has so rent away from me my leaves,

Gather them up beneath the dismal bush;
  I of that city was which to the Baptist
  Changed its first patron, wherefore he for this

Forever with his art will make it sad.
  And were it not that on the pass of Arno
  Some glimpses of him are remaining still,

Those citizens, who afterwards rebuilt it
  Upon the ashes left by Attila,
  In vain had caused their labour to be done.

Of my own house I made myself a gibbet."

Canto XIV

On the edge of the wood lies a desert of burning sand where flames rain down constantly. The shadows here are forced to adopt different positions according to their sins. Thus the poets behold supine Blasphemers and crouching Usurers, while the Sodomites are made to wander about aimlessly. Dante recognises Capaneus who died cursing Jove. The poets reach a blood-red rivulet which prompts Dante to ask about the origins of Phlegethon. Virgil replies by relating the story of the Old Man of Crete whose tears coursed down to form the four rivers of Hell.

Because the charity of my native place
  Constrained me, gathered I the scattered leaves,
  And gave them back to him, who now was hoarse.

Then came we to the confine, where disparted
  The second round is from the third, and where
  A horrible form of Justice is beheld.

Clearly to manifest these novel things,
  I say that we arrived upon a plain,
  Which from its bed rejecteth every plant;

The dolorous forest is a garland to it
  All round about, as the sad moat to that;
  There close upon the edge we stayed our feet.

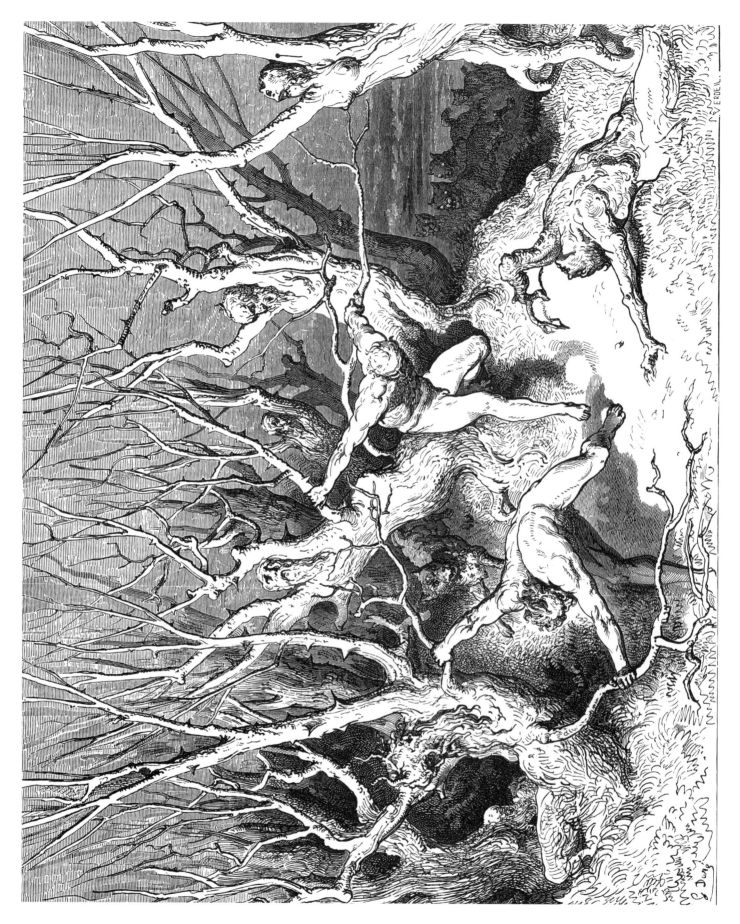

And two behold! upon our left-hand side, / Naked and scratched, fleeing so furiously, /
That of the forest, every fan they broke.

Inf. XIII, lines 115–117

The soil was of an arid and thick sand,
  Not of another fashion made than that
  Which by the feet of Cato once was pressed.

Vengeance of God, O how much oughtest thou
  By each one to be dreaded, who doth read
  That which was manifest unto mine eyes!

Of naked souls beheld I many herds,
  Who all were weeping very miserably,
  And over them seemed set a law diverse.

Supine upon the ground some folk were lying;
  And some were sitting all drawn up together,
  And others went about continually.

Those who were going round were far the more,
  And those were less who lay down to their torment,
  But had their tongues more loosed to lamentation.

O'er all the sand-waste, with a gradual fall,
  Were raining down dilated flakes of fire,
  As of the snow on Alp without a wind.

As Alexander, in those torrid parts
  Of India, beheld upon his host
  Flames fall unbroken till they reached the ground.

Whence he provided with his phalanxes
  To trample down the soil, because the vapour
  Better extinguished was while it was single;

Thus was descending the eternal heat,
  Whereby the sand was set on fire, like tinder
  Beneath the steel, for doubling of the dole.

Without repose forever was the dance
  Of miserable hands, now there, now here,
  Shaking away from off them the fresh gleeds.

"Master," began I, "thou who overcomest
  All things except the demons dire, that issued
  Against us at the entrance of the gate,

Who is that mighty one who seems to heed not
  The fire, and lieth lowering and disdainful,
  So that the rain seems not to ripen him?"

And he himself, who had become aware
  That I was questioning my Guide about him,
  Cried: "Such as I was living, am I, dead.

If Jove should weary out his smith, from whom
  He seized in anger the sharp thunderbolt,
  Wherewith upon the last day I was smitten,

And if he wearied out by turns the others
  In Mongibello at the swarthy forge,
  Vociferating, 'Help, good Vulcan, help!'

Even as he did there at the fight of Phlegra,
  And shot his bolts at me with all his might,
  He would not have thereby a joyous vengeance."

Then did my Leader speak with such great force,
  That I had never heard him speak so loud:
  "O Capaneus, in that is not extinguished

Thine arrogance, thou punished art the more;
  Not any torment, saving thine own rage,
  Would be unto thy fury pain complete."

Then he turned round to me with better lip,
  Saying: "One of the Seven Kings was he
  Who Thebes besieged, and held, and seems to hold

God in disdain, and little seems to prize him;
  But, as I said to him, his own despites
  Are for his breast the fittest ornaments.

Now follow me, and mind thou do not place
  As yet thy feet upon the burning sand,
  But always keep them close unto the wood."

Speaking no word, we came to where there gushes
  Forth from the wood a little rivulet,
  Whose redness makes my hair still stand on end.

As from the Bulicame springs the brooklet,
  The sinful women later share among them,
  So downward through the sand it went its way.

The bottom of it, and both sloping banks,
  Were made of stone, and the margins at the side;
  Whence I perceived that there the passage was.

"In all the rest which I have shown to thee
  Since we have entered in within the gate
  Whose threshold unto no one is denied,

Nothing has been discovered by thine eyes
  So notable as is the present river,
  Which all the little flames above it quenches."

O'er all the sand-waste, with a gradual fall, / Were raining down dilated flakes of fire.

Inf. XIV, lines 28–29

These words were of my Leader; whence I prayed him
  That he would give me largess of the food,
  For which he had given me largess of desire.

"In the mid-sea there sits a wasted land,"
  Said he thereafterward, "whose name is Crete,
  Under whose king the world of old was chaste.

There is a mountain there, that once was glad
  With waters and with leaves, which was called Ida;
  Now 'tis deserted, as a thing worn out.

Rhea once chose it for the faithful cradle
  Of her own son; and to conceal him better,
  Whene'er he cried, she there had clamours made.

A grand old man stands in the mount erect,
  Who holds his shoulders turned tow'rds Damietta,
  And looks at Rome as if it were his mirror.

His head is fashioned of refined gold,
  And of pure silver are the arms and breast;
  Then he is brass as far down as the fork.

From that point downward all is chosen iron,
  Save that the right foot is of kiln-baked clay,
  And more he stands on that than on the other.

Each part, except the gold, is by a fissure
  Asunder cleft, that dripping is with tears,
  Which gathered together perforate that cavern.

From rock to rock they fall into this valley;
  Acheron, Styx and Phlegethon they form;
  Then downward go along this narrow sluice

Unto that point where is no more descending.
  They form Cocytus; what that pool may be
  Thou shalt behold, so here 'tis not narrated."

And I to him: "If so the present runnel
  Doth take its rise in this way from our world,
  Why only on this verge appears it to us?"

And he to me: "Thou knowest the place is round,
  And notwithstanding thou hast journeyed far,
  Still to the left descending to the bottom,

Thou hast not yet through all the circle turned.
  Therefore if something new appear to us,
  It should not bring amazement to thy face."

And I again: "Master, where shall be found
  Lethe and Phlegethon, for of one thou'rt silent,
  And sayest the other of this rain is made?"

"In all thy questions truly thou dost please me,"
  Replied he; "but the boiling of the red
  Water might well solve one of them thou makest.

Thou shalt see Lethe, but outside this moat,
  There where the souls repair to lave themselves,
  When sin repented of has been removed."

Then said he: "It is time now to abandon
  The wood; take heed that thou come after me;
  A way the margins make that are not burning,

And over them all vapours are extinguished."

79

Canto XV

Virgil and Dante leave the burning plain by following the channel through which the Phlegethon unwinds. A company of Sodomites races towards them. One, Brunetto Latini, Guelf statesman, writer and Dante's former teacher, slows down. Brunetto prophesies that both political parties in Florence will turn against Dante. His words echo those of Ciacco in Canto VI. A cloud of smoke in the distance announces the arrival of an alien group so the Florentine sprints off to catch up with his companions.

Now bears us onward one of the hard margins,
  And so the brooklet's mist o'ershadows it,
  From fire it saves the water and the dikes.

Even as the Flemings, 'twixt Cadsand and Bruges,
  Fearing the flood that tow'rds them hurls itself,
  Their bulwarks build to put the sea to flight;

And as the Paduans along the Brenta,
  To guard their villas and their villages,
  Or ever Chiarentana feel the heat;

In such similitude had those been made,
  Albeit not so lofty nor so thick,
  Whoever he might be, the master made them.

Now were we from the forest so remote,
  I could not have discovered where it was,
  Even if backward I had turned myself,

When we a company of souls encountered,
  Who came beside the dike, and every one
  Gazed at us, as at evening we are wont

To eye each other under a new moon,
  And so towards us sharpened they their brows
  As an old tailor at the needle's eye.

Thus scrutinised by such a family,
  By some one I was recognised, who seized
  My garment's hem, and cried out, "What a marvel!"

And I, when he stretched forth his arm to me,
  On his baked aspect fastened so mine eyes,
  That the scorched countenance prevented not

His recognition by my intellect;
  And bowing down my face unto his own,
  I made reply, "Are you here, Ser Brunetto?"

And he: "May't not displease thee, O my son,
  If a brief space with thee Brunetto Latini
  Backward return and let the trail go on."

I said to him: "With all my power I ask it;
  And if you wish me to sit down with you,
  I will, if he please, for I go with him."

"O son," he said, "whoever of this herd
  A moment stops, lies then a hundred years,
  Nor fans himself when smiteth him the fire.

Therefore go on; I at thy skirts will come,
  And afterward will I rejoin my band,
  Which goes lamenting its eternal doom."

I did not dare to go down from the road
  Level to walk with him; but my head bowed
  I held as one who goeth reverently.

And he began: "What fortune or what fate
  Before the last day leadeth thee down here?
  And who is this that showeth thee the way?"

"Up there above us in the life serene,"
  I answered him, "I lost me in a valley,
  Or ever yet my age had been completed.

But yestermorn I turned my back upon it;
  This one appeared to me, returning thither,
  And homeward leadeth me along this road."

And he to me: "If thou thy star do follow,
  Thou canst not fail thee of a glorious port,
  If well I judged in the life beautiful.

And if I had not died so prematurely,
  Seeing Heaven thus benignant unto thee,
  I would have given thee comfort in the work.

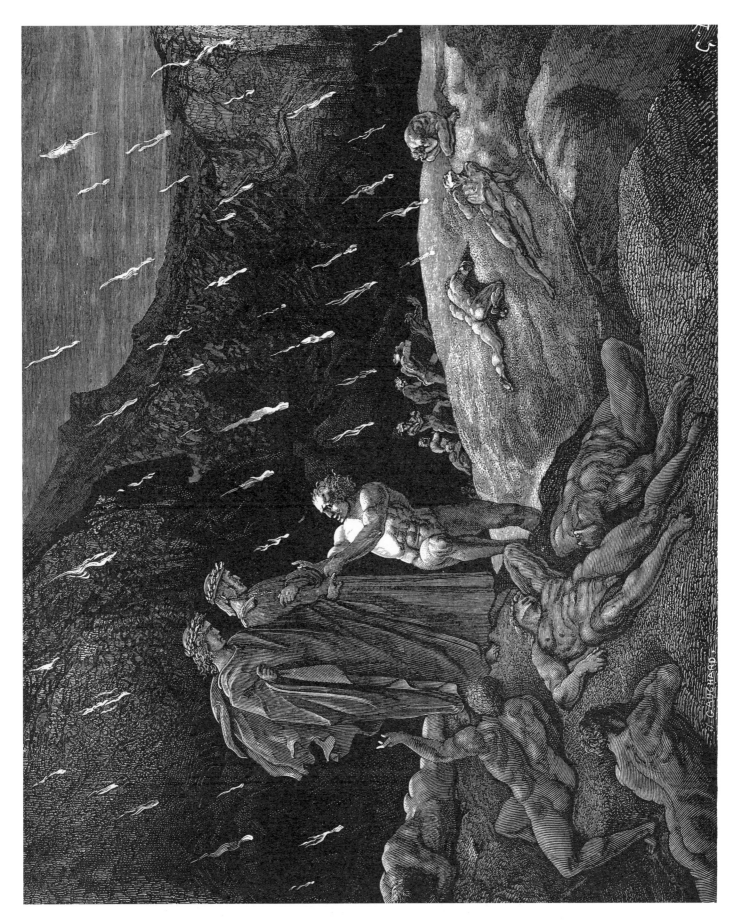

"Are you here, Ser Brunetto?"

Inf. XV, line 30

But that ungrateful and malignant people,
  Which of old time from Fesole descended,
  And smacks still of the mountain and the granite,

Will make itself, for thy good deeds, thy foe;
  And it is right; for among crabbed sorbs
  It ill befits the sweet fig to bear fruit.

Old rumour in the world proclaims them blind;
  A people avaricious, envious, proud;
  Take heed that of their customs thou do cleanse thee.

Thy fortune so much honour doth reserve thee,
  One party and the other shall be hungry
  For thee; but far from goat shall be the grass.

Their litter let the beasts of Fesole
  Make of themselves, nor let them touch the plant,
  If any still upon their dunghill rise,

In which may yet revive the consecrated
  Seed of those Romans, who remained there when
  The nest of such great malice it became."

"If my entreaty wholly were fulfilled,"
  Replied I to him, "not yet would you be
  In banishment from human nature placed;

For in my mind is fixed, and touches now
  My heart the dear and good paternal image
  Of you, when in the world from hour to hour

You taught me how a man becomes eternal;
  And how much I am grateful, while I live
  Behoves that in my language be discerned.

What you narrate of my career I write,
  And keep it to be glossed with other text
  By a Lady who can do it, if I reach her.

This much will I have manifest to you;
  Provided that my conscience do not chide me,
  For whatsoever Fortune I am ready.

Such handsel is not new unto mine ears;
  Therefore let Fortune turn her wheel around
  As it may please her, and the churl his mattock."

My Master thereupon on his right cheek
  Did backward turn himself, and looked at me;
  Then said: "He listeneth well who noteth it."

Nor speaking less on that account, I go
  With Ser Brunetto, and I ask who are
  His most known and most eminent companions.

And he to me: "To know of some is well;
  Of others it were laudable to be silent,
  For short would be the time for so much speech.

Know them in sum, that all of them were clerks,
  And men of letters great and of great fame,
  In the world tainted with the selfsame sin.

Priscian goes yonder with that wretched crowd,
  And Francis of Accorso; and thou hadst seen there
  If thou hadst had a hankering for such scurf,

That one, who by the Servant of the Servants
  From Arno was transferred to Bacchiglione,
  Where he has left his sin-excited nerves.

More would I say, but coming and discoursing
  Can be no longer; for that I behold
  New smoke uprising yonder from the sand.

A people comes with whom I may not be;
  Commended unto thee be my Tesoro,
  In which I still live, and no more I ask."

Then he turned round, and seemed to be of those
  Who at Verona run for the Green Mantle
  Across the plain; and seemed to be among them

The one who wins, and not the one who loses.

Canto XVI

Still in the Circle of Violence, Dante hears the roar of a distant waterfall. Having recognized a
fellow Florentine, three warrior Sodomites edge forward, all the while moving around him in
a circle like a turning wheel. Their spokesman introduces himself as Jacopo Rusticucci and his
two compatriots as Guido Guerra and Tegghiaio Aldobrand, both Guelf party leaders. These
illustrious citizens of Florence ask for news of their city before moving away. The rush of the
water is now deafening. Virgil removes the cord from around Dante's waist and throws it into
the abyss. Some creature stirs below before swimming upwards.

Now was I where was heard the reverberation
  Of water falling into the next round,
  Like to that humming which the beehives make,

When shadows three together started forth,
  Running, from out a company that passed
  Beneath the rain of the sharp martyrdom.

Towards us came they, and each one cried out:
  "Stop, thou; for by thy garb to us thou seemest
  To be some one of our depraved city."

Ah me! what wounds I saw upon their limbs,
  Recent and ancient by the flames burnt in!
  It pains me still but to remember it.

Unto their cries my Teacher paused attentive;
  He turned his face towards me, and "Now wait,"
  He said; "to these we should be courteous.

And if it were not for the fire that darts
  The nature of this region, I should say
  That haste were more becoming thee than them."

As soon as we stood still, they recommenced
  The old refrain, and when they overtook us,
  Formed of themselves a wheel, all three of them.

As champions stripped and oiled are wont to do,
  Watching for their advantage and their hold,
  Before they come to blows and thrusts between them,

Thus, wheeling round, did every one his visage
  Direct to me, so that in opposite wise
  His neck and feet continual journey made.

And, "If the misery of this soft place
  Bring in disdain ourselves and our entreaties,"
  Began one, "and our aspect black and blistered,

Let the renown of us thy mind incline
  To tell us who thou art, who thus securely
  Thy living feet dost move along through Hell.

He in whose footprints thou dost see me treading,
  Naked and skinless though he now may go,
  Was of a greater rank than thou dost think;

He was the grandson of the good Gualdrada;
  His name was Guido Guerra, and in life
  Much did he with his wisdom and his sword.

The other, who close by me treads the sand,
  Tegghiaio Aldobrandi is, whose fame
  Above there in the world should welcome be.

And I, who with them on the cross am placed,
  Jacopo Rusticucci was; and truly
  My savage wife, more than aught else, doth harm me."

Could I have been protected from the fire,
  Below I should have thrown myself among them,
  And think the Teacher would have suffered it;

But as I should have burned and baked myself,
  My terror overmastered my good will,
  Which made me greedy of embracing them.

Then I began: "Sorrow and not disdain
  Did your condition fix within me so,
  That tardily it wholly is stripped off,

As soon as this my Lord said unto me
  Words, on account of which I thought within me
  That people such as you are were approaching.

I of your city am; and evermore
  Your labours and your honourable names
  I with affection have retraced and heard.

I leave the gall, and go for the sweet fruits
  Promised to me by the veracious Leader;
  But to the centre first I needs must plunge."

"So may the soul for a long while conduct
  Those limbs of thine," did he make answer then,
  "And so may thy renown shine after thee,

Valour and courtesy, say if they dwell
  Within our city, as they used to do,
  Or if they wholly have gone out of it;

For Guglielmo Borsier, who is in torment
  With us of late, and goes there with his comrades,
  Doth greatly mortify us with his words."

"The new inhabitants and the sudden gains,
  Pride and extravagance have in thee engendered,
  Florence, so that thou weep'st thereat already!"

In this wise I exclaimed with face uplifted;
  And the three, taking that for my reply,
  Looked at each other, as one looks at truth.

"If other times so little it doth cost thee,"
  Replied they all, "to satisfy another,
  Happy art thou, thus speaking at thy will!

Therefore, if thou escape from these dark places,
  And come to rebehold the beauteous stars,
  When it shall pleasure thee to say, 'I was,'

See that thou speak of us unto the people."
  Then they broke up the wheel, and in their flight
  It seemed as if their agile legs were wings.

Not an Amen could possibly be said
  So rapidly as they had disappeared;
  Wherefore the Master deemed best to depart.

I followed him, and little had we gone,
  Before the sound of water was so near us,
  That speaking we should hardly have been heard.

Even as that stream which holdeth its own course
  The first from Monte Veso tow'rds the East,
  Upon the left-hand slope of Apennine,

Which is above called Acquacheta, ere
  It down descendeth into its low bed,
  And at Forli is vacant of that name,

Reverberates there above San Benedetto
  From Alps, by falling at a single leap,
  Where for a thousand there were room enough;

Thus downward from a bank precipitate,
  We found resounding that dark-tinted water,
  So that it soon the ear would have offended.

I had a cord around about me girt,
  And therewithal I whilom had designed
  To take the panther with the painted skin.

After I this had all from me unloosed,
  As my Conductor had commanded me,
  I reached it to him, gathered up and coiled,

Whereat he turned himself to the right side,
  And at a little distance from the verge,
  He cast it down into that deep abyss.

"It must needs be some novelty respond,"
  I said within myself, "to the new signal
  The Master with his eye is following so."

Ah me! how very cautious men should be
  With those who not alone behold the act,
  But with their wisdom look into the thoughts!

He said to me: "Soon there will upward come
  What I await; and what thy thought is dreaming
  Must soon reveal itself unto thy sight."

Aye to that truth which has the face of falsehood,
  A man should close his lips as far as may be,
  Because without his fault it causes shame;

But here I cannot; and, Reader, by the notes
  Of this my Comedy to thee I swear,
  So may they not be void of lasting favour,

Athwart that dense and darksome atmosphere
  I saw a figure swimming upward come,
  Marvellous unto every steadfast heart,

Even as he returns who goeth down
  Sometimes to clear an anchor, which has grappled
  Reef, or aught else that in the sea is hidden,

Who upward stretches, and draws in his feet.

Canto XVII

Geryon appears as a monstrous personification of Fraud. He has the head of an honest-looking man attached to a snake-like body with a scorpion's sting at its end. The Usurers, those who profited from lending money to others at very high interest, are sitting on the edge of the abyss with crested money pouches dangling from their necks. Dante recognizes members of the eminent Gianfigliazzi, Ubriachi and Scrovegni families. Virgil and Dante mount Geryon who descends the Eighth Circle.

"Behold the monster with the pointed tail,
  Who cleaves the hills, and breaketh walls and weapons,
  Behold him who infecteth all the world."

Thus unto me my Guide began to say,
  And beckoned him that he should come to shore,
  Near to the confine of the trodden marble;

And that uncleanly image of deceit
  Came up and thrust ashore its head and bust,
  But on the border did not drag its tail.

The face was as the face of a just man,
  Its semblance outwardly was so benign,
  And of a serpent all the trunk beside.

Two paws it had, hairy unto the armpits;
  The back, and breast, and both the sides it had
  Depicted o'er with nooses and with shields.

With colours more, groundwork or broidery
  Never in cloth did Tartars make nor Turks,
  Nor were such tissues by Arachne laid.

As sometimes wherries lie upon the shore,
  That part are in the water, part on land;
  And as among the guzzling Germans there,

The beaver plants himself to wage his war;
  So that vile monster lay upon the border,
  Which is of stone, and shutteth in the sand.

His tail was wholly quivering in the void,
  Contorting upwards the envenomed fork,
  That in the guise of scorpion armed its point.

The Guide said: "Now perforce must turn aside
  Our way a little, even to that beast
  Malevolent, that yonder coucheth him."

We therefore on the right side descended,
  And made ten steps upon the outer verge,
  Completely to avoid the sand and flame;

And after we are come to him, I see
  A little farther off upon the sand
  A people sitting near the hollow place.

Then said to me the Master: "So that full
  Experience of this round thou bear away,
  Now go and see what their condition is.

There let thy conversation be concise;
  Till thou returnest I will speak with him,
  That he concede to us his stalwart shoulders."

Thus farther still upon the outermost
  Head of that seventh circle all alone
  I went, where sat the melancholy folk.

Out of their eyes was gushing forth their woe;
  This way, that way, they helped them with their hands
  Now from the flames and now from the hot soil.

Not otherwise in summer do the dogs,
  Now with the foot, now with the muzzle, when
  By fleas, or flies, or gadflies, they are bitten.

When I had turned mine eyes upon the faces
  Of some, on whom the dolorous fire is falling,
  Not one of them I knew; but I perceived

That from the neck of each there hung a pouch,
  Which certain colour had, and certain blazon;
  And thereupon it seems their eyes are feeding.

And as I gazing round me come among them,
  Upon a yellow pouch I azure saw
  That had the face and posture of a lion.

And that uncleanly image of deceit / Came up and thrust ashore its head and bust,

Inf. XVII, lines 7–8

Proceeding then the current of my sight,
  Another of them saw I, red as blood,
  Display a goose more white than butter is.

And one, who with an azure sow and gravid
  Emblazoned had his little pouch of white,
  Said unto me: "What dost thou in this moat?

Now get thee gone; and since thou'rt still alive,
  Know that a neighbour of mine, Vitaliano,
  Will have his seat here on my left-hand side.

A Paduan am I with these Florentines;
  Full many a time they thunder in mine ears,
  Exclaiming, 'Come the sovereign cavalier,

He who shall bring the satchel with three goats;'"
  Then twisted he his mouth, and forth he thrust
  His tongue, like to an ox that licks its nose.

And fearing lest my longer stay might vex
  Him who had warned me not to tarry long,
  Backward I turned me from those weary souls.

I found my Guide, who had already mounted
  Upon the back of that wild animal,
  And said to me: "Now be both strong and bold.

Now we descend by stairways such as these;
  Mount thou in front, for I will be midway,
  So that the tail may have no power to harm thee."

Such as he is who has so near the ague
  Of quartan that his nails are blue already,
  And trembles all, but looking at the shade;

Even such became I at those proffered words;
  But shame in me his menaces produced,
  Which maketh servant strong before good master.

I seated me upon those monstrous shoulders;
  I wished to say, and yet the voice came not
  As I believed, "Take heed that thou embrace me."

But he, who other times had rescued me
  In other peril, soon as I had mounted,
  Within his arms encircled and sustained me,

And said: "Now, Geryon, bestir thyself;
  The circles large, and the descent be little;
  Think of the novel burden which thou hast."

Even as the little vessel shoves from shore,
  Backward, still backward, so he thence withdrew;
  And when he wholly felt himself afloat,

There where his breast had been he turned his tail,
  And that extended like an eel he moved,
  And with his paws drew to himself the air.

A greater fear I do not think there was
  What time abandoned Phaeton the reins,
  Whereby the heavens, as still appears, were scorched;

Nor when the wretched Icarus his flanks
  Felt stripped of feathers by the melting wax,
  His father crying, "An ill way thou takest!"

Than was my own, when I perceived myself
  On all sides in the air, and saw extinguished
  The sight of everything but of the monster.

Onward he goeth, swimming slowly, slowly;
  Wheels and descends, but I perceive it only
  By wind upon my face and from below.

I heard already on the right the whirlpool
  Making a horrible crashing under us;
  Whence I thrust out my head with eyes cast
                                    downward.

Then was I still more fearful of the abyss;
  Because I fires beheld, and heard laments,
  Whereat I, trembling, all the closer cling.

I saw then, for before I had not seen it,
  The turning and descending, by great horrors
  That were approaching upon divers sides.

As falcon who has long been on the wing,
  Who, without seeing either lure or bird,
  Maketh the falconer say, "Ah me, thou stoopest,"

Descendeth weary, whence he started swiftly,
  Thorough a hundred circles, and alights
  Far from his master, sullen and disdainful;

Even thus did Geryon place us on the bottom,
  Close to the bases of the rough-hewn rock,
  And being disencumbered of our persons,

He sped away as arrow from the string.

Onward he goeth, swimming slowly, slowly; / Wheels and descends,

Inf. XVII, lines 115–116

Canto XVIII

As the poets descend on Geryon's back in a slow gyre, Dante describes his bird's-eye view of Hell's Eighth Circle (malebolge). It has ten rocky clefts (bolgias), each one connected to the next by a curved bridge. At the edge of the first bolgia, *two lines of naked souls are moving in opposite directions – the Panders walking towards Virgil and Dante and the Seducers filing past alongside them. Dante recognizes Venedico Caccianemico, a Bolognese Guelf leader, and Jason of the Argonauts. The second* bolgia *is characterized by the foul stench of Flatterers drowning in excrement.*

There is a place in Hell called Malebolge,
  Wholly of stone and of an iron colour,
  As is the circle that around it turns.

Right in the middle of the field malign
  There yawns a well exceeding wide and deep,
  Of which its place the structure will recount.

Round, then, is that enclosure which remains
  Between the well and foot of the high, hard bank,
  And has distinct in valleys ten its bottom.

As where for the protection of the walls
  Many and many moats surround the castles,
  The part in which they are a figure forms,

Just such an image those presented there;
  And as about such strongholds from their gates
  Unto the outer bank are little bridges,

So from the precipice's base did crags
  Project, which intersected dikes and moats,
  Unto the well that truncates and collects them.

Within this place, down shaken from the back
  Of Geryon, we found us; and the Poet
  Held to the left, and I moved on behind.

Upon my right hand I beheld new anguish,
  New torments, and new wielders of the lash,
  Wherewith the foremost *Bolgia* was replete.

Down at the bottom were the sinners naked;
  This side the middle came they facing us,
  Beyond it, with us, but with greater steps;

Even as the Romans, for the mighty host,
  The year of Jubilee, upon the bridge,
  Have chosen a mode to pass the people over;

For all upon one side towards the Castle
  Their faces have, and go unto St Peter's;
  On the other side they go towards the Mountain.

This side and that, along the livid stone
  Beheld I horned demons with great scourges,
  Who cruelly were beating them behind.

Ah me! how they did make them lift their legs
  At the first blows! and sooth not any one
  The second waited for, nor for the third.

While I was going on, mine eyes by one
  Encountered were; and straight I said: "Already
  With sight of this one I am not unfed."

Therefore I stayed my feet to make him out,
  And with me the sweet Guide came to a stand,
  And to my going somewhat back assented;

And he, the scourged one, thought to hide himself,
  Lowering his face, but little it availed him;
  For said I: "Thou that castest down thine eyes,

If false are not the features which thou bearest,
  Thou art Venedico Caccianimico;
  But what doth bring thee to such pungent sauces?"

And he to me: "Unwillingly I tell it;
  But forces me thine utterance distinct,
  Which makes me recollect the ancient world.

I was the one who the fair Ghisola
  Induced to grant the wishes of the Marquis,
  Howe'er the shameless story may be told.

Not the sole Bolognese am I who weeps here;
  Nay, rather is this place so full of them,
  That not so many tongues to-day are taught

Ah me! how they did make them lift their legs / At the first blows!

Inf. XVIII, lines 37–38

'Twixt Reno and Savena to say '*sipa*;'
  And if thereof thou wishest pledge or proof,
  Bring to thy mind our avaricious heart."

While speaking in this manner, with his scourge
  A demon smote him, and said: "Get thee gone
  Pander, there are no women here for coin."

I joined myself again unto mine Escort;
  Thereafterward with footsteps few we came
  To where a crag projected from the bank.

This very easily did we ascend,
  And turning to the right along its ridge,
  From those eternal circles we departed.

When we were there, where it is hollowed out
  Beneath, to give a passage to the scourged,
  The Guide said: "Wait, and see that on thee strike

The vision of those others evil-born,
  Of whom thou hast not yet beheld the faces,
  Because together with us they have gone."

From the old bridge we looked upon the train
  Which tow'rds us came upon the other border,
  And which the scourges in like manner smite.

And the good Master, without my inquiring,
  Said to me: "See that tall one who is coming,
  And for his pain seems not to shed a tear;

Still what a royal aspect he retains!
  That Jason is, who by his heart and cunning
  The Colchians of the Ram made destitute.

He by the isle of Lemnos passed along
  After the daring women pitiless
  Had unto death devoted all their males.

There with his tokens and with ornate words
  Did he deceive Hypsipyle, the maiden
  Who first, herself, had all the rest deceived.

There did he leave her pregnant and forlorn;
  Such sin unto such punishment condemns him,
  And also for Medea is vengeance done.

With him go those who in such wise deceive;
  And this sufficient be of the first valley
  To know, and those that in its jaws it holds."

We were already where the narrow path
  Crosses athwart the second dike, and forms
  Of that a buttress for another arch.

Thence we heard people, who are making moan
  In the next *Bolgia*, snorting with their muzzles,
  And with their palms beating upon themselves

The margins were incrusted with a mould
  By exhalation from below, that sticks there,
  And with the eyes and nostrils wages war.

The bottom is so deep, no place suffices
  To give us sight of it, without ascending
  The arch's back, where most the crag impends.

Thither we came, and thence down in the moat
  I saw a people smothered in a filth
  That out of human privies seemed to flow;

And whilst below there with mine eye I search,
  I saw one with his head so foul with ordure,
  It was not clear if he were clerk or layman.

He screamed to me: "Wherefore art thou so eager
  To look at me more than the other foul ones?"
  And I to him: "Because, if I remember,

I have already seen thee with dry hair,
  And thou'rt Alessio Interminei of Lucca;
  Therefore I eye thee more than all the others."

And he thereon, belabouring his pumpkin:
  "The flatteries have submerged me here below,
  Wherewith my tongue was never surfeited."

Then said to me the Guide: "See that thou thrust
  Thy visage somewhat farther in advance,
  That with thine eyes thou well the face attain

Of that uncleanly and dishevelled drab,
  Who there doth scratch herself with filthy nails,
  And crouches now, and now on foot is standing.

Thais the harlot is it, who replied
  Unto her paramour, when he said, 'Have I
  Great gratitude from thee?' – 'Nay, marvellous;'

And herewith let our sight be satisfied."

I saw a people smothered in a filth / That out of human privies seemed to flow;

Inf. XVIII, lines 113–114

Thais the harlot is it, who replied / Unto her paramour, when he said, 'Have I /
Great gratitude from thee?' – 'Nay, marvellous;'

Inf. XVIII, lines 133–135

Canto XIX

Crossing the bridge into the third bolgia, *Virgil and Dante enter a landscape full of holes from which protrude the flaming, flailing legs of the Simonists. In life, these fraudulent ecclesiastics profited from the Church and its offices. Dante questions a pair of legs and discovers they belong to Pope Nicholas III, who mistakes him for Boniface VIII, the next pope destined to fall down that hole. According to the Simonist's eloquent prophecy, Pope Clement V is third in line. Dante expresses his moral indignation in equally ornate language. Virgil rewards his progress by carrying him to the arch above the fourth* bolgia.

O Simon Magus, O forlorn disciples,
　Ye who the things of God, which ought to be
　The brides of holiness, rapaciously

For silver and for gold do prostitute,
　Now it behoves for you the trumpet sound,
　Because in this third *Bolgia* ye abide.

We had already on the following tomb
　Ascended to that portion of the crag
　Which o'er the middle of the moat hangs plumb.

Wisdom supreme, O how great art thou showest
　In heaven, in Earth, and in the evil world,
　And with what justice doth thy power distribute!

I saw upon the sides and on the bottom
　The livid stone with perforations filled,
　All of one size, and every one was round.

To me less ample seemed they not, nor greater
　Than those that in my beautiful Saint John
　Are fashioned for the place of the baptisers,

And one of which, not many years ago,
　I broke for some one, who was drowning in it;
　Be this a seal all men to undeceive.

Out of the mouth of each one there protruded
　The feet of a transgressor, and the legs
　Up to the calf, the rest within remained.

In all of them the soles were both on fire;
　Wherefore the joints so violently quivered,
　They would have snapped asunder withes and bands.

Even as the flame of unctuous things is wont
　To move upon the outer surface only,
　So likewise was it there from heel to point.

"Master, who is that one who writhes himself,
　More than his other comrades quivering,"
　I said, "and whom a redder flame is sucking?"

And he to me: "If thou wilt have me bear thee
　Down there along that bank which lowest lies,
　From him thou'lt know his errors and himself."

And I: "What pleases thee, to me is pleasing;
　Thou art my Lord, and knowest that I depart not
　From thy desire, and knowest what is not spoken."

Straightway upon the fourth dike we arrived;
　We turned, and on the left-hand side descended
　Down to the bottom full of holes and narrow.

And the good Master yet from off his haunch
　Deposed me not, till to the hole he brought me
　Of him who so lamented with his shanks.

"Whoe'er thou art, that standest upside down,
　O doleful soul, implanted like a stake,"
　To say began I, "if thou canst, speak out."

I stood even as the friar who is confessing
　The false assassin, who, when he is fixed,
　Recalls him, so that death may be delayed.

And he cried out: "Dost thou stand there already,
　Dost thou stand there already, Boniface?
　By many years the record lied to me.

Art thou so early satiate with that wealth,
　For which thou didst not fear to take by fraud
　The beautiful Lady, and then work her woe?"

Such I became, as people are who stand,
　Not comprehending what is answered them,
　As if bemocked, and know not how to answer.

"O doleful soul, implanted like a stake," / To say began I, "if thou canst, speak out."

Inf. XIX, lines 47–48

Then said Virgilius: "Say to him straightway,
  'I am not he, I am not he thou thinkest.'"
And I replied as was imposed on me.

Whereat the spirit writhed with both his feet,
  Then, sighing, with a voice of lamentation
Said to me: "Then what wantest thou of me?

If who I am thou carest so much to know,
  That thou on that account hast crossed the bank,
Know that I vested was with the great mantle;

And truly was I son of the She-bear,
  So eager to advance the cubs, that wealth
Above, and here myself, I pocketed.

Beneath my head the others are dragged down
  Who have preceded me in simony,
Flattened along the fissure of the rock.

Below there I shall likewise fall, whenever
  That one shall come who I believed thou wast,
What time the sudden question I proposed.

But longer I my feet already toast,
  And here have been in this way upside down,
Than he will planted stay with reddened feet;

For after him shall come of fouler deed
  From tow'rds the west a Pastor without law,
Such as befits to cover him and me.

New Jason will he be, of whom we read
  In Maccabees; and as his king was pliant,
So he who governs France shall be to this one."

I do not know if I were here too bold,
  That him I answered only in this metre:
"I pray thee tell me now how great a treasure

Our Lord demanded of Saint Peter first,
  Before he put the keys into his keeping?
Truly he nothing asked but 'Follow me.'

Nor Peter nor the rest asked of Matthias
  Silver or gold, when he by lot was chosen
Unto the place the guilty soul had lost.

Therefore stay here, for thou art justly punished,
  And keep safe guard o'er the ill-gotten money,
Which caused thee to be valiant against Charles.

And were it not that still forbids it me
  The reverence for the keys superlative
Thou hadst in keeping in the gladsome life,

I would make use of words more grievous still;
  Because your avarice afflicts the world,
Trampling the good and lifting the depraved.

The Evangelist you Pastors had in mind,
  When she who sitteth upon many waters
To fornicate with kings by him was seen;

The same who with the seven heads was born,
  And power and strength from the ten horns received,
So long as virtue to her spouse was pleasing.

Ye have made yourselves a god of gold and silver;
  And from the idolater how differ ye,
Save that he one, and ye a hundred worship?

Ah, Constantine! of how much ill was mother,
  Not thy conversion, but that marriage dower
Which the first wealthy Father took from thee!"

And while I sang to him such notes as these,
  Either that anger or that conscience stung him,
He struggled violently with both his feet.

I think in sooth that it my Leader pleased,
  With such contented lip he listened ever
Unto the sound of the true words expressed.

Therefore with both his arms he took me up,
  And when he had me all upon his breast,
Remounted by the way where he descended.

Nor did he tire to have me clasped to him;
  But bore me to the summit of the arch
Which from the fourth dike to the fifth is passage.

There tenderly he laid his burden down,
  Tenderly on the crag uneven and steep,
That would have been hard passage for the goats:

Thence was unveiled to me another valley.

Canto XX

The Soothsayers or Sorcerers, a group of weeping shadows, mournfully make their way along the valley of the fourth bolgia. On Earth, they claimed they could look into the future but, in the afterlife, their heads are twisted around so completely that their tears fall on their buttocks. Virgil recognizes Amphiaraus, Tiresias, Aruns and Manto (the last one a former citizen of his Mantuan birthplace). After discussing the founding of the city, he names more of the damned.

Of a new pain behoves me to make verses
  And give material to the twentieth canto
  Of the first song, which is of the submerged.

I was already thoroughly disposed
  To peer down into the uncovered depth,
  Which bathed itself with tears of agony;

And people saw I through the circular valley,
  Silent and weeping, coming at the pace
  Which in this world the Litanies assume.

As lower down my sight descended on them,
  Wondrously each one seemed to be distorted
  From chin to the beginning of the chest;

For tow'rds the reins the countenance was turned,
  And backward it behoved them to advance,
  As to look forward had been taken from them.

Perchance indeed by violence of palsy
  Some one has been thus wholly turned awry;
  But I ne'er saw it, nor believe it can be.

As God may let thee, Reader, gather fruit
  From this thy reading, think now for thyself
  How I could ever keep my face unmoistened,

When our own image near me I beheld
  Distorted so, the weeping of the eyes
  Along the fissure bathed the hinder parts.

Truly I wept, leaning upon a peak
  Of the hard crag, so that my Escort said
  To me: "Art thou, too, of the other fools?

Here pity lives when it is wholly dead;
  Who is a greater reprobate than he
  Who feels compassion at the doom divine?

Lift up, lift up thy head, and see for whom
  Opened the earth before the Thebans' eyes;
  Wherefore they all cried: 'Whither rushest thou,

Amphiaraus? Why dost leave the war?'
  And downward ceased he not to fall amain
  As far as Minos, who lays hold on all.

See, he has made a bosom of his shoulders!
  Because he wished to see too far before him
  Behind he looks, and backward goes his way:

Behold Tiresias, who his semblance changed,
  When from a male a female he became,
  His members being all of them transformed;

And afterwards was forced to strike once more
  The two entangled serpents with his rod,
  Ere he could have again his manly plumes.

That Aruns is, who backs the other's belly,
  Who in the hills of Luni, there where grubs
  The Carrarese who houses underneath,

Among the marbles white a cavern had
  For his abode; whence to behold the stars
  And sea, the view was not cut off from him.

And she there, who is covering up her breasts,
  Which thou beholdest not, with loosened tresses,
  And on that side has all the hairy skin,

Was Manto, who made quest through many lands,
  Afterwards tarried there where I was born;
  Whereof I would thou list to me a little.

After her father had from life departed,
  And the city of Bacchus had become enslaved,
  She a long season wandered through the world.

Above in beauteous Italy lies a lake
  At the Alp's foot that shuts in Germany
  Over Tyrol, and has the name Benaco.

By a thousand springs, I think, and more, is bathed,
  'Twixt Garda and Val Camonica, Pennino,
  With water that grows stagnant in that lake.

Midway a place is where the Trentine Pastor,
  And he of Brescia, and the Veronese
  Might give his blessing, if he passed that way.

Sitteth Peschiera, fortress fair and strong,
  To front the Brescians and the Bergamasks,
  Where round about the bank descendeth lowest.

There of necessity must fall whatever
  In bosom of Benaco cannot stay,
  And grows a river down through verdant pastures.

Soon as the water doth begin to run,
  No more Benaco is it called, but Mincio,
  Far as Governo, where it falls in Po.

Not far it runs before it finds a plain
  In which it spreads itself, and makes it marshy,
  And oft 'tis wont in summer to be sickly.

Passing that way the virgin pitiless
  Land in the middle of the fen descried,
  Untilled and naked of inhabitants;

There to escape all human intercourse,
  She with her servants stayed, her arts to practise
  And lived, and left her empty body there.

The men, thereafter, who were scattered round,
  Collected in that place, which was made strong
  By the lagoon it had on every side;

They built their city over those dead bones,
  And, after her who first the place selected,
  Mantua named it, without other omen.

Its people once within more crowded were,
  Ere the stupidity of Casalodi
  From Pinamonte had received deceit.

Therefore I caution thee, if e'er thou hearest
  Originate my city otherwise,
  No falsehood may the verity defraud."

And I: "My Master, thy discourses are
  To me so certain, and so take my faith,
  That unto me the rest would be spent coals.

But tell me of the people who are passing,
  If any one note-worthy thou beholdest,
  For only unto that my mind reverts."

Then said he to me: "He who from the cheek
  Thrusts out his beard upon his swarthy shoulders
  Was, at the time when Greece was void of males,

So that there scarce remained one in the cradle,
  An augur, and with Calchas gave the moment,
  In Aulis, when to sever the first cable.

Eryphylus his name was, and so sings
  My lofty Tragedy in some part or other;
  That knowest thou well, who knowest the whole of it.

The next, who is so slender in the flanks,
  Was Michael Scott, who of a verity
  Of magical illusions knew the game.

Behold Guido Bonatti, behold Asdente,
  Who now unto his leather and his thread
  Would fain have stuck, but he too late repents.

Behold the wretched ones, who left the needle,
  The spool and rock, and made them fortune-tellers;
  They wrought their magic spells with herb and image.

But come now, for already holds the confines
  Of both the hemispheres, and under Seville
  Touches the ocean-wave, Cain and the thorns,

And yesternight the moon was round already;
  Thou shouldst remember well it did not harm thee
  From time to time within the forest deep."

Thus spake he to me, and we walked the while.

Canto XXI

Virgil and Dante stand on the arch that spans the fifth bolgia. *They see black devils running along it, with sinners over their shoulders which they cast into a ditch bubbling with pitch. These are Barrators, who sinned against the State and are now tormented by a company of pitchfork-wielding Malebranche devils. Dante hides while Virgil addresses their captain, Malacoda, declaring that Heaven wills him and another to pass. The devils exchange obscene parting salutes as a team of them escorts the poets to a different bridge (the sixth one lies broken).*

From bridge to bridge thus, speaking other things
  Of which my Comedy cares not to sing,
  We came along, and held the summit, when

We halted to behold another fissure
  Of Malebolge and other vain laments;
  And I beheld it marvellously dark.

As in the Arsenal of the Venetians
  Boils in the winter the tenacious pitch
  To smear their unsound vessels o'er again,

For sail they cannot; and instead thereof
  One makes his vessel new, and one recaulks
  The ribs of that which many a voyage has made;

One hammers at the prow, one at the stern,
  This one makes oars, and that one cordage twists,
  Another mends the mainsail and the mizzen;

Thus, not by fire, but by the art divine,
  Was boiling down below there a dense pitch
  Which upon every side the bank belimed.

I saw it, but I did not see within it
  Aught but the bubbles that the boiling raised,
  And all swell up and resubside compressed.

The while below there fixedly I gazed,
  My Leader, crying out: "Beware, beware!"
  Drew me unto himself from where I stood.

Then I turned round, as one who is impatient
  To see what it behoves him to escape,
  And whom a sudden terror doth unman,

Who, while he looks, delays not his departure;
  And I beheld behind us a black devil,
  Running along upon the crag, approach.

Ah, how ferocious was he in his aspect!
  And how he seemed to me in action ruthless,
  With open wings and light upon his feet!

His shoulders, which sharp-pointed were and high,
  A sinner did encumber with both haunches,
  And he held clutched the sinews of the feet.

From off our bridge, he said: "O Malebranche,
  Behold one of the elders of Saint Zita;
  Plunge him beneath, for I return for others

Unto that town, which is well furnished with them.
  All there are barrators, except Bonturo;
  No into Yes for money there is changed."

He hurled him down, and over the hard crag
  Turned round, and never was a mastiff loosened
  In so much hurry to pursue a thief.

The other sank, and rose again face downward;
  But the demons, under cover of the bridge,
  Cried: "Here the Santo Volto has no place!

Here swims one otherwise than in the Serchio;
  Therefore, if for our gaffs thou wishest not,
  Do not uplift thyself above the pitch."

They seized him then with more than a hundred rakes;
  They said: "It here behoves thee to dance covered,
  That, if thou canst, thou secretly mayest pilfer."

They seized him then with more than a hundred rakes;

Inf. XXI, line 52

Not otherwise the cooks their scullions make
  Immerse into the middle of the caldron
  The meat with hooks, so that it may not float.

Said the good Master to me: "That it be not
  Apparent thou art here, crouch thyself down
  Behind a jag, that thou mayest have some screen;

And for no outrage that is done to me
  Be thou afraid, because these things I know,
  For once before was I in such a scuffle."

Then he passed on beyond the bridge's head,
  And as upon the sixth bank he arrived,
  Need was for him to have a steadfast front.

With the same fury, and the same uproar,
  As dogs leap out upon a mendicant,
  Who on a sudden begs, where'er he stops,

They issued from beneath the little bridge,
  And turned against him all their grappling-irons;
  But he cried out: "Be none of you malignant!

Before those hooks of yours lay hold of me,
  Let one of you step forward, who may hear me,
  And then take counsel as to grappling me."

They all cried out: "Let Malacoda go;"
  Whereat one started, and the rest stood still,
  And he came to him, saying: "What avails it?"

"Thinkest thou, Malacoda, to behold me
  Advanced into this place," my Master said,
  "Safe hitherto from all your skill of fence,

Without the will divine, and fate auspicious?
  Let me go on, for it in Heaven is willed
  That I another show this savage road."

Then was his arrogance so humbled in him,
  That he let fall his grapnel at his feet,
  And to the others said: "Now strike him not."

And unto me my Guide: "O thou, who sittest
  Among the splinters of the bridge crouched down,
  Securely now return to me again."

Wherefore I started and came swiftly to him;
  And all the devils forward thrust themselves,
  So that I feared they would not keep their compact.

And thus beheld I once afraid the soldiers
  Who issued under safeguard from Caprona,
  Seeing themselves among so many foes.

Close did I press myself with all my person
  Beside my Leader, and turned not mine eyes
  From off their countenance, which was not good.

They lowered their rakes, and "Wilt thou have me
                         hit him,"
  They said to one another, "on the rump?"
  And answered: "Yes; see that thou nick him with it."

But the same demon who was holding parley
  With my Conductor turned him very quickly,
  And said: "Be quiet, be quiet, Scarmiglione;"

Then said to us: "You can no farther go
  Forward upon this crag, because is lying
  All shattered, at the bottom, the sixth arch.

And if it still doth please you to go onward,
  Pursue your way along upon this rock;
  Near is another crag that yields a path.

Yesterday, five hours later than this hour,
  One thousand and two hundred sixty-six
  Years were complete, that here the way was
                                  broken.

I send in that direction some of mine
  To see if any one doth air himself;
  Go ye with them; for they will not be vicious.

Step forward, Alichino and Calcabrina,"
  Began he to cry out, "and thou, Cagnazzo;
  And Barbariccia, do thou guide the ten.

Come forward, Libicocco and Draghignazzo,
  And tusked Ciriatto and Graffiacane,
  And Farfarello and mad Rubicante;

Search ye all round about the boiling pitch;
  Let these be safe as far as the next crag,
  That all unbroken passes o'er the dens."

"O me! what is it, Master, that I see?
  Pray let us go," I said, "without an escort,
  If thou knowest how, since for myself I ask none.

But he cried out: "Be none of you malignant!"

Inf. XXI, line 72

If thou art as observant as thy wont is,
  Dost thou not see that they do gnash their teeth,
  And with their brows are threatening woe to us?"

And he to me: "I will not have thee fear;
  Let them gnash on, according to their fancy,
  Because they do it for those boiling wretches."

Along the left-hand dike they wheeled about;
  But first had each one thrust his tongue between
  His teeth towards their leader for a signal;

And he had made a trumpet of his rump.

Canto XXII

*Dante compares Malacoda's salute to the kinds of military signals he knows. Any
Barrators who are seen squatting in the pitch dive underneath the surface as soon as
any devil comes near. A sinner from Navarre falls into the clutches of Graffiacan and
is torn apart. Questioned by Virgil during these antics, the Navarrese sinner tricks the
devils into momentarily looking away on the promise that he will lure others, like
Friar Gomita and Michael Zanche, to the surface. As he plunges into the pitch and
escapes, two devils rush in after him and have to be rescued by Barbarricia. A fight ensues.*

I have erewhile seen horsemen moving camp,
  Begin the storming, and their muster make,
  And sometimes starting off for their escape;

Vaunt-couriers have I seen upon your land,
  O Aretines, and foragers go forth,
  Tournaments stricken, and the joustings run,

Sometimes with trumpets and sometimes with bells,
  With kettle-drums, and signals of the castles,
  And with our own, and with outlandish things,

But never yet with bagpipe so uncouth
  Did I see horsemen move, nor infantry,
  Nor ship by any sign of land or star.

We went upon our way with the ten demons;
  Ah, savage company! but in the church
  With saints, and in the tavern with the gluttons!

Ever upon the pitch was my intent,
  To see the whole condition of that *Bolgia*,
  And of the people who therein were burned.

Even as the dolphins, when they make a sign
  To mariners by arching of the back,
  That they should counsel take to save their vessel,

Thus sometimes, to alleviate his pain,
  One of the sinners would display his back,
  And in less time conceal it than it lightens.

As on the brink of water in a ditch
  The frogs stand only with their muzzles out,
  So that they hide their feet and other bulk,

So upon every side the sinners stood;
  But ever as Barbariccia near them came,
  Thus underneath the boiling they withdrew.

I saw, and still my heart doth shudder at it,
  One waiting thus, even as it comes to pass
  One frog remains, and down another dives;

And Graffiacan, who most confronted him,
  Grappled him by his tresses smeared with pitch,
  And drew him up, so that he seemed an otter.

I knew, before, the names of all of them,
  So had I noted them when they were chosen,
  And when they called each other, listened how.

"O Rubicante, see that thou do lay
  Thy claws upon him, so that thou mayst flay him,"
  Cried all together the accursed ones.

And I: "My Master, see to it, if thou canst,
  That thou mayst know who is the luckless wight,
  Thus come into his adversaries' hands."

Near to the side of him my Leader drew,
  Asked of him whence he was; and he replied:
  "I in the kingdom of Navarre was born;

My mother placed me servant to a lord,
  For she had borne me to a ribald knave,
  Destroyer of himself and of his things.

Then I domestic was of good King Thibault;
  I set me there to practise barratry,
  For which I pay the reckoning in this heat."

And Ciriatto, from whose mouth projected,
  On either side, a tusk, as in a boar,
  Caused him to feel how one of them could rip.

Among malicious cats the mouse had come;
  But Barbariccia clasped him in his arms,
  And said: "Stand ye aside, while I enfork him."

And to my Master he turned round his head;
  "Ask him again," he said, "if more thou wish
  To know from him, before some one destroy him."

The Guide: "Now tell then of the other culprits;
  Knowest thou any one who is a Latian,
  Under the pitch?" And he: "I separated

Lately from one who was a neighbour to it;
  Would that I still were covered up with him,
  For I should fear not either claw nor hook!"

And Libicocco: "We have borne too much;"
  And with his grapnel seized him by the arm,
  So that, by rending, he tore off a tendon.

Eke Draghignazzo wished to pounce upon him
  Down at the legs; whence their Decurion
  Turned round and round about with evil look.

When they again somewhat were pacified,
  Of him, who still was looking at his wound,
  Demanded my Conductor without stay:

"Who was that one, from whom a luckless parting
  Thou sayest thou hast made, to come ashore?"
  And he replied: "It was the Friar Gomita,

He of Gallura, vessel of all fraud,
  Who had the enemies of his Lord in hand,
  And dealt so with them each exults thereat;

Money he took, and let them smoothly off,
  As he says; and in other offices
  A barrator was he, not mean but sovereign.

Foregathers with him one Don Michael Zanche
  Of Logodoro; and of Sardinia
  To gossip never do their tongues feel tired.

O me! see that one, how he grinds his teeth;
  Still farther would I speak, but am afraid
  Lest he to scratch my itch be making ready."

And the grand Provost, turned to Farfarello,
  Who rolled his eyes about as if to strike,
  Said: "Stand aside there, thou malicious bird."

"If you desire either to see or hear,"
  The terror-stricken recommenced thereon,
  "Tuscans or Lombards, I will make them come.

But let the Malebranche cease a little,
  So that these may not their revenges fear,
  And I, down sitting in this very place,

For one that I am will make seven come,
  When I shall whistle, as our custom is
  To do whenever one of us comes out."

Cagnazzo at these words his muzzle lifted,
  Shaking his head, and said: "Just hear the trick
  Which he has thought of, down to throw himself!"

Whence he, who snares in great abundance had,
  Responded: "I by far too cunning am,
  When I procure for mine a greater sadness."

Alichin held not in, but running counter
  Unto the rest, said to him: "If thou dive,
  I will not follow thee upon the gallop,

But I will beat my wings above the pitch;
  The height be left, and be the bank a shield
  To see if thou alone dost countervail us."

O thou who readest, thou shalt hear new sport!
  Each to the other side his eyes averted;
  He first, who most reluctant was to do it.

The Navarrese selected well his time;
  Planted his feet on land, and in a moment
  Leaped, and released himself from their design.

Whereat each one was suddenly stung with shame,
  But he most who was cause of the defeat;
  Therefore he moved, and cried: "Thou art o'ertakern."

But little it availed, for wings could not
  Outstrip the fear; the other one went under,
  And, flying, upward he his breast directed;

Not otherwise the duck upon a sudden
  Dives under, when the falcon is approaching,
  And upward he returneth cross and weary.

Infuriate at the mockery, Calcabrina
  Flying behind him followed close, desirous
  The other should escape, to have a quarrel.

And when the barrator had disappeared,
  He turned his talons upon his companion,
  And grappled with him right above the moat.

But sooth the other was a doughty sparhawk
  To clapperclaw him well; and both of them
  Fell in the middle of the boiling pond.

A sudden intercessor was the heat;
  But ne'ertheless of rising there was naught,
  To such degree they had their wings belimed.

Lamenting with the others, Barbariccia
  Made four of them fly to the other side
  With all their gaffs, and very speedily

This side and that they to their posts descended;
  They stretched their hooks towards the pitch-
                                        ensnared,
  Who were already baked within the crust,

And in this manner busied did we leave them.

Therefore he moved, and cried: "Thou art o'ertakern."

Inf. XXII, lines 126

But sooth the other was a doughty sparhawk / To clapperclaw him well; and both of them /
Fell in the middle of the boiling pond.

Inf. XXII, lines 139–141

Canto XXIII

*The sinner's skirmish with the devils reminds Dante of the frog, mouse and hawk
fable, where each animal successively deceives the other. Sensing danger, Virgil grabs
Dante and they run to the edge of the ravine and slide down into the sixth* bolgia.
*Looking up, they see the devils and are thankful for their escape. The weeping
Hypocrites approach in single file, wearing gilded but heavy, lead-lined cloaks. The
worst hypocrite of all, Caiaphas, Pontius Pilate's evil counsellor, stands crucified and
impaled by three stakes. Virgil is angry to discover that Malacoda lied about the bridge
in Canto XXI – they will have to climb up a rockslide instead.*

Silent, alone, and without company
  We went, the one in front, the other after,
  As go the Minor Friars along their way.

Upon the fable of Aesop was directed
  My thought, by reason of the present quarrel,
  Where he has spoken of the frog and mouse;

For 'mo' and 'issa' are not more alike
  Than this one is to that, if well we couple
  End and beginning with a steadfast mind.

And even as one thought from another springs,
  So afterward from that was born another,
  Which the first fear within me double made.

Thus did I ponder: "These on our account
  Are laughed to scorn, with injury and scoff
  So great, that much I think it must annoy them.

If anger be engrafted on ill-will,
  They will come after us more merciless
  Than dog upon the leveret which he seizes,"

I felt my hair stand all on end already
  With terror, and stood backwardly intent,
  When said I: "Master, if thou hidest not

Thyself and me forthwith, of Malebranche
  I am in dread; we have them now behind us;
  I so imagine them, I already feel them."

And he: "If I were made of leaded glass,
  Thine outward image I should not attract
  Sooner to me than I imprint the inner.

Just now thy thoughts came in among my own,
  With similar attitude and similar face,
  So that of both one counsel sole I made.

If peradventure the right bank so slope
  That we to the next *Bolgia* can descend,
  We shall escape from the imagined chase."

Not yet he finished rendering such opinion,
  When I beheld them come with outstretched wings,
  Not far remote, with will to seize upon us.

My Leader on a sudden seized me up,
  Even as a mother who by noise is wakened,
  And close beside her sees the enkindled flames,

Who takes her son, and flies, and does not stop,
  Having more care of him than of herself,
  So that she clothes her only with a shift;

And downward from the top of the hard bank
  Supine he gave him to the pendent rock,
  That one side of the other *Bolgia* walls.

Ne'er ran so swiftly water through a sluice
  To turn the wheel of any land-built mill,
  When nearest to the paddles it approaches,

As did my Master down along that border,
  Bearing me with him on his breast away,
  As his own son, and not as a companion.

Hardly the bed of the ravine below
  His feet had reached, ere they had reached the hill
  Right over us; but he was not afraid;

Hardly the bed of the ravine below / His feet had reached, ere they had reached the hill /
Right over us;

Inf. XXIII, lines 52–54

For the high Providence, which had ordained
  To place them ministers of the fifth moat,
  The power of thence departing took from all.

A painted people there below we found,
  Who went about with footsteps very slow,
  Weeping and in their semblance tired and vanquished.

They had on mantles with the hoods low down
  Before their eyes, and fashioned of the cut
  That in Cologne they for the monks are made.

Without, they gilded are so that it dazzles;
  But inwardly all leaden and so heavy
  That Frederick used to put them on of straw.

O everlastingly fatiguing mantle!
  Again we turned us, still to the left hand
  Along with them, intent on their sad plaint;

But owing to the weight, that weary folk
  Came on so tardily, that we were new
  In company at each motion of the haunch.

Whence I unto my Leader: "See thou find
  Some one who may by deed or name be known,
  And thus in going move thine eye about."

And one, who understood the Tuscan speech,
  Cried to us from behind: "Stay ye your feet,
  Ye, who so run athwart the dusky air!

Perhaps thou'lt have from me what thou demandest."
  Whereat the Leader turned him, and said: "Wait,
  And then according to his pace proceed."

I stopped, and two beheld I show great haste
  Of spirit, in their faces, to be with me;
  But the burden and the narrow way delayed them.

When they came up, long with an eye askance
  They scanned me without uttering a word.
  Then to each other turned, and said together:

"He by the action of his throat seems living;
  And if they dead are, by what privilege
  Go they uncovered by the heavy stole?"

Then said to me: "Tuscan, who to the college
  Of miserable hypocrites art come,
  Do not disdain to tell us who thou art."

And I to them: "Born was I, and grew up
  In the great town on the fair river of Arno,
  And with the body am I've always had.

But who are ye, in whom there trickles down
  Along your cheeks such grief as I behold?
  And what pain is upon you, that so sparkles?"

And one replied to me: "These orange cloaks
  Are made of lead so heavy, that the weights
  Cause in this way their balances to creak.

Frati Gaudenti were we, and Bolognese;
  I Catalano, and he Loderingo
  Named, and together taken by thy city,

As the wont is to take one man alone,
  For maintenance of its peace; and we were such
  That still it is apparent round Gardingo."

"O Friars," began I, "your iniquitous. . ."
  But said no more; for to mine eyes there rushed
  One crucified with three stakes on the ground.

When me he saw, he writhed himself all over,
  Blowing into his beard with suspirations;
  And the Friar Catalan, who noticed this,

Said to me: "This transfixed one, whom thou seest,
  Counselled the Pharisees that it was meet
  To put one man to torture for the people.

Crosswise and naked is he on the path,
  As thou perceivest; and he needs must feel,
  Whoever passes, first how much he weighs;

And in like mode his father-in-law is punished
  Within this moat, and the others of the council,
  Which for the Jews was a malignant seed."

And thereupon I saw Virgilius marvel
  O'er him who was extended on the cross
  So vilely in eternal banishment.

Then he directed to the Friar this voice:
  "Be not displeased, if granted thee, to tell us
  If to the right hand any pass slope down

By which we two may issue forth from here,
  Without constraining some of the black angels
  To come and extricate us from this deep."

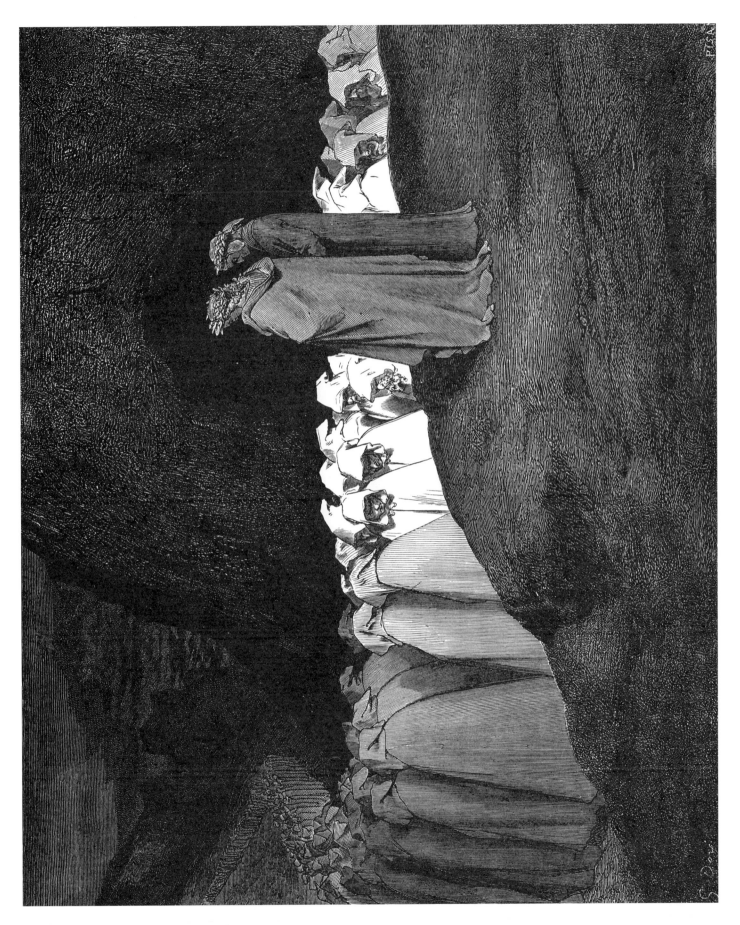

They had on mantles with the hoods low down / Before their eyes,

Inf. XXIII, lines 61–62

"This transfixed one, whom thou seest, / Counselled the Pharisees that it was meet / To put one man to torture for the people.

Inf. XXIII, lines 115–117

Then he made answer: "Nearer than thou hopest
  There is a rock, that forth from the great circle
  Proceeds, and crosses all the cruel valleys,

Save that at this 'tis broken, and does not bridge it;
  You will be able to mount up the ruin,
  That sidelong slopes and at the bottom rises."

The Leader stood awhile with head bowed down;
  Then said: "The business badly he recounted
  Who grapples with his hook the sinners yonder."

And the Friar: "Many of the Devil's vices
  Once heard I at Bologna, and among them,
  That he's a liar and the father of lies."

Thereat my Leader with great strides went on,
  Somewhat disturbed with anger in his looks;
  Whence from the heavy-laden I departed

After the prints of his beloved feet.

Canto XXIV

*Teacher and pupil begin their arduous ascent of the fallen bridge. Crossing back into
the seventh* bolgia, *they hear sounds in the darkness. Once at the top, Dante cannot
catch his breath. At the edge of the eighth* bolgia, *they behold a chaotic scene of
running Thieves being attacked by serpents. One reptile darts out and strikes a blow to
a sinner's neck. He catches fire and turns into a pile of ashes before being restored to his
mortal form – that of Vanni Fucci, a sacristy thief from Pistoia. He, too, predicts
political strife for Florence.*

In that part of the youthful year wherein
  The Sun his locks beneath Aquarius tempers,
  And now the nights draw near to half the day,

What time the hoar-frost copies on the ground
  The outward semblance of her sister white,
  But little lasts the temper of her pen,

The husbandman, whose forage faileth him,
  Rises, and looks, and seeth the champaign
  All gleaming white, whereat he beats his flank,

Returns in doors, and up and down laments,
  Like a poor wretch, who knows not what to do;
  Then he returns and hope revives again,

Seeing the world has changed its countenance
  In little time, and takes his shepherd's crook,
  And forth the little lambs to pasture drives.

Thus did the Master fill me with alarm,
  When I beheld his forehead so disturbed,
  And to the ailment came as soon the plaster.

For as we came unto the ruined bridge,
  The Leader turned to me with that sweet look
  Which at the mountain's foot I first beheld.

His arms he opened, after some advisement
  Within himself elected, looking first
  Well at the ruin, and laid hold of me.

And even as he who acts and meditates,
  For aye it seems that he provides beforehand,
  So upward lifting me towards the summit

Of a huge rock, he scanned another crag,
  Saying: "To that one grapple afterwards,
  But try first if 'tis such that it will hold thee."

This was no way for one clothed with a cloak;
  For hardly we, he light, and I pushed upward,
  Were able to ascend from jag to jag.

And had it not been, that upon that precinct
  Shorter was the ascent than on the other,
  He I know not, but I had been dead beat.

But because Malebolge tow'rds the mouth
  Of the profoundest well is all inclining,
  The structure of each valley doth import

That one bank rises and the other sinks.
  Still we arrived at length upon the point
  Wherefrom the last stone breaks itself asunder.

The breath was from my lungs so milked away,
  When I was up, that I could go no farther,
  Nay, I sat down upon my first arrival.

"Now it behoves thee thus to put off sloth,"
  My Master said; "for sitting upon down,
  Or under quilt, one cometh not to fame,

Withouten which whoso his life consumes
  Such vestige leaveth of himself on Earth,
  As smoke in air or in the water foam.

And therefore raise thee up, o'ercome the anguish
  With spirit that o'ercometh every battle,
  If with its heavy body it sink not.

A longer stairway it behoves thee mount;
  'Tis not enough from these to have departed;
  Let it avail thee, if thou understand me."

Then I uprose, showing myself provided
  Better with breath than I did feel myself,
  And said: "Go on, for I am strong and bold."

Upward we took our way along the crag,
  Which jagged was, and narrow, and difficult,
  And more precipitous far than that before.

Speaking I went, not to appear exhausted;
  Whereat a voice from the next moat came forth,
  Not well adapted to articulate words.

I know not what it said, though o'er the back
  I now was of the arch that passes there;
  But he seemed moved to anger who was speaking.

I was bent downward, but my living eyes
  Could not attain the bottom, for the dark;
  Wherefore I: "Master, see that thou arrive

At the next round, and let us descend the wall;
  For as from hence I hear and understand not,
  So I look down and nothing I distinguish."

"Other response," he said, "I make thee not,
  Except the doing; for the modest asking
  Ought to be followed by the deed in silence."

We from the bridge descended at its head,
  Where it connects itself with the eighth bank,
  And then was manifest to me the *Bolgia*;

And I beheld therein a terrible throng
  Of serpents, and of such a monstrous kind,
  That the remembrance still congeals my blood

Let Libya boast no longer with her sand;
  For if Chelydri, Jaculi and Phareae
  She breeds, with Cenchri and with Amphisbaena,

Neither so many plagues nor so malignant
  E'er showed she with all Ethiopia,
  Nor with whatever on the Red Sea is!

Among this cruel and most dismal throng
  People were running naked and affrighted.
  Without the hope of hole or heliotrope.

They had their hands with serpents bound behind them;
  These riveted upon their reins the tail
  And head, and were in front of them entwined.

And lo! at one who was upon our side
  There darted forth a serpent, which transfixed him
  There where the neck is knotted to the shoulders.

Nor 'O' so quickly e'er, nor 'I' was written,
  As he took fire, and burned; and ashes wholly
  Behoved it that in falling he became.

And when he on the ground was thus destroyed,
  The ashes drew together, and of themselves
  Into himself they instantly returned.

Even thus by the great sages 'tis confessed
  The phoenix dies, and then is born again,
  When it approaches its five-hundredth year;

On herb or grain it feeds not in its life,
  But only on tears of incense and amomum,
  And nard and myrrh are its last winding-sheet.

And as he is who falls, and knows not how,
  By force of demons who to earth down drag him,
  Or other oppilation that binds man,

Among this cruel and most dismal throng / People were running naked and affrighted.

Inf. XXIV, lines 91–92

When he arises and around him looks,
　Wholly bewildered by the mighty anguish
　Which he has suffered, and in looking sighs;

Such was that sinner after he had risen.
　Justice of God! O how severe it is,
　That blows like these in vengeance poureth down!

The Guide thereafter asked him who he was;
　Whence he replied: "I rained from Tuscany
　A short time since into this cruel gorge.

A bestial life, and not a human, pleased me,
　Even as the mule I was; I'm Vanni Fucci,
　Beast, and Pistoia was my worthy den."

And I unto the Guide: "Tell him to stir not,
　And ask what crime has thrust him here below,
　For once a man of blood and wrath I saw him."

And the sinner, who had heard, dissembled not,
　But unto me directed mind and face,
　And with a melancholy shame was painted.

Then said: "It pains me more that thou hast caught me
　Amid this misery where thou seest me,
　Than when I from the other life was taken.

What thou demandest I cannot deny;
　So low am I put down because I robbed
　The sacristy of the fair ornaments,

And falsely once 'twas laid upon another;
　But that thou mayst not such a sight enjoy,
　If thou shalt e'er be out of the dark places,

Thine ears to my announcement ope and hear:
　Pistoia first of Neri groweth meagre;
　Then Florence doth renew her men and manners;

Mars draws a vapour up from Val di Magra,
　Which is with turbid clouds enveloped round,
　And with impetuous and bitter tempest

Over Campo Picen shall be the battle;
　When it shall suddenly rend the mist asunder,
　So that each Bianco shall thereby be smitten.

And this I've said that it may give thee pain."

Canto XXV

Vanni Fucci, the militant leader from Pistoia, makes an obscene gesture towards God with his fist before being immobilized by a bevy of snakes who wrap themselves around him. When he breaks free, Cacus the Centaur gallops off in pursuit, with a fire-belching dragon on his shoulders. Three shadows appear. They are looking for Cianfa, who appears as a man-become-snake. He attacks Agnello, with whom he merges into one monstrous being. Another shadow exchanges his serpentine form with Buoso. Only Puccio Sciancato retains his shape.

At the conclusion of his words, the thief
  Lifted his hands aloft with both the figs,
  Crying: "Take that, God, for at thee I aim them."

From that time forth the serpents were my friends;
  For one entwined itself about his neck
  As if it said: "I will not thou speak more;"

And round his arms another, and rebound him,
  Clinching itself together so in front,
  That with them he could not a motion make.

Pistoia, ah, Pistoia! why resolve not
  To burn thyself to ashes and so perish,
  Since in ill-doing thou thy seed excellest?

Through all the sombre circles of this Hell,
  Spirit I saw not against God so proud,
  Not he who fell at Thebes down from the walls!

He fled away, and spake no further word;
  And I beheld a Centaur full of rage
  Come crying out: "Where is, where is the scoffer?"

I do not think Maremma has so many
  Serpents as he had all along his back,
  As far as where our countenance begins.

Upon the shoulders, just behind the nape,
  With wings wide open was a dragon lying,
  And he sets fire to all that he encounters.

My Master said: "That one is Cacus, who
  Beneath the rock upon Mount Aventine
  Created oftentimes a lake of blood.

He goes not on the same road with his brothers,
  By reason of the fraudulent theft he made
  Of the great herd, which he had near to him;

Whereat his tortuous actions ceased beneath
  The mace of Hercules, who peradventure
  Gave him a hundred, and he felt not ten."

While he was speaking thus, he had passed by,
  And spirits three had underneath us come,
  Of which nor I aware was, nor my Leader,

Until what time they shouted: "Who are you?"
  On which account our story made a halt,
  And then we were intent on them alone.

I did not know them; but it came to pass,
  As it is wont to happen by some chance,
  That one to name the other was compelled,

Exclaiming: "Where can Cianfa have remained?"
  Whence I, so that the Leader might attend,
  Upward from chin to nose my finger laid.

If thou art, Reader, slow now to believe
  What I shall say, it will no marvel be,
  For I who saw it hardly can admit it.

As I was holding raised on them my brows,
  Behold! a serpent with six feet darts forth
  In front of one, and fastens wholly on him.

With middle feet it bound him round the paunch,
  And with the forward ones his arms it seized;
  Then thrust its teeth through one cheek and the
                                                other;

117

The hindermost it stretched upon his thighs,
  And put its tail through in between the two,
  And up behind along the reins outspread it.

Ivy was never fastened by its barbs
  Unto a tree so, as this horrible reptile
  Upon the other's limbs entwined its own.

Then they stuck close, as if of heated wax
  They had been made, and intermixed their colour;
  Nor one nor other seemed now what he was;

E'en as proceedeth on before the flame
  Upward along the paper a brown colour,
  Which is not black as yet, and the white dies.

The other two looked on, and each of them
  Cried out: "O me, Agnello, how thou changest!
  Behold, thou now art neither two nor one."

Already the two heads had one become,
  When there appeared to us two figures mingled
  Into one face, wherein the two were lost.

Of the four lists were fashioned the two arms,
  The thighs and legs, the belly and the chest
  Members became that never yet were seen.

Every original aspect there was cancelled;
  Two and yet none did the perverted image
  Appear, and such departed with slow pace.

Even as a lizard, under the great scourge
  Of days canicular, exchanging hedge,
  Lightning appeareth if the road it cross;

Thus did appear, coming towards the bellies
  Of the two others, a small fiery serpent,
  Livid and black as is a peppercorn.

And in that part whereat is first received
  Our aliment, it one of them transfixed;
  Then downward fell in front of him extended.

The one transfixed looked at it, but said naught;
  Nay, rather with feet motionless he yawned,
  Just as if sleep or fever had assailed him.

He at the serpent gazed, and it at him;
  One through the wound, the other through the
                          mouth
  Smoked violently, and the smoke commingled.

Henceforth be silent Lucan, where he mentions
  Wretched Sabellus and Nassidius,
  And wait to hear what now shall be shot forth.

Be silent Ovid, of Cadmus and Arethusa;
  For if him to a snake, her to fountain,
  Converts he fabling, that I grudge him not;

Because two natures never front to front
  Has he transmuted, so that both the forms
  To interchange their matter ready were.

Together they responded in such wise,
  That to a fork the serpent cleft his tail,
  And eke the wounded drew his feet together.

The legs together with the thighs themselves
  Adhered so, that in little time the juncture
  No sign whatever made that was apparent.

He with the cloven tail assumed the figure
  The other one was losing, and his skin
  Became elastic, and the other's hard.

I saw the arms draw inward at the armpits,
  And both feet of the reptile, that were short,
  Lengthen as much as those contracted were.

Thereafter the hind feet, together twisted,
  Became the member that a man conceals,
  And of his own the wretch had two created.

While both of them the exhalation veils
  With a new colour, and engenders hair
  On one of them and depilates the other,

The one uprose and down the other fell,
  Though turning not away their impious lamps,
  Underneath which each one his muzzle changed.

He who was standing drew it tow'rds the temples,
  And from excess of matter, which came thither,
  Issued the ears from out the hollow cheeks;

What did not backward run and was retained
  Of that excess made to the face a nose,
  And the lips thickened far as was befitting.

He who lay prostrate thrusts his muzzle forward,
  And backward draws the ears into his head,
  In the same manner as the snail its horns;

"O me, Agnello, how thou changest! / Behold, thou now art neither two nor one."

Inf. XXV, lines 68–69

And so the tongue, which was entire and apt
  For speech before, is cleft, and the bi-forked
  In the other closes up, and the smoke ceases.

The soul, which to a reptile had been changed,
  Along the valley hissing takes to flight,
  And after him the other speaking sputters.

Then did he turn upon him his new shoulders,
  And said to the other: "I'll have Buoso run,
  Crawling as I have done, along this road."

In this way I beheld the seventh ballast
  Shift and reshift, and here be my excuse
  The novelty, if aught my pen transgress.

And notwithstanding that mine eyes might be
  Somewhat bewildered, and my mind dismayed,
  They could not flee away so secretly

But that I plainly saw Puccio Sciancato;
  And he it was who sole of three companions,
  Which came in the beginning, was not changed;

The other was he whom thou, Gaville, weepest.

Canto XXVI

The rocky rise above the eighth bolgia *is characterized by flickering flames, each of which contains the soul of a Deceiver. One of the flames, curiously split in two, catches Dante's attention. He is told that it houses a pair of Trojan warriors, Ulysses and Diomed, who are being jointly punished for fraudulent counselling. Virgil interrogates the pair for Dante's benefit. Ulysses recalls his final voyage, on which he sailed past the Pillars of Hercules (Strait of Gibraltar) and into the forbidden sea (Atlantic Ocean), where a whirlwind rose up and spun his vessel around before sinking it.*

Rejoice, O Florence, since thou art so great,
  That over sea and land thou beatest thy wings,
  And throughout Hell thy name is spread abroad!

Among the thieves five citizens of thine
  Like these I found, whence shame comes unto me,
  And thou thereby to no great honour risest.

But if when morn is near our dreams are true,
  Feel shalt thou in a little time from now
  What Prato, if none other, craves for thee.

And if it now were, it were not too soon;
  Would that it were, seeing it needs must be,
  For 'twill aggrieve me more the more I age.

We went our way, and up along the stairs
  The bourns had made us to descend before,
  Remounted my Conductor and drew me.

And following the solitary path
  Among the rocks and ridges of the crag,
  The foot without the hand sped not at all.

Then sorrowed I, and sorrow now again,
  When I direct my mind to what I saw,
  And more my genius curb than I am wont,

That it may run not unless virtue guide it;
  So that if some good star, or better thing,
  Have given me good, I may myself not grudge it.

As many as the hind (who on the hill
  Rests at the time when he who lights the world
  His countenance keeps least concealed from us,

While as the fly gives place unto the gnat)
  Seeth the glow-worms down along the valley,
  Perchance there where he ploughs and makes his
                                      vintage;

With flames as manifold resplendent all
  Was the eighth *Bolgia*, as I grew aware
  As soon as I was where the depth appeared.

And such as he who with the bears avenged him
  Beheld Elijah's chariot at departing,
  What time the steeds to heaven erect uprose,

For with his eye he could not follow it
  So as to see aught else than flame alone,
  Even as a little cloud ascending upward,

Thus each along the gorge of the intrenchment
  Was moving; for not one reveals the theft,
  And every flame a sinner steals away.

I stood upon the bridge uprisen to see,
  So that, if I had seized not on a rock,
  Down had I fallen without being pushed.

And the Leader, who beheld me so attent,
  Exclaimed: "Within the fires the spirits are;
  Each swathes himself with that wherewith he burns."

"My Master," I replied, "by hearing thee
  I am more sure; but I surmised already
  It might be so, and already wished to ask thee

Who is within that fire, which comes so cleft
  At top, it seems uprising from the pyre
  Where was Eteocles with his brother placed."

He answered me: "Within there are tormented
  Ulysses and Diomed, and thus together
  They unto vengeance run as unto wrath.

And there within their flame do they lament
  The ambush of the horse, which made the door
  Whence issued forth the Romans' gentle seed;

Therein is wept the craft, for which being dead
  Deidamia still deplores Achilles,
  And pain for the Palladium there is borne."

"If they within those sparks possess the power
  To speak," I said, "thee, Master, much I pray,
  And re-pray, that the prayer be worth a thousand,

That thou make no denial of awaiting
  Until the horned flame shall hither come;
  Thou seest that with desire I lean towards it."

And he to me: "Worthy is thy entreaty
  Of much applause, and therefore I accept it;
  But take heed that thy tongue restrain itself.

Leave me to speak, because I have conceived
  That which thou wishest; for they might disdain
  Perchance, since they were Greeks, discourse of
                                      thine."

When now the flame had come unto that point,
  Where to my Leader it seemed time and place,
  After this fashion did I hear him speak:

"O ye, who are twofold within one fire,
  If I deserved of you, while I was living,
  If I deserved of you or much or little

When in the world I wrote the lofty verses,
  Do not move on, but one of you declare
  Whither, being lost, he went away to die."

Then of the antique flame the greater horn,
  Murmuring, began to wave itself about
  Even as a flame doth which the wind fatigues.

Thereafterward, the summit to and fro
  Moving as if it were the tongue that spake,
  It uttered forth a voice, and said: "When I

From Circe had departed, who concealed me
  More than a year there near unto Gaeta,
  Or ever yet Aeneas named it so,

Nor fondness for my son, nor reverence
  For my old father, nor the due affection
  Which joyous should have made Penelope,

Could overcome within me the desire
  I had to be experienced of the world,
  And of the vice and virtue of mankind;

But I put forth on the high open sea
  With one sole ship, and that small company
  By which I never had deserted been.

"Within the fires the spirits are; / Each swathes himself with that wherewith he burns"

Inf. XXVI, lines 47–48

Both of the shores I saw as far as Spain,
  Far as Morocco, and the isle of Sardes,
  And the others which that sea bathes round about.

I and my company were old and slow
  When at that narrow passage we arrived
  Where Hercules his landmarks set as signals,

That man no farther onward should adventure.
  On the right hand behind me left I Seville,
  And on the other already had left Ceuta.

'O brothers, who amid a hundred thousand
  Perils,' I said, 'have come unto the West,
  To this so inconsiderable vigil

Which is remaining of your senses still
  Be ye unwilling to deny the knowledge,
  Following the sun, of the unpeopled world.

Consider ye the seed from which ye sprang;
  Ye were not made to live like unto brutes,
  But for pursuit of virtue and of knowledge.'

So eager did I render my companions,
  With this brief exhortation, for the voyage,
  That then I hardly could have held them back.

And having turned our stern unto the morning,
  We of the oars made wings for our mad flight,
  Evermore gaining on the larboard side.

Already all the stars of the other pole
  The night beheld, and ours so very low
  It did not rise above the ocean floor.

Five times rekindled and as many quenched
  Had been the splendour underneath the moon,
  Since we had entered into the deep pass,

When there appeared to us a mountain, dim
  From distance, and it seemed to me so high
  As I had never any one beheld.

Joyful were we, and soon it turned to weeping;
  For out of the new land a whirlwind rose,
  And smote upon the fore part of the ship.

Three times it made her whirl with all the waters,
  At the fourth time it made the stern uplift,
  And the prow downward go, as pleased Another,

Until the sea above us closed again."

Canto XXVII

*Another flame draws near, having recognized Virgil's Lombard accent. It asks for
tidings of its native region and pleads that its identity and life story remain undisclosed
but it is none other than Guido Da Montefeltro. This well-known deceiver joined the
Franciscan order in old age after a high-profile military career as a Ghibelline captain.
Breaking his vows, he adopted military fraud to guide Pope Boniface VIII to victory
against the Colonna family and uttered a fraudulent repentance on his deathbed,
trusting in the pontificate's fake absolution.*

Already was the flame erect and quiet,
  To speak no more, and now departed from us
  With the permission of the gentle Poet;

When yet another, which behind it came,
  Caused us to turn our eyes upon its top
  By a confused sound that issued from it.

As the Sicilian bull (that bellowed first
  With the lament of him, and that was right,
  Who with his file had modulated it)

Bellowed so with the voice of the afflicted,
  That, notwithstanding it was made of brass,
  Still it appeared with agony transfixed;

Thus, by not having any way or issue
  At first from out the fire, to its own language
  Converted were the melancholy words.

But afterwards, when they had gathered way
  Up through the point, giving it that vibration
  The tongue had given them in their passage out,

We heard it said: "O thou, at whom I aim
  My voice, and who but now wast speaking Lombard,
  Saying, 'Now go thy way, no more I urge thee,'

Because I come perchance a little late,
  To stay and speak with me let it not irk thee;
  Thou seest it irks not me, and I am burning.

If thou but lately into this blind world
  Hast fallen down from that sweet Latian land,
  Wherefrom I bring the whole of my transgression,

Say, if the Romagnuols have peace or war,
  For I was from the mountains there between
  Urbino and the yoke whence Tiber bursts."

I still was downward bent and listening,
  When my Conductor touched me on the side,
  Saying: "Speak thou: this one a Latian is."

And I, who had beforehand my reply
  In readiness, forthwith began to speak:
  "O soul, that down below there art concealed,

Romagna thine is not and never has been
  Without war in the bosom of its tyrants;
  But open war I none have left there now.

Ravenna stands as it long years has stood;
  The Eagle of Polenta there is brooding,
  So that she covers Cervia with her vans.

The city which once made the long resistance,
  And of the French a sanguinary heap,
  Beneath the Green Paws finds itself again;

Verrucchio's ancient Mastiff and the new,
  Who made such bad disposal of Montagna,
  Where they are wont make wimbles of their teeth.

The cities of Lamone and Santerno
  Governs the Lioncel of the white lair,
  Who changes sides 'twixt summer-time and winter;

And that of which the Savio bathes the flank,
  Even as it lies between the plain and mountain,
  Lives between tyranny and a free state.

Now I entreat thee tell us who thou art;
  Be not more stubborn than the rest have been,
  So may thy name hold front there in the world."

After the fire a little more had roared
  In its own fashion, the sharp point it moved
  This way and that, and then gave forth such breath:

"If I believed that my reply were made
  To one who to the world would e'er return,
  This flame without more flickering would stand still;

But inasmuch as never from this depth
  Did any one return, if I hear true,
  Without the fear of infamy I answer,

I was a man of arms, then Cordelier,
  Believing thus begirt to make amends;
  And truly my belief had been fulfilled

But for the High Priest, whom may ill betide,
  Who put me back into my former sins;
  And how and wherefore I will have thee hear.

While I was still the form of bone and pulp
  My mother gave to me, the deeds I did
  Were not those of a lion, but a fox.

The machinations and the covert ways
  I knew them all, and practised so their craft,
  That to the ends of Earth the sound went forth.

When now unto that portion of mine age
  I saw myself arrived, when each one ought
  To lower the sails, and coil away the ropes,

That which before had pleased me then displeased me;
  And penitent and confessing I surrendered,
  Ah woe is me! and it would have bestead me;

The Leader of the modern Pharisees
  Having a war near unto Lateran,
  And not with Saracens nor with the Jews,

For each one of his enemies was Christian,
  And none of them had been to conquer Acre,
  Nor merchandising in the Sultan's land,

Nor the high office, nor the sacred orders,
  In him regarded, nor in me that cord
  Which used to make those girt with it more meagre;

But even as Constantine sought out Sylvester
  To cure his leprosy, within Soracte,
  So this one sought me out as an adept

To cure him of the fever of his pride.
  Counsel he asked of me, and I was silent,
  Because his words appeared inebriate.

And then he said: 'Be not thy heart afraid;
  Henceforth I thee absolve; and thou instruct me
  How to raze Palestrina to the ground.

Heaven have I power to lock and to unlock,
  As thou dost know; therefore the keys are two,
  The which my predecessor held not dear.'

Then urged me on his weighty arguments
  There, where my silence was the worst advice;
  And said I: 'Father, since thou washest me

Of that sin into which I now must fall,
  The promise long with the fulfilment short
  Will make thee triumph in thy lofty seat.'

Francis came afterward, when I was dead,
  For me; but one of the black Cherubim
  Said to him: 'Take him not; do me no wrong;

He must come down among my servitors,
  Because he gave the fraudulent advice
  From which time forth I have been at his hair;

For who repents not cannot be absolved,
  Nor can one both repent and will at once,
  Because of the contradiction which consents not.'

O miserable me! how I did shudder
  When he seized on me, saying: 'Peradventure
  Thou didst not think that I was a logician!'

He bore me unto Minos, who entwined
  Eight times his tail about his stubborn back,
  And after he had bitten it in great rage,

Said: 'Of the thievish fire a culprit this;'
  Wherefore, here where thou seest, am I lost,
  And vested thus in going I bemoan me."

When it had thus completed its recital,
  The flame departed uttering lamentations,
  Writhing and flapping its sharp-pointed horn.

Onward we passed, both I and my Conductor,
  Up o'er the crag above another arch,
  Which the moat covers, where is paid the fee

By those who, sowing discord, win their burden.

Canto XXVIII

In the ninth bolgia, *the large crowds of the Sowers of Discord are disfigured and dismembered, many with their intestines spilling out. Several instigators of scandal and schism are named, including the Prophet Mahomet, founder of Islam, split open from crotch to chin, and Ali, his son-in-law. The sinners curse their lot and stir Dante's pity before predicting the unsavoury end of certain Italians who are still alive. The image of the medieval French troubadour Bertram De Born carrying his decapitated head in his hand is a vivid example of Dantean divine retribution or* contrapasso, *where his wits are literally 'separated' from his body.*

Who ever could, e'en with untrammelled words,
  Tell of the blood and of the wounds in full
  Which now I saw, by many times narrating?

Each tongue would for a certainty fall short
  By reason of our speech and memory,
  That have small room to comprehend so much.

If were again assembled all the people
  Which formerly upon the fateful land
  Of Puglia were lamenting for their blood

Shed by the Romans and the lingering war
  That of the rings made such illustrious spoils,
  As Livy has recorded, who errs not,

With those who felt the agony of blows
  By making counterstand to Robert Guiscard,
  And all the rest, whose bones are gathered still

At Ceperano, where a renegade
  Was each Apulian, and at Tagliacozzo,
  Where without arms the old Alardo conquered,

And one his limb transpierced, and one lopped off,
  Should show, it would be nothing to compare
  With the disgusting mode of the ninth *Bolgia*.

A cask by losing centre-piece or cant
  Was never shattered so, as I saw one
  Rent from the chin to where one breaketh wind.

Between his legs were hanging down his entrails;
  His heart was visible, and the dismal sack
  That maketh excrement of what is eaten.

While I was all absorbed in seeing him,
  He looked at me, and opened with his hands
  His bosom, saying: "See now how I rend me;

How mutilated, see, is Mahomet;
  In front of me doth Ali weeping go,
  Cleft in the face from forelock unto chin;

And all the others whom thou here beholdest,
  Disseminators of scandal and of schism
  While living were, and therefore are cleft thus.

A devil is behind here, who doth cleave us
  Thus cruelly, unto the falchion's edge
  Putting again each one of all this ream,

When we have gone around the doleful road;
  By reason that our wounds are closed again
  Ere any one in front of him repass.

But who art thou, that musest on the crag,
  Perchance to postpone going to the pain
  That is adjudged upon thine accusations?"

"Nor death hath reached him yet, nor guilt doth
                                        bring him,"
  My Master made reply, "to be tormented;
  But to procure him full experience,

Me, who am dead, behoves it to conduct him
  Down here through Hell, from circle unto circle;
  And this is true as that I speak to thee."

More than a hundred were there when they heard him,
  Who in the moat stood still to look at me,
  Through wonderment oblivious of their torture.

"Now say to Fra Dolcino, then, to arm him,
  Thou, who perhaps wilt shortly see the sun,
  If soon he wish not here to follow me,

So with provisions, that no stress of snow
  May give the victory to the Novarese,
  Which otherwise to gain would not be easy."

After one foot to go away he lifted,
  This word did Mahomet say unto me,
  Then to depart upon the ground he stretched it.

Another one, who had his throat pierced through,
  And nose cut off close underneath the brows,
  And had no longer but a single ear,

Staying to look in wonder with the others,
  Before the others did his gullet open,
  Which outwardly was red in every part,

And said: "O thou, whom guilt doth not condemn,
  And whom I once saw up in Latian land,
  Unless too great similitude deceive me,

Call to remembrance Pier da Medicina,
  If e'er thou see again the lovely plain
  That from Vercelli slopes to Marcabo,

And make it known to the best two of Fano,
  To Messer Guido and Angiolello likewise,
  That if foreseeing here be not in vain,

Cast over from their vessel shall they be,
  And drowned near unto the Cattolica,
  By the betrayal of a tyrant fell.

Between the isles of Cyprus and Majorca
  Neptune ne'er yet beheld so great a crime,
  Neither of pirates nor Argolic people.

That traitor, who sees only with one eye,
  And holds the land, which some one here with me
  Would fain be fasting from the vision of,

Will make them come unto a parley with him;
  Then will do so, that to Focara's wind
  They will not stand in need of vow or prayer."

And I to him: "Show to me and declare,
  If thou wouldst have me bear up news of thee,
  Who is this person of the bitter vision."

Then did he lay his hand upon the jaw
  Of one of his companions, and his mouth
  Oped, crying: "This is he, and he speaks not.

This one, being banished, every doubt submerged
  In Caesar by affirming the forearmed
  Always with detriment allowed delay."

O how bewildered unto me appeared,
  With tongue asunder in his windpipe slit,
  Curio, who in speaking was so bold!

And one, who both his hands dissevered had,
  The stumps uplifting through the murky air,
  So that the blood made horrible his face,

Cried out: "Thou shalt remember Mosca also,
  Who said, alas! 'A thing done has an end!'
  Which was an ill seed for the Tuscan people."

"And death unto thy race," thereto I added;
  Whence he, accumulating woe on woe,
  Departed, like a person sad and crazed.

But I remained to look upon the crowd;
  And saw a thing which I should be afraid,
  Without some further proof, even to recount,

If it were not that conscience reassures me,
  That good companion which emboldens man
  Beneath the hauberk of its feeling pure.

I truly saw, and still I seem to see it,
  A trunk without a head walk in like manner
  As walked the others of the mournful herd.

He looked at me, and opened with his hands / His bosom, saying: "See now how I rend me;"

Inf. XXVIII, lines 29–30

"Call to remembrance Pier da Medicina,"

Inf. XXVIII, lines 73

By the hair it held the head dissevered, / Hung from the hand in fashion of a lantern, /
And that upon us gazed and said: "O me!"

Inf. XXVIII, lines 121–123

And by the hair it held the head dissevered,
  Hung from the hand in fashion of a lantern,
  And that upon us gazed and said: "O me!"

It of itself made to itself a lamp,
  And they were two in one, and one in two;
  How that can be, He knows who so ordains it.

When it was come close to the bridge's foot,
  It lifted high its arm with all the head,
  To bring more closely unto us its words,

Which were: "Behold now the sore penalty,
  Thou, who dost breathing go the dead beholding;
  Behold if any be as great as this.

And so that thou may carry news of me,
  Know that Bertram de Born am I, the same
  Who gave to the Young King the evil comfort.

I made the father and the son rebellious;
  Achitophel not more with Absalom
  And David did with his accursed goadings.

Because I parted persons so united,
  Parted do I now bear my brain, alas!
  From its beginning, which is in this trunk.

Thus is observed in me the counterpoise."

Canto XXIX

When Virgil chides his pupil for showering such prolonged attention upon these
wretches, Dante argues that he is searching for someone in particular. Virgil swears
having seen Geri del Bello, first cousin to Dante's father, pointing a finger at him.
The pair continue their discussion of the sinner. In the tenth bolgia, *they find all kinds*
of shrieking, diseased and pestilent Falsifiers, frantically scratching at their sores.
Dante converses with two shadows sitting back to back, Griffolino d'Arezzo and
Capocchio. The Florentine makes jokes about the Sienese.

The many people and the divers wounds
  These eyes of mine had so inebriated,
  That they were wishful to stand still and weep;

But said Virgilius: "What dost thou still gaze at?
  Why is thy sight still riveted down there
  Among the mournful, mutilated shades?

Thou hast not done so at the other Bolge;
  Consider, if to count them thou believest,
  That two-and-twenty miles the valley winds,

And now the moon is underneath our feet;
  Henceforth the time allotted us is brief,
  And more is to be seen than what thou seest."

"If thou hadst," I made answer thereupon,
  "Attended to the cause for which I looked,
  Perhaps a longer stay thou wouldst have pardoned."

Meanwhile my Guide departed, and behind him
  I went, already making my reply,
  And superadding: "In that cavern where

I held mine eyes with such attention fixed,
  I think a spirit of my blood laments
  The sin which down below there costs so much."

Then said the Master: "Be no longer broken
  Thy thought from this time forward upon him;
  Attend elsewhere, and there let him remain;

But said Virgilius: "What dost thou still gaze at? / Why is thy sight still riveted down there /
Among the mournful, mutilated shades?"

Inf. XXIX, lines 4–6

For him I saw below the little bridge,
  Pointing at thee, and threatening with his finger
  Fiercely, and heard him called Geri del Bello.

So wholly at that time wast thou impeded
  By him who formerly held Altaforte,
  Thou didst not look that way; so he departed."

"O my Conductor, his own violent death,
  Which is not yet avenged for him," I said,
  "By any who is sharer in the shame,

Made him disdainful; whence he went away,
  As I imagine, without speaking to me,
  And thereby made me pity him the more."

Thus did we speak as far as the first place
  Upon the crag, which the next valley shows
  Down to the bottom, if there were more light.

When we were now right over the last cloister
  Of Malebolge, so that its lay-brothers
  Could manifest themselves unto our sight,

Divers lamentings pierced me through and through,
  Which with compassion had their arrows barbed,
  Whereat mine ears I covered with my hands.

What pain would be, if from the hospitals
  Of Valdichiana, 'twixt July and September,
  And of Maremma and Sardinia

All the diseases in one moat were gathered,
  Such was it here, and such a stench came from it
  As from putrescent limbs is wont to issue.

We had descended on the furthest bank
  From the long crag, upon the left hand still,
  And then more vivid was my power of sight

Down tow'rds the bottom, where the ministress
  Of the high Lord, Justice infallible,
  Punishes forgers, which she here records.

I do not think a sadder sight to see
  Was in Aegina the whole people sick,
  (When was the air so full of pestilence,

The animals, down to the little worm,
  All fell, and afterwards the ancient people,
  According as the poets have affirmed,

Were from the seed of ants restored again,)
  Than was it to behold through that dark valley
  The spirits languishing in divers heaps.

This on the belly, that upon the back
  One of the other lay, and others crawling
  Shifted themselves along the dismal road.

We step by step went onward without speech,
  Gazing upon and listening to the sick
  Who had not strength enough to lift their bodies.

I saw two sitting leaned against each other,
  As leans in heating platter against platter,
  From head to foot bespotted o'er with scabs;

And never saw I plied a currycomb
  By stable-boy for whom his master waits,
  Or him who keeps awake unwillingly,

As every one was plying fast the bite
  Of nails upon himself, for the great rage
  Of itching which no other succour had.

And the nails downward with them dragged the scab,
  In fashion as a knife the scales of bream,
  Or any other fish that has them largest.

"O thou, that with thy fingers dost dismail thee,"
  Began my Leader unto one of them,
  "And makest of them pincers now and then,

Tell me if any Latian is with those
  Who are herein; so may thy nails suffice thee
  To all eternity unto this work."

"Latians are we, whom thou so wasted seest,
  Both of us here," one weeping made reply;
  "But who art thou, that questionest about us?"

And said the Guide: "One am I who descends
  Down with this living man from cliff to cliff,
  And I intend to show Hell unto him."

Then broken was their mutual support,
  And trembling each one turned himself to me,
  With others who had heard him by rebound.

Wholly to me did the good Master gather,
  Saying: "Say unto them whate'er thou wishest."
  And I began, since he would have it so:

Such a stench came from it / As from putrescent limbs is wont to issue.

Inf. XXIX, lines 50–51

Every one was plying fast the bite / Of nails upon himself, for the great rage /
Of itching which no other succour had.

Inf. XXIX, lines 79–81

"So may your memory not steal away
  In the first world from out the minds of men,
  But so may it survive 'neath many suns,

Say to me who ye are, and of what people;
  Let not your foul and loathsome punishment
  Make you afraid to show yourselves to me."

"I of Arezzo was," one made reply,
  "And Albert of Siena had me burned;
  But what I died for does not bring me here.

'Tis true I said to him, speaking in jest,
  That I could rise by flight into the air,
  And he who had conceit, but little wit,

Would have me show to him the art; and only
  Because no Daedalus I made him, made me
  Be burned by one who held him as his son.

But unto the last *Bolgia* of the ten,
  For alchemy, which in the world I practised,
  Minos, who cannot err, has me condemned."

And to the Poet said I: "Now was ever
  So vain a people as the Sienese?
  Not for a certainty the French by far."

Whereat the other leper, who had heard me,
  Replied unto my speech: "Taking out Stricca,
  Who knew the art of moderate expenses,

And Niccolo, who the luxurious use
  Of cloves discovered earliest of all
  Within that garden where such seed takes root;

And taking out the band, among whom squandered
  Caccia d'Ascian his vineyards and vast woods,
  And where his wit the Abbagliato proffered!

But, that thou know who thus doth second thee
  Against the Sienese, make sharp thine eye
  Tow'rds me, so that my face well answer thee,

And thou shalt see I am Capocchio's shade,
  Who metals falsified by alchemy;
  Thou must remember, if I well descry thee,

How I a skilful ape of nature was."

Canto XXX

This canto conveys the mental and physical corruption of Fraud in its multiple forms.
Two mad Impersonators, Gianni Schicchi, member of the powerful Florentine
Cavalcanti family, and Myrrha, incestuous daughter of King Cinyras of Cyprus, dash
on to the scene. One bites into Capocchio's neck and drags him away. An immobile,
dehumanized Counterfeiter, Master Adam, explains how his practise was positively
encouraged by his patrons and points to the feverish shadows of two Liars, Potiphar's
wife and Sinon the Greek. The latter argues with Master Adam. The pilgrim is once
again chided for his fascination with such lowly creatures.

'Twas at the time when Juno was enraged,
  For Semele, against the Theban blood,
  As she already more than once had shown,

So reft of reason Athamas became,
  That, seeing his own wife with children twain
  Walking encumbered upon either hand,

He cried: "Spread out the nets, that I may take
  The lioness and her whelps upon the passage;"
  And then extended his unpitying claws,

Seizing the first, who had the name Learchus,
  And whirled him round, and dashed him on a rock;
  And she, with the other burthen, drowned herself;—

And at the time when fortune downward hurled
  The Trojan's arrogance, that all things dared,
  So that the king was with his kingdom crushed,

Hecuba sad, disconsolate, and captive,
  When lifeless she beheld Polyxena,
  And of her Polydorus on the shore

Of ocean was the dolorous one aware,
  Out of her senses like a dog she barked,
  So much the anguish had her mind distorted;

But not of Thebes the furies nor the Trojan
  Were ever seen in any one so cruel
  In goading beasts, and much more human members,

As I beheld two shadows pale and naked,
  Who, biting, in the manner ran along
  That a boar does, when from the sty turned loose.

One to Capocchio came, and by the nape
  Seized with its teeth his neck, so that in dragging
  It made his belly grate the solid bottom.

And the Aretine, who trembling had remained,
  Said to me: "That mad sprite is Gianni Schicchi,
  And raving goes thus harrying other people."

"O," said I to him, "so may not the other
  Set teeth on thee, let it not weary thee
  To tell us who it is, ere it dart hence."

And he to me: "That is the ancient ghost
  Of the nefarious Myrrha, who became
  Beyond all rightful love her father's lover.

She came to sin with him after this manner,
  By counterfeiting of another's form;
  As he who goeth yonder undertook,

That he might gain the lady of the herd,
  To counterfeit in himself Buoso Donati,
  Making a will and giving it due form."

And after the two maniacs had passed
  On whom I held mine eye, I turned it back
  To look upon the other evil-born.

I saw one made in fashion of a lute,
  If he had only had the groin cut off
  Just at the point at which a man is forked.

The heavy dropsy, that so disproportions
  The limbs with humours, which it ill concocts,
  That the face corresponds not to the belly,

"That mad sprite is Gianni Schicchi, / And raving goes thus harrying
other people."

Inf. XXX, lines 32–33

"That is the ancient ghost / Of the nefarious Myrrha, who became /
Beyond all rightful love her father's lover."

Inf. XXX, lines 37–39

Compelled him so to hold his lips apart
  As does the hectic, who because of thirst
  One tow'rds the chin, the other upward turns.

"O ye, who without any torment are,
  And why I know not, in the world of woe,"
  He said to us, "behold, and be attentive

Unto the misery of Master Adam;
  I had while living much of what I wished,
  And now, alas! a drop of water crave.

The rivulets, that from the verdant hills
  Of Cassentin descend down into Arno,
  Making their channels to be cold and moist,

Ever before me stand, and not in vain;
  For far more doth their image dry me up
  Than the disease which strips my face of flesh.

The rigid justice that chastises me
  Draweth occasion from the place in which
  I sinned, to put the more my sighs in flight.

There is Romena, where I counterfeited
  The currency imprinted with the Baptist,
  For which I left my body burned above.

But if I here could see the tristful soul
  Of Guido, or Alessandro, or their brother,
  For Branda's fount I would not give the sight.

One is within already, if the raving
  Shades that are going round about speak truth;
  But what avails it me, whose limbs are tied?

If I were only still so light, that in
  A hundred years I could advance one inch,
  I had already started on the way,

Seeking him out among this squalid folk,
  Although the circuit be eleven miles,
  And be not less than half a mile across.

For them am I in such a family;
  They did induce me into coining florins,
  Which had three carats of impurity."

And I to him: "Who are the two poor wretches
  That smoke like unto a wet hand in winter,
  Lying there close upon thy right-hand confines?"

"I found them here," replied he, "when I rained
  Into this chasm, and since they have not turned,
  Nor do I think they will for evermore.

One the false woman is who accused Joseph,
  The other the false Sinon, Greek of Troy;
  From acute fever they send forth such reek."

And one of them, who felt himself annoyed
  At being, peradventure, named so darkly,
  Smote with the fist upon his hardened paunch.

It gave a sound, as if it were a drum;
  And Master Adam smote him in the face,
  With arm that did not seem to be less hard,

Saying to him: "Although be taken from me
  All motion, for my limbs that heavy are,
  I have an arm unfettered for such need."

Whereat he answer made: "When thou didst go
  Unto the fire, thou hadst it not so ready:
  But hadst it so and more when thou wast coining."

The dropsical: "Thou sayest true in that;
  But thou wast not so true a witness there,
  Where thou wast questioned of the truth at Troy."

"If I spake false, thou falsifiedst the coin,"
  Said Sinon; "and for one fault I am here,
  And thou for more than any other demon."

"Remember, perjurer, about the horse,"
  He made reply who had the swollen belly,
  "And rueful be it thee the whole world knows it."

"Rueful to thee the thirst be wherewith cracks
  Thy tongue," the Greek said, "and the putrid water
  That hedges so thy paunch before thine eyes."

Then the false-coiner: "So is gaping wide
  Thy mouth for speaking evil, as 'tis wont;
  Because if I have thirst, and humour stuff me

Thou hast the burning and the head that aches,
  And to lick up the mirror of Narcissus
  Thou wouldst not want words many to invite thee."

In listening to them was I wholly fixed,
  When said the Master to me: "Now just look,
  For little wants it that I quarrel with thee."

When him I heard in anger speak to me,
  I turned me round towards him with such shame
  That still it eddies through my memory.

And as he is who dreams of his own harm,
  Who dreaming wishes it may be a dream,
  So that he craves what is, as if it were not;

Such I became, not having power to speak,
  For to excuse myself I wished, and still
  Excused myself, and did not think I did it.

"Less shame doth wash away a greater fault,"
  The Master said, "than this of thine has been;
  Therefore thyself disburden of all sadness,

And make account that I am aye beside thee,
  If e'er it come to pass that fortune bring thee
  Where there are people in a like dispute;

For a base wish it is to wish to hear it."

Canto XXXI

Dante and Virgil leave the domain of Simple Fraud and journey from the Malebolge *into Cocytus, the central lake of ice, where Complex Fraud is punished. The surrounding silence is broken by the piercing blast of Nimrod's distant horn. He and other giants are forever fixed to the pit of Hell for having violently rebelled against Jove. Only Antaeus may speak and is unchained. At Virgil's request, he picks the pair of poets up in his enormous hand and deposits them below.*

One and the selfsame tongue first wounded me,
  So that it tinged the one cheek and the other,
  And then held out to me the medicine;

Thus do I hear that once Achilles' spear,
  His and his father's, used to be the cause
  First of a sad and then a gracious boon.

We turned our backs upon the wretched valley,
  Upon the bank that girds it round about,
  Going across it without any speech.

There it was less than night, and less than day,
  So that my sight went little in advance;
  But I could hear the blare of a loud horn,

So loud it would have made each thunder faint,
  Which, counter to it following its way,
  Mine eyes directed wholly to one place.

After the dolorous discomfiture
  When Charlemagne the holy emprise lost,
  So terribly Orlando sounded not.

Short while my head turned thitherward I held
  When many lofty towers I seemed to see,
  Whereat I: "Master, say, what town is this?"

And he to me: "Because thou peerest forth
  Athwart the darkness at too great a distance,
  It happens that thou errest in thy fancy.

Well shalt thou see, if thou arrivest there,
  How much the sense deceives itself by distance;
  Therefore a little faster spur thee on."

Then tenderly he took me by the hand,
  And said: "Before we farther have advanced,
  That the reality may seem to thee

"Soul idiotic, / Keep to thy horn, and vent thyself with that, /
When wrath or other passion touches thee."

Inf. XXXI, lines 70–72

Less strange, know that these are not towers, but giants,
  And they are in the well, around the bank,
  From navel downward, one and all of them."

As, when the fog is vanishing away,
  Little by little doth the sight refigure
  Whate'er the mist that crowds the air conceals,

So, piercing through the dense and darksome air,
  More and more near approaching tow'rd the verge,
  My error fled, and fear came over me;

Because as on its circular parapets
  Montereggione crowns itself with towers,
  E'en thus the margin which surrounds the well

With one half of their bodies turreted
  The horrible giants, whom Jove menaces
  E'en now from out the heavens when he thunders.

And I of one already saw the face,
  Shoulders, and breast, and great part of the belly,
  And down along his sides both of the arms.

Certainly Nature, when she left the making
  Of animals like these, did well indeed,
  By taking such executors from Mars;

And if of elephants and whales she doth not
  Repent her, whosoever looketh subtly
  More just and more discreet will hold her for it;

For where the argument of intellect
  Is added unto evil will and power,
  No rampart can the people make against it.

His face appeared to me as long and large
  As is at Rome the pine-cone of Saint Peter's,
  And in proportion were the other bones;

So that the margin, which an apron was
  Down from the middle, showed so much of him
  Above it, that to reach up to his hair

Three Frieslanders in vain had vaunted them;
  For I beheld thirty great palms of him
  Down from the place where man his mantle buckles.

"*Raphael mai amech izabi almi,*"
  Began to clamour the ferocious mouth,
  To which were not befitting sweeter psalms.

And unto him my Guide: "Soul idiotic,
  Keep to thy horn, and vent thyself with that,
  When wrath or other passion touches thee.

Search round thy neck, and thou wilt find the belt
  Which keeps it fastened, O bewildered soul,
  And see it, where it bars thy mighty breast."

Then said to me: "He doth himself accuse;
  This one is Nimrod, by whose evil thought
  One language in the world is not still used.

Here let us leave him and not speak in vain;
  For even such to him is every language
  As his to others, which to none is known."

Therefore a longer journey did we make,
  Turned to the left, and a crossbow-shot oft
  We found another far more fierce and large.

In binding him, who might the master be
  I cannot say; but he had pinioned close
  Behind the right arm, and in front the other,

With chains, that held him so begirt about
  From the neck down, that on the part uncovered
  It wound itself as far as the fifth gyre.

"This proud one wished to make experiment
  Of his own power against the Supreme Jove,"
  My Leader said, "whence he has such a guerdon.

Ephialtes is his name; he showed great prowess.
  What time the giants terrified the gods;
  The arms he wielded never more he moves."

And I to him: "If possible, I should wish
  That of the measureless Briareus
  These eyes of mine might have experience."

Whence he replied: "Thou shalt behold Antaeus
  Close by here, who can speak and is unbound,
  Who at the bottom of all crime shall place us.

Much farther yon is he whom thou wouldst see,
  And he is bound, and fashioned like to this one,
  Save that he seems in aspect more ferocious."

There never was an earthquake of such might
  That it could shake a tower so violently,
  As Ephialtes suddenly shook himself.

"This proud one wished to make experiment / Of his own power against the Supreme Jove,"

Inf. XXXI, lines 91–92

Then was I more afraid of death than ever,
  For nothing more was needful than the fear,
  If I had not beheld the manacles.

Then we proceeded farther in advance,
  And to Antaeus came, who, full five ells
  Without the head, forth issued from the cavern.

"O thou, who in the valley fortunate,
  Which Scipio the heir of glory made,
  When Hannibal turned back with all his hosts,

Once brought'st a thousand lions for thy prey,
  And who, hadst thou been at the mighty war
  Among thy brothers, some it seems still think

The sons of Earth the victory would have gained:
  Place us below, nor be disdainful of it,
  There where the cold doth lock Cocytus up.

Make us not go to Tityus nor Typhoeus;
  This one can give of that which here is longed for;
  Therefore stoop down, and do not curl thy lip.

Still in the world can he restore thy fame;
  Because he lives, and still expects long life,
  If to itself Grace call him not untimely."

So said the Master; and in haste the other
  His hands extended and took up my Guide,—
  Hands whose great pressure Hercules once felt.

Virgilius, when he felt himself embraced,
  Said unto me: "Draw nigh, that I may take thee;"
  Then of himself and me one bundle made.

As seems the Carisenda, to behold
  Beneath the leaning side, when goes a cloud
  Above it so that opposite it hangs;

Such did Antaeus seem to me, who stood
  Watching to see him stoop, and then it was
  I could have wished to go some other way.

But lightly in the abyss, which swallows up
  Judas with Lucifer, he put us down;
  Nor thus bowed downward made he there delay,

But, as a mast does in a ship, uprose.

But lightly in the abyss, which swallows up / Judas with Lucifer, he put us down;

Inf. XXXI, lines 142–143

Canto XXXII

*As they descend into Cocytus, Virgil and Dante see more and more Traitors frozen in
the vast icy plain. Those who murdered their kindred lie in Caina, its outer margin.
The Alberti brothers, among others, are trapped in a deadly embrace. The travellers
next enter Antenora, the second division. Dante kicks the protruding head of Bocca
Degli Abati and furiously pulls his hair so he will utter his name.
A traitor to his country, the Ghibelline appeared to support the Guelf cause. He
angrily names and shames five companions. Dante glimpses two more heads, one
feasting on the brains of the other.*

If I had rhymes both rough and stridulous,
  As were appropriate to the dismal hole
  Down upon which thrust all the other rocks,

I would press out the juice of my conception
  More fully; but because I have them not,
  Not without fear I bring myself to speak;

For 'tis no enterprise to take in jest,
  To sketch the bottom of all the universe,
  Nor for a tongue that cries Mamma and Babbo.

But may those Ladies help this verse of mine,
  Who helped Amphion in enclosing Thebes,
  That from the fact the word be not diverse.

O rabble ill-begotten above all,
  Who're in the place to speak of which is hard,
  'Twere better ye had here been sheep or goats!

When we were down within the darksome well,
  Beneath the giant's feet, but lower far,
  And I was scanning still the lofty wall,

I heard it said to me: "Look how thou steppest!
  Take heed thou do not trample with thy feet
  The heads of the tired, miserable brothers!"

Whereat I turned me round, and saw before me
  And underfoot a lake, that from the frost
  The semblance had of glass, and not of water.

So thick a veil ne'er made upon its current
  In winter-time Danube in Austria,
  Nor there beneath the frigid sky the Don,

As there was here; so that if Tambernich
  Had fallen upon it, or Pietrapana,
  E'en at the edge 'twould not have given a creak.

And as to croak the frog doth place himself
  With muzzle out of water,—when is dreaming
  Of gleaning oftentimes the peasant-girl,—

Livid, as far down as where shame appears,
  Were the disconsolate shades within the ice,
  Setting their teeth unto the note of storks.

Each one his countenance held downward bent;
  From mouth the cold, from eyes the doleful heart
  Among them witness of itself procures.

When round about me somewhat I had looked,
  I downward turned me, and saw two so close,
  The hair upon their heads together mingled.

"Ye who so strain your breasts together, tell me,"
  I said, "who are you;" and they bent their necks,
  And when to me their faces they had lifted,

Their eyes, which first were only moist within,
  Gushed o'er the eyelids, and the frost congealed
  The tears between, and locked them up again.

Clamp never bound together wood with wood
  So strongly; whereat they, like two he-goats,
  Butted together, so much wrath o'ercame them.

And one, who had by reason of the cold
  Lost both his ears, still with his visage downward,
  Said: "Why dost thou so mirror thyself in us?

"Look how thou steppest! / Take heed thou do not trample with thy feet /
The heads of the tired, miserable brothers!"

Inf. XXXII, lines 19–21

If thou desire to know who these two are,
  The valley whence Bisenzio descends
  Belonged to them and to their father Albert.

They from one body came, and all Caina
  Thou shalt search through, and shalt not find a shade
  More worthy to be fixed in gelatine;

Not he in whom were broken breast and shadow
  At one and the same blow by Arthur's hand;
  Focaccia not; not he who me encumbers

So with his head I see no farther forward,
  And bore the name of Sassol Mascheroni;
  Well knowest thou who he was, if thou art Tuscan.

And that thou put me not to further speech,
  Know that I Camicion de' Pazzi was,
  And wait Carlino to exonerate me."

Then I beheld a thousand faces, made
  Purple with cold; whence o'er me comes a shudder,
  And evermore will come, at frozen ponds.

And while we were advancing tow'rds the middle,
  Where everything of weight unites together,
  And I was shivering in the eternal shade,

Whether 'twere will, or destiny, or chance,
  I know not; but in walking 'mong the heads
  I struck my foot hard in the face of one.

Weeping he growled: "Why dost thou trample me?
  Unless thou comest to increase the vengeance
  of Montaperti, why dost thou molest me?"

And I: "My Master, now wait here for me,
  That I through him may issue from a doubt;
  Then thou mayst hurry me, as thou shalt wish."

The Leader stopped; and to that one I said
  Who was blaspheming vehemently still:
  "Who art thou, that thus reprehendest others?"

"Now who art thou, that goest through Antenora
  Smiting," replied he, "other people's cheeks,
  So that, if thou wert living, 'twere too much?"

"Living I am, and dear to thee it may be,"
  Was my response, "if thou demandest fame,
  That 'mid the other notes thy name I place."

And he to me: "For the reverse I long;
  Take thyself hence, and give me no more trouble;
  For ill thou knowest to flatter in this hollow."

Then by the scalp behind I seized upon him,
  And said: "It must needs be thou name thyself,
  Or not a hair remain upon thee here."

Whence he to me: "Though thou strip off my hair,
  I will not tell thee who I am, nor show thee,
  If on my head a thousand times thou fall."

I had his hair in hand already twisted,
  And more than one shock of it had pulled out,
  He barking, with his eyes held firmly down,

When cried another: "What doth ail thee, Bocca?
  Is't not enough to clatter with thy jaws,
  But thou must bark? what devil touches thee?"

"Now," said I, "I care not to have thee speak,
  Accursed traitor; for unto thy shame
  I will report of thee veracious news."

"Begone," replied he, "and tell what thou wilt,
  But be not silent, if thou issue hence,
  Of him who had just now his tongue so prompt;

He weepeth here the silver of the French;
  'I saw,' thus canst thou phrase it, 'him of Duera
  There where the sinners stand out in the cold.'

If thou shouldst questioned be who else was there,
  Thou hast beside thee him of Beccaria,
  Of whom the gorget Florence slit asunder;

Gianni del Soldanier, I think, may be
  Yonder with Ganellon, and Tebaldello
  Who oped Faenza when the people slep."

Already we had gone away from him,
  When I beheld two frozen in one hole,
  So that one head a hood was to the other;

And even as bread through hunger is devoured,
  The uppermost on the other set his teeth,
  There where the brain is to the nape united.

Not in another fashion Tydeus gnawed
  The temples of Menalippus in disdain,
  Than that one did the skull and the other things.

Then by the scalp behind I seized upon him, / And said: "It must needs be thou name thyself, /
Or not a hair remain upon thee here."

Inf. XXXII, lines 97–99

The uppermost on the other set his teeth, / There where the brain is to the nape united.

Inf. XXXII, lines 128–129

"O thou, who showest by such bestial sign
  Thy hatred against him whom thou art eating,
  Tell me the wherefore," said I, "with this compact,

That if thou rightfully of him complain,
  In knowing who ye are, and his transgression,
  I in the world above repay thee for it,

If that wherewith I speak be not dried up."

Canto XXXIII

*The poets witness the gruesome spectacle of the Ghibelline Count Ugolino della
Gherardesca gnawing at the skull of his former collaborator, Archbishop Ruggieri.
He stops in the middle of his gory repast to tell the story of his incarceration and
murder along with that of his innocent children. The travellers venture into Ptolomea,
the third division of Lake Cocytus, where dwell those who betrayed guests and
associates. Any tears shed here freeze and lock the eyes in a fixed stare. Friar Alberigo
agrees to talk if the icy layer is removed. He declares his soul and that of another
to be dead but their bodies to be 'alive' on Earth and possessed by demons. Dante breaks
his promise.*

His mouth uplifted from his grim repast,
  That sinner, wiping it upon the hair
  Of the same head that he behind had wasted.

Then he began: "Thou wilt that I renew
  The desperate grief, which wrings my heart already
  To think of only, ere I speak of it;

But if my words be seed that may bear fruit
  Of infamy to the traitor whom I gnaw,
  Speaking and weeping shalt thou see together.

I know not who thou art, nor by what mode
  Thou hast come down here; but a Florentine
  Thou seemest to me truly, when I hear thee.

Thou hast to know I was Count Ugolino,
  And this one was Ruggieri the Archbishop;
  Now I will tell thee why I am such a neighbour.

That, by effect of his malicious thoughts,
  Trusting in him I was made prisoner,
  And after put to death, I need not say;

But ne'ertheless what thou canst not have heard,
  That is to say, how cruel was my death,
  Hear shalt thou, and shalt know if he has wronged me.

A narrow perforation in the mew,
  Which bears because of me the title of Famine,
  And in which others still must be locked up,

Had shown me through its opening many moons
  Already, when I dreamed the evil dream
  Which of the future rent for me the veil.

This one appeared to me as lord and master,
  Hunting the wolf and whelps upon the mountain
  For which the Pisans cannot Lucca see.

With sleuth-hounds gaunt, and eager, and well trained,
  Gualandi with Sismondi and Lanfianchi
  He had sent out before him to the front.

After brief course seemed unto me forespent
  The father and the sons, and with sharp tushes
  It seemed to me I saw their flanks ripped open.

When I before the morrow was awake,
  Moaning amid their sleep I heard my sons
  Who with me were, and asking after bread.

Cruel indeed art thou, if yet thou grieve not,
  Thinking of what my heart foreboded me,
  And weep'st thou not, what art thou wont to weep at?

They were awake now, and the hour drew nigh
  At which our food used to be brought to us,
  And through his dream was each one apprehensive;

And I heard locking up the under door
  Of the horrible tower; whereat without a word
  I gazed into the faces of my sons.

I wept not, I within so turned to stone;
  They wept; and darling little Anselm mine
  Said: 'Thou dost gaze so, father, what doth ail thee?'

Still not a tear I shed, nor answer made
  All of that day, nor yet the night thereafter,
  Until another sun rose on the world.

As now a little glimmer made its way
  Into the dolorous prison, and I saw
  Upon four faces my own very aspect,

Both of my hands in agony I bit;
  And, thinking that I did it from desire
  Of eating, on a sudden they uprose,

And said they: 'Father, much less pain 'twill give us
  If thou do eat of us; thyself didst clothe us
  With this poor flesh, and do thou strip it off.'

I calmed me then, not to make them more sad.
  That day we all were silent, and the next.
  Ah! obdurate Earth, wherefore didst thou not open?

When we had come unto the fourth day, Gaddo
  Threw himself down outstretched before my feet,
  Saying, 'My father, why dost thou not help me?'

And there he died; and, as thou seest me,
  I saw the three fall, one by one, between
  The fifth day and the sixth; whence I betook me,

Already blind, to groping over each,
  And three days called them after they were dead;
  Then hunger did what sorrow could not do."

When he had said this, with his eyes distorted,
  The wretched skull resumed he with his teeth,
  Which, as a dog's, upon the bone were strong.

Ah! Pisa, thou opprobrium of the people
  Of the fair land there where the 'Si' doth sound,
  Since slow to punish thee thy neighbours are,

Let the Capraia and Gorgona move,
  And make a hedge across the mouth of Arno
  That every person in thee it may drown!

For if Count Ugolino had the fame
  Of having in thy castles thee betrayed,
  Thou shouldst not on such cross have put his sons.

Guiltless of any crime, thou modern Thebes!
  Their youth made Uguccione and Brigata,
  And the other two my song doth name above!

We passed still farther onward, where the ice
  Another people ruggedly enswathes,
  Not downward turned, but all of them reversed.

Weeping itself there does not let them weep,
  And grief that finds a barrier in the eyes
  Turns itself inward to increase the anguish;

Because the earliest tears a cluster form,
  And, in the manner of a crystal visor,
  Fill all the cup beneath the eyebrow full.

And notwithstanding that, as in a callus,
  Because of cold all sensibility
  Its station had abandoned in my face,

Still it appeared to me I felt some wind;
  Whence I: "My Master, who sets this in motion?
  Is not below here every vapour quenched?"

Whence he to me: "Full soon shalt thou be where
  Thine eye shall answer make to thee of this,
  Seeing the cause which raineth down the blast."

"I calmed me then, not to make them more sad."

Inf. XXXIII, line 64

"Gaddo / Threw himself down outstretched before my feet, / Saying, 'My father, why dost thou not help me?'"

Inf. XXXIII, lines 67–69

"Then hunger did what sorrow could not do."

Inf. XXXIII, line 75

And one of the wretches of the frozen crust
  Cried out to us: "O souls so merciless
  That the last post is given unto you,

Lift from mine eyes the rigid veils, that I
  May vent the sorrow which impregns my heart
  A little, e'er the weeping recongeal."

Whence I to him: "If thou wouldst have me help thee
  Say who thou wast; and if I free thee not,
  May I go to the bottom of the ice."

Then he replied: "I am Friar Alberigo;
  He am I of the fruit of the bad garden,
  Who here a date am getting for my fig."

"O," said I to him, "now art thou, too, dead?"
  And he to me: "How may my body fare
  Up in the world, no knowledge I possess.

Such an advantage has this Ptolomaea,
  That oftentimes the soul descendeth here
  Sooner than Atropos in motion sets it.

And, that thou mayest more willingly remove
  From off my countenance these glassy tears,
  Know that as soon as any soul betrays

As I have done, his body by a demon
  Is taken from him, who thereafter rules it,
  Until his time has wholly been revolved.

Itself down rushes into such a cistern;
  And still perchance above appears the body
  Of yonder shade, that winters here behind me.

This thou shouldst know, if thou hast just come down;
  It is Ser Branca d' Oria, and many years
  Have passed away since he was thus locked up."

"I think," said I to him, "thou dost deceive me;
  For Branca d' Oria is not dead as yet,
  And eats, and drinks, and sleeps, and puts on clothes."

"In moat above," said he, "of Malebranche,
  There where is boiling the tenacious pitch,
  As yet had Michel Zanche not arrived,

When this one left a devil in his stead
  In his own body and one near of kin,
  Who made together with him the betrayal.

But hitherward stretch out thy hand forthwith,
  Open mine eyes;"—and open them I did not,
  And to be rude to him was courtesy.

Ah, Genoese! ye men at variance
  With every virtue, full of every vice
  Wherefore are ye not scattered from the world?

For with the vilest spirit of Romagna
  I found of you one such, who for his deeds
  In soul already in Cocytus bathes,

And still above in body seems alive!

Canto XXXIV

Across the lake can be glimpsed the shape of Lucifer like a windmill through the distant fog. The impotent creature stands alone in Judecca, the fourth division, immobile from the chest down, flapping his wings, each of his three faces chewing one of humankind's worst sinners – Judas Iscariot, who betrayed Christ, and Brutus and Cassius, joint conspirators against Caesar. Virgil carries Dante in piggyback fashion as they climb down Lucifer's back and thighs. Having passed through the centre of the Earth, they struggle back up to a cave where a path will lead them to the safety of Mount Purgatory.

"'*Vexilla Regis prodeunt Inferni*'
 Towards us; therefore look in front of thee,"
 My Master said, "if thou discernest him."

As, when there breathes a heavy fog, or when
 Our hemisphere is darkening into night,
 Appears far off a mill the wind is turning,

Methought that such a building then I saw;
 And, for the wind, I drew myself behind
 My Guide, because there was no other shelter.

Now was I, and with fear in verse I put it,
 There where the shades were wholly covered up,
 And glimmered through like unto straws in glass.

Some prone are lying, others stand erect,
 This with the head, and that one with the soles;
 Another, bow-like, face to feet inverts.

When in advance so far we had proceeded,
 That it my Master pleased to show to me
 The creature who once had the beauteous semblance,

He from before me moved and made me stop,
 Saying: "Behold Dis, and behold the place
 Where thou with fortitude must arm thyself."

How frozen I became and powerless then,
 Ask it not, Reader, for I write it not,
 Because all language would be insufficient.

I did not die, and I alive remained not;
 Think for thyself now, hast thou aught of wit,
 What I became, being of both deprived.

The Emperor of the kingdom dolorous
 From his mid-breast forth issued from the ice;
 And better with a giant I compare

Than do the giants with those arms of his;
 Consider now how great must be that whole,
 Which unto such a part conforms itself.

Were he as fair once, as he now is foul,
 And lifted up his brow against his Maker,
 Well may proceed from him all tribulation.

O, what a marvel it appeared to me,
 When I beheld three faces on his head!
 The one in front, and that vermilion was;

Two were the others, that were joined with this
 Above the middle part of either shoulder,
 And they were joined together at the crest;

And the right-hand one seemed 'twixt white and yellow;
 The left was such to look upon as those
 Who come from where the Nile falls valley-ward.

Underneath each came forth two mighty wings,
 Such as befitting were so great a bird;
 Sails of the sea I never saw so large.

"Behold Dis, and behold the place / Where thou with fortitude must arm thyself."

Inf. XXXIV, lines 20–21

No feathers had they, but as of a bat
  Their fashion was; and he was waving them,
  So that three winds proceeded forth therefrom.

Thereby Cocytus wholly was congealed.
  With six eyes did he weep, and down three chins
  Trickled the tear-drops and the bloody drivel.

At every mouth he with his teeth was crunching
  A sinner, in the manner of a brake,
  So that he three of them tormented thus.

To him in front the biting was as naught
  Unto the clawing, for sometimes the spine
  Utterly stripped of all the skin remained.

"That soul up there which has the greatest pain,"
  The Master said, "is Judas Iscariot;
  With head inside, he plies his legs without.

Of the two others, who head downward are,
  The one who hangs from the black jowl is Brutus;
  See how he writhes himself, and speaks no word.

And the other, who so stalwart seems, is Cassius.
  But night is reascending, and 'tis time
  That we depart, for we have seen the whole."

As seemed him good, I clasped him round the neck,
  And he the vantage seized of time and place,
  And when the wings were opened wide apart,

He laid fast hold upon the shaggy sides;
  From fell to fell descended downward then
  Between the thick hair and the frozen crust.

When we were come to where the thigh revolves
  Exactly on the thickness of the haunch,
  The Guide, with labour and with hard-drawn breath,

Turned round his head where he had had his legs,
  And grappled to the hair, as one who mounts,
  So that to Hell I thought we were returning.

"Keep fast thy hold, for by such stairs as these,"
  The Master said, panting as one fatigued,
  "Must we perforce depart from so much evil."

Then through the opening of a rock he issued,
  And down upon the margin seated me;
  Then tow'rds me he outstretched his wary step.

I lifted up mine eyes and thought to see
  Lucifer in the same way I had left him;
  And I beheld him upward hold his legs.

And if I then became disquieted,
  Let stolid people think who do not see
  What the point is beyond which I had passed.

"Rise up," the Master said, "upon thy feet;
  The way is long, and difficult the road,
  And now the sun to middle-tierce returns."

It was not any palace corridor
  There where we were, but dungeon natural,
  With floor uneven and unease of light.

"Ere from the abyss I tear myself away,
  My Master," said I when I had arisen,
  "To draw me from an error speak a little;

Where is the ice? and how is this one fixed
  Thus upside down? and how in such short time
  From eve to morn has the sun made his transit?"

And he to me: "Thou still imaginest
  Thou art beyond the centre, where I grasped
  The hair of the fell worm, who mines the world.

That side thou wast, so long as I descended;
  When round I turned me, thou didst pass the point
  To which things heavy draw from every side,

And now beneath the hemisphere art come
  Opposite that which overhangs the vast
  Dry-land, and 'neath whose cope was put to death

The Man who without sin was born and lived.
  Thou hast thy feet upon the little sphere
  Which makes the other face of the Judecca.

Here it is morn when it is evening there;
  And he who with his hair a stairway made us
  Still fixed remaineth as he was before.

Upon this side he fell down out of heaven;
  And all the land, that whilom here emerged,
  For fear of him made of the sea a veil,

And came to our hemisphere; and peradventure
  To flee from him, what on this side appears
  Left the place vacant here, and back recoiled."

A place there is below, from Beelzebub
  As far receding as the tomb extends,
  Which not by sight is known, but by the sound

Of a small rivulet, that there descendeth
  Through chasm within the stone, which it has gnawed
  With course that winds about and slightly falls.

The Guide and I into that hidden road
  Now entered, to return to the bright world;
  And without care of having any rest

We mounted up, he first and I the second,
  Till I beheld through a round aperture
  Some of the beauteous things that Heaven doth bear;

Thence we came forth to rebehold the stars.

The Guide and I into that hidden road / Now entered, to return to the bright world;

Inf. XXXIV, lines 133–134

Thence we came forth to rebehold the stars.

Inf. XXXIV, line 139

Purgatorio

Having escaped from Hell, Dante and Virgil arrive on the shores of Mount Purgatory and begin clambering up the rock face until they reach the two terraces of Ante-Purgatory, where souls not yet satisfactorily reconciled with God must wait to begin their ascent. The angelic guardian of Peter's Gate, the entrance to Purgatory, marks Dante's forehead with seven Ps, one for each capital sin, before the poets wend their way up the northern side of the mountain into the seven terraces purging Pride, Envy, Wrath, Sloth, Covetousness, Gluttony and Lust. Once all his markings have been wiped away by the sweep of angel wings, Dante is able to scale the summit and finds himself in the Earthly Paradise. Reunited with Beatrice, he prepares to enter Paradise.

Contents

Canto I

Having emerged from Hell, Dante and Virgil find themselves on the shores of Purgatory. They are gruffly challenged by the guardian of the mountain, Cato of Utica, a Roman statesman famous for his Stoic virtue. Mistaking them for doomed souls escaped from Hell, he asks whether there has been a shift in the order of the universe. Virgil explains that Dante still lives and is there at the command of a lady from Heaven. He then prepares Dante for his ascent by washing his face and tying a reed girdle around his waist to safeguard him against Pride, the source of all sin.

To run o'er better waters hoists its sail
  The little vessel of my genius now,
  That leaves behind itself a sea so cruel;

And of that second kingdom will I sing
  Wherein the human spirit doth purge itself,
  And to ascend to heaven becometh worthy.

But let dead Poesy here rise again,
  O holy Muses, since that I am yours,
  And here Calliope somewhat ascend,

My song accompanying with that sound,
  Of which the miserable magpies felt
  The blow so great, that they despaired of pardon.

Sweet colour of the oriental sapphire,
  That was upgathered in the cloudless aspect
  Of the pure air, as far as the first circle,

Unto mine eyes did recommence delight
  Soon as I issued forth from the dead air,
  Which had with sadness filled mine eyes and breast.

The beauteous planet, that to love incites,
  Was making all the orient to laugh,
  Veiling the Fishes that were in her escort.

To the right hand I turned, and fixed my mind
  Upon the other pole, and saw four stars
  Ne'er seen before save by the primal people.

Rejoicing in their flamelets seemed the heaven.
  O thou septentrional and widowed site,
  Because thou art deprived of seeing these!

When from regarding them I had withdrawn,
  Turning a little to the other pole,
  There where the Wain had disappeared already,

I saw beside me an old man alone,
  Worthy of so much reverence in his look,
  That more owes not to father any son.

A long beard and with white hair intermingled
  He wore, in semblance like unto the tresses,
  Of which a double list fell on his breast.

The rays of the four consecrated stars
  Did so adorn his countenance with light,
  That him I saw as were the sun before him.

"Who are you? ye who, counter the blind river,
  Have fled away from the eternal prison?"
  Moving those venerable plumes, he said:

"Who guided you? or who has been your lamp
  In issuing forth out of the night profound,
  That ever black makes the infernal valley?

The laws of the abyss, are they thus broken?
  Or is there changed in heaven some council new,
  That being damned ye come unto my crags?"

Then did my Leader lay his grasp upon me,
  And with his words, and with his hands and signs,
  Reverent he made in me my knees and brow;

Then answered him: "I came not of myself;
  A Lady from Heaven descended, at whose prayers
  I aided this one with my company.

But since it is thy will more be unfolded
  Of our condition, how it truly is,
  Mine cannot be that this should be denied thee.

This one has never his last evening seen,
  But by his folly was so near to it
  That very little time was there to turn.

The beauteous planet, that to love incites, / Was making all the orient to laugh, /
Veiling the Fishes that were in her escort.

Purg. I, lines 19–21

I saw beside me an old man alone, / Worthy of so much reverence in his look, /
That more owes not to father any son.

Purg. I, lines 31-33

As I have said, I unto him was sent
  To rescue him, and other way was none
  Than this to which I have myself betaken.

I've shown him all the people of perdition,
  And now those spirits I intend to show
  Who purge themselves beneath thy guardianship.

How I have brought him would be long to tell thee.
  Virtue descendeth from on high that aids me
  To lead him to behold thee and to hear thee.

Now may it please thee to vouchsafe his coming;
  He seeketh Liberty, which is so dear,
  As knoweth he who life for her refuses.

Thou know'st it; since, for her, to thee not bitter
  Was death in Utica, where thou didst leave
  The vesture, that will shine so, the great day.

By us the eternal edicts are not broken;
  Since this one lives, and Minos binds not me;
  But of that circle I, where are the chaste

Eyes of thy Marcia, who in looks still prays thee,
  O holy breast, to hold her as thine own;
  For her love, then, incline thyself to us.

Permit us through thy sevenfold realm to go;
  I will take back this grace from thee to her,
  If to be mentioned there below thou deignest."

"Marcia so pleasing was unto mine eyes
  While I was on the other side," then said he,
  "That every grace she wished of me I granted;

Now that she dwells beyond the evil river,
  She can no longer move me, by that law
  Which, when I issued forth from there, was made.

But if a Lady of Heaven do move and rule thee,
  As thou dost say, no flattery is needful;
  Let it suffice thee that for her thou ask me.

Go, then, and see thou gird this one about
  With a smooth rush, and that thou wash his face,
  So that thou cleanse away all stain therefrom,

For 'twere not fitting that the eye o'ercast
  By any mist should go before the first
  Angel, who is of those of Paradise.

This little island round about its base
  Below there, yonder, where the billow beats it,
  Doth rushes bear upon its washy ooze;

No other plant that putteth forth the leaf,
  Or that doth indurate, can there have life,
  Because it yieldeth not unto the shocks.

Thereafter be not this way your return;
  The sun, which now is rising, will direct you
  To take the mount by easier ascent."

With this he vanished; and I raised me up
  Without a word, and wholly drew myself
  Unto my Guide, and turned mine eyes to him.

And he began: "Son, follow thou my steps;
  Let us turn back, for on this side declines
  The plain unto its lower boundaries."

The dawn was vanquishing the matin hour
  Which fled before it, so that from afar
  I recognised the trembling of the sea.

Along the solitary plain we went
  As one who unto the lost road returns,
  And till he finds it seems to go in vain.

As soon as we were come to where the dew
  Fights with the sun, and, being in a part
  Where shadow falls, little evaporates,

Both of his hands upon the grass outspread
  In gentle manner did my Master place;
  Whence I, who of his action was aware,

Extended unto him my tearful cheeks;
  There did he make in me uncovered wholly
  That hue which Hell had covered up in me.

Then came we down upon the desert shore
  Which never yet saw navigate its waters
  Any that afterward had known return.

There he begirt me as the other pleased;
  O marvellous! for even as he culled
  The humble plant, such it sprang up again

Suddenly there where he uprooted it.

Canto II

From the shores of Purgatory, Dante watches the arrival of the ship carrying the souls of those recently saved. Piloted by a gleaming winged angel, the vessel first emerges over the curve of the Earth. The crew is joyfully singing the hymn In exitu Israel de Aegypto! *(When Israel Came Out of Egypt) because they have left behind a place of evil for a new life in God's promised land. The souls notice that Dante is alive. Casella the musician stops to play one of Dante's own compositions – a performance which Cato brusquely interrupts, chiding them for wasting time.*

Already had the sun the horizon reached
  Whose circle of meridian covers o'er
  Jerusalem with its most lofty point,

And night that opposite to him revolves
  Was issuing forth from Ganges with the Scales
  That fall from out her hand when she exceedeth;

So that the white and the vermilion cheeks
  Of beautiful Aurora, where I was,
  By too great age were changing into orange.

We still were on the border of the sea,
  Like people who are thinking of their road,
  Who go in heart and with the body stay;

And lo! as when, upon the approach of morning,
  Through the gross vapours Mars grows fiery red
  Down in the West upon the ocean floor,

Appeared to me—may I again behold it!—
  A light along the sea so swiftly coming,
  Its motion by no flight of wing is equalled;

From which when I a little had withdrawn
  Mine eyes, that I might question my Conductor,
  Again I saw it brighter grown and larger.

Then on each side of it appeared to me
  I knew not what of white, and underneath it
  Little by little there came forth another.

My Master yet had uttered not a word
  While the first whiteness into wings unfolded;
  But when he clearly recognised the pilot,

He cried: "Make haste, make haste to bow the knee!
  Behold the Angel of God! fold thou thy hands!
  Henceforward shalt thou see such officers!

See how he scorneth human arguments,
  So that nor oar he wants, nor other sail
  Than his own wings, between so distant shores.

See how he holds them pointed up to heaven,
  Fanning the air with the eternal pinions,
  That do not moult themselves like mortal hair!"

Then as still nearer and more near us came
  The Bird Divine, more radiant he appeared,
  So that near by the eye could not endure him,

But down I cast it; and he came to shore
  With a small vessel, very swift and light,
  So that the water swallowed naught thereof.

Upon the stern stood the Celestial Pilot;
  Beatitude seemed written in his face,
  And more than a hundred spirits sat within.

"In exitu Israel de Aegypto!"
  They chanted all together in one voice,
  With whatso in that psalm is after written.

Then made he sign of holy rood upon them,
  Whereat all cast themselves upon the shore,
  And he departed swiftly as he came.

The throng which still remained there unfamiliar
  Seemed with the place, all round about them gazing,
  As one who in new matters makes essay.

On every side was darting forth the day.
  The sun, who had with his resplendent shafts
  From the mid-heaven chased forth the Capricorn,

When the new people lifted up their faces
  Towards us, saying to us: "If ye know,
  Show us the way to go unto the mountain."

But when he clearly recognised the pilot, / He cried: "Make haste, make haste to bow the knee! /
Behold the Angel of God!"

Purg. II, lines 27–29

Beatitude seemed written in his face,

Purg. II, line 44

And answer made Virgilius: "Ye believe
  Perchance that we have knowledge of this place,
  But we are strangers even as yourselves.

Just now we came, a little while before you,
  Another way, which was so rough and steep,
  That mounting will henceforth seem sport to us."

The souls who had, from seeing me draw breath,
  Become aware that I was still alive,
  Pallid in their astonishment became;

And as to messenger who bears the olive
  The people throng to listen to the news,
  And no one shows himself afraid of crowding,

So at the sight of me stood motionless
  Those fortunate spirits, all of them, as if
  Oblivious to go and make them fair.

One from among them saw I coming forward,
  As to embrace me, with such great affection,
  That it incited me to do the like.

O empty shadows, save in aspect only!
  Three times behind it did I clasp my hands,
  As oft returned with them to my own breast!

I think with wonder I depicted me;
  Whereat the shadow smiled and backward drew;
  And I, pursuing it, pressed farther forward.

Gently it said that I should stay my steps;
  Then knew I who it was, and I entreated
  That it would stop awhile to speak with me.

It made reply to me: "Even as I loved thee
  In mortal body, so I love thee free;
  Therefore I stop; but wherefore goest thou?"

"My own Casella! to return once more
  There where I am, I make this journey," said I;
  "But how from thee has so much time be taken?"

And he to me: "No outrage has been done me,
  If he who takes both when and whom he pleases
  Has many times denied to me this passage,

For of a righteous will his own is made.
  He, sooth to say, for three months past has taken
  Whoever wished to enter with all peace;

Whence I, who now had turned unto that shore
  Where salt the waters of the Tiber grow,
  Benignantly by him have been received.

Unto that outlet now his wing is pointed,
  Because for evermore assemble there
  Those who tow'rds Acheron do not descend."

And I: "If some new law take not from thee
  Memory or practice of the song of love,
  Which used to quiet in me all my longings,

Thee may it please to comfort therewithal
  Somewhat this soul of mine, that with its body
  Hitherward coming is so much distressed."

"Love, that within my mind discourses with me,"
  Forthwith began he so melodiously,
  The melody within me still is sounding.

My Master, and myself, and all that people
  Which with him were, appeared as satisfied
  As if naught else might touch the mind of any.

We all of us were moveless and attentive
  Unto his notes; and lo! the grave old man,
  Exclaiming: "What is this, ye laggard spirits?

What negligence, what standing still is this?
  Run to the mountain to strip off the slough,
  That lets not God be manifest to you."

Even as when, collecting grain or tares,
  The doves, together at their pasture met,
  Quiet, nor showing their accustomed pride,

If aught appear of which they are afraid,
  Upon a sudden leave their food alone,
  Because they are assailed by greater care;

So that fresh company did I behold
  The song relinquish, and go tow'rds the hill,
  As one who goes, and knows not whitherward;

Nor was our own departure less in haste.

Canto III

*As Virgil and Dante clamber up the lower slopes of the mountain, the Florentine notices
that the rays of the rising sun cast his shadow but pass through Virgil's airy body. With
a pang, he remembers that Virgil's spirit is dead and damned. In the First Terrace of
Ante-Purgatory, the poets encounter the Excommunicate (including the Emperor
Manfred). Although detained by God outside of Purgatory for having been lazy with
their faith, these souls endure the delay patiently in the hope of securing divine
satisfaction, after which time they will be allowed to ascend the mountain.*

Inasmuch as the instantaneous flight
  Had scattered them asunder o'er the plain,
  Turned to the mountain whither reason spurs us,

I pressed me close unto my faithful comrade,
  And how without him had I kept my course?
  Who would have led me up along the mountain?

He seemed to me within himself remorseful;
  O noble conscience, and without a stain,
  How sharp a sting is trivial fault to thee!

After his feet had laid aside the haste
  Which mars the dignity of every act,
  My mind, that hitherto had been restrained,

Let loose its faculties as if delighted,
  And I my sight directed to the hill
  That highest tow'rds the heaven uplifts itself.

The sun, that in our rear was flaming red,
  Was broken in front of me into the figure
  Which had in me the stoppage of its rays;

Unto one side I turned me, with the fear
  Of being left alone, when I beheld
  Only in front of me the ground obscured.

"Why dost thou still mistrust?" my Comforter
  Began to say to me turned wholly round;
  "Dost thou not think me with thee, and that I
                  guide thee?

'Tis evening there already where is buried
  The body within which I cast a shadow;
  'Tis from Brundusium ta'en, and Naples has it.

Now if in front of me no shadow fall,
  Marvel not at it more than at the heavens,
  Because one ray impedeth not another

To suffer torments, both of cold and heat,
  Bodies like this that Power provides, which wills
  That how it works be not unveiled to us.

Insane is he who hopeth that our reason
  Can traverse the illimitable way,
  Which the one Substance in three Persons follows!

Mortals, remain contented at the 'Quia;'
  For if ye had been able to see all,
  No need there were for Mary to give birth;

And ye have seen desiring without fruit,
  Those whose desire would have been quieted,
  Which evermore is given them for a grief.

I speak of Aristotle and of Plato,
  And many others;"—and here bowed his head,
  And more he said not, and remained disturbed.

We came meanwhile unto the mountain's foot;
  There so precipitate we found the rock,
  That nimble legs would there have been in vain.

'Twixt Lerici and Turbia, the most desert,
  The most secluded pathway is a stair
  Easy and open, if compared with that.

"Who knoweth now upon which hand the hill
  Slopes down," my Master said, his footsteps staying,
  "So that who goeth without wings may mount?"

And while he held his eyes upon the ground
  Examining the nature of the path,
  And I was looking up around the rock,

On the left hand appeared to me a throng
  Of souls, that moved their feet in our direction,
  And did not seem to move, they came so slowly.

"Lift up thine eyes," I to the Master said;
  "Behold, on this side, who will give us counsel,
  If thou of thine own self can have it not."

Then he looked at me, and with frank expression
  Replied: "Let us go there, for they come slowly,
  And thou be steadfast in thy hope, sweet son."

Still was that people as far off from us,
  After a thousand steps of ours I say,
  As a good thrower with his hand would reach,

When they all crowded unto the hard masses
  Of the high bank, and motionless stood and close,
  As he stands still to look who goes in doubt.

"O happy dead! O spirits elect already!"
  Virgilius made beginning, "by that peace
  Which I believe is waiting for you all,

Tell us upon what side the mountain slopes,
  So that the going up be possible,
  For to lose time irks him most who most knows."

As sheep come issuing forth from out the fold
  By ones and twos and threes, and the others stand
  Timidly, holding down their eyes and nostrils,

And what the foremost does the others do,
  Huddling themselves against her, if she stop,
  Simple and quiet and the wherefore know not;

So moving to approach us thereupon
  I saw the leader of that fortunate flock,
  Modest in face and dignified in gait.

As soon as those in the advance saw broken
  The light upon the ground at my right side,
  So that from me the shadow reached the rock,

They stopped, and backward drew themselves
                                    somewhat;
  And all the others, who came after them,
  Not knowing why nor wherefore, did the same.

"Without your asking, I confess to you
  This is a human body which you see,
  Whereby the sunshine on the ground is cleft.

Marvel ye not thereat, but be persuaded
  That not without a power which comes from Heaven
  Doth he endeavour to surmount this wall."

The Master thus; and said those worthy people:
  "Return ye then, and enter in before us,"
  Making a signal with the back o' the hand

And one of them began: "Whoe'er thou art,
  Thus going turn thine eyes, consider well
  If e'er thou saw me in the other world."

I turned me tow'rds him, and looked at him closely;
  Blond was he, beautiful, and of noble aspect,
  But one of his eyebrows had a blow divided.

When with humility I had disclaimed
  E'er having seen him, "Now behold!" he said,
  And showed me high upon his breast a wound.

Then said he with a smile: "I am Manfredi,
  The grandson of the Empress Costanza;
  Therefore, when thou returnest, I beseech thee

Go to my daughter beautiful, the mother
  Of Sicily's honour and of Aragon's,
  And the truth tell her, if aught else be told.

After I had my body lacerated
  By these two mortal stabs, I gave myself
  Weeping to Him, who willingly doth pardon.

Horrible my iniquities had been;
  But Infinite Goodness hath such ample arms,
  That it receives whatever turns to it.

Had but Cosenza's pastor, who in chase
  Of me was sent by Clement at that time,
  In God read understandingly this page,

The bones of my dead body still would be
  At the bridge-head, near unto Benevento,
  Under the safeguard of the heavy cairn.

Now the rain bathes and moveth them the wind,
  Beyond the realm, almost beside the Verde,
  Where he transported them with tapers quenched.

On the left hand appeared to me a throng / Of souls, that moved their feet in our direction, /
And did not seem to move,

Purg. III, lines 58–60

By malison of theirs is not so lost
  Eternal Love, that it cannot return,
  So long as hope has anything of green.

True is it, who in contumacy dies
  Of Holy Church, though penitent at last,
  Must wait upon the outside this bank

Thirty times told the time that he has been
  In his presumption, unless such decree
  Shorter by means of righteous prayers become.

See now if thou hast power to make me happy,
  By making known unto my good Costanza
  How thou hast seen me, and this ban beside,

For those on Earth can much advance us here."

Canto IV

*Virgil and Dante walk with the excommunicated souls along the terrace until they
reach a steep rock face on the side of the mountain. The poets enter the Second Terrace
of Ante-Purgatory which is occupied by the Late Repentant (the first sub-group of
which are the Indolent). The Florentine instrument-maker Belacqua explains to them
that, although such souls remained within the bosom of the Church, they chose a tardy
repentance and must now endure a delay equal in length to the duration of their
earthly lives before being pardoned. Dante wonders why the sun is always on their left
and Virgil explains the paradox to him.*

Whenever by delight or else by pain,
  That seizes any faculty of ours,
  Wholly to that the soul collects itself,

It seemeth that no other power it heeds;
  And this against that error is which thinks
  One soul above another kindles in us.

And hence, whenever aught is heard or seen
  Which keeps the soul intently bent upon it,
  Time passes on, and we perceive it not,

Because one faculty is that which listens,
  And other that which the soul keeps entire;
  This is as if in bonds, and that is free.

Of this I had experience positive
  In hearing and in gazing at that spirit;
  For fifty full degrees uprisen was

The sun, and I had not perceived it, when
  We came to where those souls with one accord
  Cried out unto us: "Here is what you ask."

A greater opening ofttimes hedges up
  With but a little forkful of his thorns
  The villager, what time the grape imbrowns,

Than was the passage-way through which ascended
  Only my Leader and myself behind him,
  After that company departed from us.

One climbs Sanleo and descends in Noli,
  And mounts the summit of Bismantova,
  With feet alone; but here one needs must fly;

With the swift pinions and the plumes I say
  Of great desire, conducted after him
  Who gave me hope, and made a light for me.

We mounted upward through the rifted rock,
  And on each side the border pressed upon us,
  And feet and hands the ground beneath required.

When we were come upon the upper rim
  Of the high bank, out on the open slope,
  "My Master," said I, "what way shall we take?"

And he to me: "No step of thine descend;
  Still up the mount behind me win thy way,
  Till some sage escort shall appear to us."

The summit was so high it vanquished sight,
  And the hillside precipitous far more
  Than line from middle quadrant to the centre.

Spent with fatigue was I, when I began:
  "O my sweet Father! turn thee and behold
  How I remain alone, unless thou stay!"

"O son," he said, "up yonder drag thyself,"
  Pointing me to a terrace somewhat higher,
  Which on that side encircles all the hill.

These words of his so spurred me on, that I
  Strained every nerve, behind him scrambling up,
  Until the circle was beneath my feet.

Thereon ourselves we seated both of us
  Turned to the East, from which we had ascended,
  For all men are delighted to look back.

To the low shores mine eyes I first directed,
  Then to the sun uplifted them, and wondered
  That on the left hand we were smitten by it.

The Poet well perceived that I was wholly
  Bewildered at the chariot of the light,
  Where 'twixt us and the Aquilon it entered.

Whereon he said to me: "If Castor and Pollux
  Were in the company of yonder mirror,
  That up and down conducteth with its light,

Thou wouldst behold the zodiac's jagged wheel
  Revolving still more near unto the Bears,
  Unless it swerved aside from its old track.

How that may be wouldst thou have power to think,
  Collected in thyself, imagine Zion
  Together with this mount on earth to stand,

So that they both one sole horizon have,
  And hemispheres diverse; whereby the road
  Which Phaeton, alas! knew not to drive,

Thou'lt see how of necessity must pass
  This on one side, when that upon the other,
  If thine intelligence right clearly heed."

"Truly, my Master," said I, "never yet
  Saw I so clearly as I now discern,
  There where my wit appeared incompetent,

That the mid-circle of supernal motion,
  Which in some art is the Equator called,
  And aye remains between the Sun and Winter,

For reason which thou sayest, departeth hence
  Tow'rds the Septentrion, what time the Hebrews
  Beheld it tow'rds the region of the heat.

But, if it pleaseth thee, I fain would learn
  How far we have to go; for the hill rises
  Higher than eyes of mine have power to rise."

And he to me: "This mount is such, that ever
  At the beginning down below 'tis tiresome,
  And aye the more one climbs, the less it hurts.

Therefore, when it shall seem so pleasant to thee,
  That going up shall be to thee as easy
  As going down the current in a boat,

Then at this pathway's ending thou wilt be;
  There to repose thy panting breath expect;
  No more I answer; and this I know for true."

And as he finished uttering these words,
  A voice close by us sounded: "Peradventure
  Thou wilt have need of sitting down ere that."

At sound thereof each one of us turned round,
  And saw upon the left hand a great rock,
  Which neither I nor he before had noticed.

Thither we drew; and there were persons there
  Who in the shadow stood behind the rock,
  As one through indolence is wont to stand.

And one of them, who seemed to me fatigued,
  Was sitting down, and both his knees embraced,
  Holding his face low down between them bowed.

We mounted upward through the rifted rock, / And on each side the border pressed upon us,

Purg. IV, lines 31–32

Thither we drew; and there were persons there / Who in the shadow stood behind the rock, /
As one through indolence is wont to stand.

Purg. IV, lines 103–105

PURGATORIO – CANTO IV

"O my sweet Lord," I said, "do turn thine eye
  On him who shows himself more negligent
  Then even Sloth herself his sister were."

Then he turned round to us, and he gave heed,
  Just lifting up his eyes above his thigh,
  And said: "Now go thou up, for thou art valiant."

Then knew I who he was; and the distress,
  That still a little did my breathing quicken,
  My going to him hindered not; and after

I came to him he hardly raised his head,
  Saying: "Hast thou seen clearly how the sun
  O'er thy left shoulder drives his chariot?"

His sluggish attitude and his curt words
  A little unto laughter moved my lips;
  Then I began: "Belacqua, I grieve not

For thee henceforth; but tell me, wherefore seated
  In this place art thou? Waitest thou an escort?
  Or has thy usual habit seized upon thee?"

And he: "O brother, what's the use of climbing?
  Since to my torment would not let me go
  The Angel of God, who sitteth at the gate.

First heaven must needs so long revolve me round
  Outside thereof, as in my life it did,
  Since the good sighs I to the end postponed,

Unless, e'er that, some prayer may bring me aid
  Which rises from a heart that lives in grace;
  What profit others that in heaven are heard not?"

Meanwhile the Poet was before me mounting,
  And saying: "Come now; see the sun has touched
  Meridian, and from the shore the night

Covers already with her foot Morocco."

Canto V

*In the Second Terrace of Ante-Purgatory, Dante and Virgil meet a group of the Late
Repentants, who are singing the* Miserere. *Although they had died under violent
circumstances or had otherwise met an untimely death, they had still managed to
repent. Dante converses with Jacopo del Cassero, a Guelf supporter from Fano;
Buonconte da Montefeltro, son of Guido from Hell's* Canto XXVII; *and Lady Pia dei
Tolomei, a Sienese aristocrat murdered by her husband, to whom she was forcibly
betrothed. They ask Dante to assist them when he is back in the world again.*

I had already from those shades departed,
  And followed in the footsteps of my Guide,
  When from behind, pointing his finger at me,

One shouted: "See, it seems as if shone not
  The sunshine on the left of him below,
  And like one living seems he to conduct him."

Mine eyes I turned at utterance of these words,
  And saw them watching with astonishment
  But me, but me, and the light which was broken!

"Why doth thy mind so occupy itself,"
  The Master said, "that thou thy pace dost slacken?
  What matters it to thee what here is whispered?

Come after me, and let the people talk;
  Stand like a steadfast tower, that never wags
  Its top for all the blowing of the winds;

For evermore the man in whom is springing
  Thought upon thought, removes from him the mark,
  Because the force of one the other weakens."

What could I say in answer but "I come"?
  I said it somewhat with that colour tinged
  Which makes a man of pardon sometimes worthy.

Meanwhile along the mountain-side across
  Came people in advance of us a little,
  Singing the *Miserere* verse by verse.

When they became aware I gave no place
  For passage of the sunshine through my body,
  They changed their song into a long, hoarse "Oh!"

And two of them, in form of messengers,
  Ran forth to meet us, and demanded of us,
  "Of your condition make us cognisant."

And said my Master: "Ye can go your way
  And carry back again to those who sent you,
  That this one's body is of very flesh.

If they stood still because they saw his shadow,
  As I suppose, enough is answered them;
  Him let them honour, it may profit them."

Vapours enkindled saw I ne'er so swiftly
  At early nightfall cleave the air serene,
  Nor, at the set of sun, the clouds of August,

But upward they returned in briefer time,
  And, on arriving, with the others wheeled
  Tow'rds us, like troops that run without a rein.

"This folk that presses unto us is great,
  And cometh to implore thee," said the Poet;
  "So still go onward, and in going listen."

"O soul that goest to beatitude
  With the same members wherewith thou wast born,"
  Shouting they came, "a little stay thy steps,

Look, if thou e'er hast any of us seen,
  So that o'er yonder thou bear news of him;
  Ah, why dost thou go on? Ah, why not stay?

Long since we all were slain by violence,
  And sinners even to the latest hour;
  Then did a light from heaven admonish us,

So that, both penitent and pardoning, forth
  From life we issued reconciled to God,
  Who with desire to see Him stirs our hearts."

And I: "Although I gaze into your faces,
  No one I recognize; but if may please you
  Aught I have power to do, ye well-born spirits,

Speak ye, and I will do it, by that peace
  Which, following the feet of such a Guide,
  From world to world makes itself sought by me."

And one began: "Each one has confidence
  In thy good offices without an oath,
  Unless the I cannot cut off the I will;

Whence I, who speak alone before the others,
  Pray thee, if ever thou dost see the land
  That 'twixt Romagna lies and that of Charles,

Thou be so courteous to me of thy prayers
  In Fano, that they pray for me devoutly,
  That I may purge away my grave offences.

From thence was I; but the deep wounds, through which
  Issued the blood wherein I had my seat,
  Were dealt me in bosom of the Antenori,

There where I thought to be the most secure;
  'Twas he of Este had it done, who held me
  In hatred far beyond what justice willed.

But if towards the Mira I had fled,
  When I was overtaken at Oriaco,
  I still should be o'er yonder where men breathe.

I ran to the lagoon, and reeds and mire
  Did so entangle me I fell, and saw there
  A lake made from my veins upon the ground."

Then said another: "Ah, be that desire
  Fulfilled that draws thee to the lofty mountain,
  As thou with pious pity aidest mine.

I was of Montefeltro, and am Buonconte;
  Giovanna, nor none other cares for me;
  Hence among these I go with downcast front."

And I to him: "What violence or what chance
  Led thee astray so far from Campaldino,
  That never has thy sepulture been known?"

"Oh," he replied, "at Casentino's foot
  A river crosses named Archiano, born
  Above the Hermitage in Apennine.

Meanwhile along the mountain-side across / Came people in advance of us a little, /
Singing the *Miserere* verse by verse.

Purg. V, lines 22–24

There where the name thereof becometh void
　Did I arrive, pierced through and through the throat,
　Fleeing on foot, and bloodying the plain;

There my sight lost I, and my utterance
　Ceased in the name of Mary, and thereat
　I fell, and tenantless my flesh remained.

Truth will I speak, repeat it to the living;
　God's Angel took me up, and he of hell
　Shouted: 'O thou from heaven, why dost thou rob me?

Thou bearest away the eternal part of him,
　For one poor little tear, that takes him from me;
　But with the rest I'll deal in other fashion!'

Well knowest thou how in the air is gathered
　That humid vapour which to water turns,
　Soon as it rises where the cold doth grasp it.

He joined that evil will, which aye seeks evil,
　To intellect, and moved the mist and wind
　By means of power, which his own nature gave;

Thereafter, when the day was spent, the valley
　From Pratomagno to the great yoke covered
　With fog, and made the heaven above intent,

So that the pregnant air to water changed;
　Down fell the rain, and to the gullies came
　Whate'er of it earth tolerated not;

And as it mingled with the mighty torrents,
　Towards the royal river with such speed
　It headlong rushed, that nothing held it back.

My frozen body near unto its outlet
　The robust Archian found, and into Arno
　Thrust it, and loosened from my breast the cross

I made of me, when agony o'ercame me;
　It rolled me on the banks and on the bottom,
　Then with its booty covered and begirt me."

"Ah, when thou hast returned unto the world,
　And rested thee from thy long journeying,"
　After the second followed the third spirit,

"Do thou remember me who am the Pia;
　Siena made me, unmade me Maremma;
　He knoweth it, who had encircled first,

Espousing me, my finger with his gem."

Canto VI

Dante is besieged by a crowd of unshriven souls, all of whom ask for his help through
prayer. He questions Virgil about its efficacy but the heathen can only give the pilgrim a
superficial answer, and it is evident that Beatrice will be the one to reveal to Dante the
more profound aspects of the Christian faith. Sordello, a Mantuan troubadour, acquaints
the poets further with the inhabitants and the organization of Ante-Purgatory. Dante
starts to inveigh against the political factions keeping Italy divided and then launches
into a savage and ironic criticism on Florence and its perpetual shifts of power.

Whene'er is broken up the game of Zara,
　He who has lost remains behind despondent,
　The throws repeating, and in sadness learns;

The people with the other all depart;
　One goes in front, and one behind doth pluck him,
　And at his side one brings himself to mind;

"God's Angel took me up, and he of hell / Shouted: 'O thou from heaven, why dost thou
rob me?"

Purg. V, lines 104–105

"Do thou remember me who am the Pia; / Siena made me, unmade me Maremma;"

Purg. V, lines 133–134

He pauses not, and this and that one hears;
  They crowd no more to whom his hand he stretches,
  And from the throng he thus defends himself.

Even such was I in that dense multitude,
  Turning to them this way and that my face,
  And, promising, I freed myself therefrom.

There was the Aretine, who from the arms
  Untamed of Ghin di Tacco had his death,
  And he who fleeing from pursuit was drowned.

There was imploring with his hands outstretched
  Frederick Novello, and that one of Pisa
  Who made the good Marzucco seem so strong.

I saw Count Orso; and the soul divided
  By hatred and by envy from its body,
  As it declared, and not for crime committed,

Pierre de la Brosse I say; and here provide
  While still on Earth the Lady of Brabant,
  So that for this she be of no worse flock!

As soon as I was free from all those shades
  Who only prayed that some one else may pray,
  So as to hasten their becoming holy,

Began I: "It appears that thou deniest,
  O light of mine, expressly in some text,
  That orison can bend decree of Heaven;

And ne'ertheless these people pray for this.
  Might then their expectation bootless be?
  Or is to me thy saying not quite clear?"

And he to me: "My writing is explicit,
  And not fallacious is the hope of these,
  If with sane intellect 'tis well regarded;

For top of judgment doth not vail itself,
  Because the fire of love fulfils at once
  What he must satisfy who here installs him.

And there, where I affirmed that proposition,
  Defect was not amended by a prayer,
  Because the prayer from God was separate.

Verily, in so deep a questioning
  Do not decide, unless she tell it thee,
  Who light 'twixt truth and intellect shall be.

I know not if thou understand; I speak
  Of Beatrice; her shalt thou see above,
  Smiling and happy, on this mountain's top."

And I: "Good Leader, let us make more haste,
  For I no longer tire me as before;
  And see, e'en now the hill a shadow casts."

"We will go forward with this day" he answered,
  "As far as now is possible for us;
  But otherwise the fact is than thou thinkest.

Ere thou art up there, thou shalt see return
  Him, who now hides himself behind the hill,
  So that thou dost not interrupt his rays.

But yonder there behold! a soul that stationed
  All, all alone is looking hitherward;
  It will point out to us the quickest way."

We came up unto it; O Lombard soul,
  How lofty and disdainful thou didst bear thee,
  And grand and slow in moving of thine eyes!

Nothing whatever did it say to us,
  But let us go our way, eying us only
  After the manner of a couchant lion;

Still near to it Virgilius drew, entreating
  That it would point us out the best ascent;
  And it replied not unto his demand,

But of our native land and of our life
  It questioned us; and the sweet Guide began:
  "Mantua,"—and the shade, all in itself recluse,

Rose tow'rds him from the place where first it was,
  Saying: "O Mantuan, I am Sordello
  Of thine own land!" and one embraced the other.

Ah! servile Italy, grief's hostelry!
  A ship without a pilot in great tempest!
  No Lady thou of Provinces, but brothel!

That noble soul was so impatient, only
  At the sweet sound of his own native land,
  To make its citizen glad welcome there;

And now within thee are not without war
  Thy living ones, and one doth gnaw the other
  Of those whom one wall and one fosse shut in!

Search, wretched one, all round about the shores
　Thy seaboard, and then look within thy bosom,
　If any part of thee enjoyeth peace!

What boots it, that for thee Justinian
　The bridle mend, if empty be the saddle?
　Withouten this the shame would be the less.

Ah! people, thou that oughtest to be devout,
　And to let Caesar sit upon the saddle,
　If well thou hearest what God teacheth thee,

Behold how fell this wild beast has become,
　Being no longer by the spur corrected,
　Since thou hast laid thy hand upon the bridle.

O German Albert! who abandonest
　Her that has grown recalcitrant and savage,
　And oughtest to bestride her saddle-bow,

May a just judgment from the stars down fall
　Upon thy blood, and be it new and open,
　That thy successor may have fear thereof;

Because thy father and thyself have suffered,
　By greed of those transalpine lands distrained,
　The garden of the empire to be waste.

Come and behold Montecchi and Cappelletti,
　Monaldi and Fillippeschi, careless man!
　Those sad already, and these doubt-depressed!

Come, cruel one! come and behold the oppression
　Of thy nobility, and cure their wounds,
　And thou shalt see how safe is Santafiore!

Come and behold thy Rome, that is lamenting,
　Widowed, alone, and day and night exclaims,
　"My Caesar, why hast thou forsaken me?"

Come and behold how loving are the people;
　And if for us no pity moveth thee,
　Come and be made ashamed of thy renown!

And if it lawful be, O Jove Supreme!
　Who upon Earth for us wast crucified,
　Are thy just eyes averted otherwhere?

Or preparation is 't, that, in the abyss
　Of thine own counsel, for some good thou makest
　From our perception utterly cut off?

For all the towns of Italy are full
　Of tyrants, and becometh a Marcellus
　Each peasant churl who plays the partisan!

My Florence! well mayst thou contented be
　With this digression, which concerns thee not,
　Thanks to thy people who such forethought take!

Many at heart have justice, but shoot slowly,
　That unadvised they come not to the bow,
　But on their very lips thy people have it!

Many refuse to bear the common burden;
　But thy solicitous people answereth
　Without being asked, and crieth: "I submit."

Now be thou joyful, for thou hast good reason;
　Thou affluent, thou in peace, thou full of wisdom!
　If I speak true, the event conceals it not.

Athens and Lacedaemon, they who made
　The ancient laws, and were so civilized,
　Made towards living well a little sign

Compared with thee, who makest such fine-spun
　Provisions, that to middle of November
　Reaches not what thou in October spinnest.

How oft, within the time of thy remembrance,
　Laws, money, offices, and usages
　Hast thou remodelled, and renewed thy members?

And if thou mind thee well, and see the light,
　Thou shalt behold thyself like a sick woman,
　Who cannot find repose upon her down,

But by her tossing wardeth off her pain.

Canto VII

Sordello asks the travellers who they are. When he discovers the great Classical poet's identity, he drops down on his knees and enquires about Virgil's fate. Sordello explains the Rule of the Mountain, which forbids any climbing after dark, and takes the poets to a beautiful valley, where he identifies distinguished members of the Preoccupied, the third sub-group of the Late Repentant – Rudolph of Hapsburg, Ottocar II and Wenceslas IV of Bohemia, Henry of Navarre, Philip of France, Peter III of Aragon, Henry III of England and William, Marquis of Monferrat and Canavese. Their worldly cares caused them to neglect their spiritual duties and they now continue to fret over family or state matters.

After the gracious and glad salutations
  Had three and four times been reiterated,
  Sordello backward drew and said, "Who are you?"

"Or ever to this mountain were directed
  The souls deserving to ascend to God,
  My bones were buried by Octavian.

I am Virgilius; and for no crime else
  Did I lose heaven, than for not having faith;"
  In this wise then my Leader made reply.

As one who suddenly before him sees
  Something whereat he marvels, who believes
  And yet does not, saying, "It is! it is not!"

So he appeared; and then bowed down his brow,
  And with humility returned towards him,
  And, where inferiors embrace, embraced him.

"O glory of the Latians, thou," he said,
  "Through whom our language showed what it
                      could do
  O pride eternal of the place I came from,

What merit or what grace to me reveals thee?
  If I to hear thy words be worthy, tell me
  If thou dost come from Hell, and from what cloister."

"Through all the circles of the doleful realm,"
  Responded he, "have I come hitherward;
  Heaven's power impelled me, and with that I come.

I by not doing, not by doing, lost
  The sight of that high sun which thou desirest,
  And which too late by me was recognized.

A place there is below not sad with torments,
  But darkness only, where the lamentations
  Have not the sound of wailing, but are sighs.

There dwell I with the little innocents
  Snatched by the teeth of Death, or ever they
  Were from our human sinfulness exempt.

There dwell I among those who the three saintly
  Virtues did not put on, and without vice
  The others knew and followed all of them.

But if thou know and can, some indication
  Give us by which we may the sooner come
  Where Purgatory has its right beginning."

He answered: "No fixed place has been assigned us;
  'Tis lawful for me to go up and round;
  So far as I can go, as guide I join thee.

But see already how the day declines,
  And to go up by night we are not able;
  Therefore 'tis well to think of some fair sojourn.

Souls are there on the right hand here withdrawn;
  If thou permit me I will lead thee to them,
  And thou shalt know them not without delight."

So he appeared; and then bowed down his brow, / And with humility returned towards him, /
And, where inferiors embrace, embraced him.

Purg. VII, lines 13–15

"How is this?" was the answer; "should one wish
  To mount by night would he prevented be
  By others? or mayhap would not have power?"

And on the ground the good Sordello drew
  His finger, saying, "See, this line alone
  Thou couldst not pass after the sun is gone;

Not that aught else would hindrance give, however,
  To going up, save the nocturnal darkness;
  This with the want of power the will perplexes.

We might indeed therewith return below,
  And, wandering, walk the hill-side round about,
  While the horizon holds the day imprisoned."

Thereon my Lord, as if in wonder, said:
  "Do thou conduct us thither, where thou sayest
  That we can take delight in tarrying."

Little had we withdrawn us from that place,
  When I perceived the mount was hollowed out
  In fashion as the valleys here are hollowed.

"Thitherward," said that shade, "will we repair,
  Where of itself the hill-side makes a lap,
  And there for the new day will we await."

'Twixt hill and plain there was a winding path
  Which led us to the margin of that dell,
  Where dies the border more than half away.

Gold and fine silver, and scarlet and pearl-white,
  The Indian wood resplendent and serene,
  Fresh emerald the moment it is broken,

By herbage and by flowers within that hollow
  Planted, each one in colour would be vanquished,
  As by its greater vanquished is the less.

Nor in that place had nature painted only,
  But of the sweetness of a thousand odours
  Made there a mingled fragrance and unknown.

"*Salve Regina*," on the green and flowers
  There seated, singing, spirits I beheld,
  Which were not visible outside the valley.

"Before the scanty sun now seeks his nest,"
  Began the Mantuan who had led us thither,
  "Among them do not wish me to conduct you.

Better from off this ledge the acts and faces
  Of all of them will you discriminate,
  Than in the plain below received among them.

He who sits highest, and the semblance bears
  Of having what he should have done neglected,
  And to the others' song moves not his lips,

Rudolph the Emperor was, who had the power
  To heal the wounds that Italy have slain,
  So that through others slowly she revives.

The other, who in look doth comfort him,
  Governed the region where the water springs,
  The Moldau bears the Elbe, and Elbe the sea.

His name was Ottocar; and in swaddling-clothes
  Far better he than bearded Winceslaus
  His son, who feeds in luxury and ease.

And the small-nosed, who close in council seems
  With him that has an aspect so benign,
  Died fleeing and disflowering the lily;

Look there, how he is beating at his breast!
  Behold the other one, who for his cheek
  Sighing has made of his own palm a bed;

Father and father-in-law of France's Pest
  Are they, and know his vicious life and lewd,
  And hence proceeds the grief that so doth pierce them.

He who appears so stalwart, and chimes in,
  Singing, with that one of the manly nose,
  The cord of every valour wore begirt;

And if as King had after him remained
  The stripling who in rear of him is sitting,
  Well had the valour passed from vase to vase,

Which cannot of the other heirs be said.
  Frederick and Jacomo possess the realms,
  But none the better heritage possesses.

Not oftentimes upriseth through the branches
  The probity of man; and this He wills
  Who gives it, so that we may ask of Him.

Eke to the large-nosed reach my words, no less
  Than to the other, Pier, who with him sings;
  Whence Provence and Apulia grieve already

"*Salve Regina,*" on the green and flowers / There seated, singing, spirits I beheld,

Purg. VII, lines 82–83

The plant is as inferior to its seed,
  As more than Beatrice and Margaret
  Costanza boasteth of her husband still.

Behold the monarch of the simple life,
  Harry of England, sitting there alone;
  He in his branches has a better issue.

He who the lowest on the ground among them
  Sits looking upward, is the Marquis William,
  For whose sake Alessandria and her war

Make Monferrat and Canavese weep."

Canto VIII

At nightfall, the fretful souls of the Preoccupied sing Te Lucis Ante *as they are still liable to temptation in Ante-Purgatory. Two green-robed angels with fiery swords descend as divine protection until the light of the sun can once again illuminate their path. Judge Nino Visconti recognizes Dante who notices that the Four Stars (Justice, Prudence, Temperance and Fortitude) seen before daybreak have now set and three new ones (Faith, Hope and Charity) have risen in their place. The angels drive out an intruding serpent. Dante speaks with Conrad Malaspina.*

'Twas now the hour that turneth back desire
  In those who sail the sea, and melts the heart,
  The day they've said to their sweet friends farewell,

And the new pilgrim penetrates with love,
  If he doth hear from far away a bell
  That seemeth to deplore the dying day,

When I began to make of no avail
  My hearing, and to watch one of the souls
  Uprisen, that begged attention with its hand.

It joined and lifted upward both its palms,
  Fixing its eyes upon the orient,
  As if it said to God, "Naught else I care for."

"*Te lucis ante*" so devoutly issued
  Forth from its mouth, and with such dulcet notes,
  It made me issue forth from my own mind.

And then the others, sweetly and devoutly,
  Accompanied it through all the hymn entire,
  Having their eyes on the supernal wheels.

Here, Reader, fix thine eyes well on the truth,
  For now indeed so subtile is the veil,
  Surely to penetrate within is easy.

I saw that army of the gentle-born
  Thereafterward in silence upward gaze,
  As if in expectation, pale and humble;

And from on high come forth and down descend,
  I saw two Angels with two flaming swords,
  Truncated and deprived of their points.

Green as the little leaflets just now born
  Their garments were, which, by their verdant pinions
  Beaten and blown abroad, they trailed behind.

One just above us came to take his station,
  And one descended to the opposite bank,
  So that the people were contained between them.

Clearly in them discerned I the blond head;
  But in their faces was the eye bewildered,
  As faculty confounded by excess.

"From Mary's bosom both of them have come,"
  Sordello said, "as guardians of the valley
  Against the serpent, that will come anon."

Whereupon I, who knew not by what road,
  Turned round about, and closely drew myself,
  Utterly frozen, to the faithful shoulders.

And once again Sordello: "Now descend we
  'Mid the grand shades, and we will speak to them;
  Right pleasant will it be for them to see you."

Only three steps I think that I descended,
  And was below, and saw one who was looking
  Only at me, as if he fain would know me.

Already now the air was growing dark,
  But not so that between his eyes and mine
  It did not show what it before locked up.

Tow'rds me he moved, and I tow'rds him did move;
  Noble Judge Nino! how it me delighted,
  When I beheld thee not among the damned!

No greeting fair was left unsaid between us;
  Then asked he: "How long is it since thou camest
  O'er the far waters to the mountain's foot?"

"Oh!" said I to him, "through the dismal places
  I came this morn; and am in the first life,
  Albeit the other, going thus, I gain."

And on the instant my reply was heard,
  He and Sordello both shrank back from me,
  Like people who are suddenly bewildered.

One to Virgilius, and the other turned
  To one who sat there, crying, "Up, Currado!
  Come and behold what God in grace has willed!"

Then, turned to me: "By that especial grace
  Thou owest unto Him, who so conceals
  His own first wherefore, that it has no ford,

When thou shalt be beyond the waters wide,
  Tell my Giovanna that she pray for me,
  Where answer to the innocent is made.

I do not think her mother loves me more,
  Since she has laid aside her wimple white,
  Which she, unhappy, needs must wish again.

Through her full easily is comprehended
  How long in woman lasts the fire of love,
  If eye or touch do not relight it often.

So fair a hatchment will not make for her
  The Viper marshalling the Milanese
  A-field, as would have made Gallura's Cock."

In this wise spake he, with the stamp impressed
  Upon his aspect of that righteous zeal
  Which measurably burneth in the heart.

My greedy eyes still wandered up to heaven,
  Still to that point where slowest are the stars,
  Even as a wheel the nearest to its axle.

And my Conductor: "Son, what dost thou gaze at
  Up there?" And I to him: "At those three torches
  With which this hither pole is all on fire."

And he to me: "The four resplendent stars
  Thou sawest this morning are down yonder low,
  And these have mounted up to where those were."

As he was speaking, to himself Sordello
  Drew him, and said, "Lo there our Adversary!"
  And pointed with his finger to look thither.

Upon the side on which the little valley
  No barrier hath, a serpent was; perchance
  The same which gave to Eve the bitter food.

'Twixt grass and flowers came on the evil streak,
  Turning at times its head about, and licking
  Its back like to a beast that smoothes itself.

I did not see, and therefore cannot say
  How the celestial falcons 'gan to move,
  But well I saw that they were both in motion.

Hearing the air cleft by their verdant wings,
  The serpent fled, and round the Angels wheeled,
  Up to their stations flying back alike.

The shade that to the Judge had near approached
  When he had called, throughout that whole assault
  Had not a moment loosed its gaze on me.

"So may the light that leadeth thee on high
  Find in thine own free-will as much of wax
  As needful is up to the highest azure,"

Hearing the air cleft by their verdant wings, / The serpent fled, and round the
Angels wheeled,

Purg. VIII, lines 106–107

Began it, "if some true intelligence
  Of Valdimagra or its neighbourhood
  Thou knowest, tell it me, who once was great there.

Currado Malaspina was I called;
  I'm not the elder, but from him descended;
  To mine I bore the love which here refineth."

"O," said I unto him, "through your domains
  I never passed, but where is there a dwelling
  Throughout all Europe, where they are not known?

That fame, which doeth honour to your house,
  Proclaims its Signors and proclaims its land,
  So that he knows of them who ne'er was there.

And, as I hope for heaven, I swear to you
  Your honoured family in naught abates
  The glory of the purse and of the sword.

It is so privileged by use and nature,
  That though a guilty head misguide the world,
  Sole it goes right, and scorns the evil way."

And he: "Now go; for the sun shall not lie
  Seven times upon the pillow which the Ram
  With all his four feet covers and bestrides,

Before that such a courteous opinion
  Shall in the middle of thy head be nailed
  With greater nails than of another's speech,

Unless the course of justice standeth still."

Canto IX

*Dante dreams that he is being carried away by an eagle but it is Saint Lucia, one of
the three blessed ladies from Hell's Canto II, who is bearing him up to the Angel of the
Church at Peter's Gate. Dante is invited to walk up the gate's steps (symbolizing the
three parts of penitence – confession, contrition and satisfaction). With his sword, the
angel marks the seven capital sins as Ps (for* peccatum *or 'sin') on Dante's forehead.
One at a time, each P will be erased as his soul is purged of that particular sin. The
poets enter Purgatory to the strains of the hymn* Te Deum Laudamus.*

The concubine of old Tithonus now
  Gleamed white upon the eastern balcony,
  Forth from the arms of her sweet paramour;

With gems her forehead all relucent was,
  Set in the shape of that cold animal
  Which with its tail doth smite amain the nations,

And of the steps, with which she mounts, the Night
  Had taken two in that place where we were,
  And now the third was bending down its wings;

When I, who something had of Adam in me,
  Vanquished by sleep, upon the grass reclined,
  There were all five of us already sat.

Just at the hour when her sad lay begins
  The little swallow, near unto the morning,
  Perchance in memory of her former woes,

And when the mind of man, a wanderer
  More from the flesh, and less by thought imprisoned,
  Almost prophetic in its visions is,

The concubine of old Tithonus now / Gleamed white upon the eastern balcony,

Purg. IX, lines 1–2

Terrible as the lightning he descended, / And snatched me upward even to the fire.

Purg. IX, lines 29–30

In dreams it seemed to me I saw suspended
  An eagle in the sky, with plumes of gold,
  With wings wide open, and intent to stoop,

And this, it seemed to me, was where had been
  By Ganymede his kith and kin abandoned,
  When to the high consistory he was rapt.

I thought within myself, perchance he strikes
  From habit only here, and from elsewhere
  Disdains to bear up any in his feet.

Then wheeling somewhat more, it seemed to me,
  Terrible as the lightning he descended,
  And snatched me upward even to the fire.

Therein it seemed that he and I were burning,
  And the imagined fire did scorch me so,
  That of necessity my sleep was broken.

Not otherwise Achilles started up,
  Around him turning his awakened eyes,
  And knowing not the place in which he was,

What time from Chiron stealthily his mother
  Carried him sleeping in her arms to Scyros,
  Wherefrom the Greeks withdrew him afterwards,

Than I upstarted, when from off my face
  Sleep fled away; and pallid I became,
  As doth the man who freezes with affright.

Only my Comforter was at my side,
  And now the sun was more than two hours high,
  And turned towards the sea-shore was my face.

"Be not intimidated," said my Lord,
  "Be reassured, for all is well with us;
  Do not restrain, but put forth all thy strength.

Thou hast at length arrived at Purgatory;
  See there the cliff that closes it around;
  See there the entrance, where it seems disjoined.

Whilom at dawn, which doth precede the day,
  When inwardly thy spirit was asleep
  Upon the flowers that deck the land below,

There came a Lady and said: 'I am Lucia;
  Let me take this one up, who is asleep;
  So will I make his journey easier for him.'

Sordello and the other noble shapes
  Remained; she took thee, and, as day grew bright,
  Upward she came, and I upon her footsteps.

She laid thee here; and first her beauteous eyes
  That open entrance pointed out to me;
  Then she and sleep together went away."

In guise of one whose doubts are reassured,
  And who to confidence his fear doth change,
  After the truth has been discovered to him,

So did I change; and when without disquiet
  My Leader saw me, up along the cliff
  He moved, and I behind him, tow'rd the height.

Reader, thou seest well how I exalt
  My theme, and therefore if with greater art
  I fortify it, marvel not thereat.

Nearer approached we, and were in such place,
  That there, where first appeared to me a rift
  Like to a crevice that disparts a wall,

I saw a portal, and three stairs beneath,
  Diverse in colour, to go up to it,
  And a gate-keeper, who yet spake no word.

And as I opened more and more mine eyes,
  I saw him seated on the highest stair,
  Such in the face that I endured it not.

And in his hand he had a naked sword,
  Which so reflected back the sunbeams tow'rds us,
  That oft in vain I lifted up mine eyes.

"Tell it from where you are, what is't you wish?"
  Began he to exclaim; "where is the escort?
  Take heed your coming hither harm you not!"

"A Lady of Heaven, with these things conversant,"
  My Master answered him, "but even now
  Said to us, 'Thither go; there is the portal.'"

"And may she speed your footsteps in all good,"
  Again began the courteous janitor;
  "Come forward then unto these stairs of ours."

Thither did we approach; and the first stair
  Was marble white, so polished and so smooth,
  I mirrored myself therein as I appear.

I saw him seated on the highest stair, / Such in the face that I endured it not. /
And in his hand he had a naked sword,

Purg. IX, lines 80–82

The second, tinct of deeper hue than perse,
   Was of a calcined and uneven stone,
   Cracked all asunder lengthwise and across.

The third, that uppermost rests massively,
   Porphyry seemed to me, as flaming red
   As blood that from a vein is spirting forth.

Both of his feet was holding upon this
   The Angel of God, upon the threshold seated,
   Which seemed to me a stone of diamond.

Along the three stairs upward with good will
   Did my Conductor draw me, saying: "Ask
   Humbly that he the fastening may undo."

Devoutly at the holy feet I cast me,
   For mercy's sake besought that he would open,
   But first upon my breast three times I smote.

Seven Ps upon my forehead he described
   With the sword's point, and, "Take heed that thou
                                             wash
   These wounds, when thou shalt be within," he said.

Ashes, or earth that dry is excavated,
   Of the same colour were with his attire,
   And from beneath it he drew forth two keys.

One was of gold, and the other was of silver;
   First with the white, and after with the yellow,
   Plied he the door, so that I was content.

"Whenever faileth either of these keys
   So that it turn not rightly in the lock,"
   He said to us, "this entrance doth not open.

More precious one is, but the other needs
   More art and intellect ere it unlock,
   For it is that which doth the knot unloose.

From Peter I have them; and he bade me err
   Rather in opening than in keeping shut,
   If people but fall down before my feet."

Then pushed the portals of the sacred door,
   Exclaiming: "Enter; but I give you warning
   That forth returns whoever looks behind."

And when upon their hinges were turned round
   The swivels of that consecrated gate,
   Which are of metal, massive and sonorous,

Roared not so loud, nor so discordant seemed
   Tarpeia, when was ta'en from it the good
   Metellus, wherefore meagre it remained.

At the first thunder-peal I turned attentive,
   And "*Te Deum laudamus*" seemed to hear
   In voices mingled with sweet melody.

Exactly such an image rendered me
   That which I heard, as we are wont to catch,
   When people singing with the organ stand;

For now we hear, and now hear not, the words.

Canto X

As the gate shuts behind them, the two poets struggle up a very steep, narrow cleft to the First Cornice, where the sin of Pride is being redeemed. The ledge wraps around the base of the mountain and seems deserted at first but for reliefs showing examples of great Humility (the Whip of Pride) carved into the rock face, such as the Virgin Mary, King David and the Emperor Trajan. The penitent Proud approach, bent double under the weight of enormous boulders. Just as these individuals elevated themselves above others in life, they must now submit to being humble.

When we had crossed the threshold of the door
  Which the perverted love of souls disuses,
  Because it makes the crooked way seem straight,

Re-echoing I heard it closed again;
  And if I had turned back mine eyes upon it,
  What for my failing had been fit excuse?

We mounted upward through a rifted rock,
  Which undulated to this side and that,
  Even as a wave receding and advancing.

"Here it behoves us use a little art,"
  Began my Leader, "to adapt ourselves
  Now here, now there, to the receding side."

And this our footsteps so infrequent made,
  That sooner had the moon's decreasing disk
  Regained its bed to sink again to rest,

Than we were forth from out that needle's eye;
  But when we free and in the open were,
  There where the mountain backward piles itself,

I wearied out, and both of us uncertain
  About our way, we stopped upon a plain
  More desolate than roads across the deserts.

From where its margin borders on the void,
  To foot of the high bank that ever rises,
  A human body three times told would measure;

And far as eye of mine could wing its flight,
  Now on the left, and on the right flank now,
  The same this cornice did appear to me.

Thereon our feet had not been moved as yet,
  When I perceived the embankment round about,
  Which all right of ascent had interdicted,

To be of marble white, and so adorned
  With sculptures, that not only Polycletus,
  But Nature's self, had there been put to shame.

The Angel, who came down to Earth with tidings
  Of peace, that had been wept for many a year,
  And opened Heaven from its long interdict,

In front of us appeared so truthfully
  There sculptured in a gracious attitude,
  He did not seem an image that is silent.

One would have sworn that he was saying, "*Ave;*"
  For she was there in effigy portrayed
  Who turned the key to ope the exalted love,

And in her mien this language had impressed,
  "*Ecce ancilla Dei,*" as distinctly
  As any figure stamps itself in wax.

"Keep not thy mind upon one place alone,"
  The gentle Master said, who had me standing
  Upon that side where people have their hearts;

Whereat I moved mine eyes, and I beheld
  In rear of Mary, and upon that side
  Where he was standing who conducted me,

Another story on the rock imposed;
  Wherefore I passed Virgilius and drew near,
  So that before mine eyes it might be set.

There sculptured in the self-same marble were
  The cart and oxen, drawing the holy ark,
  Wherefore one dreads an office not appointed.

People appeared in front, and all of them
  In seven choirs divided, of two senses
  Made one say "No," the other, "Yes, they sing."

Likewise unto the smoke of the frankincense,
  Which there was imaged forth, the eyes and nose
  Were in the yes and no discordant made.

Preceded there the vessel benedight,
  Dancing with girded loins, the humble Psalmist,
  And more and less than King was he in this.

Opposite, represented at the window
  Of a great palace, Michal looked upon him,
  Even as a woman scornful and afflicted.

I moved my feet from where I had been standing,
  To examine near at hand another story,
  Which after Michal glimmered white upon me.

There the high glory of the Roman Prince
  Was chronicled, whose great beneficence
  Moved Gregory to his great victory;

'Tis of the Emperor Trajan I am speaking;
  And a poor widow at his bridle stood,
  In attitude of weeping and of grief.

Around about him seemed it thronged and full
  Of cavaliers, and the eagles in the gold
  Above them visibly in the wind were moving.

The wretched woman in the midst of these
  Seemed to be saying: "Give me vengeance, Lord,
  For my dead son, for whom my heart is breaking."

And he to answer her: "Now wait until
  I shall return." And she: "My Lord," like one
  In whom grief is impatient, "shouldst thou not

Return?" And he: "Who shall be where I am
  Will give it thee." And she: "Good deed of others
  What boots it thee, if thou neglect thine own?"

Whence he: "Now comfort thee, for it behoves me
  That I discharge my duty ere I move;
  Justice so wills, and pity doth retain me."

He who on no new thing has ever looked
  Was the creator of this visible language,
  Novel to us, for here it is not found.

While I delighted me in contemplating
  The images of such humility,
  And dear to look on for their Maker's sake,

"Behold, upon this side, but rare they make
  Their steps," the Poet murmured, "many people;
  These will direct us to the lofty stairs."

Mine eyes, that in beholding were intent
  To see new things, of which they curious are,
  In turning round towards him were not slow.

But still I wish not, Reader, thou shouldst swerve
  From thy good purposes, because thou hearest
  How God ordaineth that the debt be paid;

Attend not to the fashion of the torment,
  Think of what follows; think that at the worst
  It cannot reach beyond the mighty sentence.

"Master," began I, "that which I behold
  Moving towards us seems to me not persons,
  And what I know not, so in sight I waver."

And he to me: "The grievous quality
  Of this their torment bows them so to Earth,
  That my own eyes at first contended with it;

But look there fixedly, and disentangle
  By sight what cometh underneath those stones;
  Already canst thou see how each is stricken."

O ye proud Christians! wretched, weary ones!
  Who, in the vision of the mind infirm
  Confidence have in your backsliding steps,

Do ye not comprehend that we are worms,
  Born to bring forth the angelic butterfly
  That flieth unto judgment without screen?

Why floats aloft your spirit high in air?
  Like are ye unto insects undeveloped,
  Even as the worm in whom formation fails!

As to sustain a ceiling or a roof,
  In place of corbel, oftentimes a figure
  Is seen to join its knees unto its breast,

The wretched woman in the midst of these / Seemed to be saying: "Give me vengeance, Lord, / For my dead son, for whom my heart is breaking."

Purg. X, lines 82–84

Which makes of the unreal real anguish
  Arise in him who sees it, fashioned thus
  Beheld I those, when I had ta'en good heed.

True is it, they were more or less bent down,
  According as they more or less were laden;
  And he who had most patience in his looks

Weeping did seem to say, "I can no more!"

Canto XI

*Dante overhears the penitent Proud reciting their own version of the Lord's Prayer
as they approach. Having sinned through pride in their birthright, abilities and
worldly powers, they must now seek to recover their spiritual innocence. Omberto
Aldobrandesco, a member of the great Ghibelline family, advises the poets to turn
right and follow him to the next flight of steps. The manuscript painter Oderisi of
Gubbio gives a discourse on the vanity of temporal fame. He points to Provenzan
Salvani, a despotic Sienese nobleman, whose one great gesture of Humility led him
straight here instead of being detained in Ante-Purgatory in the company of the
Late Repentant. Oderisi predicts Dante's coming exile.*

"Our Father, thou who dwellest in the heavens,
  Not circumscribed, but from the greater love
  Thou bearest to the first effects on high,

Praised be thy name and thine omnipotence
  By every creature, as befitting is
  To render thanks to thy sweet effluence.

Come unto us the peace of thy dominion,
  For unto it we cannot of ourselves,
  If it come not, with all our intellect.

Even as thine own Angels of their will
  Make sacrifice to thee, Hosanna singing,
  So may all men make sacrifice of theirs.

Give unto us this day our daily manna,
  Withouten which in this rough wilderness
  Backward goes he who toils most to advance.

And even as we the trespass we have suffered
  Pardon in one another, pardon thou
  Benignly, and regard not our desert.

Our virtue, which is easily o'ercome,
  Put not to proof with the old Adversary,
  But thou from him who spurs it so, deliver.

This last petition verily, dear Lord,
  Not for ourselves is made, who need it not,
  But for their sake who have remained behind us."

Thus for themselves and us good furtherance
  Those shades imploring, went beneath a weight
  Like unto that of which we sometimes dream,

Unequally in anguish round and round
  And weary all, upon that foremost cornice,
  Purging away the smoke-stains of the world.

If there good words are always said for us,
  What may not here be said and done for them,
  By those who have a good root to their will?

Well may we help them wash away the marks
  That hence they carried, so that clean and light
  They may ascend unto the starry wheels!

"Ah! so may pity and justice you disburden
　Soon, that ye may have power to move the wing,
　That shall uplift you after your desire,

Show us on which hand tow'rd the stairs the way
　Is shortest, and if more than one the passes,
　Point us out that which least abruptly falls;

For he who cometh with me, through the burden
　Of Adam's flesh wherewith he is invested,
　Against his will is chary of his climbing."

The words of theirs which they returned to those
　That he whom I was following had spoken,
　It was not manifest from whom they came,

But it was said: "To the right hand come with us
　Along the bank, and ye shall find a pass
　Possible for living person to ascend.

And were I not impeded by the stone,
　Which this proud neck of mine doth subjugate,
　Whence I am forced to hold my visage down,

Him, who still lives and does not name himself,
　Would I regard, to see if I may know him
　And make him piteous unto this burden.

A Latian was I, and born of a great Tuscan;
　Guglielmo Aldobrandeschi was my father;
　I know not if his name were ever with you.

The ancient blood and deeds of gallantry
　Of my progenitors so arrogant made me
　That, thinking not upon the common mother,

All men I held in scorn to such extent
　I died therefor, as know the Sienese,
　And every child in Campagnatico.

I am Omberto; and not to me alone
　Has pride done harm, but all my kith and kin
　Has with it dragged into adversity.

And here must I this burden bear for it
　Till God be satisfied, since I did not
　Among the living, here among the dead."

Listening I downward bent my countenance;
　And one of them, not this one who was speaking,
　Twisted himself beneath the weight that cramps him,

And looked at me, and knew me, and called out,
　Keeping his eyes laboriously fixed
　On me, who all bowed down was going with them.

"O," asked I him, "art thou not Oderisi,
　Agobbio's honour, and honour of that art
　Which is in Paris called illuminating?"

"Brother," said he, "more laughing are the leaves
　Touched by the brush of Franco Bolognese;
　All his the honour now, and mine in part.

In sooth I had not been so courteous
　While I was living, for the great desire
　Of excellence, on which my heart was bent.

Here of such pride is paid the forfeiture;
　And yet I should not be here, were it not
　That, having power to sin, I turned to God.

O thou vain glory of the human powers,
　How little green upon thy summit lingers,
　If't be not followed by an age of grossness!

In painting Cimabue thought that he
　Should hold the field, now Giotto has the cry,
　So that the other's fame is growing dim.

So has one Guido from the other taken
　The glory of our tongue, and he perchance
　Is born, who from the nest shall chase them both.

Naught is this mundane rumour but a breath
　Of wind, that comes now this way and now that,
　And changes name, because it changes side.

What fame shalt thou have more, if old peel off
　From thee thy flesh, than if thou hadst been dead
　Before thou left the 'pappo' and the 'dindi,'

Ere pass a thousand years? which is a shorter
　Space to the eterne, than twinkling of an eye
　Unto the circle that in heaven wheels slowest.

With him, who takes so little of the road
　In front of me, all Tuscany resounded;
　And now he scarce is lisped of in Siena,

Where he was lord, what time was overthrown
　The Florentine delirium, that superb
　Was at that day as now 'tis prostitute.

Your reputation is the colour of grass
  Which comes and goes, and that discolours it
  By which it issues green from out the earth."

And I: "Thy true speech fills my heart with good
  Humility, and great tumour thou assuagest;
  But who is he, of whom just now thou spakest?"

"That," he replied, "is Provenzan Salvani,
  And he is here because he had presumed
  To bring Siena all into his hands.

He has gone thus, and goeth without rest
  E'er since he died; such money renders back
  In payment he who is on Earth too daring."

And I: "If every spirit who awaits
  The verge of life before that he repent,
  Remains below there and ascends not hither,

(Unless good orison shall him bestead,)
  Until as much time as he lived be passed,
  How was the coming granted him in largess?"

"When he in greatest splendour lived," said he,
  "Freely upon the Campo of Siena,
  All shame being laid aside, he placed himself;

And there to draw his friend from the duress
  Which in the prison-house of Charles he suffered,
  He brought himself to tremble in each vein.

I say no more, and know that I speak darkly;
  Yet little time shall pass before thy neighbours
  Will so demean themselves that thou canst gloss it.

This action has released him from those confines."

Canto XII

*Knowing he is guilty of being proud, Dante makes a point of stooping as he walks
along the First Cornice looking at the carved images that depict the sin and fall of
Pride (most notably Satan, Briareus, Thymbraeus, Pallas, Mars, Nimrod, Niobe,
Saul, Arachne and Rehoboam). The shimmering Angel of Humility salutes the poets
and erases one P with the gentle brush of its wings as it utters the beatitude, Beati
Pauperes Spiritu. The pilgrim's feet suddenly feel lighter as he is escorted by the Pass
of Pardon into the Second Cornice through a staircase in the rock.*

Abreast, like oxen going in a yoke,
  I with that heavy-laden soul went on,
  As long as the sweet pedagogue permitted;

But when he said, "Leave him, and onward pass,
  For here 'tis good that with the sail and oars,
  As much as may be, each push on his barque;"

Upright, as walking wills it, I redressed
  My person, notwithstanding that my thoughts
  Remained within me downcast and abashed.

I had moved on, and followed willingly
  The footsteps of my Master, and we both
  Already showed how light of foot we were,

When unto me he said: "Cast down thine eyes;
  'Twere well for thee, to alleviate the way,
  To look upon the bed beneath thy feet."

As, that some memory may exist of them,
  Above the buried dead their tombs in earth
  Bear sculptured on them what they were before;

Abreast, like oxen going in a yoke, / I with that heavy-laden soul went on,

Purg. XII, lines 1–2

Whence often there we weep for them afresh,
  From pricking of remembrance, which alone
  To the compassionate doth set its spur;

So saw I there, but of a better semblance
  In point of artifice, with figures covered
  Whate'er as pathway from the mount projects.

I saw that one who was created noble
  More than all other creatures, down from heaven
  Flaming with lightnings fall upon one side.

I saw Briareus smitten by the dart
  Celestial, lying on the other side,
  Heavy upon the earth by mortal frost.

I saw Thymbraeus, Pallas saw, and Mars,
  Still clad in armour round about their father,
  Gaze at the scattered members of the giants.

I saw, at foot of his great labour, Nimrod,
  As if bewildered, looking at the people
  Who had been proud with him in Sennaar.

O Niobe! with what afflicted eyes
  Thee I beheld upon the pathway traced,
  Between thy seven and seven children slain!

O Saul! how fallen upon thy proper sword
  Didst thou appear there lifeless in Gilboa,
  That felt thereafter neither rain nor dew!

O mad Arachne! so I thee beheld
  E'en then half spider, sad upon the shreds
  Of fabric wrought in evil hour for thee!

O Rehoboam! no more seems to threaten
  Thine image there; but full of consternation
  A chariot bears it off, when none pursues!

Displayed moreo'er the adamantine pavement
  How unto his own mother made Alcmaeon
  Costly appear the luckless ornament;

Displayed how his own sons did throw themselves
  Upon Sennacherib within the temple,
  And how, he being dead, they left him there;

Displayed the ruin and the cruel carnage
  That Tomyris wrought, when she to Cyrus said,
  "Blood didst thou thirst for, and with blood I glut thee!"

Displayed how routed fled the Assyrians
  After that Holofernes had been slain,
  And likewise the remainder of that slaughter.

I saw there Troy in ashes and in caverns;
  O Ilion! thee, how abject and debased,
  Displayed the image that is there discerned!

Whoe'er of pencil master was or stile,
  That could portray the shades and traits which there
  Would cause each subtile genius to admire?

Dead seemed the dead, the living seemed alive;
  Better than I saw not who saw the truth,
  All that I trod upon while bowed I went.

Now wax ye proud, and on with looks uplifted,
  Ye sons of Eve, and bow not down your faces
  So that ye may behold your evil ways!

More of the mount by us was now encompassed,
  And far more spent the circuit of the sun,
  Than had the mind preoccupied imagined,

When he, who ever watchful in advance
  Was going on, began: "Lift up thy head,
  'Tis no more time to go thus meditating.

Lo there an Angel who is making haste
  To come towards us; lo, returning is
  From service of the day the sixth handmaiden.

With reverence thine acts and looks adorn,
  So that he may delight to speed us upward;
  Think that this day will never dawn again."

I was familiar with his admonition
  Ever to lose no time; so on this theme
  He could not unto me speak covertly.

Towards us came the being beautiful
  Vested in white, and in his countenance
  Such as appears the tremulous morning star.

His arms he opened, and opened then his wings;
  "Come," said he, "near at hand here are the steps,
  And easy from henceforth is the ascent."

At this announcement few are they who come!
  O human creatures, born to soar aloft,
  Why fall ye thus before a little wind?

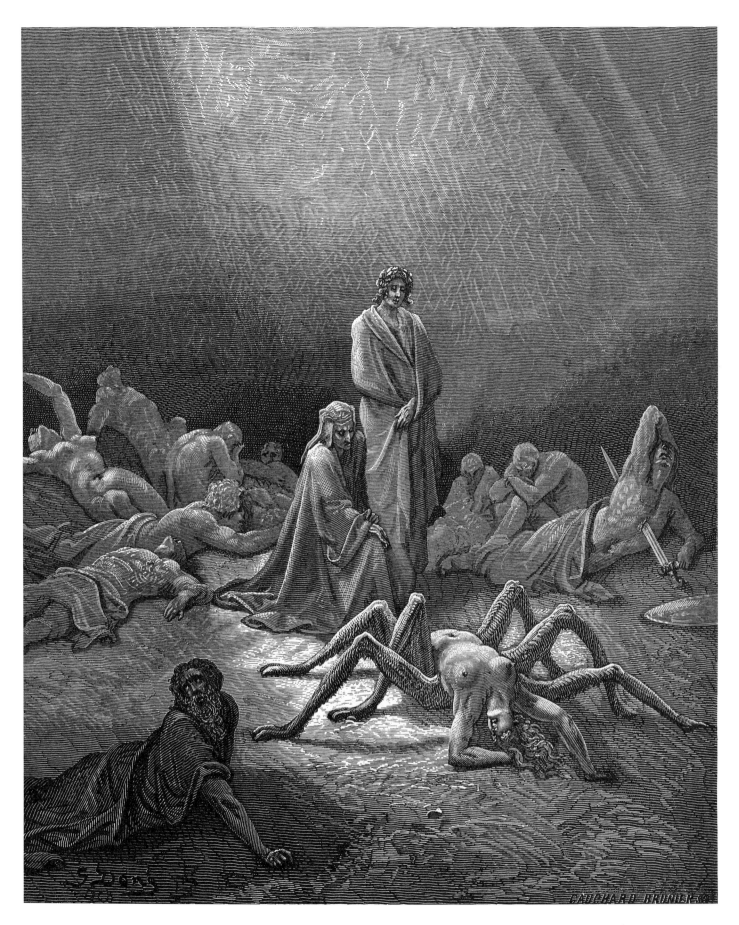

O mad Arachne! so I thee beheld / E'en then half spider,

Purg. XII, lines 43–44

He led us on to where the rock was cleft;
  There smote upon my forehead with his wings,
  Then a safe passage promised unto me.

As on the right hand, to ascend the mount
  Where seated is the church that lordeth it
  O'er the well-guided, above Rubaconte,

The bold abruptness of the ascent is broken
  By stairways that were made there in the age
  When still were safe the ledger and the stave,

E'en thus attempered is the bank which falls
  Sheer downward from the second circle there;
  But on this, side and that the high rock graze.

As we were turning thitherward our persons,
  "*Beati pauperes spiritu,*" voices
  Sang in such wise that speech could tell it not.

Ah me! how different are these entrances
  From the Infernal! for with anthems here
  One enters, and below with wild laments.

We now were hunting up the sacred stairs,
  And it appeared to me by far more easy
  Than on the plain it had appeared before.

Whence I: "My Master, say, what heavy thing
  Has been uplifted from me, so that hardly
  Aught of fatigue is felt by me in walking?"

He answered: "When the Ps which have remained
  Still on thy face almost obliterate
  Shall wholly, as the first is, be erased,

Thy feet will be so vanquished by good will,
  That not alone they shall not feel fatigue,
  But urging up will be to them delight."

Then did I even as they do who are going
  With something on the head to them unknown,
  Unless the signs of others make them doubt,

Wherefore the hand to ascertain is helpful,
  And seeks and finds, and doth fulfill the office
  Which cannot be accomplished by the sight;

And with the fingers of the right hand spread
  I found but six the letters, that had carved
  Upon my temples he who bore the keys;

Upon beholding which my Leader smiled.

Canto XIII

Dante and Virgil reach the Second Cornice, where the sin of Envy is being purged, to find it deserted. Virgil looks up at the sun for guidance. The poets suddenly hear voices in the air (the Whip of Envy), crying out Christian and pagan examples of Generosity, the opposing virtue. They see the penitent Envious sitting down, dressed in sackcloth, their eyelids sewn shut as they implore the charity of the saints. Dante talks to the spirit of Sapia Bigozzi of Siena, who rejoiced when her countrymen suffered defeat at the battle of Colle against the Florentines.

We were upon the summit of the stairs,
  Where for the second time is cut away
  The mountain, which ascending shriveth all.

There in like manner doth a cornice bind
  The hill all round about, as does the first,
  Save that its arc more suddenly is curved.

Shade is there none, nor sculpture that appears;
  So seems the bank, and so the road seems smooth,
  With but the livid colour of the stone.

"If to inquire we wait for people here,"
  The Poet said, "I fear that peradventure
  Too much delay will our election have."

Then steadfast on the sun his eyes he fixed,
  Made his right side the centre of his motion,
  And turned the left part of himself about.

"O thou sweet light! with trust in whom I enter
  Upon this novel journey, do thou lead us,"
  Said he, "as one within here should be led.

Thou warmest the world, thou shinest over it;
  If other reason prompt not otherwise,
  Thy rays should evermore our leaders be!"

As much as here is counted for a mile,
  So much already there had we advanced
  In little time, by dint of ready will;

And tow'rds us there were heard to fly, albeit
  They were not visible, spirits uttering
  Unto Love's table courteous invitations,

The first voice that passed onward in its flight,
  "*Vinum non habent,*" said in accents loud,
  And went reiterating it behind us.

And ere it wholly grew inaudible
  Because of distance, passed another, crying,
  "I am Orestes!" and it also stayed not.

"O," said I, "Father, these, what voices are they?"
  And even as I asked, behold the third,
  Saying: "Love those from whom ye have had evil!"

And the good Master said: "This circle scourges
  The sin of envy, and on that account
  Are drawn from love the lashes of the scourge.

The bridle of another sound shall be;
  I think that thou wilt hear it, as I judge,
  Before thou comest to the Pass of Pardon.

But fix thine eyes athwart the air right steadfast,
  And people thou wilt see before us sitting,
  And each one close against the cliff is seated."

Then wider than at first mine eyes I opened;
  I looked before me, and saw shades with mantles
  Not from the colour of the stone diverse.

And when we were a little farther onward,
  I heard a cry of, "Mary, pray for us!"
  A cry of, "Michael, Peter, and all Saints!"

I do not think there walketh still on Earth
  A man so hard, that he would not be pierced
  With pity at what afterward I saw.

For when I had approached so near to them
  That manifest to me their acts became,
  Drained was I at the eyes by heavy grief.

Covered with sackcloth vile they seemed to me,
  And one sustained the other with his shoulder,
  And all of them were by the bank sustained.

Thus do the blind, in want of livelihood,
  Stand at the doors of churches asking alms,
  And one upon another leans his head,

So that in others pity soon may rise,
  Not only at the accent of their words,
  But at their aspect, which no less implores.

And as unto the blind the sun comes not,
  So to the shades, of whom just now I spake,
  Heaven's light will not be bounteous of itself;

For all their lids an iron wire transpierces,
  And sews them up, as to a sparhawk wild
  Is done, because it will not quiet stay.

To me it seemed, in passing, to do outrage,
  Seeing the others without being seen;
  Wherefore I turned me to my counsel sage.

Well knew he what the mute one wished to say,
  And therefore waited not for my demand,
  But said: "Speak, and be brief, and to the point."

I had Virgilius upon that side
  Of the embankment from which one may fall,
  Since by no border 'tis engarlanded;

Upon the other side of me I had
  The shades devout, who through the horrible seam
  Pressed out the tears so that they bathed their cheeks.

To them I turned me, and, "O people, certain,"
  Began I, "of beholding the high light,
  Which your desire has solely in its care,

So may grace speedily dissolve the scum
  Upon your consciences, that limpidly
  Through them descend the river of the mind,

Tell me, for dear 'twill be to me and gracious,
  If any soul among you here is Latian,
  And 'twill perchance be good for him I learn it."

"O brother mine, each one is citizen
  Of one true city; but thy meaning is,
  Who may have lived in Italy a pilgrim."

By way of answer this I seemed to hear
  A little farther on than where I stood,
  Whereat I made myself still nearer heard.

Among the rest I saw a shade that waited
  In aspect, and should any one ask how,
  Its chin it lifted upward like a blind man.

"Spirit," I said, "who stoopest to ascend,
  If thou art he who did reply to me,
  Make thyself known to me by place or name."

"Sienese was I," it replied, "and with
  The others here recleanse my guilty life,
  Weeping to Him to lend himself to us.

Sapient I was not, although I Sapia
  Was called, and I was at another's harm
  More happy far than at my own good fortune.

And that thou mayst not think that I deceive thee,
  Hear if I was as foolish as I tell thee.
  The arc already of my years descending,

My fellow-citizens near unto Colle
  Were joined in battle with their adversaries,
  And I was praying God for what he willed.

Routed were they, and turned into the bitter
  Passes of flight; and I, the chase beholding,
  A joy received unequalled by all others;

So that I lifted upward my bold face
  Crying to God, 'Henceforth I fear thee not,'
  As did the blackbird at the little sunshine.

Peace I desired with God at the extreme
  Of my existence, and as yet would not
  My debt have been by penitence discharged,

Had it not been that in remembrance held me
  Pier Pettignano in his holy prayers,
  Who out of charity was grieved for me.

But who art thou, that into our conditions
  Questioning goest, and hast thine eyes unbound
  As I believe, and breathing dost discourse?"

Covered with sackcloth vile they seemed to me, / And one sustained the other with his shoulder, / And all of them were by the bank sustained.

Purg. XIII, lines 58–60

"Sienese was I," it replied, "and with / The others here recleanse my guilty life",

Purg. XIII, lines 106–107

"Mine eyes," I said, "will yet be here ta'en from me,
  But for short space; for small is the offence
  Committed by their being turned with envy.

Far greater is the fear, wherein suspended
  My soul is, of the torment underneath,
  For even now the load down there weighs on me."

And she to me: "Who led thee, then, among us
  Up here, if to return below thou thinkest?"
  And I: "He who is with me, and speaks not;

And living am I; therefore ask of me,
  Spirit elect, if thou wouldst have me move
  O'er yonder yet my mortal feet for thee."

"O, this is such a novel thing to hear,"
  She answered, "that great sign it is God loves thee;
  Therefore with prayer of thine sometimes assist me.

And I implore, by what thou most desirest,
  If e'er thou treadest the soil of Tuscany,
  Well with my kindred reinstate my fame.

Them wilt thou see among that people vain
  Who hope in Talamone, and will lose there
  More hope than in discovering the Diana;

But there still more the admirals will lose."

Canto XIV

Two blind souls detect Dante's presence with much excitement and ask the pilgrim
his whereabouts. Hearing his accent, one of the Romagnol nobles, Guido del Duca of
Brettinoro from the Onesti family of Ravenna, delivers an invective against the towns
along the river Arno and accuses prominent local families of corruption. The other,
Renier da Calboli, criticizes Romagna. As Dante and Virgil take their leave, they hear
disembodied voices crying out examples that will serve as the Bridle of Envy:
the stories of Cain who murdered his brother, Abel; and Aglaurus, the princess who
was turned to stone because of envy.

"Who is this one that goes about our mountain,
  Or ever Death has given him power of flight,
  And opes his eyes and shuts them at his will?"

"I know not who, but know he's not alone;
  Ask him thyself, for thou art nearer to him,
  And gently, so that he may speak, accost him."

Thus did two spirits, leaning tow'rds each other,
  Discourse about me there on the right hand;
  Then held supine their faces to address me.

And said the one: "O soul, that, fastened still
  Within the body, tow'rds the heaven art going,
  For charity console us, and declare

Whence comest and who art thou; for thou mak'st us
  As much to marvel at this grace of thine
  As must a thing that never yet has been."

And I: "Through midst of Tuscany there wanders
  A streamlet that is born in Falterona,
  And not a hundred miles of course suffice it;

From thereupon do I this body bring.
  To tell you who I am were speech in vain,
  Because my name as yet makes no great noise."

"If well thy meaning I can penetrate
  With intellect of mine," then answered me
  He who first spake, "thou speakest of the Arno."

And said the other to him: "Why concealed
  This one the appellation of that river,
  Even as a man doth of things horrible?"

And thus the shade that questioned was of this
  Himself acquitted: "I know not; but truly
  'Tis fit the name of such a valley perish;

For from its fountain-head (where is so pregnant
  The Alpine mountain whence is cleft Peloro
  That in few places it that mark surpasses)

To where it yields itself in restoration
  Of what the heaven doth of the sea dry up,
  Whence have the rivers that which goes with them,

Virtue is like an enemy avoided
  By all, as is a serpent, through misfortune
  Of place, or through bad habit that impels them;

On which account have so transformed their nature
  The dwellers in that miserable valley,
  It seems that Circe had them in her pasture.

'Mid ugly swine, of acorns worthier
  Than other food for human use created,
  It first directeth its impoverished way.

Curs findeth it thereafter, coming downward,
  More snarling than their puissance demands,
  And turns from them disdainfully its muzzle.

It goes on falling, and the more it grows,
  The more it finds the dogs becoming wolves,
  This maledict and misadventurous ditch.

Descended then through many a hollow gulf,
  It finds the foxes so replete with fraud,
  They fear no cunning that may master them.

Nor will I cease because another hears me;
  And well 'twill be for him, if still he mind him
  Of what a truthful spirit to me unravels.

Thy grandson I behold, who doth become
  A hunter of those wolves upon the bank
  Of the wild stream, and terrifies them all.

He sells their flesh, it being yet alive;
  Thereafter slaughters them like ancient beeves;
  Many of life, himself of praise, deprives.

Blood-stained he issues from the dismal forest;
  He leaves it such, a thousand years from now
  In its primeval state 'tis not re-wooded."

As at the announcement of impending ills
  The face of him who listens is disturbed,
  From whate'er side the peril seize upon him;

So I beheld that other soul, which stood
  Turned round to listen, grow disturbed and sad,
  When it had gathered to itself the word.

The speech of one and aspect of the other
  Had me desirous made to know their names,
  And question mixed with prayers I made thereof,

Whereat the spirit which first spake to me
  Began again: "Thou wishest I should bring me
  To do for thee what thou'lt not do for me;

But since God willeth that in thee shine forth
  Such grace of his, I'll not be chary with thee;
  Know, then, that I Guido del Duca am.

My blood was so with envy set on fire,
  That if I had beheld a man make merry,
  Thou wouldst have seen me sprinkled o'er with pallor.

From my own sowing such the straw I reap!
  O human race! why dost thou set thy heart
  Where interdict of partnership must be?

This is Renier; this is the boast and honour
  Of the house of Calboli, where no one since
  Has made himself the heir of his desert.

And not alone his blood is made devoid,
  'Twixt Po and mount, and sea-shore and the Reno,
  Of good required for truth and for diversion;

For all within these boundaries is full
  Of venomous roots, so that too tardily
  By cultivation now would they diminish.

Where is good Lizio, and Arrigo Manardi,
  Pier Traversaro, and Guido di Carpigna,
  O Romagnuoli into bastards turned?

When in Bologna will a Fabbro rise?
  When in Faenza a Bernardin di Fosco,
  The noble scion of ignoble seed?

Be not astonished, Tuscan, if I weep,
  When I remember, with Guido da Prata,
  Ugolin d' Azzo, who was living with us,

Frederick Tignoso and his company,
  The house of Traversara, and th' Anastagi,
  And one race and the other is extinct;

The dames and cavaliers, the toils and ease
  That filled our souls with love and courtesy,
  There where the hearts have so malicious grown!

O Brettinoro! why dost thou not flee,
  Seeing that all thy family is gone,
  And many people, not to be corrupted?

Bagnacaval does well in not begetting
  And ill does Castrocaro, and Conio worse,
  In taking trouble to beget such Counts.

Will do well the Pagani, when their Devil
  Shall have departed; but not therefore pure
  Will testimony of them e'er remain.

O Ugolin de' Fantoli, secure
  Thy name is, since no longer is awaited
  One who, degenerating, can obscure it!

But go now, Tuscan, for it now delights me
  To weep far better than it does to speak,
  So much has our discourse my mind distressed."

We were aware that those beloved souls
  Heard us depart; therefore, by keeping silent,
  They made us of our pathway confident.

When we became alone by going onward,
  Thunder, when it doth cleave the air, appeared
  A voice, that counter to us came, exclaiming:

"Shall slay me whosoever findeth me!"
  And fled as the reverberation dies
  If suddenly the cloud asunder bursts.

As soon as hearing had a truce from this,
  Behold another, with so great a crash,
  That it resembled thunderings following fast:

"I am Aglaurus, who became a stone!"
  And then, to press myself close to the Poet,
  I backward, and not forward, took a step.

Already on all sides the air was quiet;
  And said he to me: "That was the hard curb
  That ought to hold a man within his bounds;

But you take in the bait so that the hook
  Of the old Adversary draws you to him,
  And hence availeth little curb or call.

The heavens are calling you, and wheel around you,
  Displaying to you their eternal beauties,
  And still your eye is looking on the ground;

Whence He, who all discerns, chastises you."

Canto XV

*Dante is dazzled by the Angel of Generosity shining from the West, who effaces
the second P and leads him through the Pass. As they are proceeding the singing of*
Beati Misericordes *can be heard behind them. Virgil delivers his first great speech
on Love. At the entrance to the Third Cornice, where the sin of Wrath is purged,
Dante is shown three visions of the virtue of Meekness – the finding of the Christ
child in the temple; Pisistratus forgiving the man who embraced his daughter; and
the martyrdom of Saint Stephen. Thick, black smoke, the penance of the Wrathful,
suddenly envelops the poets from across the terrace.*

As much as 'twixt the close of the third hour
  And dawn of day appeareth of that sphere
  Which aye in fashion of a child is playing,

So much it now appeared, towards the night,
  Was of his course remaining to the sun;
  There it was evening, and 'twas midnight here;

And the rays smote the middle of our faces,
  Because by us the mount was so encircled,
  That straight towards the west we now were going

When I perceived my forehead overpowered
  Beneath the splendour far more than at first,
  And stupor were to me the things unknown,

Whereat towards the summit of my brow
  I raised my hands, and made myself the visor
  Which the excessive glare diminishes.

As when from off the water, or a mirror,
  The sunbeam leaps unto the opposite side,
  Ascending upward in the selfsame measure

That it descends, and deviates as far
  From falling of a stone in line direct,
  (As demonstrate experiment and art,)

So it appeared to me that by a light
  Refracted there before me I was smitten;
  On which account my sight was swift to flee.

"What is that, Father sweet, from which I cannot
  So fully screen my sight that it avail me,"
  Said I, "and seems towards us to be moving?"

"Marvel thou not, if dazzle thee as yet
  The family of heaven," he answered me;
  "An angel 'tis, who comes to invite us upward.

Soon will it be, that to behold these things
  Shall not be grievous, but delightful to thee
  As much as nature fashioned thee to feel."

When we had reached the Angel benedight,
  With joyful voice he said: "Here enter in
  To stairway far less steep than are the others."

We mounting were, already thence departed,
  And "*Beati misericordes*" was
  Behind us sung, "Rejoice, thou that o'ercomest!"

My Master and myself, we two alone
  Were going upward, and I thought, in going,
  Some profit to acquire from words of his;

And I to him directed me, thus asking:
  "What did the spirit of Romagna mean,
  Mentioning interdict and partnership?"

Whence he to me: "Of his own greatest failing
  He knows the harm; and therefore wonder not
  If he reprove us, that we less may rue it.

Because are thither pointed your desires
  Where by companionship each share is lessened,
  Envy doth ply the bellows to your sighs.

But if the love of the supernal sphere
  Should upwardly direct your aspiration,
  There would not be that fear within your breast;

Then saw I people hot in fire of wrath, / With stones a young man slaying, clamorously /
Still crying to each other, "Kill him, kill him!"

Purg. XV, lines 106–108

For there, as much the more as one says 'Our,'
  So much the more of good each one possesses,
  And more of charity in that cloister burns."

"I am more hungering to be satisfied,"
  I said, "than if I had before been silent,
  And more of doubt within my mind I gather.

How can it be, that boon distributed
  The more possessors can more wealthy make
  Therein, than if by few it be possessed?"

And he to me: "Because thou fixest still
  Thy mind entirely upon earthly things,
  Thou pluckest darkness from the very light.

That goodness infinite and ineffable
  Which is above there, runneth unto love,
  As to a lucid body comes the sunbeam.

So much it gives itself as it finds ardour,
  So that as far as charity extends,
  O'er it increases the eternal valour.

And the more people thitherward aspire,
  More are there to love well, and more they love there,
  And, as a mirror, one reflects the other.

And if my reasoning appease thee not,
  Thou shalt see Beatrice; and she will fully
  Take from thee this and every other longing.

Endeavour, then, that soon may be extinct,
  As are the two already, the five wounds
  That close themselves again by being painful."

Even as I wished to say, "Thou dost appease me,"
  I saw that I had reached another circle,
  So that my eager eyes made me keep silence.

There it appeared to me that in a vision
  Ecstatic on a sudden I was rapt,
  And in a temple many persons saw;

And at the door a woman, with the sweet
  Behaviour of a mother, saying: "Son,
  Why in this manner hast thou dealt with us?

Lo, sorrowing, thy father and myself
  Were seeking for thee;"—and as here she ceased,
  That which appeared at first had disappeared.

Then I beheld another with those waters
  Adown her cheeks which grief distils whenever
  From great disdain of others it is born,

And saying: "If of that city thou art lord,
  For whose name was such strife among the gods,
  And whence doth every science scintillate,

Avenge thyself on those audacious arms
  That clasped our daughter, O Pisistratus;"
  And the lord seemed to me benign and mild

To answer her with aspect temperate:
  "What shall we do to those who wish us ill,
  If he who loves us be by us condemned?"

Then saw I people hot in fire of wrath,
  With stones a young man slaying, clamorously
  Still crying to each other, "Kill him! kill him!"

And him I saw bow down, because of death
  That weighed already on him, to the Earth,
  But of his eyes made ever gates to heaven,

Imploring the high Lord, in so great strife,
  That he would pardon those his persecutors,
  With such an aspect as unlocks compassion.

Soon as my soul had outwardly returned
  To things external to it which are true,
  Did I my not false errors recognize.

My Leader, who could see me bear myself
  Like to a man that rouses him from sleep,
  Exclaimed: "What ails thee, that thou canst not stand?

But hast been coming more than half a league
  Veiling thine eyes, and with thy legs entangled,
  In guise of one whom wine or sleep subdues?"

"O my sweet Father, if thou listen to me,
  I'll tell thee," said I, "what appeared to me,
  When thus from me my legs were ta'en away."

And he: "If thou shouldst have a hundred masks
  Upon thy face, from me would not be shut
  Thy cogitations, howsoever small.

What thou hast seen was that thou mayst not fail
  To ope thy heart unto the waters of peace,
  Which from the eternal fountain are diffused.

I did not ask, 'What ails thee?' as he does
  Who only looketh with the eyes that see not
  When of the soul bereft the body lies,

But asked it to give vigour to thy feet;
  Thus must we needs urge on the sluggards, slow
  To use their wakefulness when it returns."

We passed along, athwart the twilight peering
  Forward as far as ever eye could stretch
  Against the sunbeams serotine and lucent;

And lo! by slow degrees a smoke approached
  In our direction, sombre as the night,
  Nor was there place to hide one's self therefrom.

This of our eyes and the pure air bereft us.

Canto XVI

*As the poets stumble through the blinding, suffocating smoke, Virgil hears the voices of
the penitent Wrathful singing their prayer, the* Agnus Dei *(the Lamb of God). Their
punishment is apt because anger blinds judgement and suffocates all feeling. The spirit
of Marco the Lombard guides the poets through the cloud as he outlines the political
factors corrupting the world, plays down the influences of fate on human affairs, affirms
the divine notion of free will and laments the lack of good political and religious leaders.
The smoke thins out with the approach of the third angel.*

Darkness of hell, and of a night deprived
  Of every planet under a poor sky,
  As much as may be tenebrous with cloud,

Ne'er made unto my sight so thick a veil,
  As did that smoke which there enveloped us,
  Nor to the feeling of so rough a texture;

For not an eye it suffered to stay open;
  Whereat mine escort, faithful and sagacious,
  Drew near to me and offered me his shoulder.

E'en as a blind man goes behind his guide,
  Lest he should wander, or should strike against
  Aught that may harm or peradventure kill him,

So went I through the bitter and foul air,
  Listening unto my Leader, who said only,
  "Look that from me thou be not separated."

Voices I heard, and every one appeared
  To supplicate for peace and misericord
  The Lamb of God who takes away our sins.

Still "*Agnus Dei*" their exordium was;
  One word there was in all, and metre one,
  So that all harmony appeared among them.

"Master," I said, "are spirits those I hear?"
  And he to me: "Thou apprehendest truly,
  And they the knot of anger go unloosing."

"Now who art thou, that cleavest through our smoke
  And art discoursing of us even as though
  Thou didst by calends still divide the time?"

After this manner by a voice was spoken;
  Whereon my Master said: "Do thou reply,
  And ask if on this side the way go upward."

"Now who art thou, that cleavest through our smoke / And art discoursing of us even as
though / Thou didst by calends still divide the time?"

Purg. XVI, lines 25–27

And I: "O creature that dost cleanse thyself
  To return beautiful to Him who made thee,
  Thou shalt hear marvels if thou follow me."

"Thee will I follow far as is allowed me,"
  He answered; "and if smoke prevent our seeing,
  Hearing shall keep us joined instead thereof."

Thereon began I: "With that swathing band
  Which death unwindeth am I going upward,
  And hither came I through the infernal anguish.

And if God in his grace has me infolded,
  So that he wills that I behold his court
  By method wholly out of modern usage,

Conceal not from me who ere death thou wast,
  But tell it me, and tell me if I go
  Right for the pass, and be thy words our escort."

"Lombard was I, and I was Marco called;
  The world I knew, and loved that excellence,
  At which has each one now unbent his bow.

For mounting upward, thou art going right."
  Thus he made answer, and subjoined: "I pray thee
  To pray for me when thou shalt be above."

And I to him: "My faith I pledge to thee
  To do what thou dost ask me; but am bursting
  Inly with doubt, unless I rid me of it.

First it was simple, and is now made double
  By thy opinion, which makes certain to me,
  Here and elsewhere, that which I couple with it.

The world forsooth is utterly deserted
  By every virtue, as thou tellest me,
  And with iniquity is big and covered;

But I beseech thee point me out the cause,
  That I may see it, and to others show it;
  For one in the heavens, and here below one puts it."

A sigh profound, that grief forced into Ai!
  He first sent forth, and then began he: "Brother,
  The world is blind, and sooth thou comest from it!

Ye who are living every cause refer
  Still upward to the heavens, as if all things
  They of necessity moved with themselves.

If this were so, in you would be destroyed
  Free will, nor any justice would there be
  In having joy for good, or grief for evil.

The heavens your movements do initiate,
  I say not all; but granting that I say it,
  Light has been given you for good and evil,

And free volition; which, if some fatigue
  In the first battles with the heavens it suffers,
  Afterwards conquers all, if well 'tis nurtured.

To greater force and to a better nature,
  Though free, ye subject are, and that creates
  The mind in you the heavens have not in charge.

Hence, if the present world doth go astray,
  In you the cause is, be it sought in you;
  And I therein will now be thy true spy.

Forth from the hand of Him, who fondles it
  Before it is, like to a little girl
  Weeping and laughing in her childish sport,

Issues the simple soul, that nothing knows,
  Save that, proceeding from a joyous Maker,
  Gladly it turns to that which gives it pleasure.

Of trivial good at first it tastes the savour;
  Is cheated by it, and runs after it,
  If guide or rein turn not aside its love.

Hence it behoved laws for a rein to place,
  Behoved a king to have, who at the least
  Of the true city should discern the tower.

The laws exist, but who sets hand to them?
  No one; because the shepherd who precedes
  Can ruminate, but cleaveth not the hoof;

Wherefore the people that perceives its guide
  Strike only at the good for which it hankers,
  Feeds upon that, and farther seeketh not.

Clearly canst thou perceive that evil guidance
  The cause is that has made the world depraved,
  And not that nature is corrupt in you.

Rome, that reformed the world, accustomed was
  Two suns to have, which one road and the other,
  Of God and of the world, made manifest.

"Thee will I follow far as is allowed me," / He answered; "and if smoke prevent our seeing, /
Hearing shall keep us joined instead thereof."

Purg. XVI, lines 34–36

One has the other quenched, and to the crosier
  The sword is joined, and ill beseemeth it
  That by main force one with the other go,

Because, being joined, one feareth not the other;
  If thou believe not, think upon the grain,
  For by its seed each herb is recognized.

In the land laved by Po and Adige,
  Valour and courtesy used to be found,
  Before that Frederick had his controversy;

Now in security can pass that way
  Whoever will abstain, through sense of shame,
  From speaking with the good, or drawing near them.

True, three old men are left, in whom upbraids
  The ancient age the new, and late they deem it
  That God restore them to the better life:

Currado da Palazzo, and good Gherardo,
  And Guido da Castel, who better named is,
  In fashion of the French, the simple Lombard:

Say thou henceforward that the Church of Rome,
  Confounding in itself two governments,
  Falls in the mire, and soils itself and burden."

"O Marco mine," I said, "thou reasonest well;
  And now discern I why the sons of Levi
  Have been excluded from the heritage.

But what Gherardo is it, who, as sample
  Of a lost race, thou sayest has remained
  In reprobation of the barbarous age?"

"Either thy speech deceives me, or it tempts me,"
  He answered me; "for speaking Tuscan to me,
  It seems of good Gherardo naught thou knowest.

By other surname do I know him not,
  Unless I take it from his daughter Gaia.
  May God be with you, for I come no farther.

Behold the dawn, that through the smoke rays out,
  Already whitening; and I must depart—
  Yonder the Angel is—ere he appear."

Thus did he speak, and would no farther hear me.

Canto XVII

*Dante emerges from the smoke cloud as the sun is setting and experiences three visions
which will serve as the Bridle for his Wrath. The Angel of Meekness utters the
benediction,* Beati Pacifici, *and erases the third P before indicating the stairway to the
Fourth Cornice. The two poets rest for the night and Virgil passes the time by arguing
that Love lies at the root of every action, whether good or bad. He shows Dante that
all seven capital sins stem from deviations of Love, including the excessive love of
things that are not God.*

Remember, Reader, if e'er in the Alps
  A mist o'ertook thee, through which thou couldst see
  Not otherwise than through its membrane mole,

How, when the vapours humid and condensed
  Begin to dissipate themselves, the sphere
  Of the sun feebly enters in among them,

And thy imagination will be swift
  In coming to perceive how I re-saw
  The sun at first, that was already setting.

Thus, to the faithful footsteps of my Master
  Mating mine own, I issued from that cloud
  To rays already dead on the low shores.

O thou, Imagination, that dost steal us
  So from without sometimes, that man perceives not,
  Although around may sound a thousand trumpets,

Who moveth thee, if sense impel thee not?
  Moves thee a light, which in the heaven takes form,
  By self, or by a will that downward guides it.

Of her impiety, who changed her form
  Into the bird that most delights in singing,
  In my imagining appeared the trace;

And hereupon my mind was so withdrawn
  Within itself, that from without there came
  Nothing that then might be received by it.

Then reigned within my lofty fantasy
  One crucified, disdainful and ferocious
  In countenance, and even thus was dying.

Around him were the great Ahasuerus,
  Esther his wife, and the just Mordecai,
  Who was in word and action so entire.

And even as this image burst asunder
  Of its own self, in fashion of a bubble
  In which the water it was made of fails,

There rose up in my vision a young maiden
  Bitterly weeping, and she said: "O queen,
  Why hast thou wished in anger to be naught?

Thou'st slain thyself, Lavinia not to lose;
  Now hast thou lost me; I am she who mourns,
  Mother, at thine ere at another's ruin."

As sleep is broken, when upon a sudden
  New light strikes in upon the eyelids closed,
  And broken quivers ere it dieth wholly,

So this imagining of mine fell down
  As soon as the effulgence smote my face,
  Greater by far than what is in our wont.

I turned me round to see where I might be,
  When said a voice, "Here is the passage up;"
  Which from all other purposes removed me,

And made my wish so full of eagerness
  To look and see who was it that was speaking,
  It never rests till meeting face to face;

But as before the sun, which quells the sight,
  And in its own excess its figure veils,
  Even so my power was insufficient here.

"This is a spirit divine, who in the way
  Of going up directs us without asking,
  And who with his own light himself conceals.

He does with us as man doth with himself;
  For he who sees the need, and waits the asking,
  Malignly leans already tow'rds denial.

Accord we now our feet to such inviting,
  Let us make haste to mount ere it grow dark;
  For then we could not till the day return."

Thus my Conductor said; and I and he
  Together turned our footsteps to a stairway;
  And I, as soon as the first step I reached,

Near me perceived a motion as of wings,
  And fanning in the face, and saying, "'*Beati
  Pacifici*,' who are without ill anger."

Already over us were so uplifted
  The latest sunbeams, which the night pursues,
  That upon many sides the stars appeared.

"O manhood mine, why dost thou vanish so?"
  I said within myself; for I perceived
  The vigour of my legs was put in truce.

We at the point were where no more ascends
  The stairway upward, and were motionless,
  Even as a ship, which at the shore arrives;

And I gave heed a little, if I might hear
  Aught whatsoever in the circle new;
  Then to my Master turned me round and said:

"Say, my sweet Father, what delinquency
  Is purged here in the circle where we are?
  Although our feet may pause, pause not thy speech."

And he to me: "The love of good, remiss
  In what it should have done, is here restored;
  Here plied again the ill-belated oar;

But still more openly to understand,
  Turn unto me thy mind, and thou shalt gather
  Some profitable fruit from our delay.

Neither Creator nor a creature ever,
  Son," he began, "was destitute of love
  Natural or spiritual; and thou knowest it.

The natural was ever without error;
  But err the other may by evil object,
  Or by too much, or by too little vigour.

While in the first it well directed is,
  And in the second moderates itself,
  It cannot be the cause of sinful pleasure;

But when to ill it turns, and, with more care
  Or lesser than it ought, runs after good,
  'Gainst the Creator works his own creation.

Hence thou mayst comprehend that love must be
  The seed within yourselves of every virtue,
  And every act that merits punishment.

Now inasmuch as never from the welfare
  Of its own subject can love turn its sight,
  From their own hatred all things are secure;

And since we cannot think of any being
  Standing alone, nor from the First divided,
  Of hating Him is all desire cut off.

Hence if, discriminating, I judge well,
  The evil that one loves is of one's neighbour,
  And this is born in three modes in your clay.

There are, who, by abasement of their neighbour,
  Hope to excel, and therefore only long
  That from his greatness he may be cast down;

There are, who power, grace, honour, and renown
  Fear they may lose because another rises,
  Thence are so sad that the reverse they love;

And there are those whom injury seems to chafe,
  So that it makes them greedy for revenge,
  And such must needs shape out another's harm.

This threefold love is wept for down below;
  Now of the other will I have thee hear,
  That runneth after good with measure faulty.

Each one confusedly a good conceives
  Wherein the mind may rest, and longeth for it;
  Therefore to overtake it each one strives.

If languid love to look on this attract you,
  Or in attaining unto it, this cornice,
  After just penitence, torments you for it.

There's other good that does not make man happy;
  'Tis not felicity, 'tis not the good
  Essence, of every good the fruit and root.

The love that yields itself too much to this
  Above us is lamented in three circles;
  But how tripartite it may be described,

I say not, that thou seek it for thyself."

Canto XVIII

Virgil continues the discourse begun in Canto XVII by addressing the origin and nature of Love, the concept of the rational soul (as distinct from the material body) and determinism versus free will. Just as Dante is drifting off to sleep, he is awakened by the noisy spirits of the Slothful. Apathetic or indifferent to life, their penance now demands ceaseless activity as they rush around the Fourth Cornice, crying out examples of active Zeal, the opposing virtue, which serve as the Whip and Bridle for their meditation. The Abbot of San Zeno gives Virgil directions. Dante falls into a slumber.

An end had put unto his reasoning
  The lofty Teacher, and attent was looking
  Into my face, if I appeared content;

And I, whom a new thirst still goaded on,
  Without was mute, and said within: "Perchance
  The too much questioning I make annoys him."

But that true Father, who had comprehended
  The timid wish, that opened not itself,
  By speaking gave me hardihood to speak.

Whence I: "My sight is, Master, vivified
  So in thy light, that clearly I discern
  Whate'er thy speech importeth or describes.

Therefore I thee entreat, sweet Father dear,
  To teach me love, to which thou dost refer
  Every good action and its contrary."

"Direct," he said, "towards me the keen eyes
  Of intellect, and clear will be to thee
  The error of the blind, who would be leaders.

The soul, which is created apt to love,
  Is mobile unto everything that pleases,
  Soon as by pleasure she is waked to action.

Your apprehension from some real thing
  An image draws, and in yourselves displays it
  So that it makes the soul turn unto it.

And if, when turned, towards it she incline,
  Love is that inclination; it is nature,
  Which is by pleasure bound in you anew

Then even as the fire doth upward move
  By its own form, which to ascend is born,
  Where longest in its matter it endures,

So comes the captive soul into desire,
  Which is a motion spiritual, and ne'er rests
  Until she doth enjoy the thing beloved.

Now may apparent be to thee how hidden
  The truth is from those people, who aver
  All love is in itself a laudable thing;

Because its matter may perchance appear
  Aye to be good; but yet not each impression
  Is good, albeit good may be the wax."

"Thy words, and my sequacious intellect,"
  I answered him, "have love revealed to me;
  But that has made me more impregned with doubt;

For if love from without be offered us,
  And with another foot the soul go not,
  If right or wrong she go, 'tis not her merit."

And he to me: "What reason seeth here,
  Myself can tell thee; beyond that await
  For Beatrice, since 'tis a work of faith.

Every substantial form, that segregate
  From matter is, and with it is united,
  Specific power has in itself collected,

Which without act is not perceptible,
  Nor shows itself except by its effect,
  As life does in a plant by the green leaves.

But still, whence cometh the intelligence
  Of the first notions, man is ignorant,
  And the affection for the first allurements,

Which are in you as instinct in the bee
  To make its honey; and this first desire
  Merit of praise or blame containeth not.

Now, that to this all others may be gathered,
  Innate within you is the power that counsels,
  And it should keep the threshold of assent.

This is the principle, from which is taken
  Occasion of desert in you, according
  As good and guilty loves it takes and winnows.

Those who, in reasoning, to the bottom went,
  Were of this innate liberty aware,
  Therefore bequeathed they Ethics to the world.

Supposing, then, that from necessity
  Springs every love that is within you kindled,
  Within yourselves the power is to restrain it.

The noble virtue Beatrice understands
  By the free will; and therefore see that thou
  Bear it in mind, if she should speak of it."

The moon, belated almost unto midnight,
  Now made the stars appear to us more rare,
  Formed like a bucket, that is all ablaze,

And counter to the heavens ran through those paths
  Which the sun sets aflame, when he of Rome
  Sees it 'twixt Sardes and Corsicans go down;

And that patrician shade, for whom is named
  Pietola more than any Mantuan town,
  Had laid aside the burden of my lading;

Whence I, who reason manifest and plain
  In answer to my questions had received,
  Stood like a man in drowsy reverie.

But taken from me was this drowsiness
  Suddenly by a people, that behind
  Our backs already had come round to us.

And as, of old, Ismenus and Asopus
  Beside them saw at night the rush and throng,
  If but the Thebans were in need of Bacchus,

So they along that circle curve their step,
  From what I saw of those approaching us,
  Who by good-will and righteous love are ridden.

Full soon they were upon us, because running
  Moved onward all that mighty multitude,
  And two in the advance cried out, lamenting,

"Mary in haste unto the mountain ran,
  And Caesar, that he might subdue Ilerda,
  Thrust at Marseilles, and then ran into Spain."

"Quick! quick! so that the time may not be lost
  By little love!" forthwith the others cried,
  "For ardour in well-doing freshens grace!"

"O folk, in whom an eager fervour now
  Supplies perhaps delay and negligence,
  Put by you in well-doing, through lukewarmness,

This one who lives, and truly I lie not,
  Would fain go up, if but the sun relight us;
  So tell us where the passage nearest is."

These were the words of him who was my Guide;
  And some one of those spirits said: "Come on
  Behind us, and the opening shalt thou find;

So full of longing are we to move onward,
  That stay we cannot; therefore pardon us,
  If thou for churlishness our justice take.

I was San Zeno's Abbot at Verona,
  Under the empire of good Barbarossa,
  Of whom still sorrowing Milan holds discourse;

And he has one foot in the grave already,
  Who shall erelong lament that monastery,
  And sorry be of having there had power,

Because his son, in his whole body sick,
  And worse in mind, and who was evil-born,
  He put into the place of its true pastor."

But taken from me was this drowsiness / Suddenly by a people, that behind /
Our backs already had come round to us.

Purg. XVIII, lines 88–90

If more he said, or silent was, I know not,
  He had already passed so far beyond us;
  But this I heard, and to retain it pleased me.

And he who was in every need my succour
  Said: "Turn thee hitherward; see two of them
  Come fastening upon slothfulness their teeth."

In rear of all they shouted: "Sooner were
  The people dead to whom the sea was opened,
  Than their inheritors the Jordan saw;

And those who the fatigue did not endure
  Unto the issue, with Anchises' son,
  Themselves to life withouten glory offered."

Then when from us so separated were
  Those shades, that they no longer could be seen,
  Within me a new thought did entrance find,

Whence others many and diverse were born;
  And so I lapsed from one into another,
  That in a reverie mine eyes I closed,

And meditation into dream transmuted.

Canto XIX

Dante has another dream: this time, an ugly, misshapen woman is singing to him.
Under his gaze, she becomes a beautiful Siren. He is enchanted but Virgil breaks the spell.
The Angel of Zeal, guardian of the Fourth Cornice, utters the benediction, "Blessed Are
They Who Mourn", wipes off the fourth P and takes the poets to the next level. In the
Fifth Cornice, lie the prostrate (and praying) souls of the penitent Covetous who
worshipped wealth and power above all things. The fettered spirit of Pope Adrian V
(Ottobuono Fieschi) confesses his sins and asks after his niece, Alagia.

It was the hour when the diurnal heat
  No more can warm the coldness of the moon,
  Vanquished by Earth, or peradventure Saturn,

When geomancers their Fortuna Major
  See in the orient before the dawn
  Rise by a path that long remains not dim,

There came to me in dreams a stammering woman,
  Squint in her eyes, and in her feet distorted,
  With hands dissevered and of sallow hue.

I looked at her; and as the sun restores
  The frigid members which the night benumbs,
  Even thus my gaze did render voluble

Her tongue, and made her all erect thereafter
  In little while, and the lost countenance
  As love desires it so in her did colour.

When in this wise she had her speech unloosed,
  She 'gan to sing so, that with difficulty
  Could I have turned my thoughts away from her.

"I am," she sang, "I am the Siren sweet
  Who mariners amid the main unman,
  So full am I of pleasantness to hear.

I drew Ulysses from his wandering way
  Unto my song, and he who dwells with me
  Seldom departs so wholly I content him."

Her mouth was not yet closed again, before
  Appeared a Lady saintly and alert
  Close at my side to put her to confusion.

"Virgilius, O Virgilius! who is this?"
  Sternly she said; and he was drawing near
  With eyes still fixed upon that modest one.

She seized the other and in front laid open,
  Rending her garments, and her belly showed me;
  This waked me with the stench that issued from it.

I turned mine eyes, and good Virgilius said:
  "At least thrice have I called thee; rise and come;
  Find we the opening by which thou mayst enter."

I rose; and full already of high day
  Were all the circles of the Sacred Mountain,
  And with the new sun at our back we went.

Following behind him, I my forehead bore
  Like unto one who has it laden with thought,
  Who makes himself the half arch of a bridge,

When I heard say, "Come, here the passage is,"
  Spoken in a manner gentle and benign,
  Such as we hear not in this mortal region.

With open wings, which of a swan appeared,
  Upward he turned us who thus spake to us,
  Between the two walls of the solid granite.

He moved his pinions afterwards and fanned us,
  Affirming those 'qui lugent' to be blessed,
  For they shall have their souls with comfort filled.

"What aileth thee, that aye to Earth thou gazest?"
  To me my Guide began to say, we both
  Somewhat beyond the Angel having mounted.

And I: "With such misgiving makes me go
  A vision new, which bends me to itself,
  So that I cannot from the thought withdraw me."

"Didst thou behold," he said, "that old enchantress,
  Who sole above us henceforth is lamented?
  Didst thou behold how man is freed from her?

Suffice it thee, and smite earth with thy heels,
  Thine eyes lift upward to the lure, that whirls
  The Eternal King with revolutions vast."

Even as the hawk, that first his feet surveys,
  Then turns him to the call and stretches forward,
  Through the desire of food that draws him thither,

Such I became, and such, as far as cleaves
  The rock to give a way to him who mounts,
  Went on to where the circling doth begin.

On the fifth circle when I had come forth,
  People I saw upon it who were weeping,
  Stretched prone upon the ground, all downward
                                              turned.

"*Adhaesit pavimento anima mea,*"
  I heard them say with sighings so profound,
  That hardly could the words be understood.

"O ye elect of God, whose sufferings
  Justice and Hope both render less severe,
  Direct ye us towards the high ascents."

"If ye are come secure from this prostration,
  And wish to find the way most speedily,
  Let your right hands be evermore outside."

Thus did the Poet ask, and thus was answered
  By them somewhat in front of us; whence I
  In what was spoken divined the rest concealed,

And unto my Lord's eyes mine eyes I turned;
  Whence he assented with a cheerful sign
  To what the sight of my desire implored.

When of myself I could dispose at will,
  Above that creature did I draw myself,
  Whose words before had caused me to take note,

Saying: "O Spirit, in whom weeping ripens
  That without which to God we cannot turn,
  Suspend awhile for me thy greater care.

Who wast thou, and why are your backs turned
                                              upwards,
  Tell me, and if thou wouldst that I procure thee
  Anything there whence living I departed."

And he to me: "Wherefore our backs the heaven
  Turns to itself, know shalt thou; but beforehand
  '*Scias quod ego fui successor Petri.*'

"What aileth thee, that aye to Earth thou gazest?" / To me my Guide began to say, we both /
Somewhat beyond the Angel having mounted.

Purg. XIX , lines 52–54

Between Siestri and Chiaveri descends
  A river beautiful, and of its name
  The title of my blood its summit makes.

A month and little more essayed I how
  Weighs the great cloak on him from mire who
                                    keeps it,
  For all the other burdens seem a feather.

Tardy, ah woe is me! was my conversion;
  But when the Roman Shepherd I was made,
  Then I discovered life to be a lie.

I saw that there the heart was not at rest,
  Nor farther in that life could one ascend;
  Whereby the love of this was kindled in me.

Until that time a wretched soul and parted
  From God was I, and wholly avaricious;
  Now, as thou seest, I here am punished for it.

What avarice does is here made manifest
  In the purgation of these souls converted,
  And no more bitter pain the Mountain has.

Even as our eye did not uplift itself
  Aloft, being fastened upon earthly things,
  So justice here has merged it in the earth.

As avarice had extinguished our affection
  For every good, whereby was action lost,
  So justice here doth hold us in restraint,

Bound and imprisoned by the feet and hands;
  And so long as it pleases the just Lord
  Shall we remain immovable and prostrate.”

I on my knees had fallen, and wished to speak;
  But even as I began, and he was ’ware,
  Only by listening, of my reverence,

“What cause,” he said, “has downward bent thee thus?”
  And I to him: “For your own dignity,
  Standing, my conscience stung me with remorse.”

“Straighten thy legs, and upward raise thee, brother,”
  He answered: “Err not, fellow-servant am I
  With thee and with the others to one power.

If e’er that holy, evangelic sound,
  Which sayeth ‘neque nubent,’ thou hast heard,
  Well canst thou see why in this wise I speak.

Now go; no longer will I have thee linger,
  Because thy stay doth incommode my weeping,
  With which I ripen that which thou hast said.

On Earth I have a grandchild named Alagia,
  Good in herself, unless indeed our house
  Malevolent may make her by example,

And she alone remains to me on Earth.”

"What cause," he said, "has downward bent thee thus?" / And I to him: "For your own dignity,
/ Standing, my conscience stung me with remorse."

Purg. XIX, lines 130–132

Canto XX

As the two poets make their way through the Fifth Cornice, they hear someone
proclaiming examples of the virtue opposed to Covetousness. The voice cites Mary,
Fabricius and Saint Nicholas. This spirit is Hugh Capet, founder of the Capetian
dynasty. He goes on to denounce the crimes of his descendants. Speaking of the souls, he
explains that they recite virtuous prayers by day but at night they engage in criticism
of the covetousness of prominent figures such as Pygmalion and Midas. The travellers
carry on with their journey until the mountain of Purgatory suddenly shakes from top
to bottom. All the prostrate souls sing Gloria in excelsis Deo. *Dante is intrigued.*

Ill strives the will against a better will;
  Therefore, to pleasure him, against my pleasure
  I drew the sponge not saturate from the water.

Onward I moved, and onward moved my Leader,
  Through vacant places, skirting still the rock,
  As on a wall close to the battlements;

For they that through their eyes pour drop by drop
  The malady which all the world pervades,
  On the other side too near the verge approach.

Accursed mayst thou be, thou old she-wolf,
  That more than all the other beasts hast prey,
  Because of hunger infinitely hollow!

O heaven, in whose gyrations some appear
  To think conditions here below are changed,
  When will he come through whom she shall depart?

Onward we went with footsteps slow and scarce,
  And I attentive to the shades I heard
  Piteously weeping and bemoaning them;

And I by peradventure heard "Sweet Mary!"
  Uttered in front of us amid the weeping
  Even as a woman does who is in child-birth;

And in continuance: "How poor thou wast
  Is manifested by that hostelry
  Where thou didst lay thy sacred burden down."

Thereafterward I heard: "O good Fabricius,
  Virtue with poverty didst thou prefer
  To the possession of great wealth with vice."

So pleasurable were these words to me
  That I drew farther onward to have knowledge
  Touching that spirit whence they seemed to come.

He furthermore was speaking of the largess
  Which Nicholas unto the maidens gave,
  In order to conduct their youth to honour.

"O soul that dost so excellently speak,
  Tell me who wast thou," said I, "and why only
  Thou dost renew these praises well deserved?

Not without recompense shall be thy word,
  If I return to finish the short journey
  Of that life which is flying to its end."

And he: "I'll tell thee, not for any comfort
  I may expect from earth, but that so much
  Grace shines in thee or ever thou art dead.

I was the root of that malignant plant
  Which overshadows all the Christian world,
  So that good fruit is seldom gathered from it;

But if Douay and Ghent, and Lille and Bruges
  Had Power, soon vengeance would be taken on it;
  And this I pray of Him who judges all.

Hugh Capet was I called upon the Earth;
  From me were born the Louises and Philips,
  By whom in later days has France been governed.

I was the son of a Parisian butcher,
  What time the ancient kings had perished all,
  Excepting one, contrite in cloth of gray.

Onward we went with footsteps slow and scarce, / And I attentive to the shades I heard /
Piteously weeping and bemoaning them;

Purg. XX, lines 16–18

I found me grasping in my hands the rein
 Of the realm's government, and so great power
 Of new acquest, and so with friends abounding,

That to the widowed diadem promoted
 The head of mine own offspring was, from whom
 The consecrated bones of these began.

So long as the great dowry of Provence
 Out of my blood took not the sense of shame,
 'Twas little worth, but still it did no harm.

Then it began with falsehood and with force
 Its rapine; and thereafter, for amends,
 Took Ponthieu, Normandy, and Gascony.

Charles came to Italy, and for amends
 A victim made of Conradin, and then
 Thrust Thomas back to heaven, for amends.

A time I see, not very distant now,
 Which draweth forth another Charles from France,
 The better to make known both him and his.

Unarmed he goes, and only with the lance
 That Judas jousted with; and that he thrusts
 So that he makes the paunch of Florence burst.

He thence not land, but sin and infamy,
 Shall gain, so much more grievous to himself
 As the more light such damage he accounts.

The other, now gone forth, ta'en in his ship,
 See I his daughter sell, and chaffer for her
 As corsairs do with other female slaves.

What more, O Avarice, canst thou do to us,
 Since thou my blood so to thyself hast drawn,
 It careth not for its own proper flesh?

That less may seem the future ill and past,
 I see the flower-de-luce Alagna enter,
 And Christ in his own Vicar captive made.

I see him yet another time derided;
 I see renewed the vinegar and gall,
 And between living thieves I see him slain.

I see the modern Pilate so relentless,
 This does not sate him, but without decretal
 He to the temple bears his sordid sails!

When, O my Lord! shall I be joyful made
 By looking on the vengeance which, concealed,
 Makes sweet thine anger in thy secrecy?

What I was saying of that only bride
 Of the Holy Ghost, and which occasioned thee
 To turn towards me for some commentary,

So long has been ordained to all our prayers
 As the day lasts; but when the night comes on,
 Contrary sound we take instead thereof.

At that time we repeat Pygmalion,
 Of whom a traitor, thief, and parricide
 Made his insatiable desire of gold;

And the misery of avaricious Midas,
 That followed his inordinate demand,
 At which forevermore one needs but laugh.

The foolish Achan each one then records,
 And how he stole the spoils; so that the wrath
 Of Joshua still appears to sting him here.

Then we accuse Sapphira with her husband,
 We laud the hoof-beats Heliodorus had,
 And the whole mount in infamy encircles

Polymnestor who murdered Polydorus.
 Here finally is cried: 'O Crassus, tell us,
 For thou dost know, what is the taste of gold?'

Sometimes we speak, one loud, another low,
 According to desire of speech, that spurs us
 To greater now and now to lesser pace.

But in the good that here by day is talked of,
 Erewhile alone I was not; yet near by
 No other person lifted up his voice."

From him already we departed were,
 And made endeavour to o'ercome the road
 As much as was permitted to our power,

When I perceived, like something that is falling,
 The mountain tremble, whence a chill seized on me,
 As seizes him who to his death is going.

Certes so violently shook not Delos,
 Before Latona made her nest therein
 To give birth to the two eyes of the heaven.

Then upon all sides there began a cry,
　　Such that the Master drew himself towards me,
　　Saying, "Fear not, while I am guiding thee."

"*Gloria in excelsis Deo*," all
　　Were saying, from what near I comprehended,
　　Where it was possible to hear the cry.

We paused immovable and in suspense,
　　Even as the shepherds who first heard that song,
　　Until the trembling ceased, and it was finished.

Then we resumed again our holy path,
　　Watching the shades that lay upon the ground,
　　Already turned to their accustomed plaint.

No ignorance ever with so great a strife
　　Had rendered me importunate to know,
　　If erreth not in this my memory,

As meditating then I seemed to have;
　　Nor out of haste to question did I dare,
　　Nor of myself I there could aught perceive;

So I went onward timorous and thoughtful.

Canto XXI

*Dante and Virgil are walking along the Fifth Cornice when the spirit of the Latin
poet Publius Papinius Statius catches up with them. He explains that Mount
Purgatory shakes with joy every time a soul is released into Paradise. The latest
trembling was for himself, risen after 500 years of lying prostrate among the
Covetous. He only regrets not having met the author of the* Aeneid *to whom much
of his work owes a debt. When Dante reveals his companion's identity, Statius bends
down to embrace the feet of Virgil who protests by reminding him that both are
mere shadows.*

The natural thirst, that ne'er is satisfied
　　Excepting with the water for whose grace
　　The woman of Samaria besought,

Put me in travail, and haste goaded me
　　Along the encumbered path behind my Leader
　　And I was pitying that righteous vengeance;

And lo! in the same manner as Luke writeth
　　That Christ appeared to two upon the way
　　From the sepulchral cave already risen,

A shade appeared to us, and came behind us,
　　Down gazing on the prostrate multitude,
　　Nor were we ware of it, until it spake,

Saying, "My brothers, may God give you peace!"
　　We turned us suddenly, and Virgilius rendered
　　To him the countersign thereto conforming.

Thereon began he: "In the blessed council,
　　Thee may the court veracious place in peace,
　　That me doth banish in eternal exile!"

"How," said he, and the while we went with speed,
　　"If ye are shades whom God deigns not on high,
　　Who up his stairs so far has guided you?"

And said my Teacher: "If thou note the marks
　　Which this one bears, and which the Angel traces
　　Well shalt thou see he with the good must reign.

But because she who spinneth day and night
  For him had not yet drawn the distaff off,
  Which Clotho lays for each one and compacts,

His soul, which is thy sister and my own,
  In coming upwards could not come alone,
  By reason that it sees not in our fashion.

Whence I was drawn from out the ample throat
  Of Hell to be his guide, and I shall guide him
  As far on as my school has power to lead.

But tell us, if thou knowest, why such a shudder
  Erewhile the mountain gave, and why together
  All seemed to cry, as far as its moist feet?"

In asking he so hit the very eye
  Of my desire, that merely with the hope
  My thirst became the less unsatisfied.

"Naught is there," he began, "that without order
  May the religion of the mountain feel,
  Nor aught that may be foreign to its custom.

Free is it here from every permutation;
  What from itself heaven in itself receiveth
  Can be of this the cause, and naught beside;

Because that neither rain, nor hail, nor snow,
  Nor dew, nor hoar-frost any higher falls
  Than the short, little stairway of three steps.

Dense clouds do not appear, nor rarefied,
  Nor coruscation, nor the daughter of Thaumas,
  That often upon Earth her region shifts;

No arid vapour any farther rises
  Than to the top of the three steps I spake of,
  Whereon the Vicar of Peter has his feet.

Lower down perchance it trembles less or more,
  But, for the wind that in the earth is hidden
  I know not how, up here it never trembled.

It trembles here, whenever any soul
  Feels itself pure, so that it soars, or moves
  To mount aloft, and such a cry attends it.

Of purity the will alone gives proof,
  Which, being wholly free to change its convent,
  Takes by surprise the soul, and helps it fly.

First it wills well; but the desire permits not,
  Which divine justice with the self-same will
  There was to sin, upon the torment sets.

And I, who have been lying in this pain
  Five hundred years and more, but just now felt
  A free volition for a better seat.

Therefore thou heardst the earthquake, and the pious
  Spirits along the mountain rendering praise
  Unto the Lord, that soon he speed them upwards."

So said he to him; and since we enjoy
  As much in drinking as the thirst is great,
  I could not say how much it did me good.

And the wise Leader: "Now I see the net
  That snares you here, and how ye are set free,
  Why the Earth quakes, and wherefore ye rejoice.

Now who thou wast be pleased that I may know;
  And why so many centuries thou hast here
  Been lying, let me gather from thy words."

"In days when the good Titus, with the aid
  Of the supremest King, avenged the wounds
  Whence issued forth the blood by Judas sold,

Under the name that most endures and honours,
  Was I on Earth," that spirit made reply,
  "Greatly renowned, but not with faith as yet.

My vocal spirit was so sweet, that Rome
  Me, a Thoulousian, drew unto herself,
  Where I deserved to deck my brows with myrtle.

Statius the people name me still on Earth;
  I sang of Thebes, and then of great Achilles;
  But on the way fell with my second burden.

The seeds unto my ardour were the sparks
  Of that celestial flame which heated me,
  Whereby more than a thousand have been fired;

Of the Aeneid speak I, which to me
  A mother was, and was my nurse in song;
  Without this weighed I not a drachma's weight.

And to have lived upon the Earth what time
  Virgilius lived, I would accept one sun
  More than I must ere issuing from my ban."

These words towards me made Virgilius turn
  With looks that in their silence said, "Be silent!"
  But yet the power that wills cannot do all things;

For tears and laughter are such pursuivants
  Unto the passion from which each springs forth,
  In the most truthful least the will they follow.

I only smiled, as one who gives the wink;
  Whereat the shade was silent, and it gazed
  Into mine eyes, where most expression dwells;

And, "As thou well mayst consummate a labour
  So great," it said, "why did thy face just now
  Display to me the lightning of a smile?"

Now am I caught on this side and on that;
  One keeps me silent, one to speak conjures me,
  Wherefore I sigh, and I am understood.

"Speak," said my Master, "and be not afraid
  Of speaking, but speak out, and say to him
  What he demands with such solicitude."

Whence I: "Thou peradventure marvellest,
  O antique spirit, at the smile I gave;
  But I will have more wonder seize upon thee.

This one, who guides on high these eyes of mine,
  Is that Virgilius, from whom thou didst learn
  To sing aloud of men and of the Gods.

If other cause thou to my smile imputedst,
  Abandon it as false, and trust it was
  Those words which thou hast spoken concerning him."

Already he was stooping to embrace
  My Teacher's feet; but he said to him: "Brother,
  Do not; for shade thou art, and shade beholdest."

And he uprising: "Now canst thou the sum
  Of love which warms me to thee comprehend,
  When this our vanity I disremember,

Treating a shadow as substantial thing."

Canto XXII

*Statius takes the visitors out of the Fifth Cornice through the Pass of Pardon and
on to the next level. The Angel of Liberality erases the fifth P and blesses those
who thirst for righteousness. Statius explains that his sin was not Avarice but the
opposite. He also discusses his conversion to Christianity and the penalty he paid
for keeping it secret. On the Sixth Cornice, where Gluttony is purged, they
behold a fruit-laden tree and a cascade of water. From the tree issues a voice that
forbids any eating of the fruit and shouts examples of the virtues of Moderation.*

Already was the Angel left behind us,
  The Angel who to the sixth round had turned us,
  Having erased one mark from off my face;

And those who have in justice their desire
  Had said to us, "*Beati*," in their voices,
  With "*sitio*," and without more ended it.

And I, more light than through the other passes,
  Went onward so, that without any labour
  I followed upward the swift-footed spirits;

When thus Virgilius began: "The love
  Kindled by virtue aye another kindles,
  Provided outwardly its flame appear.

Hence from the hour that Juvenal descended
  Among us into the infernal Limbo,
  Who made apparent to me thy affection,

My kindliness towards thee was as great
  As ever bound one to an unseen person,
  So that these stairs will now seem short to me.

But tell me, and forgive me as a friend,
  If too great confidence let loose the rein,
  And as a friend now hold discourse with me;

How was it possible within thy breast
  For avarice to find place, 'mid so much wisdom
  As thou wast filled with by thy diligence?"

These words excited Statius at first
  Somewhat to laughter; afterward he answered:
  "Each word of thine is love's dear sign to me.

Verily oftentimes do things appear
  Which give fallacious matter to our doubts,
  Instead of the true causes which are hidden!

Thy question shows me thy belief to be
  That I was niggard in the other life,
  It may be from the circle where I was;

Therefore know thou, that avarice was removed
  Too far from me; and this extravagance
  Thousands of lunar periods have punished.

And were it not that I my thoughts uplifted,
  When I the passage heard where thou exclaimest,
  As if indignant, unto human nature,

'To what impellest thou not, O cursed hunger
  Of gold, the appetite of mortal men?'
  Revolving I should feel the dismal joustings.

Then I perceived the hands could spread too wide
  Their wings in spending, and repented me
  As well of that as of my other sins;

How many with shorn hair shall rise again
  Because of ignorance, which from this sin
  Cuts off repentance living and in death!

And know that the transgression which rebuts
  By direct opposition any sin
  Together with it here its verdure dries.

Therefore if I have been among that folk
  Which mourns its avarice, to purify me,
  For its opposite has this befallen me."

"Now when thou sangest the relentless weapons
  Of the twofold affliction of Jocasta,"
  The singer of the Songs Bucolic said,

"From that which Clio there with thee preludes,
  It does not seem that yet had made thee faithful
  That faith without which no good works suffice.

If this be so, what candles or what sun
  Scattered thy darkness so that thou didst trim
  Thy sails behind the Fisherman thereafter?"

And he to him: "Thou first directedst me
  Towards Parnassus, in its grots to drink,
  And first concerning God didst me enlighten.

Thou didst as he who walketh in the night,
  Who bears his light behind, which helps him not,
  But wary makes the persons after him,

When thou didst say: 'The age renews itself,
  Justice returns, and man's primeval time,
  And a new progeny descends from heaven.'

Through thee I Poet was, through thee a Christian;
  But that thou better see what I design,
  To colour it will I extend my hand.

Already was the world in every part
  Pregnant with the true creed, disseminated
  By messengers of the eternal kingdom;

And thy assertion, spoken of above,
  With the new preachers was in unison;
  Whence I to visit them the custom took.

Then they became so holy in my sight,
  That, when Domitian persecuted them,
  Not without tears of mine were their laments;

And all the while that I on Earth remained,
  Them I befriended, and their upright customs
  Made me disparage all the other sects.

And ere I led the Greeks unto the rivers
  Of Thebes, in poetry, I was baptized,
  But out of fear was covertly a Christian,

For a long time professing paganism;
  And this lukewarmness caused me the fourth circle
  To circuit round more than four centuries.

Thou, therefore, who hast raised the covering
  That hid from me whatever good I speak of,
  While in ascending we have time to spare,

Tell me, in what place is our friend Terentius,
  Caecilius, Plautus, Varro, if thou knowest;
  Tell me if they are damned, and in what alley."

"These, Persius and myself, and others many,"
  Replied my Leader, "with that Grecian are
  Whom more than all the rest the Muses suckled,

In the first circle of the prison blind;
  Ofttimes we of the mountain hold discourse
  Which has our nurses ever with itself.

Euripides is with us, Antiphon,
  Simonides, Agatho, and many other
  Greeks who of old their brows with laurel decked.

There some of thine own people may be seen,
  Antigone, Deiphile and Argia,
  And there Ismene mournful as of old.

There she is seen who pointed out Langia;
  There is Tiresias' daughter, and there Thetis,
  And there Deidamia with her sisters."

Silent already were the poets both,
  Attent once more in looking round about,
  From the ascent and from the walls released;

And four handmaidens of the day already
  Were left behind, and at the pole the fifth
  Was pointing upward still its burning horn,

What time my Guide: "I think that tow'rds the edge
  Our dexter shoulders it behoves us turn,
  Circling the mount as we are wont to do."

Thus in that region custom was our ensign;
  And we resumed our way with less suspicion
  For the assenting of that worthy soul

They in advance went on, and I alone
  Behind them, and I listened to their speech,
  Which gave me lessons in the art of song.

But soon their sweet discourses interrupted
  A tree which midway in the road we found,
  With apples sweet and grateful to the smell.

And even as a fir-tree tapers upward
  From bough to bough, so downwardly did that;
  I think in order that no one might climb it.

On that side where our pathway was enclosed
  Fell from the lofty rock a limpid water,
  And spread itself abroad upon the leaves.

The Poets twain unto the tree drew near,
  And from among the foliage a voice
  Cried: "Of this food ye shall have scarcity."

Then said: "More thoughtful Mary was of making
  The marriage feast complete and honourable,
  Than of her mouth which now for you responds;

And for their drink the ancient Roman women
  With water were content; and Daniel
  Disparaged food, and understanding won.

The primal age was beautiful as gold;
  Acorns it made with hunger savorous,
  And nectar every rivulet with thirst.

Honey and locusts were the aliments
  That fed the Baptist in the wilderness;
  Whence he is glorious, and so magnified

As by the Evangel is revealed to you."

Canto XXIII

Near the tree, the three poets hear Labia Mea, Domine *before being overtaken by a group of former Gluttons, now starved spirits. Dante recognizes Forese Donati, his former boon companion, by his voice as the wasted face is unfamiliar to him. The pilgrim expresses great surprise at not seeing his friend detained in Ante-Purgatory among the Indolent – after all, he was a late repentant and recently deceased. Forese admits his purgation has been greatly accelerated by his devoted wife Nella's incessant prayers and attacks contemporary Florentine women for their extravagance. Dante explains the reason for his journey.*

The while among the verdant leaves mine eyes
  I riveted, as he is wont to do
  Who wastes his life pursuing little birds,

My more than Father said unto me: "Son,
  Come now; because the time that is ordained us
  More usefully should be apportioned out."

I turned my face and no less soon my steps
  Unto the Sages, who were speaking so
  They made the going of no cost to me;

And lo! were heard a song and a lament,
  "*Labia mea, Domine,*" in fashion
  Such that delight and dolence it brought forth.

"O my sweet Father, what is this I hear?"
  Began I; and he answered: "Shades that go
  Perhaps the knot unloosing of their debt."

In the same way that thoughtful pilgrims do,
  Who, unknown people on the road o'ertaking,
  Turn themselves round to them, and do not stop,

Even thus, behind us with a swifter motion
  Coming and passing onward, gazed upon us
  A crowd of spirits silent and devout.

Each in his eyes was dark and cavernous,
  Pallid in face, and so emaciate
  That from the bones the skin did shape itself.

I do not think that so to merest rind
  Could Erisichthon have been withered up
  By famine, when most fear he had of it.

Thinking within myself I said: "Behold,
  This is the folk who lost Jerusalem,
  When Mary made a prey of her own son."

Their sockets were like rings without the gems;
  Whoever in the face of men reads 'omo'
  Might well in these have recognised the 'm.'

Who would believe the odour of an apple,
  Begetting longing, could consume them so,
  And that of water, without knowing how?

I still was wondering what so famished them,
  For the occasion not yet manifest
  Of their emaciation and sad squalor;

And lo! from out the hollow of his head
  His eyes a shade turned on me, and looked keenly;
  Then cried aloud: "What grace to me is this?"

Never should I have known him by his look;
  But in his voice was evident to me
  That which his aspect had suppressed within it.

This spark within me wholly re-enkindled
  My recognition of his altered face,
  And I recalled the features of Forese.

"Ah, do not look at this dry leprosy,"
  Entreated he, "which doth my skin discolour,
  Nor at default of flesh that I may have;

But tell me truth of thee, and who are those
  Two souls, that yonder make for thee an escort;
  Do not delay in speaking unto me."

"That face of thine, which dead I once bewept,
  Gives me for weeping now no lesser grief,"
  I answered him, "beholding it so changed!

But tell me, for God's sake, what thus denudes you?
  Make me not speak while I am marvelling,
  For ill speaks he who's full of other longings."

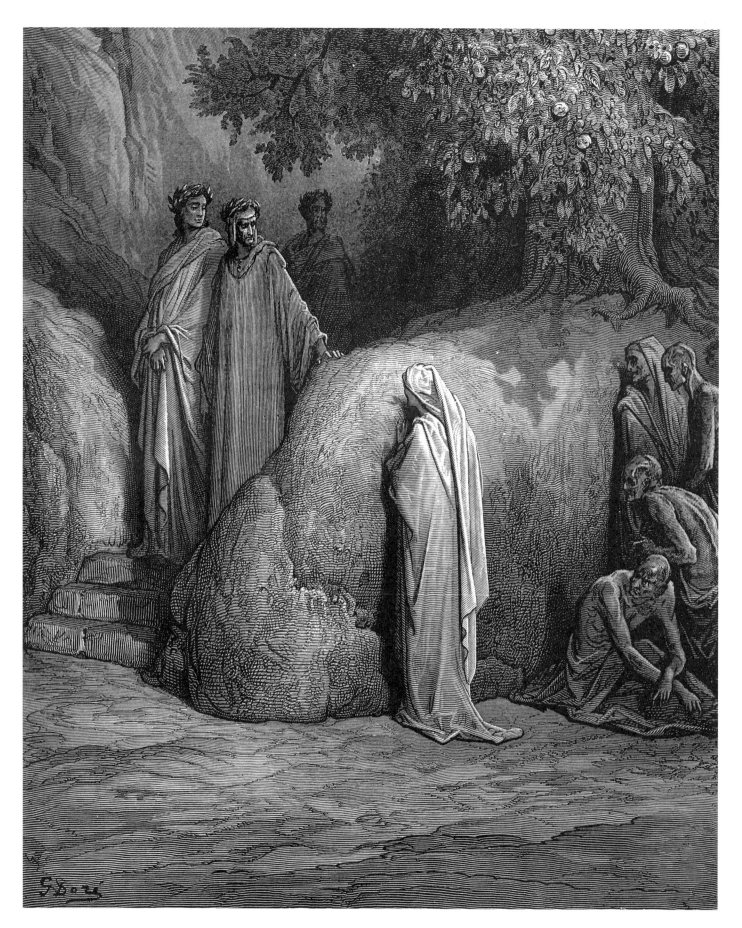

"Ah, do not look at this dry leprosy," / Entreated he, "which doth my skin discolour, /
Nor at default of flesh that I may have;"

Purg. XXIII, lines 49–51

And he to me: "From the eternal council
  Falls power into the water and the tree
  Behind us left, whereby I grow so thin.

All of this people who lamenting sing,
  For following beyond measure appetite
  In hunger and thirst are here re-sanctified.

Desire to eat and drink enkindles in us
  The scent that issues from the apple-tree,
  And from the spray that sprinkles o'er the verdure;

And not a single time alone, this ground
  Encompassing, is refreshed our pain,—
  I say our pain, and ought to say our solace,—

For the same wish doth lead us to the tree
  Which led the Christ rejoicing to say '*Eli*,'
  When with his veins he liberated us."

And I to him: "Forese, from that day
  When for a better life thou changedst worlds,
  Up to this time five years have not rolled round.

If sooner were the power exhausted in thee
  Of sinning more, than thee the hour surprised
  Of that good sorrow which to God reweds us,

How hast thou come up hitherward already?
  I thought to find thee down there underneath,
  Where time for time doth restitution make."

And he to me: "Thus speedily has led me
  To drink of the sweet wormwood of these torments,
  My Nella with her overflowing tears;

She with her prayers devout and with her sighs
  Has drawn me from the coast where one awaits,
  And from the other circles set me free.

So much more dear and pleasing is to God
  My little widow, whom so much I loved,
  As in good works she is the more alone;

For the Barbagia of Sardinia
  By far more modest in its women is
  Than the Barbagia I have left her in.

O brother sweet, what wilt thou have me say?
  A future time is in my sight already,
  To which this hour will not be very old,

When from the pulpit shall be interdicted
  To the unblushing womankind of Florence
  To go about displaying breast and paps.

What savages were e'er, what Saracens,
  Who stood in need, to make them covered go,
  Of spiritual or other discipline?

But if the shameless women were assured
  Of what swift Heaven prepares for them, already
  Wide open would they have their mouths to howl;

For if my foresight here deceive me not,
  They shall be sad ere he has bearded cheeks
  Who now is hushed to sleep with lullaby.

O brother, now no longer hide thee from me;
  See that not only I, but all these people
  Are gazing there, where thou dost veil the sun."

Whence I to him: "If thou bring back to mind
  What thou with me hast been and I with thee,
  The present memory will be grievous still.

Out of that life he turned me back who goes
  In front of me, two days agone when round
  The sister of him yonder showed herself,"

And to the sun I pointed. "Through the deep
  Night of the truly dead has this one led me,
  With this true flesh, that follows after him.

Thence his encouragements have led me up,
  Ascending and still circling round the mount
  That you doth straighten, whom the world made
                       crooked.

He says that he will bear me company,
  Till I shall be where Beatrice will be;
  There it behoves me to remain without him.

This is Virgilius, who thus says to me,"
  And him I pointed at; "the other is
  That shade for whom just now shook every slope

Your realm, that from itself discharges him."

Canto XXIV

*Forese rejoices that his sister, Piccarda, is in Heaven and points to Bonagiunta of
Lucca, a thirteenth-century poet. Dante and Bonagiunta discuss the state of poetry and
the Florentine school's* dolce stil nuovo *(sweet new style), which conceives of Love as a
power of divine origin, devoid of the sensual elements of courtly love. At the second
tree, a voice rehearses examples from the Bridle of Gluttony. The Angel of Temperance
wipes off the sixth P, utters the benediction, "Blessed Are They Who Hunger After
Righteousness" and shows the way to the next cornice by the Pass of Pardon.*

Nor speech the going, nor the going that
  Slackened; but talking we went bravely on,
  Even as a vessel urged by a good wind.

And shadows, that appeared things doubly dead,
  From out the sepulchres of their eyes betrayed
  Wonder at me, aware that I was living.

And I, continuing my colloquy,
  Said: "Peradventure he goes up more slowly
  Than he would do, for other people's sake.

But tell me, if thou knowest, where is Piccarda;
  Tell me if any one of note I see
  Among this folk that gazes at me so."

"My sister, who, 'twixt beautiful and good,
  I know not which was more, triumphs rejoicing
  Already in her crown on high Olympus."

So said he first, and then: "'Tis not forbidden
  To name each other here, so milked away
  Is our resemblance by our dieting.

This," pointing with his finger, "is Bonagiunta,
  Bonagiunta, of Lucca; and that face
  Beyond him there, more peaked than the others,

Has held the holy Church within his arms;
  From Tours was he, and purges by his fasting
  Bolsena's eels and the Vernaccia wine."

He named me many others one by one;
  And all contented seemed at being named,
  So that for this I saw not one dark look.

I saw for hunger bite the empty air
  Ubaldin dalla Pila, and Boniface,
  Who with his crook had pastured many people.

I saw Messer Marchese, who had leisure
  Once at Forli for drinking with less dryness,
  And he was one who ne'er felt satisfied.

But as he does who scans, and then doth prize
  One more than others, did I him of Lucca,
  Who seemed to take most cognizance of me.

He murmured, and I know not what Gentucca
  From that place heard I, where he felt the wound
  Of justice, that doth macerate them so.

"O soul," I said, "that seemest so desirous
  To speak with me, do so that I may hear thee,
  And with thy speech appease thyself and me."

"A maid is born, and wears not yet the veil,"
  Began he, "who to thee shall pleasant make
  My city, howsoever men may blame it.

Thou shalt go on thy way with this prevision;
  If by my murmuring thou hast been deceived,
  True things hereafter will declare it to thee.

But say if him I here behold, who forth
  Evoked the new-invented rhymes, beginning,
  'Ladies, that have intelligence of love?'"

And I to him: "One am I, who, whenever
  Love doth inspire me, note, and in that measure
  Which he within me dictates, singing go."

And shadows, that appeared things doubly dead, / From out the sepulchres of their eyes
betrayed / Wonder at me, aware that I was living.

Purg. XXIV, lines 4–6

"O brother, now I see," he said, "the knot
  Which me, the Notary, and Guittone held
  Short of the sweet new style that now I hear.

I do perceive full clearly how your pens
  Go closely following after him who dictates,
  Which with our own forsooth came not to pass;

And he who sets himself to go beyond,
  No difference sees from one style to another;"
  And as if satisfied, he held his peace.

Even as the birds, that winter tow'rds the Nile,
  Sometimes into a phalanx form themselves,
  Then fly in greater haste, and go in file;

In such wise all the people who were there,
  Turning their faces, hurried on their steps,
  Both by their leanness and their wishes light.

And as a man, who weary is with trotting,
  Lets his companions onward go, and walks,
  Until he vents the panting of his chest;

So did Forese let the holy flock
  Pass by, and came with me behind it, saying,
  "When will it be that I again shall see thee?"

"How long," I answered, "I may live, I know not;
  Yet my return will not so speedy be,
  But I shall sooner in desire arrive;

Because the place where I was set to live
  From day to day of good is more depleted,
  And unto dismal ruin seems ordained."

"Now go," he said, "for him most guilty of it
  At a beast's tail behold I dragged along
  Towards the valley where is no repentance.

Faster at every step the beast is going,
  Increasing evermore until it smites him,
  And leaves the body vilely mutilated.

Not long those wheels shall turn," and he uplifted
  His eyes to heaven, "ere shall be clear to thee
  That which my speech no farther can declare.

Now stay behind; because the time so precious
  Is in this kingdom, that I lose too much
  By coming onward thus abreast with thee."

As sometimes issues forth upon a gallop
  A cavalier from out a troop that ride,
  And seeks the honour of the first encounter,

So he with greater strides departed from us;
  And on the road remained I with those two,
  Who were such mighty marshals of the world.

And when before us he had gone so far
  Mine eyes became to him such pursuivants
  As was my understanding to his words,

Appeared to me with laden and living boughs
  Another apple-tree, and not far distant,
  From having but just then turned thitherward.

People I saw beneath it lift their hands,
  And cry I know not what towards the leaves,
  Like little children eager and deluded,

Who pray, and he they pray to doth not answer,
  But, to make very keen their appetite,
  Holds their desire aloft, and hides it not.

Then they departed as if undeceived;
  And now we came unto the mighty tree
  Which prayers and tears so manifold refuses.

"Pass farther onward without drawing near;
  The tree of which Eve ate is higher up,
  And out of that one has this tree been raised."

Thus said I know not who among the branches;
  Whereat Virgilius, Statius, and myself
  Went crowding forward on the side that rises.

"Be mindful," said he, "of the accursed ones
  Formed of the cloud-rack, who inebriate
  Combated Theseus with their double breasts;

And of the Jews who showed them soft in drinking,
  Whence Gideon would not have them for
                                    companions
  When he tow'rds Midian the hills descended."

Thus, closely pressed to one of the two borders,
  On passed we, hearing sins of gluttony,
  Followed forsooth by miserable gains;

Then set at large upon the lonely road,
  A thousand steps and more we onward went,
  In contemplation, each without a word.

People I saw beneath it lift their hands, / And cry I know not what towards the leaves,

Purg. XXIV, lines 106–107

"What go ye thinking thus, ye three alone?"
  Said suddenly a voice, whereat I started
  As terrified and timid beasts are wont.

I raised my head to see who this might be,
  And never in a furnace was there seen
  Metals or glass so lucent and so red

As one I saw who said: "If it may please you
  To mount aloft, here it behoves you turn;
  This way goes he who goeth after peace."

His aspect had bereft me of my sight,
  So that I turned me back unto my Teachers,
  Like one who goeth as his hearing guides him.

And as, the harbinger of early dawn,
  The air of May doth move and breathe out
                                          fragrance,
  Impregnate all with herbage and with flowers,

So did I feel a breeze strike in the midst
  My front, and felt the moving of the plumes
  That breathed around an odour of ambrosia;

And heard it said: "Blessed are they whom grace
  So much illumines, that the love of taste
  Excites not in their breasts too great desire,

Hungering at all times so far as is just."

Canto XXV

As the three poets venture up the steep and rocky stairs, Dante enquires how the
penitent can look so emaciated whilst lacking a physical form. Statius embarks
on a scientific and theological lecture about the origin of the rational human soul
and its relation to the material body, before and after death. The trio come to a
wall of fire, the Seventh Cornice, and hear Summae Deus Clementiae *coming*
from the blaze that is purifying the penitent Lustful. The spirits cry out
examples of virgin Chastity, the opposing virtue, and then praise chasteness
within marriage.

Now was it the ascent no hindrance brooked,
  Because the sun had his meridian circle
  To Taurus left, and night to Scorpio;

Wherefore as doth a man who tarries not,
  But goes his way, whate'er to him appear,
  If of necessity the sting transfix him,

In this wise did we enter through the gap,
  Taking the stairway, one before the other,
  Which by its narrowness divides the climbers.

And as the little stork that lifts its wing
  With a desire to fly, and does not venture
  To leave the nest, and lets it downward droop,

Even such was I, with the desire of asking
  Kindled and quenched, unto the motion coming
  He makes who doth address himself to speak.

Not for our pace, though rapid it might be,
  My father sweet forbore, but said: "Let fly
  The bow of speech thou to the barb hast drawn."

With confidence I opened then my mouth,
  And I began: "How can one meagre grow
  There where the need of nutriment applies not?"

"If thou wouldst call to mind how Meleager
  Was wasted by the wasting of a brand,
  This would not," said he, "be to thee so sour;

And wouldst thou think how at each tremulous
                                    motion
  Trembles within a mirror your own image;
  That which seems hard would mellow seem to thee.

But that thou mayst content thee in thy wish
  Lo Statius here; and him I call and pray
  He now will be the healer of thy wounds."

"If I unfold to him the eternal vengeance,"
  Responded Statius, "where thou present art,
  Be my excuse that I can naught deny thee."

Then he began: "Son, if these words of mine
  Thy mind doth contemplate and doth receive,
  They'll be thy light unto the How thou sayest.

The perfect blood, which never is drunk up
  Into the thirsty veins, and which remaineth
  Like food that from the table thou removest,

Takes in the heart for all the human members
  Virtue informative, as being that
  Which to be changed to them goes through the veins

Again digest, descends it where 'tis better
  Silent to be than say; and then drops thence
  Upon another's blood in natural vase.

There one together with the other mingles,
  One to be passive meant, the other active
  By reason of the perfect place it springs from;

And being conjoined, begins to operate,
  Coagulating first, then vivifying
  What for its matter it had made consistent.

The active virtue, being made a soul
  As of a plant, (in so far different,
  This on the way is, that arrived already,)

Then works so much, that now it moves and feels
  Like a sea-fungus, and then undertakes
  To organize the powers whose seed it is.

Now, Son, dilates and now distends itself
  The virtue from the generator's heart,
  Where nature is intent on all the members.

But how from animal it man becomes
  Thou dost not see as yet; this is a point
  Which made a wiser man than thou once err

So far, that in his doctrine separate
  He made the soul from possible intellect,
  For he no organ saw by this assumed.

Open thy breast unto the truth that's coming,
  And know that, just as soon as in the foetus
  The articulation of the brain is perfect,

The primal Motor turns to it well pleased
  At so great art of nature, and inspires
  A spirit new with virtue all replete,

Which what it finds there active doth attract
  Into its substance, and becomes one soul,
  Which lives, and feels, and on itself revolves.

And that thou less may wonder at my word,
  Behold the sun's heat, which becometh wine,
  Joined to the juice that from the vine distils.

Whenever Lachesis has no more thread,
  It separates from the flesh, and virtually
  Bears with itself the human and divine;

The other faculties are voiceless all;
  The memory, the intelligence, and the will
  In action far more vigorous than before.

Without a pause it falleth of itself
  In marvellous way on one shore or the other;
  There of its roads it first is cognizant.

Soon as the place there circumscribeth it,
  The virtue informative rays round about,
  As, and as much as, in the living members.

And even as the air, when full of rain,
  By alien rays that are therein reflected,
  With divers colours shows itself adorned,

So there the neighbouring air doth shape itself
  Into that form which doth impress upon it
  Virtually the soul that has stood still.

And then in manner of the little flame,
  Which followeth the fire where'er it shifts,
  After the spirit followeth its new form.

Since afterwards it takes from this its semblance,
  It is called shade; and thence it organizes
  Thereafter every sense, even to the sight.

Thence is it that we speak, and thence we laugh;
  Thence is it that we form the tears and sighs,
  That on the mountain thou mayhap hast heard.

According as impress us our desires
  And other affections, so the shade is shaped,
  And this is cause of what thou wonderest at."

And now unto the last of all the circles
  Had we arrived, and to the right hand turned,
  And were attentive to another care.

There the embankment shoots forth flames of fire,
  And upward doth the cornice breathe a blast
  That drives them back, and from itself sequesters.

Hence we must needs go on the open side,
  And one by one; and I did fear the fire
  On this side, and on that the falling down.

My Leader said: "Along this place one ought
  To keep upon the eyes a tightened rein,
  Seeing that one so easily might err."

"*Summae Deus clementiae*," in the bosom
  Of the great burning chanted then I heard,
  Which made me no less eager to turn round;

And spirits saw I walking through the flame;
  Wherefore I looked, to my own steps and theirs
  Apportioning my sight from time to time.

After the close which to that hymn is made,
  Aloud they shouted, "*Virum non cognosco*;"
  Then recommenced the hymn with voices low.

This also ended, cried they: "To the wood
  Diana ran, and drove forth Helice
  Therefrom, who had of Venus felt the poison."

Then to their song returned they; then the wives
  They shouted, and the husbands who were chaste.
  As virtue and the marriage vow imposes.

And I believe that them this mode suffices,
  For all the time the fire is burning them;
  With such care is it needful, and such food,

That the last wound of all should be closed up.

There the embankment shoots forth flames of fire, / And upward doth the cornice breathe a
blast / That drives them back, and from itself sequesters.

Purg. XXV, lines 112–114

"*Summae Deus clementiae,*" in the bosom / Of the great burning chanted then I heard, /
Which made me no less eager to turn round;

Purg. XXV, lines 121–123

And spirits saw I walking through the flame; / Wherefore I looked, to my own steps and theirs / Apportioning my sight from time to time.

Purg. XXV, lines 124–126

Canto XXVI

*In the Seventh Cornice, the fact that Dante is alive excites a great deal of interest. He
starts talking to one of the souls but they are interrupted. Two groups, the naturally
and unnaturally Lustful, exchange embraces and then each group calls out 'Sodom
and Gomorrah' while the 'hermaphrodites' refer to the bestial example of Pasiphae.
When the soul identifies himself as Guido Guinicelli, Dante praises him as the
father of the* dolce stil nuovo. *He in turn yields to Arnaut Daniel, who speaks in his
native Provençal.*

While on the brink thus one before the other
  We went upon our way, oft the good Master
  Said: "Take thou heed! suffice it that I warn thee."

On the right shoulder smote me now the sun,
  That, raying out, already the whole west
  Changed from its azure aspect into white.

And with my shadow did I make the flame
  Appear more red; and even to such a sign
  Shades saw I many, as they went, give heed.

This was the cause that gave them a beginning
  To speak of me; and to themselves began they
  To say: "That seems not a factitious body!"

Then towards me, as far as they could come,
  Came certain of them, always with regard
  Not to step forth where they would not be burned.

"O thou who goest, not from being slower
  But reverent perhaps, behind the others,
  Answer me, who in thirst and fire am burning.

Nor to me only is thine answer needful;
  For all of these have greater thirst for it
  Than for cold water Ethiop or Indian.

Tell us how is it that thou makest thyself
  A wall unto the sun, as if thou hadst not
  Entered as yet into the net of death."

Thus one of them addressed me, and I straight
  Should have revealed myself, were I not bent
  On other novelty that then appeared.

For through the middle of the burning road
  There came a people face to face with these,
  Which held me in suspense with gazing at them.

There see I hastening upon either side
  Each of the shades, and kissing one another
  Without a pause, content with brief salute.

Thus in the middle of their brown battalions
  Muzzle to muzzle one ant meets another
  Perchance to spy their journey or their fortune.

No sooner is the friendly greeting ended,
  Or ever the first footstep passes onward,
  Each one endeavours to outcry the other;

The new-come people: "Sodom and Gomorrah!"
  The rest: "Into the cow Pasiphae enters,
  So that the bull unto her lust may run!"

Then as the cranes, that to Riphaean mountains
  Might fly in part, and part towards the sands,
  These of the frost, those of the sun avoidant,

One folk is going, and the other coming,
  And weeping they return to their first songs,
  And to the cry that most befitteth them;

And close to me approached, even as before,
  The very same who had entreated me,
  Attent to listen in their countenance.

I, who their inclination twice had seen,
  Began: "O souls secure in the possession,
  Whene'er it may be, of a state of peace,

Neither unripe nor ripened have remained
  My members upon Earth, but here are with me
  With their own blood and their articulations.

I go up here to be no longer blind;
  A Lady is above, who wins this grace,
  Whereby the mortal through your world I bring.

But as your greatest longing satisfied
  May soon become, so that the Heaven may house you
  Which full of love is, and most amply spreads,

Tell me, that I again in books may write it,
  Who are you, and what is that multitude
  Which goes upon its way behind your backs?"

Not otherwise with wonder is bewildered
  The mountaineer, and staring round is dumb,
  When rough and rustic to the town he goes,

Than every shade became in its appearance;
  But when they of their stupor were disburdened,
  Which in high hearts is quickly quieted,

"Blessed be thou, who of our border-lands,"
  He recommenced who first had questioned us,
  "Experience freightest for a better life.

The folk that comes not with us have offended
  In that for which once Caesar, triumphing,
  Heard himself called in contumely, 'Queen.'

Therefore they separate, exclaiming, 'Sodom!'
  Themselves reproving, even as thou hast heard,
  And add unto their burning by their shame.

Our own transgression was hermaphrodite;
  But because we observed not human law,
  Following like unto beasts our appetite,

In our opprobrium by us is read,
  When we part company, the name of her
  Who bestialized herself in bestial wood.

Now knowest thou our acts, and what our crime was;
  Wouldst thou perchance by name know who we are,
  There is not time to tell, nor could I do it.

Thy wish to know me shall in sooth be granted;
  I'm Guido Guinicelli, and now purge me,
  Having repented ere the hour extreme."

The same that in the sadness of Lycurgus
  Two sons became, their mother re-beholding,
  Such I became, but rise not to such height,

The moment I heard name himself the father
  Of me and of my betters, who had ever
  Practised the sweet and gracious rhymes of love;

And without speech and hearing thoughtfully
  For a long time I went, beholding him,
  Nor for the fire did I approach him nearer.

When I was fed with looking, utterly
  Myself I offered ready for his service,
  With affirmation that compels belief.

And he to me: "Thou leavest footprints such
  In me, from what I hear, and so distinct,
  Lethe cannot efface them, nor make dim.

But if thy words just now the truth have sworn,
  Tell me what is the cause why thou displayest
  In word and look that dear thou holdest me?"

And I to him: "Those dulcet lays of yours
  Which, long as shall endure our modern fashion,
  Shall make for ever dear their very ink!"

"O brother," said he, "he whom I point out,"
  And here he pointed at a spirit in front,
  "Was of the mother tongue a better smith.

Verses of love and proses of romance,
  He mastered all; and let the idiots talk,
  Who think the Lemosin surpasses him.

To clamour more than truth they turn their faces,
  And in this way establish their opinion,
  Ere art or reason has by them been heard.

Thus many ancients with Guittone did,
  From cry to cry still giving him applause,
  Until the truth has conquered with most persons.

Now, if thou hast such ample privilege
  'Tis granted thee to go unto the cloister
  Wherein is Christ the abbot of the college,

To him repeat for me a Paternoster,
  So far as needful to us of this world,
  Where power of sinning is no longer ours."

Then, to give place perchance to one behind,
  Whom he had near, he vanished in the fire
  As fish in water going to the bottom.

I moved a little tow'rds him pointed out,
  And said that to his name my own desire
  An honourable place was making ready.

He of his own free will began to say:
  '*Tan m' abellis vostre cortes deman,*
  Que jeu nom' puesc ni vueill a vos cobrire;

Jeu sui Arnaut, que plor e vai chantan;
  Consiros vei la passada folor,
  E vei jauzen lo jorn qu' esper denan.

Ara vus prec per aquella valor,
  Que vus condus al som de la scalina,
  *Sovenga vus a temprar ma dolor.'**

Then hid him in the fire that purifies them.

* *So pleases me your courteous demand,*
  I cannot and I will not hide me from you.
I am Arnaut, who weep and singing go;
  Contrite I see the folly of the past,
  And joyous see the hoped-for day before me.
Therefore do I implore you, by that power
  Which guides you to the summit of the stairs,
  Be mindful to assuage my suffering!

Canto XXVII

The three poets are met by the Angel of Chastity who chants the beatitude Beati mundo corde *and tells them that they must first pass through the flames. Dante is filled with terror, but Virgil persuades him to go on. He emerges to the words "Venite, benedicti Patris mei" and an angel urges them to press on while it is light. When night falls, the trio stops to rest. Dante dreams of Leah (the Active Life) and Rachel (the Contemplative Life) – complimentary halves of the Christian whole. On gaining the final stair and reaching the Earthly Paradise, Virgil crowns Dante master of himself.*

As when he vibrates forth his earliest rays,
  In regions where his Maker shed his blood,
  (The Ebro falling under lofty Libra,

And waters in the Ganges burnt with noon,)
  So stood the Sun; hence was the day departing,
  When the glad Angel of God appeared to us.

Outside the flame he stood upon the verge,
  And chanted forth, "*Beati mundo corde,*"
  In voice by far more living than our own.

Then: "No one farther goes, souls sanctified,
  If first the fire bite not; within it enter,
  And be not deaf unto the song beyond."

When we were close beside him thus he said;
  Wherefore e'en such became I, when I heard him,
  As he is who is put into the grave.

Upon my clasped hands I straightened me,
  Scanning the fire, and vividly recalling
  The human bodies I had once seen burned.

Towards me turned themselves my good Conductors,
  And unto me Virgilius said: "My son,
  Here may indeed be torment, but not death.

Remember thee, remember! and if I
  On Geryon have safely guided thee,
  What shall I do now I am nearer God?

Believe for certain, shouldst thou stand a full
 Millennium in the bosom of this flame,
 It could not make thee bald a single hair.

And if perchance thou think that I deceive thee,
 Draw near to it, and put it to the proof
 With thine own hands upon thy garment's hem.

Now lay aside, now lay aside all fear,
 Turn hitherward, and onward come securely;"
 And I still motionless, and 'gainst my conscience!

Seeing me stand still motionless and stubborn,
 Somewhat disturbed he said: "Now look thou, Son,
 'Twixt Beatrice and thee there is this wall."

As at the name of Thisbe oped his lids
 The dying Pyramus, and gazed upon her,
 What time the mulberry became vermilion,

Even thus, my obduracy being softened,
 I turned to my wise Guide, hearing the name
 That in my memory evermore is welling.

Whereat he wagged his head, and said: "How now?
 Shall we stay on this side?" then smiled as one
 Does at a child who's vanquished by an apple.

Then into the fire in front of me he entered,
 Beseeching Statius to come after me,
 Who a long way before divided us.

When I was in it, into molten glass
 I would have cast me to refresh myself,
 So without measure was the burning there!

And my sweet Father, to encourage me,
 Discoursing still of Beatrice went on,
 Saying: "Her eyes I seem to see already!"

A voice, that on the other side was singing,
 Directed us, and we, attent alone
 On that, came forth where the ascent began.

"*Venite, benedicti Patris mei,*"
 Sounded within a splendour, which was there
 Such it o'ercame me, and I could not look.

"The sun departs," it added, "and night cometh;
 Tarry ye not, but onward urge your steps,
 So long as yet the west becomes not dark."

Straight forward through the rock the path ascended
 In such a way that I cut off the rays
 Before me of the sun, that now was low.

And of few stairs we yet had made assay,
 Ere by the vanished shadow the sun's setting
 Behind us we perceived, I and my Sages.

And ere in all its parts immeasurable
 The horizon of one aspect had become,
 And Night her boundless dispensation held,

Each of us of a stair had made his bed;
 Because the nature of the mount took from us
 The power of climbing, more than the delight.

Even as in ruminating passive grow
 The goats, who have been swift and venturesome
 Upon the mountain-tops ere they were fed,

Hushed in the shadow, while the sun is hot,
 Watched by the herdsman, who upon his staff
 Is leaning, and in leaning tendeth them;

And as the shepherd, lodging out of doors,
 Passes the night beside his quiet flock,
 Watching that no wild beast may scatter it,

Such at that hour were we, all three of us,
 I like the goat, and like the herdsmen they,
 Begirt on this side and on that by rocks.

Little could there be seen of things without;
 But through that little I beheld the stars
 More luminous and larger than their wont.

Thus ruminating, and beholding these,
 Sleep seized upon me,—sleep, that oftentimes
 Before a deed is done has tidings of it.

It was the hour, I think, when from the East
 First on the mountain Citherea beamed,
 Who with the fire of love seems always burning;

Youthful and beautiful in dreams methought
 I saw a lady walking in a meadow,
 Gathering flowers; and singing she was saying:

"Know whosoever may my name demand
 That I am Leah, and go moving round
 My beauteous hands to make myself a garland.

Youthful and beautiful in dreams methought / I saw a lady walking in a meadow, /
Gathering flowers;

Purg. XXVII, lines 97–99

To please me at the mirror, here I deck me,
  But never does my sister Rachel leave
  Her looking-glass, and sitteth all day long.

To see her beauteous eyes as eager is she,
  As I am to adorn me with my hands;
  Her, seeing, and me, doing satisfies."

And now before the antelucan splendours
  That unto pilgrims the more grateful rise,
  As, home-returning, less remote they lodge,

The darkness fled away on every side,
  And slumber with it; whereupon I rose,
  Seeing already the great Masters risen.

"That apple sweet, which through so many branches
  The care of mortals goeth in pursuit of,
  To-day shall put in peace thy hungerings."

Speaking to me, Virgilius of such words
  As these made use; and never were there guerdons
  That could in pleasantness compare with these.

Such longing upon longing came upon me
  To be above, that at each step thereafter
  For flight I felt in me the pinions growing.

When underneath us was the stairway all
  Run o'er, and we were on the highest step,
  Virgilius fastened upon me his eyes,

And said: "The temporal fire and the eternal,
  Son, thou hast seen, and to a place art come
  Where of myself no farther I discern.

By intellect and art I here have brought thee;
  Take thine own pleasure for thy guide henceforth;
  Beyond the steep ways and the narrow art thou.

Behold the sun, that shines upon thy forehead;
  Behold the grass, the flowerets, and the shrubs
  Which of itself alone this land produces.

Until rejoicing come the beauteous eyes
  Which weeping caused me to come unto thee,
  Thou canst sit down, and thou canst walk among them.

Expect no more or word or sign from me;
  Free and upright and sound is thy free-will,
  And error were it not to do its bidding;

Thee o'er thyself I therefore crown and mitre!"

Canto XXVIII

Dante enters the Sacred Wood and finds Matilda picking flowers by a stream. She explains that Adam and Eve were created in the Garden of Eden and that the gentle breeze is caused by the motion of the nine heavenly spheres upon the Earth. This Earthly Paradise represents the recovery of the original innocence that poets and men have so longingly recalled across the ages as if from memory. The water present is not fed by rain but by the twin fountains of Lethe, the river of Oblivion, and Eunoe, the river of Good Remembrance.

Eager already to search in and round
  The heavenly forest, dense and living-green,
  Which tempered to the eyes the new-born day,

Withouten more delay I left the bank,
  Taking the level country slowly, slowly
  Over the soil that everywhere breathes fragrance.

A softly-breathing air, that no mutation
　　Had in itself, upon the forehead smote me
　　No heavier blow than of a gentle wind,

Whereat the branches, lightly tremulous,
　　Did all of them bow downward toward that side
　　Where its first shadow casts the Holy Mountain;

Yet not from their upright direction swayed,
　　So that the little birds upon their tops
　　Should leave the practice of each art of theirs;

But with full ravishment the hours of prime,
　　Singing, received they in the midst of leaves,
　　That ever bore a burden to their rhymes,

Such as from branch to branch goes gathering on
　　Through the pine forest on the shore of Chiassi,
　　When Eolus unlooses the Sirocco.

Already my slow steps had carried me
　　Into the ancient wood so far, that I
　　Could not perceive where I had entered it.

And lo! my further course a stream cut off,
　　Which tow'rd the left hand with its little waves
　　Bent down the grass that on its margin sprang.

All waters that on Earth most limpid are
　　Would seem to have within themselves some mixture
　　Compared with that which nothing doth conceal,

Although it moves on with a brown, brown current
　　Under the shade perpetual, that never
　　Ray of the sun lets in, nor of the moon.

With feet I stayed, and with mine eyes I passed
　　Beyond the rivulet, to look upon
　　The great variety of the fresh may.

And there appeared to me (even as appears
　　Suddenly something that doth turn aside
　　Through very wonder every other thought)

A lady all alone, who went along
　　Singing and culling floweret after floweret,
　　With which her pathway was all painted over.

"Ah, beauteous lady, who in rays of love
　　Dost warm thyself, if I may trust to looks,
　　Which the heart's witnesses are wont to be,

May the desire come unto thee to draw
　　Near to this river's bank," I said to her,
　　"So much that I might hear what thou art singing.

Thou makest me remember where and what
　　Proserpina that moment was when lost
　　Her mother her, and she herself the Spring."

As turns herself, with feet together pressed
　　And to the ground, a lady who is dancing,
　　And hardly puts one foot before the other,

On the vermilion and the yellow flowerets
　　She turned towards me, not in other wise
　　Than maiden who her modest eyes casts down;

And my entreaties made to be content,
　　So near approaching, that the dulcet sound
　　Came unto me together with its meaning

As soon as she was where the grasses are.
　　Bathed by the waters of the beauteous river,
　　To lift her eyes she granted me the boon.

I do not think there shone so great a light
　　Under the lids of Venus, when transfixed
　　By her own son, beyond his usual custom!

Erect upon the other bank she smiled,
　　Bearing full many colours in her hands,
　　Which that high land produces without seed.

Apart three paces did the river make us;
　　But Hellespont, where Xerxes passed across,
　　(A curb still to all human arrogance,)

More hatred from Leander did not suffer
　　For rolling between Sestos and Abydos,
　　Than that from me, because it oped not then.

"Ye are new-comers; and because I smile,"
　　Began she, "peradventure, in this place
　　Elect to human nature for its nest,

Some apprehension keeps you marvelling;
　　But the psalm 'Delectasti' giveth light
　　Which has the power to uncloud your intellect.

And thou who foremost art, and didst entreat me,
　　Speak, if thou wouldst hear more; for I came ready
　　To all thy questionings, as far as needful."

Already my slow steps had carried me / Into the ancient wood so far, that I /
Could not perceive where I had entered it.

Purg. XXVIII, lines 22–24

"The water," said I, "and the forest's sound,
  Are combating within me my new faith
  In something which I heard opposed to this."

Whence she: "I will relate how from its cause
  Proceedeth that which maketh thee to wonder,
  And purge away the cloud that smites upon thee.

The Good Supreme, sole in itself delighting,
  Created man good, and this goodly place
  Gave him as hansel of eternal peace.

By his default short while he sojourned here;
  By his default to weeping and to toil
  He changed his innocent laughter and sweet play.

That the disturbance which below is made
  By exhalations of the land and water,
  (Which far as may be follow after heat,)

Might not upon mankind wage any war,
  This mount ascended tow'rds the heaven so high,
  And is exempt, from there where it is locked.

Now since the universal atmosphere
  Turns in a circuit with the primal motion
  Unless the circle is broken on some side,

Upon this height, that all is disengaged
  In living ether, doth this motion strike
  And make the forest sound, for it is dense;

And so much power the stricken plant possesses
  That with its virtue it impregns the air,
  And this, revolving, scatters it around;

And yonder Earth, according as 'tis worthy
  In self or in its clime, conceives and bears
  Of divers qualities the divers trees;

It should not seem a marvel then on earth,
  This being heard, whenever any plant
  Without seed manifest there taketh root.

And thou must know, this holy table-land
  In which thou art is full of every seed,
  And fruit has in it never gathered there.

The water which thou seest springs not from vein
  Restored by vapour that the cold condenses,
  Like to a stream that gains or loses breath;

But issues from a fountain safe and certain,
  Which by the will of God as much regains
  As it discharges, open on two sides.

Upon this side with virtue it descends,
  Which takes away all memory of sin;
  On that, of every good deed done restores it.

Here Lethe, as upon the other side
  Eunoe, it is called; and worketh not
  If first on either side it be not tasted.

This every other savour doth transcend;
  And notwithstanding slaked so far may be
  Thy thirst, that I reveal to thee no more,

I'll give thee a corollary still in grace,
  Nor think my speech will be to thee less dear
  If it spread out beyond my promise to thee.

Those who in ancient times have feigned in song
  The Age of Gold and its felicity,
  Dreamed of this place perhaps upon Parnassus.

Here was the human race in innocence;
  Here evermore was Spring, and every fruit;
  This is the nectar of which each one speaks."

Then backward did I turn me wholly round
  Unto my Poets, and saw that with a smile
  They had been listening to these closing words;

Then to the beautiful lady turned mine eyes.

Canto XXIX

The first allegorical masque, the triumphant Pageant of the Sacrament, draws near.
A company dressed in white, like a Corpus Christi procession, is carrying seven
candlesticks (the gifts of the Holy Spirit), followed by twenty-four elders crowned with
lilies (the books of the Old Testament) and four winged creatures (the Beasts of the
Apocalypse). Its centrepiece is a chariot pulled by a Griffin (half-eagle/half-lion and, as
such, the union of Christ's divine and human nature) with three damsels (the
Theological Virtues) on the right and four (the Cardinal Virtues) on the left. Behind
everyone is an old man (the Book of the Revelation of Saint John).

Singing like unto an enamoured lady
  She, with the ending of her words, continued:
  "Beati quorum tecta sunt peccata."

And even as Nymphs, that wandered all alone
  Among the sylvan shadows, sedulous
  One to avoid and one to see the sun,

She then against the stream moved onward, going
  Along the bank, and I abreast of her,
  Her little steps with little steps attending.

Between her steps and mine were not a hundred,
  When equally the margins gave a turn,
  In such a way, that to the East I faced.

Nor even thus our way continued far
  Before the lady wholly turned herself
  Unto me, saying, "Brother, look and listen!"

And lo! a sudden lustre ran across
  On every side athwart the spacious forest,
  Such that it made me doubt if it were lightning.

But since the lightning ceases as it comes,
  And that continuing brightened more and more,
  Within my thought I said, "What thing is this?"

And a delicious melody there ran
  Along the luminous air, whence holy zeal
  Made me rebuke the hardihood of Eve;

For there where Earth and heaven obedient were,
  The woman only, and but just created,
  Could not endure to stay 'neath any veil;

Underneath which had she devoutly stayed,
  I sooner should have tasted those delights
  Ineffable, and for a longer time.

While 'mid such manifold first-fruits I walked
  Of the eternal pleasure all enrapt,
  And still solicitous of more delights,

In front of us like an enkindled fire
  Became the air beneath the verdant boughs,
  And the sweet sound as singing now was heard.

O Virgins sacrosanct! if ever hunger,
  Vigils, or cold for you I have endured,
  The occasion spurs me their reward to claim!

Now Helicon must needs pour forth for me,
  And with her choir Urania must assist me,
  To put in verse things difficult to think.

A little farther on, seven trees of gold
  In semblance the long space still intervening
  Between ourselves and them did counterfeit;

But when I had approached so near to them
  The common object, which the sense deceives,
  Lost not by distance any of its marks,

The faculty that lends discourse to reason
  Did apprehend that they were candlesticks,
  And in the voices of the song *"Hosanna!"*

Above them flamed the harness beautiful,
  Far brighter than the moon in the serene
  Of midnight, at the middle of her month.

I turned me round, with admiration filled,
  To good Virgilius, and he answered me
  With visage no less full of wonderment.

Then back I turned my face to those high things,
  Which moved themselves towards us so sedately,
  They had been distanced by new-wedded brides.

The lady chid me: "Why dost thou burn only
  So with affection for the living lights,
  And dost not look at what comes after them?"

Then saw I people, as behind their leaders,
  Coming behind them, garmented in white,
  And such a whiteness never was on Earth.

The water on my left flank was resplendent,
  And back to me reflected my left side,
  E'en as a mirror, if I looked therein.

When I upon my margin had such post
  That nothing but the stream divided us,
  Better to see I gave my steps repose;

And I beheld the flamelets onward go,
  Leaving behind themselves the air depicted,
  And they of trailing pennons had the semblance,

So that it overhead remained distinct
  With sevenfold lists, all of them of the colours
  Whence the sun's bow is made, and Delia's girdle.

These standards to the rearward longer were
  Than was my sight; and, as it seemed to me,
  Ten paces were the outermost apart.

Under so fair a heaven as I describe
  The four and twenty Elders, two by two,
  Came on incoronate with flower-de-luce.

They all of them were singing: "Blessed thou
  Among the daughters of Adam art, and blessed
  For evermore shall be thy loveliness."

After the flowers and other tender grasses
  In front of me upon the other margin
  Were disencumbered of that race elect,

Even as in heaven star followeth after star,
  There came close after them four animals,
  Incoronate each one with verdant leaf.

Plumed with six wings was every one of them,
  The plumage full of eyes; the eyes of Argus
  If they were living would be such as these.

Reader! to trace their forms no more I waste
  My rhymes; for other spendings press me so,
  That I in this cannot be prodigal.

But read Ezekiel, who depicteth them
  As he beheld them from the region cold
  Coming with cloud, with whirlwind, and with fire;

And such as thou shalt find them in his pages,
  Such were they here; saving that in their plumage
  John is with me, and differeth from him.

The interval between these four contained
  A chariot triumphal on two wheels,
  Which by a Griffin's neck came drawn along;

And upward he extended both his wings
  Between the middle list and three and three,
  So that he injured none by cleaving it.

So high they rose that they were lost to sight;
  His limbs were gold, so far as he was bird,
  And white the others with vermilion mingled.

Not only Rome with no such splendid car
  E'er gladdened Africanus, or Augustus,
  But poor to it that of the Sun would be,—

That of the Sun, which swerving was burnt up
  At the importunate orison of Earth,
  When Jove was so mysteriously just.

Three maidens at the right wheel in a circle
  Came onward dancing; one so very red
  That in the fire she hardly had been noted.

The second was as if her flesh and bones
  Had all been fashioned out of emerald;
  The third appeared as snow but newly fallen.

And now they seemed conducted by the white,
  Now by the red, and from the song of her
  The others took their step, or slow or swift.

Upon the left hand four made holiday
  Vested in purple, following the measure
  Of one of them with three eyes in her head.

The four and twenty Elders, two by two, / Came on incoronate with flower-de-luce.

Purg. XXIX, lines 83–84

Came onward dancing; one so very red / That in the fire she hardly had been noted. /
The second was as if her flesh and bones / Had all been fashioned out of emerald; /
The third appeared as snow but newly fallen.

Purg. XXIX, lines 122–126

In rear of all the group here treated of
  Two old men I beheld, unlike in habit,
  But like in gait, each dignified and grave.

One showed himself as one of the disciples
  Of that supreme Hippocrates, whom nature
  Made for the animals she holds most dear;

Contrary care the other manifested,
  With sword so shining and so sharp, it caused
  Terror to me on this side of the river.

Thereafter four I saw of humble aspect,
  And behind all an aged man alone
  Walking in sleep with countenance acute.

And like the foremost company these seven
  Were habited; yet of the flower-de-luce
  No garland round about the head they wore,

But of the rose, and other flowers vermilion;
  At little distance would the sight have sworn
  That all were in a flame above their brows.

And when the car was opposite to me
  Thunder was heard; and all that folk august
  Seemed to have further progress interdicted,

There with the vanward ensigns standing still.

Canto XXX

The Pageant of the Sacrament procession comes to a halt and the elders rush over to the chariot as one hundred angels chant the Benedictus *overhead and toss flowers into the air. Acclaimed by all, the veiled figure of Beatrice suddenly appears on the chariot, symbol and image of the Holy Host and the sacramental principle by which God grants new and eternal life. Dante is overcome by this long-awaited reunion with his beloved and turns to Virgil for reassurance but finds that he is gone. Beatrice scolds Dante for having strayed from the path of Truth and salvation.*

When the Septentrion of the highest heaven
  (Which never either setting knew or rising,
  Nor veil of other cloud than that of sin,

And which made every one therein aware
  Of his own duty, as the lower makes
  Whoever turns the helm to come to port)

Motionless halted, the veracious people,
  That came at first between it and the Griffin,
  Turned themselves to the car, as to their peace.

And one of them, as if by Heaven commissioned,
  Singing, "*Veni, sponsa, de Libano*"
  Shouted three times, and all the others after.

Even as the Blessed at the final summons
  Shall rise up quickened each one from his cavern,
  Uplifting light the reinvested flesh,

So upon that celestial chariot
  A hundred rose '*ad vocem tanti senis,*'
  Ministers and messengers of life eternal.

They all were saying, "*Benedictus qui venis,*"
  And, scattering flowers above and round about,
  "*Manibus o date lilia plenis.*"

Ere now have I beheld, as day began,
  The eastern hemisphere all tinged with rose,
  And the other heaven with fair serene adorned;

And the sun's face, uprising, overshadowed
  So that by tempering influence of vapours
  For a long interval the eye sustained it;

Thus in the bosom of a cloud of flowers
  Which from those hands angelical ascended,
  And downward fell again inside and out,

Over her snow-white veil with olive cinct
  Appeared a lady under a green mantle,
  Vested in colour of the living flame.

And my own spirit, that already now
  So long a time had been, that in her presence
  Trembling with awe it had not stood abashed,

Without more knowledge having by mine eyes,
  Through occult virtue that from her proceeded
  Of ancient love the mighty influence felt.

As soon as on my vision smote the power
  Sublime, that had already pierced me through
  Ere from my boyhood I had yet come forth,

To the left hand I turned with that reliance
  With which the little child runs to his mother,
  When he has fear, or when he is afflicted,

To say unto Virgilius: "Not a drachm
  Of blood remains in me, that does not tremble;
  I know the traces of the ancient flame."

But us Virgilius of himself deprived
  Had left, Virgilius, sweetest of all fathers,
  Virgilius, to whom I for safety gave me:

Nor whatsoever lost the ancient mother
  Availed my cheeks now purified from dew,
  That weeping they should not again be darkened.

"Dante, because Virgilius has departed
  Do not weep yet, do not weep yet awhile;
  For by another sword thou need'st must weep."

E'en as an admiral, who on poop and prow
  Comes to behold the people that are working
  In other ships, and cheers them to well-doing,

Upon the left hand border of the car,
  When at the sound I turned of my own name,
  Which of necessity is here recorded,

I saw the Lady, who erewhile appeared
  Veiled underneath the angelic festival,
  Direct her eyes to me across the river.

Although the veil, that from her head descended,
  Encircled with the foliage of Minerva,
  Did not permit her to appear distinctly,

In attitude still royally majestic
  Continued she, like unto one who speaks,
  And keeps his warmest utterance in reserve:

"Look at me well; in sooth I'm Beatrice!
  How didst thou deign to come unto the Mountain?
  Didst thou not know that man is happy here?"

Mine eyes fell downward into the clear fountain,
  But, seeing myself therein, I sought the grass,
  So great a shame did weigh my forehead down.

As to the son the mother seems superb,
  So she appeared to me; for somewhat bitter
  Tasteth the savour of severe compassion.

Silent became she, and the Angels sang
  Suddenly, "*In te, Domine, speravi:*"
  But beyond 'pedes meos' did not pass.

Even as the snow among the living rafters
  Upon the back of Italy congeals,
  Blown on and drifted by Sclavonian winds,

And then, dissolving, trickles through itself
  Whene'er the land that loses shadow breathes,
  So that it seems a fire that melts a taper;

E'en thus was I without a tear or sigh,
  Before the song of those who sing for ever
  After the music of the eternal spheres.

But when I heard in their sweet melodies
  Compassion for me, more than had they said,
  "O wherefore, lady, dost thou thus upbraid him?"

The ice, that was about my heart congealed,
  To air and water changed, and in my anguish
  Through mouth and eyes came gushing from my breast.

She, on the right-hand border of the car
  Still firmly standing, to those holy beings
  Thus her discourse directed afterwards:

Appeared a lady under a green mantle, / Vested in colour of the living flame.

Purg. XXX, lines 32–33

"Ye keep your watch in the eternal day,
  So that nor night nor sleep can steal from you
  One step the ages make upon their path;

Therefore my answer is with greater care,
  That he may hear me who is weeping yonder,
  So that the sin and dole be of one measure.

Not only by the work of those great wheels,
  That destine every seed unto some end,
  According as the stars are in conjunction,

But by the largess of celestial graces,
  Which have such lofty vapours for their rain
  That near to them our sight approaches not,

Such had this man become in his new life
  Potentially, that every righteous habit
  Would have made admirable proof in him;

But so much more malignant and more savage
  Becomes the land untilled and with bad seed,
  The more good earthly vigour it possesses.

Some time did I sustain him with my look;
  Revealing unto him my youthful eyes,
  I led him with me turned in the right way.

As soon as ever of my second age
  I was upon the threshold and changed life,
  Himself from me he took and gave to others.

When from the flesh to spirit I ascended,
  And beauty and virtue were in me increased,
  I was to him less dear and less delightful;

And into ways untrue he turned his steps,
  Pursuing the false images of good,
  That never any promises fulfil;

Nor prayer for inspiration me availed,
  By means of which in dreams and otherwise
  I called him back, so little did he heed them.

So low he fell, that all appliances
  For his salvation were already short,
  Save showing him the people of perdition.

For this I visited the gates of death,
  And unto him, who so far up has led him,
  My intercessions were with weeping borne.

God's lofty fiat would be violated,
  If Lethe should be passed, and if such viands
  Should tasted be, withouten any scot

Of penitence, that gushes forth in tears."

Canto XXXI

Beatrice's rebuke prompts Dante to confess his sins before fainting with shame. On regaining consciousness, he finds Matilda pulling him towards the river Lethe to plunge his head in so that he is forced to drink – all remembrance of sin will now be forgotten. The Cardinal Virtues take him to Beatrice. Dante gazes into the eyes of his beloved, where he sees the reflection of the split nature of the Griffin which mirrors the duality (human/divine) of God's Incarnate Love for us through the figure of Christ. A mystical union takes place between Dante and Beatrice accompanied by the prayers of the Theological Virtues.

"O thou who art beyond the sacred river,"
  Turning to me the point of her discourse,
  That edgewise even had seemed to me so keen,

She recommenced, continuing without pause,
  "Say, say if this be true; to such a charge,
  Thy own confession needs must be conjoined."

My faculties were in so great confusion,
  That the voice moved, but sooner was extinct
  Than by its organs it was set at large.

Awhile she waited; then she said: "What thinkest?
  Answer me; for the mournful memories
  In thee not yet are by the waters injured."

Confusion and dismay together mingled
  Forced such a Yes! from out my mouth, that sight
  Was needful to the understanding of it.

Even as a cross-bow breaks, when 'tis discharged
  Too tensely drawn the bowstring and the bow,
  And with less force the arrow hits the mark,

So I gave way beneath that heavy burden,
  Outpouring in a torrent tears and sighs,
  And the voice flagged upon its passage forth.

Whence she to me: "In those desires of mine
  Which led thee to the loving of that good,
  Beyond which there is nothing to aspire to,

What trenches lying traverse or what chains
  Didst thou discover, that of passing onward
  Thou shouldst have thus despoiled thee of the hope?

And what allurements or what vantages
  Upon the forehead of the others showed,
  That thou shouldst turn thy footsteps unto them?"

After the heaving of a bitter sigh,
  Hardly had I the voice to make response,
  And with fatigue my lips did fashion it.

Weeping I said: "The things that present were
  With their false pleasure turned aside my steps,
  Soon as your countenance concealed itself."

And she: "Shouldst thou be silent, or deny
  What thou confessest, not less manifest
  Would be thy fault, by such a Judge 'tis known.

But when from one's own cheeks comes bursting forth
  The accusal of the sin, in our tribunal
  Against the edge the wheel doth turn itself.

But still, that thou mayst feel a greater shame
  For thy transgression, and another time
  Hearing the Sirens thou mayst be more strong,

Cast down the seed of weeping and attend;
  So shalt thou hear, how in an opposite way
  My buried flesh should have directed thee.

Never to thee presented art or nature
  Pleasure so great as the fair limbs wherein
  I was enclosed, which scattered are in earth.

And if the highest pleasure thus did fail thee
  By reason of my death, what mortal thing
  Should then have drawn thee into its desire?

Thou oughtest verily at the first shaft
  Of things fallacious to have risen up
  To follow me, who was no longer such.

Thou oughtest not to have stooped thy pinions
                                        downward
  To wait for further blows, or little girl,
  Or other vanity of such brief use.

The callow birdlet waits for two or three,
  But to the eyes of those already fledged,
  In vain the net is spread or shaft is shot."

Even as children silent in their shame
  Stand listening with their eyes upon the ground,
  And conscious of their fault, and penitent;

So was I standing; and she said: "If thou
  In hearing sufferest pain, lift up thy beard
  And thou shalt feel a greater pain in seeing."

With less resistance is a robust holm
  Uprooted, either by a native wind
  Or else by that from regions of Iarbas,

Than I upraised at her command my chin;
  And when she by the beard the face demanded,
  Well I perceived the venom of her meaning.

And as my countenance was lifted up,
  Mine eye perceived those creatures beautiful
  Had rested from the strewing of the flowers;

And, still but little reassured, mine eyes
  Saw Beatrice turned round towards the monster,
  That is one person only in two natures.

Beneath her veil, beyond the margent green,
  She seemed to me far more her ancient self
  To excel, than others here, when she was here.

So pricked me then the thorn of penitence,
  That of all other things the one which turned me
  Most to its love became the most my foe.

Such self-conviction stung me at the heart
  O'erpowered I fell, and what I then became
  She knoweth who had furnished me the cause.

Then, when the heart restored my outward sense,
  The lady I had found alone, above me
  I saw, and she was saying, "Hold me, hold me."

Up to my throat she in the stream had drawn me,
  And, dragging me behind her, she was moving
  Upon the water lightly as a shuttle.

When I was near unto the blessed shore,
  "*Asperges me*," I heard so sweetly sung,
  Remember it I cannot, much less write it.

The beautiful lady opened wide her arms,
  Embraced my head, and plunged me underneath,
  Where I was forced to swallow of the water.

Then forth she drew me, and all dripping brought
  Into the dance of the four beautiful,
  And each one with her arm did cover me.

'We here are Nymphs, and in the Heaven are stars;
  Ere Beatrice descended to the world,
  We as her handmaids were appointed her.

We'll lead thee to her eyes; but for the pleasant
  Light that within them is, shall sharpen thine
  The three beyond, who more profoundly look.'

Thus singing they began; and afterwards
  Unto the Griffin's breast they led me with them,
  Where Beatrice was standing, turned towards us.

"See that thou dost not spare thine eyes," they said;
  "Before the emeralds have we stationed thee,
  Whence Love aforetime drew for thee his weapons."

A thousand longings, hotter than the flame,
  Fastened mine eyes upon those eyes relucent,
  That still upon the Griffin steadfast stayed.

As in a glass the sun, not otherwise
  Within them was the twofold monster shining,
  Now with the one, now with the other nature.

Think, Reader, if within myself I marvelled,
  When I beheld the thing itself stand still,
  And in its image it transformed itself.

While with amazement filled and jubilant,
  My soul was tasting of the food, that while
  It satisfies us makes us hunger for it,

Themselves revealing of the highest rank
  In bearing, did the other three advance,
  Singing to their angelic saraband.

The beautiful lady opened wide her arms, / Embraced my head, and plunged me underneath, /
Where I was forced to swallow of the water.

Purg. XXXI, lines 100–102

"Turn, Beatrice, O turn thy holy eyes,"
  Such was their song, "unto thy faithful one,
  Who has to see thee ta'en so many steps.

In grace do us the grace that thou unveil
  Thy face to him, so that he may discern
  The second beauty which thou dost conceal."

O splendour of the living light eternal!
  Who underneath the shadow of Parnassus
  Has grown so pale, or drunk so at its cistern,

He would not seem to have his mind encumbered
  Striving to paint thee as thou didst appear,
  Where the harmonious heaven o'ershadowed thee,

When in the open air thou didst unveil?

Canto XXXII

*Beatrice descends from the chariot before the Tree of Knowledge. An allegorical scene
follows, where the Griffin binds the chariot pole (Christ, the Second Adam) to the tree
(the First, fallen Adam) which bursts into bloom (Christ's redemption of mankind).
Dante is shown a second allegorical masque, the Pageant of Church and Empire. The
Eagle (pagan Rome) attacks the tree (the early Christians) and the appearance of a fox
(heresy) precedes that of a dragon (the schism with Islam) tearing through the floor of
the chariot (the Church). The broken vehicle sprouts forth several heads (the Beast of
the Apocalypse) and a prostitute (the perfidious papacy in Avignon) dallies with a giant
(the corrupt French kings).*

So steadfast and attentive were mine eyes
  In satisfying their decennial thirst,
  That all my other senses were extinct,

And upon this side and on that they had
  Walls of indifference, so the holy smile
  Drew them unto itself with the old net

When forcibly my sight was turned away
  Towards my left hand by those goddesses,
  Because I heard from them a "Too intently!"

And that condition of the sight which is
  In eyes but lately smitten by the sun
  Bereft me of my vision some short while;

But to the less when sight re-shaped itself,
  I say the less in reference to the greater
  Splendour from which perforce I had withdrawn,

I saw upon its right wing wheeled about
  The glorious host returning with the sun
  And with the sevenfold flames upon their faces.

As underneath its shields, to save itself,
  A squadron turns, and with its banner wheels,
  Before the whole thereof can change its front,

That soldiery of the celestial kingdom
  Which marched in the advance had wholly passed us
  Before the chariot had turned its pole.

Then to the wheels the maidens turned themselves,
  And the Griffin moved his burden benedight,
  But so that not a feather of him fluttered.

The lady fair who drew me through the ford
  Followed with Statius and myself the wheel
  Which made its orbit with the lesser arc.

So passing through the lofty forest, vacant
  By fault of her who in the serpent trusted,
  Angelic music made our steps keep time.

Perchance as great a space had in three flights
  An arrow loosened from the string o'erpassed,
  As we had moved when Beatrice descended.

I heard them murmur altogether, "Adam!"
  Then circled they about a tree despoiled
  Of blooms and other leafage on each bough.

Its tresses, which so much the more dilate
  As higher they ascend, had been by Indians
  Among their forests marvelled at for height.

"Blessed art thou, O Griffin, who dost not
  Pluck with thy beak these branches sweet to taste,
  Since appetite by this was turned to evil."

After this fashion round the tree robust
  The others shouted; and the twofold creature:
  "Thus is preserved the seed of all the just."

And turning to the pole which he had dragged,
  He drew it close beneath the widowed bough,
  And what was of it unto it left bound.

In the same manner as our trees (when downward
  Falls the great light, with that together mingled
  Which after the celestial Lasca shines)

Begin to swell, and then renew themselves,
  Each one with its own colour, ere the Sun
  Harness his steeds beneath another star:

Less than of rose and more than violet
  A hue disclosing, was renewed the tree
  That had erewhile its boughs so desolate.

I never heard, nor here below is sung,
  The hymn which afterward that people sang,
  Nor did I bear the melody throughout.

Had I the power to paint how fell asleep
  Those eyes compassionless, of Syrinx hearing,
  Those eyes to which more watching cost so dear,

Even as a painter who from model paints
  I would portray how I was lulled asleep;
  He may, who well can picture drowsihood.

Therefore I pass to what time I awoke,
  And say a splendour rent from me the veil
  Of slumber, and a calling: "Rise, what dost thou?"

As to behold the apple-tree in blossom
  Which makes the Angels greedy for its fruit,
  And keeps perpetual bridals in the Heaven,

Peter and John and James conducted were,
  And, overcome, recovered at the word
  By which still greater slumbers have been broken,

And saw their school diminished by the loss
  Not only of Elias, but of Moses,
  And the apparel of their Master changed;

So I revived, and saw that piteous one
  Above me standing, who had been conductress
  Aforetime of my steps beside the river,

And all in doubt I said, "Where's Beatrice?"
  And she: "Behold her seated underneath
  The leafage new, upon the root of it.

Behold the company that circles her;
  The rest behind the Griffin are ascending
  With more melodious song, and more profound."

And if her speech were more diffuse I know not,
  Because already in my sight was she
  Who from the hearing of aught else had shut me.

Alone she sat upon the very earth,
  Left there as guardian of the chariot
  Which I had seen the biform monster fasten.

Encircling her, a cloister made themselves
  The seven Nymphs, with those lights in their hands
  Which are secure from Aquilon and Auster.

"Short while shalt thou be here a forester,
  And thou shalt be with me for evermore
  A citizen of that Rome where Christ is Roman.

Therefore, for that world's good which liveth ill,
  Fix on the car thine eyes, and what thou seest,
  Having returned to Earth, take heed thou write."

Thus Beatrice; and I, who at the feet
  Of her commandments all devoted was,
  My mind and eyes directed where she willed.

Never descended with so swift a motion
  Fire from a heavy cloud, when it is raining
  From out the region which is most remote,

As I beheld the bird of Jove descend
  Down through the tree, rending away the bark,
  As well as blossoms and the foliage new,

And he with all his might the chariot smote,
  Whereat it reeled, like vessel in a tempest
  Tossed by the waves, now starboard and now
                              larboard.

Thereafter saw I leap into the body
  Of the triumphal vehicle a Fox,
  That seemed unfed with any wholesome food.

But for his hideous sins upbraiding him,
  My Lady put him to as swift a flight
  As such a fleshless skeleton could bear.

Then by the way that it before had come,
  Into the chariot's chest I saw the Eagle
  Descend, and leave it feathered with his plumes.

And such as issues from a heart that mourns,
  A voice from Heaven there issued, and it said:
  "My little bark, how badly art thou freighted!"

Methought, then, that the earth did yawn between
  Both wheels, and I saw rise from it a Dragon,
  Who through the chariot upward fixed his tail,

And as a wasp that draweth back its sting,
  Drawing unto himself his tail malign,
  Drew out the floor, and went his way rejoicing.

That which remained behind, even as with grass
  A fertile region, with the feathers, offered
  Perhaps with pure intention and benign,

Reclothed itself, and with them were reclothed
  The pole and both the wheels so speedily,
  A sigh doth longer keep the lips apart.

Transfigured thus the holy edifice
  Thrust forward heads upon the parts of it,
  Three on the pole and one at either corner.

The first were horned like oxen; but the four
  Had but a single horn upon the forehead;
  A monster such had never yet been seen!

Firm as a rock upon a mountain high,
  Seated upon it, there appeared to me
  A shameless whore, with eyes swift glancing round,

And, as if not to have her taken from him,
  Upright beside her I beheld a giant;
  And ever and anon they kissed each other.

But because she her wanton, roving eye
  Turned upon me, her angry paramour
  Did scourge her from her head unto her feet.

Then full of jealousy, and fierce with wrath,
  He loosed the monster, and across the forest
  Dragged it so far, he made of that alone

A shield unto the whore and the strange beast.

Upright beside her I beheld a giant; / And ever and anon they kissed each other.

Purg. XXXII, lines 152–153

Canto XXXIII

Beatrice and her retinue lament the sorrowful state of the Church but soon press on
through the forest, followed by Dante, Matilda and Statius. Calling the pilgrim to her
side, she discusses all the pageants he has seen and prophesies the eventual deliverance
of Christendom. Dante is asked to chronicle all he has experienced for posterity. In the
final purgation ritual, Matilda leads Dante to the double fountainhead of Lethe and
Eunoe so he may drink from it and eliminate from his memory not only the guilt of
sin but the fact of having sinned. Invigorated, he feels ready to ascend to Paradise.

"*Deus venerunt gentes,*" alternating
　Now three, now four, melodious psalmody
　The maidens in the midst of tears began;

And Beatrice, compassionate and sighing,
　Listened to them with such a countenance,
　That scarce more changed was Mary at the cross.

But when the other virgins place had given
　For her to speak, uprisen to her feet
　With colour as of fire, she made response:

"'*Modicum, et non videbitis me;*
　Et iterum,' my sisters predilect,
　'*Modicum, et vos videbitis me.*'"

Then all the seven in front of her she placed;
　And after her, by beckoning only, moved
　Me and the lady and the sage who stayed.

So she moved onward; and I do not think
　That her tenth step was placed upon the ground,
　When with her eyes upon mine eyes she smote,

And with a tranquil aspect, "Come more quickly,"
　To me she said, "that, if I speak with thee,
　To listen to me thou mayst be well placed."

As soon as I was with her as I should be,
　She said to me: "Why, brother, dost thou not
　Venture to question now, in coming with me?"

As unto those who are too reverential,
　Speaking in presence of superiors,
　Who drag no living utterance to their teeth,

It me befell, that without perfect sound
　Began I: "My necessity, Madonna,
　You know, and that which thereunto is good."

And she to me: "Of fear and bashfulness
　Henceforward I will have thee strip thyself,
　So that thou speak no more as one who dreams.

Know that the vessel which the serpent broke
　Was, and is not; but let him who is guilty
　Think that God's vengeance does not fear a sop.

Without an heir shall not for ever be
　The Eagle that left his plumes upon the car,
　Whence it became a monster, then a prey;

For verily I see, and hence narrate it,
　The stars already near to bring the time,
　From every hindrance safe, and every bar,

Within which a Five-hundred, Ten and Five,
　One sent from God, shall slay the thievish woman
　And that same giant who is sinning with her.

And peradventure my dark utterance,
　Like Themis and the Sphinx, may less persuade thee,
　Since, in their mode, it clouds the intellect;

But soon the facts shall be the Naiades
　Who shall this difficult enigma solve,
　Without destruction of the flocks and harvests.

Note thou; and even as by me are uttered
　These words, so teach them unto those who live
　That life which is a running unto death;

And bear in mind, whene'er thou writest them,
  Not to conceal what thou hast seen the plant,
  That twice already has been pillaged here.

Whoever pillages or shatters it,
  With blasphemy of deed offendeth God,
  Who made it holy for his use alone.

For biting that, in pain and in desire
  Five thousand years and more the first-born soul
  Craved Him, who punished in himself the bite.

Thy genius slumbers, if it deem it not
  For special reason so pre-eminent
  In height, and so inverted in its summit.

And if thy vain imaginings had not been
  Water of Elsa round about thy mind,
  And Pyramus to the mulberry, their pleasure,

Thou by so many circumstances only
  The justice of the interdict of God
  Morally in the tree wouldst recognize.

But since I see thee in thine intellect
  Converted into stone and stained with sin,
  So that the light of my discourse doth daze thee,

I will too, if not written, at least painted,
  Thou bear it back within thee, for the reason
  That cinct with palm the pilgrim's staff is borne."

And I: "As by a signet is the wax
  Which does not change the figure stamped upon it,
  My brain is now imprinted by yourself.

But wherefore so beyond my power of sight
  Soars your desirable discourse, that aye
  The more I strive, so much the more I lose it?"

"That thou mayst recognize," she said, "the school
  Which thou hast followed, and mayst see how far
  Its doctrine follows after my discourse,

And mayst behold your path from the divine
  Distant as far as separated is
  From Earth the heaven that highest hastens on."

Whence her I answered: "I do not remember
  That ever I estranged myself from you,
  Nor have I conscience of it that reproves me."

"And if thou art not able to remember,"
  Smiling she answered, "recollect thee now
  That thou this very day hast drunk of Lethe;

And if from smoke a fire may be inferred,
  Such an oblivion clearly demonstrates
  Some error in thy will elsewhere intent.

Truly from this time forward shall my words
  Be naked, so far as it is befitting
  To lay them open unto thy rude gaze."

And more coruscant and with slower steps
  The sun was holding the meridian circle,
  Which, with the point of view, shifts here and there

When halted (as he cometh to a halt,
  Who goes before a squadron as its escort,
  If something new he find upon his way)

The ladies seven at a dark shadow's edge,
  Such as, beneath green leaves and branches black,
  The Alp upon its frigid border wears.

In front of them the Tigris and Euphrates
  Methought I saw forth issue from one fountain,
  And slowly part, like friends, from one another.

"O light, O glory of the human race!
  What stream is this which here unfolds itself
  From out one source, and from itself withdraws?"

For such a prayer, 'twas said unto me, "Pray
  Matilda that she tell thee;" and here answered,
  As one does who doth free himself from blame,

The beautiful lady: "This and other things
  Were told to him by me; and sure I am
  The water of Lethe has not hid them from him."

And Beatrice: "Perhaps a greater care,
  Which oftentimes our memory takes away,
  Has made the vision of his mind obscure.

But Eunoë behold, that yonder rises;
  Lead him to it, and, as thou art accustomed,
  Revive again the half-dead virtue in him."

Like gentle soul, that maketh no excuse,
  But makes its own will of another's will
  As soon as by a sign it is disclosed,

Even so, when she had taken hold of me,
  The beautiful lady moved, and unto Statius
  Said, in her womanly manner, "Come with him."

If, Reader, I possessed a longer space
  For writing it, I yet would sing in part
  Of the sweet draught that ne'er would satiate me;

But inasmuch as full are all the leaves
  Made ready for this second canticle,
  The curb of art no farther lets me go.

From the most holy water I returned
  Regenerate, in the manner of new trees
  That are renewed with a new foliage,

Pure and disposed to mount unto the stars.

If, Reader, I possessed a longer space / For writing it, I yet would sing in part /
Of the sweet draught that ne'er would satiate me;

Purg. XXXIII, lines 136–138

Paradiso

The final phase of the journey takes Dante through the Ten Heavens – The Moon, Mercury, Venus, the Sun, Jupiter, Saturn, the Fixed Stars, the Primum Mobile and the Empyrean. With Beatrice, he meets those who broke their vows, those who courted Fame, the souls of Lovers, the Fathers of the Church, Christian Martyrs and Crusaders, the Just and the Contemplative. Reaching the Fixed Stars he witnesses the Triumph of Christ, the Virgin Mary, the Apostles, angels, saints and martyrs. He is tested on Faith by Saint Peter, on Hope by Saint James and on Charity by Saint John. In the Primum Mobile, which governs all the Heavens, Dante sees hierarchies of angels. Finally, he reaches the Empyrean where the tiered souls of the blessed form the White Rose of Paradise. Dante finally gazes upon his Maker and understands the indefinable divine mystery.

Contents

Canto I

Dante still finds himself in the natural world after drinking from the waters of Eunoe in the Garden of Eden (Purgatory, Canto XXXIII). Beatrice, who is at his side, turns to gaze into the midday sun of the Spring Equinox, the noblest time of the day within the perfect season. Blinded by its brilliance, Dante appeals to Apollo, the pagan sun god, to help him look at it unflinchingly. Upon hearing the music of the cosmos in motion, Dante realizes that he and Beatrice have risen above the Earth into the heavens helped by the universal law of gravity.

The glory of Him who moveth everything
  Doth penetrate the universe, and shine
  In one part more and in another less.

Within that heaven which most his light receives
  Was I, and things beheld which to repeat
  Nor knows, nor can, who from above descends;

Because in drawing near to its desire
  Our intellect ingulphs itself so far,
  That after it the memory cannot go.

Truly whatever of the holy realm
  I had the power to treasure in my mind
  Shall now become the subject of my song.

O good Apollo, for this last emprise
  Make of me such a vessel of thy power
  As giving the beloved laurel asks!

One summit of Parnassus hitherto
  Has been enough for me, but now with both
  I needs must enter the arena left.

Enter into my bosom, thou, and breathe
  As at the time when Marsyas thou didst draw
  Out of the scabbard of those limbs of his.

O power divine, lend'st thou thyself to me
  So that the shadow of the blessed realm
  Stamped in my brain I can make manifest,

Thou'lt see me come unto thy darling tree,
  And crown myself thereafter with those leaves
  Of which the theme and thou shall make me worthy.

So seldom, Father, do we gather them
  For triumph or of Caesar or of Poet,
  (The fault and shame of human inclinations,)

That the Peneian foliage should bring forth
  Joy to the joyous Delphic deity,
  When any one it makes to thirst for it.

A little spark is followed by great flame;
  Perchance with better voices after me
  Shall prayer be made that Cyrrha may respond!

To mortal men by passages diverse
  Uprises the world's lamp; but by that one
  Which circles four uniteth with three crosses,

With better course and with a better star
  Conjoined it issues, and the mundane wax
  Tempers and stamps more after its own fashion.

Almost that passage had made morning there
  And evening here, and there was wholly white
  That hemisphere, and black the other part,

When Beatrice towards the left-hand side
  I saw turned round, and gazing at the sun;
  Never did eagle fasten so upon it!

And even as a second ray is wont
  To issue from the first and reascend,
  Like to a pilgrim who would fain return,

Thus of her action, through the eyes infused
  In my imagination, mine I made,
  And sunward fixed mine eyes beyond our wont.

There much is lawful which is here unlawful
  Unto our powers, by virtue of the place
  Made for the human species as its own.

Not long I bore it, nor so little while
  But I beheld it sparkle round about
  Like iron that comes molten from the fire;

And suddenly it seemed that day to day
  Was added, as if He who has the power
  Had with another sun the heaven adorned.

With eyes upon the everlasting wheels
  Stood Beatrice all intent, and I, on her
  Fixing my vision from above removed,

Such at her aspect inwardly became
  As Glaucus, tasting of the herb that made him
  Peer of the other gods beneath the sea.

To represent transhumanise in words
  Impossible were; the example, then, suffice
  Him for whom Grace the experience reserves.

If I was merely what of me thou newly
  Createdst, Love who governest the heaven,
  Thou knowest, who didst lift me with thy light!

When now the wheel, which thou dost make eternal
  Desiring thee, made me attentive to it
  By harmony thou dost modulate and measure,

Then seemed to me so much of heaven enkindled
  By the sun's flame, that neither rain nor river
  E'er made a lake so widely spread abroad.

The newness of the sound and the great light
  Kindled in me a longing for their cause,
  Never before with such acuteness felt;

Whence she, who saw me as I saw myself,
  To quiet in me my perturbed mind,
  Opened her mouth, ere I did mine to ask,

And she began: "Thou makest thyself so dull
  With false imagining, that thou seest not
  What thou wouldst see if thou hadst shaken it off.

Thou art not upon Earth, as thou believest;
  But lightning, fleeing its appropriate site,
  Ne'er ran as thou, who thitherward returnest."

If of my former doubt I was divested
  By these brief little words more smiled than spoken,
  I in a new one was the more ensnared;

And said: "Already did I rest content
  From great amazement; but am now amazed
  In what way I transcend these bodies light."

Whereupon she, after a pitying sigh,
  Her eyes directed tow'rds me with that look
  A mother casts on a delirious child;

And she began: "All things whate'er they be
  Have order among themselves, and this is form,
  That makes the universe resemble God.

Here do the higher creatures see the footprints
  Of the Eternal Power, which is the end
  Whereto is made the law already mentioned.

In the order that I speak of are inclined
  All natures, by their destinies diverse,
  More or less near unto their origin;

Hence they move onward unto ports diverse
  O'er the great sea of being; and each one
  With instinct given it which bears it on.

This bears away the fire towards the moon;
  This is in mortal hearts the motive power
  This binds together and unites the Earth.

Nor only the created things that are
  Without intelligence this bow shoots forth,
  But those that have both intellect and love.

The Providence that regulates all this
  Makes with its light the heaven forever quiet,
  Wherein that turns which has the greatest haste.

And thither now, as to a site decreed,
  Bears us away the virtue of that cord
  Which aims its arrows at a joyous mark.

True is it, that as oftentimes the form
  Accords not with the intention of the art,
  Because in answering is matter deaf,

So likewise from this course doth deviate
  Sometimes the creature, who the power possesses,
  Though thus impelled, to swerve some other way,

(In the same wise as one may see the fire
  Fall from a cloud,) if the first impetus
  Earthward is wrested by some false delight.

Thou shouldst not wonder more, if well I judge,
  At thine ascent, than at a rivulet
  From some high mount descending to the lowland.

Marvel it would be in thee, if deprived
  Of hindrance, thou wert seated down below,
  As if on Earth the living fire were quiet."

Thereat she heavenward turned again her face.

Canto II

*Dante stops to warn the shallow reader to turn back because from now on his journey
will take him through unfamiliar territory. He fixes his eyes on Beatrice and together
they rise up beyond the sphere of fire into the First Heaven, the sphere of the Moon,
the one furthest away from the Empyrean and thus the most unstable, at a speed
approaching that of light. They penetrate its substance as light through water, as God
incarnated himself in man or as a saved soul enters God. Beatrice explains that the
markings on the lunar surface are due to the varying densities of energy of the celestial
beings who are rotating the various spheres.*

O Ye, who in some pretty little boat,
  Eager to listen, have been following
  Behind my ship, that singing sails along,

Turn back to look again upon your shores;
  Do not put out to sea, lest peradventure,
  In losing me, you might yourselves be lost.

The sea I sail has never yet been passed;
  Minerva breathes, and pilots me Apollo,
  And Muses nine point out to me the Bears.

Ye other few who have the neck uplifted
  Betimes to th' bread of Angels upon which
  One liveth here and grows not sated by it,

Well may you launch upon the deep salt-sea
  Your vessel, keeping still my wake before you
  Upon the water that grows smooth again.

Those glorious ones who unto Colchos passed
  Were not so wonder-struck as you shall be,
  When Jason they beheld a ploughman made!

The con-created and perpetual thirst
  For the realm deiform did bear us on,
  As swift almost as ye the heavens behold.

Upward gazed Beatrice, and I at her;
  And in such space perchance as strikes a bolt
  And flies, and from the notch unlocks itself,

Arrived I saw me where a wondrous thing
  Drew to itself my sight; and therefore she
  From whom no care of mine could be concealed,

Towards me turning, blithe as beautiful,
  Said unto me: "Fix gratefully thy mind
  On God, who unto the first star has brought us."

It seemed to me a cloud encompassed us,
  Luminous, dense, consolidate and bright
  As adamant on which the sun is striking.

Into itself did the eternal pearl
  Receive us, even as water doth receive
  A ray of light, remaining still unbroken.

If I was body, (and we here conceive not
  How one dimension tolerates another,
  Which needs must be if body enter body,)

More the desire should be enkindled in us
  That essence to behold, wherein is seen
  How God and our own nature were united.

There will be seen what we receive by faith,
  Not demonstrated, but self-evident
  In guise of the first truth that man believes.

I made reply: "Madonna, as devoutly
  As most I can do I give thanks to Him
  Who has removed me from the mortal world.

But tell me what the dusky spots may be
  Upon this body, which below on Earth
  Make people tell that fabulous tale of Cain?"

Somewhat she smiled; and then, "If the opinion
  Of mortals be erroneous," she said,
  "Where'er the key of sense doth not unlock,

Certes, the shafts of wonder should not pierce thee
  Now, forasmuch as, following the senses,
  Thou seest that the reason has short wings.

But tell me what thou think'st of it thyself."
  And I: "What seems to us up here diverse,
  Is caused, I think, by bodies rare and dense."

And she: "Right truly shalt thou see immersed
  In error thy belief, if well thou hearest
  The argument that I shall make against it.

Lights many the eighth sphere displays to you
  Which in their quality and quantity
  May noted be of aspects different.

If this were caused by rare and dense alone,
  One only virtue would there be in all
  Or more or less diffused, or equally.

Virtues diverse must be perforce the fruits
  Of formal principles; and these, save one,
  Of course would by thy reasoning be destroyed.

Besides, if rarity were of this dimness
  The cause thou askest, either through and through
  This planet thus attenuate were of matter,

Or else, as in a body is apportioned
  The fat and lean, so in like manner this
  Would in its volume interchange the leaves.

Were it the former, in the sun's eclipse
  It would be manifest by the shining through
  Of light, as through aught tenuous interfused.

This is not so; hence we must scan the other,
  And if it chance the other I demolish,
  Then falsified will thy opinion be.

But if this rarity go not through and through,
  There needs must be a limit, beyond which
  Its contrary prevents the further passing,

And thence the foreign radiance is reflected,
  Even as a colour cometh back from glass,
  The which behind itself concealeth lead.

Now thou wilt say the sunbeam shows itself
  More dimly there than in the other parts,
  By being there reflected farther back.

From this reply experiment will free thee
  If e'er thou try it, which is wont to be
  The fountain to the rivers of your arts.

Three mirrors shalt thou take, and two remove
  Alike from thee, the other more remote
  Between the former two shall meet thine eyes.

Turned towards these, cause that behind thy back
  Be placed a light, illuming the three mirrors
  And coming back to thee by all reflected.

Though in its quantity be not so ample
  The image most remote, there shalt thou see
  How it perforce is equally resplendent.

Now, as beneath the touches of warm rays
  Naked the subject of the snow remains
  Both of its former colour and its cold,

Thee thus remaining in thy intellect,
  Will I inform with such a living light,
  That it shall tremble in its aspect to thee.

Within the heaven of the divine repose
  Revolves a body, in whose virtue lies
  The being of whatever it contains.

The following heaven, that has so many eyes,
  Divides this being by essences diverse,
  Distinguished from it, and by it contained.

The other spheres, by various differences,
  All the distinctions which they have within them
  Dispose unto their ends and their effects.

Thus do these organs of the world proceed,
  As thou perceivest now, from grade to grade;
  Since from above they take, and act beneath.

Observe me well, how through this place I come
  Unto the truth thou wishest, that hereafter
  Thou mayst alone know how to keep the ford

The power and motion of the holy spheres,
  As from the artisan the hammer's craft,
  Forth from the blessed motors must proceed.

The heaven, which lights so manifold make fair,
  From the Intelligence profound, which turns it,
  The image takes, and makes of it a seal.

And even as the soul within your dust
  Through members different and accommodated
  To faculties diverse expands itself,

So likewise this Intelligence diffuses
  Its virtue multiplied among the stars.
  Itself revolving on its unity.

Virtue diverse doth a diverse alloyage
  Make with the precious body that it quickens,
  In which, as life in you, it is combined.

From the glad nature whence it is derived,
  The mingled virtue through the body shines,
  Even as gladness through the living pupil.

From this proceeds whate'er from light to light
  Appeareth different, not from dense and rare:
  This is the formal principle that produces,

According to its goodness, dark and bright."

Canto III

Dante discerns faces in the wan light and mistakes them for reflections. Among the souls of those who broke or recanted holy vows are Piccarda dei Donati, sister of Corso and Forese (Purgatory, Cantos XXIII and XXIV), and the Empress Constance, mother of Frederick II of Sicily. Both chose a life of celibacy but were removed from their nunnery to contract a political marriage. Although occupying the lowliest sphere, such spirits are delighted with the degree of joy accorded them by God. Dante is overpowered by Beatrice's radiance as the glory of the Empyrean momentarily shines through her.

That Sun, which erst with love my bosom warmed,
  Of beauteous truth had unto me discovered,
  By proving and reproving, the sweet aspect.

And, that I might confess myself convinced
  And confident, so far as was befitting,
  I lifted more erect my head to speak.

But there appeared a vision, which withdrew me
  So close to it, in order to be seen,
  That my confession I remembered not.

Such as through polished and transparent glass,
  Or waters crystalline and undisturbed,
  But not so deep as that their bed be lost,

Saw I many faces prompt to speak,

Par. III, lines 16

Come back again the outlines of our faces
  So feeble, that a pearl on forehead white
  Comes not less speedily unto our eyes;

Such saw I many faces prompt to speak,
  So that I ran in error opposite
  To that which kindled love 'twixt man and fountain.

As soon as I became aware of them,
  Esteeming them as mirrored semblances,
  To see of whom they were, mine eyes I turned,

And nothing saw, and once more turned them forward
  Direct into the light of my sweet Guide,
  Who smiling kindled in her holy eyes.

"Marvel thou not," she said to me, "because
  I smile at this thy puerile conceit,
  Since on the truth it trusts not yet its foot,

But turns thee, as 'tis wont, on emptiness.
  True substances are these which thou beholdest,
  Here relegate for breaking of some vow.

Therefore speak with them, listen and believe;
  For the true light, which giveth peace to them,
  Permits them not to turn from it their feet."

And I unto the shade that seemed most wishful
  To speak directed me, and I began,
  As one whom too great eagerness bewilders:

"O well-created spirit, who in the rays
  Of life eternal dost the sweetness taste
  Which being untasted ne'er is comprehended,

Grateful 'twill be to me, if thou content me
  Both with thy name and with your destiny."
  Whereat she promptly and with laughing eyes:

"Our charity doth never shut the doors
  Against a just desire, except as one
  Who wills that all her court be like herself.

I was a virgin sister in the world;
  And if thy mind doth contemplate me well,
  The being more fair will not conceal me from thee,

But thou shalt recognise I am Piccarda,
  Who, stationed here among these other blessed,
  Myself am blessed in the slowest sphere.

All our affections, that alone inflamed
  Are in the pleasure of the Holy Ghost,
  Rejoice at being of his order formed;

And this allotment, which appears so low,
  Therefore is given us, because our vows
  Have been neglected and in some part void."

Whence I to her: "In your miraculous aspects
  There shines I know not what of the divine,
  Which doth transform you from our first conceptions.

Therefore I was not swift in my remembrance;
  But what thou tellest me now aids me so,
  That the refiguring is easier to me.

But tell me, ye who in this place are happy,
  Are you desirous of a higher place,
  To see more or to make yourselves more friends?"

First with those other shades she smiled a little;
  Thereafter answered me so full of gladness,
  She seemed to burn in the first fire of love:

"Brother, our will is quieted by virtue
  Of charity, that makes us wish alone
  For what we have, nor gives us thirst for more.

If to be more exalted we aspired,
  Discordant would our aspirations be
  Unto the will of Him who here secludes us;

Which thou shalt see finds no place in these circles,
  If being in charity is needful here,
  And if thou lookest well into its nature;

Nay, 'tis essential to this blest existence
  To keep itself within the will divine,
  Whereby our very wishes are made one;

So that, as we are station above station
  Throughout this realm, to all the realm 'tis pleasing,
  As to the King, who makes his will our will.

And his will is our peace; this is the sea
  To which is moving onward whatsoever
  It doth create, and all that nature makes."

Then it was clear to me how everywhere
  In heaven is Paradise, although the grace
  Of good supreme there rain not in one measure.

But as it comes to pass, if one food sates,
  And for another still remains the longing,
  We ask for this, and that decline with thanks,

E'en thus did I; with gesture and with word,
  To learn from her what was the web wherein
  She did not ply the shuttle to the end.

"A perfect life and merit high in-heaven
  A lady o'er us," said she, "by whose rule
  Down in your world they vest and veil themselves,

That until death they may both watch and sleep
  Beside that Spouse who every vow accepts
  Which charity conformeth to his pleasure.

To follow her, in girlhood from the world
  I fled, and in her habit shut myself,
  And pledged me to the pathway of her sect.

Then men accustomed unto evil more
  Than unto good, from the sweet cloister tore me;
  God knows what afterward my life became.

This other splendour, which to thee reveals
  Itself on my right side, and is enkindled
  With all the illumination of our sphere,

What of myself I say applies to her;
  A nun was she, and likewise from her head
  Was ta'en the shadow of the sacred wimple.

But when she too was to the world returned
  Against her wishes and against good usage,
  Of the heart's veil she never was divested.

Of great Costanza this is the effulgence,
  Who from the second wind of Suabia
  Brought forth the third and latest puissance."

Thus unto me she spake, and then began
  "*Ave Maria*" singing, and in singing
  Vanished, as through deep water something heavy.

My sight, that followed her as long a time
  As it was possible, when it had lost her
  Turned round unto the mark of more desire,

And wholly unto Beatrice reverted;
  But she such lightnings flashed into mine eyes,
  That at the first my sight endured it not;

And this in questioning more backward made me.

Canto IV

Dante is baffled. Firstly, how can those souls forced to break their vows be given a reduced level of merit? Secondly, could Plato's notion of the soul's return to its native star be correct? Beatrice gives a theological answer to the second question. In answer to the first question, Beatrice discusses two kinds of Will. The Absolute Will of Lawrence and Mutius and the Conditioned Will of Piccarda and Constance, which changes according to circumstances. It is that which has bound them to the Moon. Dante then asks if it is possible to atone for broken vows through good deeds.

Between two viands, equally removed
  And tempting, a free man would die of hunger
  Ere either he could bring unto his teeth.

So would a lamb between the ravenings
  Of two fierce wolves stand fearing both alike;
  And so would stand a dog between two does.

Hence, if I held my peace, myself I blame not,
  Impelled in equal measure by my doubts,
  Since it must be so, nor do I commend.

I held my peace; but my desire was painted
  Upon my face, and questioning with that
  More fervent far than by articulate speech.

Beatrice did as Daniel had done
  Relieving Nebuchadnezzar from the wrath
  Which rendered him unjustly merciless,

And said: "Well see I how attracteth thee
  One and the other wish, so that thy care
  Binds itself so that forth it does not breathe.

Thou arguest, if good will be permanent,
  The violence of others, for what reason
  Doth it decrease the measure of my merit?

Again for doubting furnish thee occasion
  Souls seeming to return unto the stars,
  According to the sentiment of Plato.

These are the questions which upon thy wish
  Are thrusting equally; and therefore first
  Will I treat that which hath the most of gall.

He of the Seraphim most absorbed in God,
  Moses, and Samuel, and whichever John
  Thou mayst select, I say, and even Mary,

Have not in any other heaven their seats,
  Than have those spirits that just appeared to thee,
  Nor of existence more or fewer years;

But all make beautiful the primal circle,
  And have sweet life in different degrees,
  By feeling more or less the eternal breath.

They showed themselves here, not because allotted
  This sphere has been to them, but to give sign
  Of the celestial which is least exalted.

To speak thus is adapted to your mind,
  Since only through the sense it apprehendeth
  What then it worthy makes of intellect.

On this account the Scripture condescends
  Unto your faculties, and feet and hands
  To God attributes, and means something else;

And Holy Church under an aspect human
  Gabriel and Michael represent to you,
  And him who made Tobias whole again.

That which Timaeus argues of the soul
  Doth not resemble that which here is seen,
  Because it seems that as he speaks he thinks.

He says the soul unto its star returns,
  Believing it to have been severed thence
  Whenever nature gave it as a form.

Perhaps his doctrine is of other guise
  Than the words sound, and possibly may be
  With meaning that is not to be derided.

If he doth mean that to these wheels return
  The honour of their influence and the blame,
  Perhaps his bow doth hit upon some truth.

This principle ill understood once warped
  The whole world nearly, till it went astray
  Invoking Jove and Mercury and Mars.

The other doubt which doth disquiet thee
  Less venom has, for its malevolence
  Could never lead thee otherwhere from me.

That as unjust our justice should appear
  In eyes of mortals, is an argument
  Of faith, and not of sin heretical.

But still, that your perception may be able
  To thoroughly penetrate this verity,
  As thou desirest, I will satisfy thee.

If it be violence when he who suffers
  Co-operates not with him who uses force,
  These souls were not on that account excused;

For will is never quenched unless it will,
  But operates as nature doth in fire
  If violence a thousand times distort it.

Hence, if it yieldeth more or less, it seconds
  The force; and these have done so, having power
  Of turning back unto the holy place.

If their will had been perfect, like to that
  Which Lawrence fast upon his gridiron held,
  And Mutius made severe to his own hand,

It would have urged them back along the road
  Whence they were dragged, as soon as they were free;
  But such a solid will is all too rare.

And by these words, if thou hast gathered them
  As thou shouldst do, the argument is refuted
  That would have still annoyed thee many times.

But now another passage runs across
  Before thine eyes, and such that by thyself
  Thou couldst not thread it ere thou wouldst be weary.

I have for certain put into thy mind
  That soul beatified could never lie,
  For it is near the primal Truth,

And then thou from Piccarda might'st have heard
  Costanza kept affection for the veil,
  So that she seemeth here to contradict me.

Many times, brother, has it come to pass,
  That, to escape from peril, with reluctance
  That has been done it was not right to do,

E'en as Alcmaeon (who, being by his father
  Thereto entreated, his own mother slew)
  Not to lose pity pitiless became.

At this point I desire thee to remember
  That force with will commingles, and they cause
  That the offences cannot be excused.

Will absolute consenteth not to evil;
  But in so far consenteth as it fears,
  If it refrain, to fall into more harm.

Hence when Piccarda uses this expression,
  She meaneth the will absolute, and I
  The other, so that both of us speak truth."

Such was the flowing of the holy river
  That issued from the fount whence springs all truth;
  This put to rest my wishes one and all.

"O love of the first lover, O divine,"
  Said I forthwith, "whose speech inundates me
  And warms me so, it more and more revives me,

My own affection is not so profound
  As to suffice in rendering grace for grace;
  Let Him, who sees and can, thereto respond.

Well I perceive that never sated is
  Our intellect unless the Truth illume it,
  Beyond which nothing true expands itself.

It rests therein, as wild beast in his lair,
  When it attains it; and it can attain it;
  If not, then each desire would frustrate be.

Therefore springs up, in fashion of a shoot,
  Doubt at the foot of truth; and this is nature,
  Which to the top from height to height impels us.

This doth invite me, this assurance give me
  With reverence, Lady, to inquire of you
  Another truth, which is obscure to me.

I wish to know if man can satisfy you
  For broken vows with other good deeds, so
  That in your balance they will not be light."

Beatrice gazed upon me with her eyes
  Full of the sparks of love, and so divine,
  That, overcome my power, I turned my back

And almost lost myself with eyes downcast.

Canto V

The stories of Piccarda and Constance have raised the subject of vows and how best to obey them. Impressed by the illuminated state of Dante's mind, Beatrice declares that every vow to God is defined by two aspects: the thing sworn and the surrender of one's will. The latter condition underpins everything but the content of what is pledged may be altered, provided that an individual gives up something even dearer in exchange. Beatrice and Dante ascend into the Second Heaven, the sphere of Mercury, where crowds of luminous souls flock to them. Beatrice urges Dante to question one of them.

"If in the heat of love I flame upon thee
  Beyond the measure that on Earth is seen,
  So that the valour of thine eyes I vanquish,

Marvel thou not thereat; for this proceeds
  From perfect sight, which as it apprehends
  To the good apprehended moves its feet.

Well I perceive how is already shining
  Into thine intellect the eternal light,
  That only seen enkindles always love;

And if some other thing your love seduce,
  'Tis nothing but a vestige of the same,
  Ill understood, which there is shining through.

Thou fain wouldst know if with another service
  For broken vow can such return be made
  As to secure the soul from further claim."

This Canto thus did Beatrice begin;
  And, as a man who breaks not off his speech,
  Continued thus her holy argument:

"The greatest gift that in his largess God
  Creating made, and unto his own goodness
  Nearest conformed, and that which he doth prize

Most highly, is the freedom of the will,
  Wherewith the creatures of intelligence
  Both all and only were and are endowed.

Now wilt thou see, if thence thou reasonest,
  The high worth of a vow, if it he made
  So that when thou consentest God consents:

For, closing between God and man the compact,
  A sacrifice is of this treasure made,
  Such as I say, and made by its own act.

What can be rendered then as compensation?
  Think'st thou to make good use of what thou'st
               offered,
  With gains ill gotten thou wouldst do good deed.

Now art thou certain of the greater point;
  But because Holy Church in this dispenses,
  Which seems against the truth which I have
              shown thee,

Behoves thee still to sit awhile at table,
  Because the solid food which thou hast taken
  Requireth further aid for thy digestion.

Open thy mind to that which I reveal,
  And fix it there within; for 'tis not knowledge,
  The having heard without retaining it.

In the essence of this sacrifice two things
  Convene together; and the one is that
  Of which 'tis made, the other is the agreement.

This last for evermore is cancelled not
  Unless complied with, and concerning this
  With such precision has above been spoken.

Therefore it was enjoined upon the Hebrews
  To offer still, though sometimes what was offered
  Might be commuted, as thou ought'st to know.

The other, which is known to thee as matter,
  May well indeed be such that one errs not
  If it for other matter be exchanged.

But let none shift the burden on his shoulder
  At his arbitrament, without the turning
  Both of the white and of the yellow key;

And every permutation deem as foolish,
  If in the substitute the thing relinquished,
  As the four is in six, be not contained.

Therefore whatever thing has so great weight
  In value that it drags down every balance,
  Cannot be satisfied with other spending.

Let mortals never take a vow in jest;
  Be faithful and not blind in doing that,
  As Jephthah was in his first offering,

Whom more beseemed to say, 'I have done wrong,
  Than to do worse by keeping; and as foolish
  Thou the great leader of the Greeks wilt find,

Whence wept Iphigenia her fair face,
  And made for her both wise and simple weep,
  Who heard such kind of worship spoken of.'

Christians, be ye more serious in your movements;
  Be ye not like a feather at each wind,
  And think not every water washes you.

Ye have the Old and the New Testament,
  And the Pastor of the Church who guideth you
  Let this suffice you unto your salvation.

If evil appetite cry aught else to you,
  Be ye as men, and not as silly sheep,
  So that the Jew among you may not mock you.

Be ye not as the lamb that doth abandon
  Its mother's milk, and frolicsome and simple
  Combats at its own pleasure with itself."

Thus Beatrice to me even as I write it;
  Then all desireful turned herself again
  To that part where the world is most alive.

Her silence and her change of countenance
  Silence imposed upon my eager mind,
  That had already in advance new questions;

And as an arrow that upon the mark
  Strikes ere the bowstring quiet hath become,
  So did we speed into the second realm.

My Lady there so joyful I beheld,
  As into the brightness of that heaven she entered,
  More luminous thereat the planet grew;

And if the star itself was changed and smiled,
  What became I, who by my nature am
  Exceeding mutable in every guise!

As, in a fish-pond which is pure and tranquil,
  The fishes draw to that which from without
  Comes in such fashion that their food they deem it;

So I beheld more than a thousand splendours
  Drawing towards us, and in each was heard:
  "Lo, this is she who shall increase our love."

And as each one was coming unto us,
  Full of beatitude the shade was seen,
  By the effulgence clear that issued from it.

Think, Reader, if what here is just beginning
  No farther should proceed, how thou wouldst have
  An agonizing need of knowing more;

And of thyself thou'lt see how I from these
  Was in desire of hearing their conditions,
  As they unto mine eyes were manifest.

"O thou well-born, unto whom Grace concedes
  To see the thrones of the eternal triumph,
  Or ever yet the warfare be abandoned

With light that through the whole of heaven is spread
  Kindled are we, and hence if thou desirest
  To know of us, at thine own pleasure sate thee."

Thus by some one among those holy spirits
  Was spoken, and by Beatrice: "Speak, speak
  Securely, and believe them even as Gods."

"Well I perceive how thou dost nest thyself
  In thine own light, and drawest it from thine eyes,
  Because they coruscate when thou dost smile,

But know not who thou art, nor why thou hast,
  Spirit august, thy station in the sphere
  That veils itself to men in alien rays."

This said I in direction of the light
  Which first had spoken to me; whence it became
  By far more lucent than it was before.

So I beheld more than a thousand splendours / Drawing towards us,

Par. V, lines 103–104

Even as the sun, that doth conceal himself
  By too much light, when heat has worn away
  The tempering influence of the vapours dense,

By greater rapture thus concealed itself
  In its own radiance the figure saintly,
  And thus close, close enfolded answered me

In fashion as the following Canto sings.

Canto VI

*The Emperor Justinian of Constantinople is chosen as the mouthpiece for a glorious
Roman Empire as Dante concedes that secular and religious elements functioned
well during his reign. Justinian moved the seat of the empire from Rome to
Byzantium, codified Roman law after converting to Christianity, and here recounts
the history of the mighty empire, from its foundation up to the time of
Charlemagne. He explains that the souls around him performed noble deeds which
were sadly marred by a desire for personal advancement. Now freed from the desire
for greater reward, they bask in God's eternal mercy. Among them is Romeo,
adviser to Raymond Berenger IV, Count of Provence.*

"After that Constantine the eagle turned
  Against the course of heaven, which it had followed
  Behind the ancient who Lavinia took,

Two hundred years and more the bird of God
  In the extreme of Europe held itself,
  Near to the mountains whence it issued first;

And under shadow of the sacred plumes
  It governed there the world from hand to hand,
  And, changing thus, upon mine own alighted.

Caesar I was, and am Justinian,
  Who, by the will of primal Love I feel,
  Took from the laws the useless and redundant;

And ere unto the work I was attent,
  One nature to exist in Christ, not more,
  Believed, and with such faith was I contented.

But blessed Agapetus, he who was
  The supreme pastor, to the faith sincere
  Pointed me out the way by words of his.

Him I believed, and what was his assertion
  I now see clearly, even as thou seest
  Each contradiction to be false and true.

As soon as with the Church I moved my feet,
  God in his grace it pleased with this high task
  To inspire me, and I gave me wholly to it,

And to my Belisarius I commended
  The arms, to which was heaven's right hand so joined
  It was a signal that I should repose.

Now here to the first question terminates
  My answer; but the character thereof
  Constrains me to continue with a sequel,

In order that thou see with how great reason
  Men move against the standard sacrosanct,
  Both who appropriate and who oppose it.

Behold how great a power has made it worthy
  Of reverence, beginning from the hour
  When Pallas died to give it sovereignty.

Thou knowest it made in Alba its abode
　Three hundred years and upward, till at last
　The three to three fought for it yet again.

Thou knowest what it achieved from Sabine wrong
　Down to Lucretia's sorrow, in seven kings
　O'ercoming round about the neighboring nations;

Thou knowest what it achieved, borne by the Romans
　Illustrious against Brennus, against Pyrrhus,
　Against the other princes and confederates.

Torquatus thence and Quinctius, who from locks
　Unkempt was named, Decii and Fabii,
　Received the fame I willingly embalm;

It struck to earth the pride of the Arabians,
　Who, following Hannibal, had passed across
　The Alpine ridges, Po, from which thou glidest;

Beneath it triumphed while they yet were young
　Pompey and Scipio, and to the hill
　Beneath which thou wast born it bitter seemed;

Then, near unto the time when heaven had willed
　To bring the whole world to its mood serene,
　Did Caesar by the will of Rome assume it.

What it achieved from Var unto the Rhine,
　Isere beheld and Saone, beheld the Seine,
　And every valley whence the Rhone is filled;

What it achieved when it had left Ravenna,
　And leaped the Rubicon, was such a flight
　That neither tongue nor pen could follow it.

Round towards Spain it wheeled its legions; then
　Towards Durazzo, and Pharsalia smote
　That to the calid Nile was felt the pain.

Antandros and the Simois, whence it started,
　It saw again, and there where Hector lies,
　And ill for Ptolemy then roused itself.

From thence it came like lightning upon Juba;
　Then wheeled itself again into your West,
　Where the Pompeian clarion it heard.

From what it wrought with the next standard-bearer
　Brutus and Cassius howl in Hell together,
　And Modena and Perugia dolent were;

Still doth the mournful Cleopatra weep
　Because thereof, who, fleeing from before it,
　Took from the adder sudden and black death.

With him it ran even to the Red Sea shore;
　With him it placed the world in so great peace,
　That unto Janus was his temple closed.

But what the standard that has made me speak
　Achieved before, and after should achieve
　Throughout the mortal realm that lies beneath it,

Becometh in appearance mean and dim,
　If in the hand of the third Caesar seen
　With eye unclouded and affection pure,

Because the living Justice that inspires me
　Granted it, in the hand of him I speak of,
　The glory of doing vengeance for its wrath.

Now here attend to what I answer thee;
　Later it ran with Titus to do vengeance
　Upon the vengeance of the ancient sin.

And when the tooth of Lombardy had bitten
　The Holy Church, then underneath its wings
　Did Charlemagne victorious succor her.

Now hast thou power to judge of such as those
　Whom I accused above, and of their crimes,
　Which are the cause of all your miseries.

To the public standard one the yellow lilies
　Opposes, the other claims it for a party,
　So that 'tis hard to see which sins the most.

Let, let the Ghibellines ply their handicraft
　Beneath some other standard; for this ever
　Ill follows he who it and justice parts.

And let not this new Charles e'er strike it down,
　He and his Guelfs, but let him fear the talons
　That from a nobler lion stripped the fell.

Already oftentimes the sons have wept
　The father's crime; and let him not believe
　That God will change His scutcheon for the lilies.

This little planet doth adorn itself
　With the good spirits that have active been,
　That fame and honour might come after them;

And whensoever the desires mount thither,
  Thus deviating, must perforce the rays
  Of the true love less vividly mount upward.

But in commensuration of our wages
  With our desert is portion of our joy,
  Because we see them neither less nor greater.

Herein doth living Justice sweeten so
  Affection in us, that for evermore
  It cannot warp to any iniquity.

Voices diverse make up sweet melodies;
  So in this life of ours the seats diverse
  Render sweet harmony among these spheres;

And in the compass of this present pearl
  Shineth the sheen of Romeo, of whom
  The grand and beauteous work was ill rewarded.

But the Provencals who against him wrought,
  They have not laughed, and therefore ill goes he
  Who makes his hurt of the good deeds of others.

Four daughters, and each one of them a queen,
  Had Raymond Berenger, and this for him
  Did Romeo, a poor man and a pilgrim;

And then malicious words incited him
  To summon to a reckoning this just man,
  Who rendered to him seven and five for ten.

Then he departed poor and stricken in years,
  And if the world could know the heart he had,
  In begging bit by bit his livelihood,

Though much it laud him, it would laud him more."

Canto VII

Justinian and the other spirits spin out of sight. Beatrice explains that just vengeance was exacted for the Fall through the Crucifixion, but that even though Christ's human nature was justly punished, his divinity had been wronged. Dante begins to understand that God wished to accomplish the redemption of mankind through the gift of his only son. A discussion follows about the mystery of the Resurrection of the Body: what God created as first matter – life, the angels and the spheres – is eternal; what decays are things not directly made by his hand.

"*Osanna sanctus Deus Sabaoth,*
  Superillustrans claritate tua
  Felices ignes horum malahoth!"

In this wise, to his melody returning,
  This substance, upon which a double light
  Doubles itself, was seen by me to sing,

And to their dance this and the others moved,
  And in the manner of swift-hurrying sparks
  Veiled themselves from me with a sudden distance.

Doubting was I, and saying, "Tell her, tell her,"
  Within me, "tell her," saying, "tell my Lady,"
  Who slakes my thirst with her sweet effluences;

And yet that reverence which doth lord it over
  The whole of me only by B and ICE,
  Bowed me again like unto one who drowses.

Short while did Beatrice endure me thus;
  And she began, lighting me with a smile
  Such as would make one happy in the fire:

"According to infallible advisement,
  After what manner a just vengeance justly
  Could be avenged has put thee upon thinking,

But I will speedily thy mind unloose;
  And do thou listen, for these words of mine
  Of a great doctrine will a present make thee.

By not enduring on the power that wills
  Curb for his good, that man who ne'er was born,
  Damning himself damned all his progeny;

Whereby the human species down below
  Lay sick for many centuries in great error,
  Till to descend it pleased the Word of God

To where the nature, which from its own Maker
  Estranged itself, he joined to him in person
  By the sole act of his eternal love.

Now unto what is said direct thy sight;
  This nature when united to its Maker,
  Such as created, was sincere and good;

But by itself alone was banished forth
  From Paradise, because it turned aside
  Out of the way of truth and of its life.

Therefore the penalty the cross held out,
  If measured by the nature thus assumed,
  None ever yet with so great justice stung,

And none was ever of so great injustice,
  Considering who the Person was that suffered,
  Within whom such a nature was contracted.

From one act therefore issued things diverse;
  To God and to the Jews one death was pleasing;
  Earth trembled at it and the Heaven was opened.

It should no longer now seem difficult
  To thee, when it is said that a just vengeance
  By a just court was afterward avenged.

But now do I behold thy mind entangled
  From thought to thought within a knot, from which
  With great desire it waits to free itself.

Thou sayest, 'Well discern I what I hear;
  But it is hidden from me why God willed
  For our redemption only this one mode.'

Buried remaineth, brother, this decree
  Unto the eyes of every one whose nature
  Is in the flame of love not yet adult.

Verily, inasmuch as at this mark
  One gazes long and little is discerned,
  Wherefore this mode was worthiest will I say.

Goodness Divine, which from itself doth spurn
  All envy, burning in itself so sparkles
  That the eternal beauties it unfolds.

Whate'er from this immediately distils
  Has afterwards no end, for ne'er removed
  Is its impression when it sets its seal.

Whate'er from this immediately rains down
  Is wholly free, because it is not subject
  Unto the influences of novel things.

The more conformed thereto, the more it pleases;
  For the blest ardour that irradiates all things
  In that most like itself is most vivacious.

With all of these things has advantaged been
  The human creature; and if one be wanting,
  From his nobility he needs must fall.

'Tis sin alone which doth disfranchise him,
  And render him unlike the Good Supreme,
  So that he little with its light is blanched,

And to his dignity no more returns,
  Unless he fill up where transgression empties
  With righteous pains for criminal delights.

Your nature when it sinned so utterly
  In its own seed, out of these dignities
  Even as out of Paradise was driven,

Nor could itself recover, if thou notest
  With nicest subtilty, by any way,
  Except by passing one of these two fords:

Either that God through clemency alone
  Had pardon granted, or that man himself
  Had satisfaction for his folly made.

Fix now thine eye deep into the abyss
  Of the eternal counsel, to my speech
  As far as may be fastened steadfastly!

Man in his limitations had not power
  To satisfy, not having power to sink
  In his humility obeying then,

Far as he disobeying thought to rise;
  And for this reason man has been from power
  Of satisfying by himself excluded.

Therefore it God behoved in his own ways
  Man to restore unto his perfect life,
  I say in one, or else in both of them.

But since the action of the doer is
  So much more grateful, as it more presents
  The goodness of the heart from which it issues,

Goodness Divine, that doth imprint the world,
  Has been contented to proceed by each
  And all its ways to lift you up again;

Nor 'twixt the first day and the final night
  Such high and such magnificent proceeding
  By one or by the other was or shall be;

For God more bounteous was himself to give
  To make man able to uplift himself,
  Than if he only of himself had pardoned;

And all the other modes were insufficient
  For justice, were it not the Son of God
  Himself had humbled to become incarnate.

Now, to fill fully each desire of thine,
  Return I to elucidate one place,
  In order that thou there mayst see as I do.

Thou sayst: 'I see the air, I see the fire,
  The water, and the earth, and all their mixtures
  Come to corruption, and short while endure;

And these things notwithstanding were created;'
  Therefore if that which I have said were true,
  They should have been secure against corruption.

The Angels, brother, and the land sincere
  In which thou art, created may be called
  Just as they are in their entire existence;

But all the elements which thou hast named,
  And all those things which out of them are made,
  By a created virtue are informed.

Created was the matter which they have;
  Created was the informing influence
  Within these stars that round about them go.

The soul of every brute and of the plants
  By its potential temperament attracts
  The ray and motion of the holy lights;

But your own life immediately inspires
  Supreme Beneficence, and enamours it
  So with herself, it evermore desires her.

And thou from this mayst argue furthermore
  Your resurrection, if thou think again
  How human flesh was fashioned at that time

When the first parents both of them were made."

Canto VIII

*As Dante and Beatrice ascend into the orbit of Venus, the Third Heaven, he is awed by
the increasing loveliness of her face. Here they encounter the souls of those who loved
with a passion so ardent it verged on madness. Chastened, they celebrate their place in
the hierarchy of bliss. Charles Martel discourses on the way in which heredity is
subservient to the workings of Providence, so that ancestors are not the only factor in a
person's character. He ends by speaking of how men would not go astray if they
followed what is laid down for them by nature.*

The world used in its peril to believe
  That the fair Cypria delirious love
  Rayed out, in the third epicycle turning;

Wherefore not only unto her paid honour
  Of sacrifices and of votive cry
  The ancient nations in the ancient error,

But both Dione honoured they and Cupid,
  That as her mother, this one as her son,
  And said that he had sat in Dido's lap;

And they from her, whence I beginning take,
  Took the denomination of the star
  That woos the sun, now following, now in front.

I was not ware of our ascending to it;
  But of our being in it gave full faith
  My Lady whom I saw more beauteous grow.

And as within a flame a spark is seen,
  And as within a voice a voice discerned,
  When one is steadfast, and one comes and goes,

Within that light beheld I other lamps
  Move in a circle, speeding more and less,
  Methinks in measure of their inward vision.

From a cold cloud descended never winds,
  Or visible or not, so rapidly
  They would not laggard and impeded seem

To any one who had those lights divine
  Seen come towards us, leaving the gyration
  Begun at first in the high Seraphim.

And behind those that most in front appeared
  Sounded "*Osanna!*" so that never since
  To hear again was I without desire.

Then unto us more nearly one approached,
  And it alone began: "We all are ready
  Unto thy pleasure, that thou joy in us.

We turn around with the celestial Princes,
  One gyre and one gyration and one thirst,
  To whom thou in the world of old didst say,

'Ye who, intelligent, the third heaven are moving;'
  And are so full of love, to pleasure thee
  A little quiet will not be less sweet."

After these eyes of mine themselves had offered
  Unto my Lady reverently, and she
  Content and certain of herself had made them,

Back to the light they turned, which so great promise
  Made of itself, and "Say, who art thou?" was
  My voice, imprinted with a great affection.

O how and how much I beheld it grow
  With the new joy that superadded was
  Unto its joys, as soon as I had spoken!

Thus changed, it said to me: "The world possessed me
  Short time below; and, if it had been more,
  Much evil will be which would not have been.

My gladness keepeth me concealed from thee,
  Which rayeth round about me, and doth hide me
  Like as a creature swathed in its own silk.

Much didst thou love me, and thou hadst good reason;
  For had I been below, I should have shown thee
  Somewhat beyond the foliage of my love.

That left-hand margin, which doth bathe itself
  In Rhone, when it is mingled with the Sorgue,
  Me for its lord awaited in due time,

And that horn of Ausonia, which is towned
  With Bari, with Gaeta and Catona,
  Whence Tronto and Verde in the sea disgorge.

Already flashed upon my brow the crown
  Of that dominion which the Danube waters
  After the German borders it abandons;

And beautiful Trinacria, that is murky
  'Twixt Pachino and Peloro, (on the gulf
  Which greatest scath from Eurus doth receive,)

Not through Typhoeus, but through nascent sulphur,
  Would have awaited her own monarchs still,
  Through me from Charles descended and from
                                    Rudolph,

If evil lordship, that exasperates ever
  The subject populations, had not moved
  Palermo to the outcry of 'Death! death!'

And if my brother could but this foresee,
  The greedy poverty of Catalonia
  Straight would he flee, that it might not molest him;

For verily 'tis needful to provide,
  Through him or other, so that on his bark
  Already freighted no more freight be placed.

His nature, which from liberal covetous
  Descended, such a soldiery would need
  As should not care for hoarding in a chest."

"Because I do believe the lofty joy
  Thy speech infuses into me, my Lord,
  Where every good thing doth begin and end

Thou seest as I see it, the more grateful
  Is it to me; and this too hold I dear,
  That gazing upon God thou dost discern it.

Glad hast thou made me; so make clear to me,
  Since speaking thou hast stirred me up to doubt,
  How from sweet seed can bitter issue forth."

This I to him; and he to me: "If I
  Can show to thee a truth, to what thou askest
  Thy face thou'lt hold as thou dost hold thy back.

The Good which all the realm thou art ascending
  Turns and contents, maketh its providence
  To be a power within these bodies vast;

And not alone the natures are foreseen
  Within the mind that in itself is perfect,
  But they together with their preservation.

For whatsoever thing this bow shoots forth
  Falls foreordained unto an end foreseen,
  Even as a shaft directed to its mark.

If that were not, the heaven which thou dost walk
  Would in such manner its effects produce,
  That they no longer would be arts, but ruins.

This cannot be, if the Intelligences
  That keep these stars in motion are not maimed,
  And maimed the First that has not made them perfect.

Wilt thou this truth have clearer made to thee?"
  And I: "Not so; for 'tis impossible
  That nature tire, I see, in what is needful."

Whence he again: "Now say, would it be worse
  For men on Earth were they not citizens?"
  "Yes," I replied; "and here I ask no reason."

"And can they be so, if below they live not
  Diversely unto offices diverse?
  No, if your master writeth well for you."

So came he with deductions to this point;
  Then he concluded: "Therefore it behoves
  The roots of your effects to be diverse.

Hence one is Solon born, another Xerxes,
  Another Melchisedec, and another he
  Who, flying through the air, his son did lose.

Revolving Nature, which a signet is
  To mortal wax, doth practise well her art,
  But not one inn distinguish from another;

Thence happens it that Esau differeth
  In seed from Jacob; and Quirinus comes
  From sire so vile that he is given to Mars.

"That left-hand margin, which doth bathe itself / In Rhone, when it is mingled with the Sorgue, / Me for its lord awaited in due time,"

Par. VIII, lines 58–60

A generated nature its own way
  Would always make like its progenitors,
  If Providence divine were not triumphant.

Now that which was behind thee is before thee;
  But that thou know that I with thee am pleased,
  With a corollary will I mantle thee.

Evermore nature, if it fortune find
  Discordant to it, like each other seed
  Out of its region, maketh evil thrift;

And if the world below would fix its mind
  On the foundation which is laid by nature,
  Pursuing that, 'twould have the people good.

But you unto religion wrench aside
  Him who was born to gird him with the sword,
  And make a king of him who is for sermons;

Therefore your footsteps wander from the road."

Canto IX

Dante hears stories of human love transformed into an adoration for God. He meets
Cunizza da Romano, sister of the tyrant Ezzelino and mistress of Sordello
(Purgatory, Cantos VI and VII), and also Foulquet of Marseilles, a troubadour poet
famous for his verse and love affairs. Both souls deliver damning speeches about
temporal affairs: Cunizza predicts disaster for Treviso and its surroundings whilst
Foulquet denounces the Church for its failings and indicts the city of Florence. They
finally express jubilance at being where they are and comprehend that God's will,
which is Love, governs the cosmos.

Beautiful Clemence, after that thy Charles
  Had me enlightened, he narrated to me
  The treacheries his seed should undergo;

But said: "Be still and let the years roll round;"
  So I can only say, that lamentation
  Legitimate shall follow on your wrongs.

And of that holy light the life already
  Had to the Sun which fills it turned again,
  As to that good which for each thing sufficeth.

Ah, souls deceived, and creatures impious,
  Who from such good do turn away your hearts,
  Directing upon vanity your foreheads!

And now, behold, another of those splendours
  Approached me, and its will to pleasure me
  It signified by brightening outwardly.

The eyes of Beatrice, that fastened were
  Upon me, as before, of dear assent
  To my desire assurance gave to me.

"Ah, bring swift compensation to my wish,
  Thou blessed spirit," I said, "and give me proof
  That what I think in thee I can reflect!"

Whereat the light, that still was new to me,
  Out of its depths, whence it before was singing,
  As one delighted to do good, continued:

"Within that region of the land depraved
  Of Italy, that lies between Rialto
  And fountain-heads of Brenta and of Piava,

Rises a hill, and mounts not very high,
  Wherefrom descended formerly a torch
  That made upon that region great assault.

Out of one root were born both I and it;
  Cunizza was I called, and here I shine
  Because the splendour of this star o'ercame me.

But gladly to myself the cause I pardon
  Of my allotment, and it does not grieve me;
  Which would perhaps seem strong unto your vulgar.

Of this so luculent and precious jewel,
  Which of our heaven is nearest unto me,
  Great fame remained; and ere it die away

This hundredth year shall yet quintupled be.
  See if man ought to make him excellent,
  So that another life the first may leave!

And thus thinks not the present multitude
  Shut in by Adige and Tagliamento,
  Nor yet for being scourged is penitent.

But soon 'twill be that Padua in the marsh
  Will change the water that Vicenza bathes,
  Because the folk are stubborn against duty;

And where the Sile and Cagnano join
  One lordeth it, and goes with lofty head,
  For catching whom e'en now the net is making.

Feltro moreover of her impious pastor
  Shall weep the crime, which shall so monstrous be
  That for the like none ever entered Malta.

Ample exceedingly would be the vat
  That of the Ferrarese could hold the blood,
  And weary who should weigh it ounce by ounce,

Of which this courteous priest shall make a gift
  To show himself a partisan; and such gifts
  Will to the living of the land conform.

Above us there are mirrors, Thrones you call them,
  From which shines out on us God Judicant,
  So that this utterance seems good to us."

Here it was silent, and it had the semblance
  Of being turned elsewhither, by the wheel
  On which it entered as it was before.

The other joy, already known to me,
  Became a thing transplendent in my sight,
  As a fine ruby smitten by the sun.

Through joy effulgence is acquired above,
  As here a smile; but down below, the shade
  Outwardly darkens, as the mind is sad.

"God seeth all things, and in Him, blest spirit,
  Thy sight is," said I, "so that never will
  Of his can possibly from thee be hidden;

Thy voice, then, that for ever makes the heavens
  Glad, with the singing of those holy fires
  Which of their six wings make themselves a cowl,

Wherefore does it not satisfy my longings?
  Indeed, I would not wait thy questioning
  If I in thee were as thou art in me."

"The greatest of the valleys where the water
  Expands itself," forthwith its words began,
  "That sea excepted which the earth engarlands,

Between discordant shores against the sun
  Extends so far, that it meridian makes
  Where it was wont before to make the horizon.

I was a dweller on that valley's shore
  'Twixt Ebro and Magra that with journey short
  Doth from the Tuscan part the Genoese.

With the same sunset and same sunrise nearly
  Sit Buggia and the city whence I was,
  That with its blood once made the harbour hot.

Folco that people called me unto whom
  My name was known; and now with me this heaven
  Imprints itself, as I did once with it;

For more the daughter of Belus never burned,
  Offending both Sichaeus and Creusa,
  Than I, so long as it became my locks,

Nor yet that Rodophean, who deluded
  was by Demophoon, nor yet Alcides,
  When Iole he in his heart had locked.

Yet here is no repenting, but we smile,
  Not at the fault, which comes not back to mind,
  But at the power which ordered and foresaw.

Here we behold the art that doth adorn
  With such affection, and the good discover
  Whereby the world above turns that below.

But that thou wholly satisfied mayst bear
  Thy wishes hence which in this sphere are born,
  Still farther to proceed behoveth me.

Thou fain wouldst know who is within this light
  That here beside me thus is scintillating,
  Even as a sunbeam in the limpid water.

Then know thou, that within there is at rest
  Rahab, and being to our order joined,
  With her in its supremest grade 'tis sealed.

Into this heaven, where ends the shadowy cone
  Cast by your world, before all other souls
  First of Christ's triumph was she taken up.

Full meet it was to leave her in some heaven,
  Even as a palm of the high victory
  Which he acquired with one palm and the other,

Because she favoured the first glorious deed
  Of Joshua upon the Holy Land,
  That little stirs the memory of the Pope.

Thy city, which an offshoot is of him
  Who first upon his Maker turned his back,
  And whose ambition is so sorely wept,

Brings forth and scatters the accursed flower
  Which both the sheep and lambs hath led astray
  Since it has turned the shepherd to a wolf.

For this the Evangel and the mighty Doctors
  Are derelict, and only the Decretals
  So studied that it shows upon their margins.

On this are Pope and Cardinals intent;
  Their meditations reach not Nazareth,
  There where his pinions Gabriel unfolded;

But Vatican and the other parts elect
  Of Rome, which have a cemetery been
  Unto the soldiery that followed Peter

Shall soon be free from this adultery."

Canto X

Beatrice and Dante leave the shadow of the Earth as they ascend into the sphere of the Sun, the Fourth Heaven. The souls of leading theologians, historians, teachers and philosophers form a revolving circle of light, symbol of the indivisible Truth of God, around Beatrice and Dante. The pilgrim can find no words to describe the beauty of their singing. Saint Thomas Aquinas, author of the Summa Theologiae, *names the other luminaries – Albertus Magnus, Gratian, Peter Lombard, Solomon, Dionysius the Areopagite, Paulus Orosius, Boethius, Isidore of Seville, the Venerable Bede, Richard of Saint Victor and Sigier of Brabant.*

Looking into his Son with all the Love
  Which each of them eternally breathes forth,
  The Primal and unutterable Power

Whate'er before the mind or eye revolves
  With so much order made, there can be none
  Who this beholds without enjoying Him.

Lift up then, Reader, to the lofty wheels
  With me thy vision straight unto that part
  Where the one motion on the other strikes,

And there begin to contemplate with joy
  That Master's art, who in himself so loves it
  That never doth his eye depart therefrom.

Behold how from that point goes branching off
  The oblique circle, which conveys the planets,
  To satisfy the world that calls upon them;

And if their pathway were not thus inflected,
  Much virtue in the heavens would be in vain,
  And almost every power below here dead.

If from the straight line distant more or less
  Were the departure, much would wanting be
  Above and underneath of mundane order.

Remain now, Reader, still upon thy bench,
  In thought pursuing that which is foretasted,
  If thou wouldst jocund be instead of weary.

I've set before thee; henceforth feed thyself,
  For to itself diverteth all my care
  That theme whereof I have been made the scribe.

The greatest of the ministers of nature,
  Who with the power of heaven the world imprints
  And measures with his light the time for us,

With that part which above is called to mind
  Conjoined, along the spirals was revolving,
  Where each time earlier he presents himself;

And I was with him; but of the ascending
  I was not conscious, saving as a man
  Of a first thought is conscious ere it come;

And Beatrice, she who is seen to pass
  From good to better, and so suddenly
  That not by time her action is expressed,

How lucent in herself must she have been!
  And what was in the sun, wherein I entered,
  Apparent not by colour but by light,

I, though I call on genius, art, and practice,
  Cannot so tell that it could be imagined;
  Believe one can, and let him long to see it.

And if our fantasies too lowly are
  For altitude so great, it is no marvel,
  Since o'er the sun was never eye could go.

Such in this place was the fourth family
  Of the high Father, who forever sates it,
  Showing how he breathes forth and how begets.

And Beatrice began: "Give thanks, give thanks
  Unto the Sun of Angels, who to this
  Sensible one has raised thee by his grace!"

Never was heart of mortal so disposed
  To worship, nor to give itself to God
  With all its gratitude was it so ready,

As at those words did I myself become;
  And all my love was so absorbed in Him,
  That in oblivion Beatrice was eclipsed.

Nor this displeased her; but she smiled at it
  So that the splendour of her laughing eyes
  My single mind on many things divided.

Lights many saw I, vivid and triumphant,
  Make us a centre and themselves a circle,
  More sweet in voice than luminous in aspect.

Thus girt about the daughter of Latona
  We sometimes see, when pregnant is the air,
  So that it holds the thread which makes her zone.

Within the court of Heaven, whence I return,
  Are many jewels found, so fair and precious
  They cannot be transported from the realm;

And of them was the singing of those lights.
  Who takes not wings that he may fly up thither,
  The tidings thence may from the dumb await!

As soon as singing thus those burning suns
  Had round about us whirled themselves three times,
  Like unto stars neighbouring the steadfast poles,

Ladies they seemed, not from the dance released,
  But who stop short, in silence listening
  Till they have gathered the new melody.

And within one I heard beginning: "When
  The radiance of grace, by which is kindled
  True love, and which thereafter grows by loving,

Within thee multiplied is so resplendent
  That it conducts thee upward by that stair,
  Where without reascending none descends,

Who should deny the wine out of his vial
  Unto thy thirst, in liberty were not
  Except as water which descends not seaward.

Fain wouldst thou know with what plants is enflowered
  This garland that encircles with delight
  The Lady fair who makes thee strong for heaven.

Of the lambs was I of the holy flock
  Which Dominic conducteth by a road
  Where well one fattens if he strayeth not.

He who is nearest to me on the right
  My brother and master was; and he Albertus
  Is of Cologne, I Thomas of Aquinum.

If thou of all the others wouldst be certain,
  Follow behind my speaking with thy sight
  Upward along the blessed garland turning.

That next effulgence issues from the smile
  Of Gratian, who assisted both the courts
  In such wise that it pleased in Paradise.

The other which near by adorns our choir
  That Peter was who, e'en as the poor widow,
  Offered his treasure unto Holy Church.

The fifth light, that among us is the fairest,
  Breathes forth from such a love, that all the world
  Below is greedy to learn tidings of it.

Within it is the lofty mind, where knowledge
  So deep was put, that, if the true be true,
  To see so much there never rose a second.

Thou seest next the lustre of that taper,
  Which in the flesh below looked most within
  The angelic nature and its ministry.

Within that other little light is smiling
  The advocate of the Christian centuries,
  Out of whose rhetoric Augustine was furnished.

Now if thou trainest thy mind's eye along
  From light to light pursuant of my praise,
  With thirst already of the eighth thou waitest.

By seeing every good therein exults
  The sainted soul, which the fallacious world
  Makes manifest to him who listeneth well;

The body whence 'twas hunted forth is lying
  Down in Cieldauro, and from martyrdom
  And banishment it came unto this peace.

See farther onward flame the burning breath
  Of Isidore, of Beda, and of Richard
  Who was in contemplation more than man.

This, whence to me returneth thy regard,
  The light is of a spirit unto whom
  In his grave meditations death seemed slow.

It is the light eternal of Sigier,
  Who, reading lectures in the Street of Straw,
  Did syllogize invidious verities."

Then, as a horologe that calleth us
  What time the Bride of God is rising up
  With matins to her Spouse that he may love her,

Wherein one part the other draws and urges,
  Ting! ting! resounding with so sweet a note,
  That swells with love the spirit well disposed,

Thus I beheld the glorious wheel move round,
  And render voice to voice, in modulation
  And sweetness that can not be comprehended,

Excepting there where joy is made eternal.

Canto XI

*Dante weighs up the secondary aims of earthly life with the absolute values of eternal
life. He listens to the Dominican scholar and theologian Saint Thomas Aquinas reveal
that Providence has chosen two princes to guide the Roman Catholic Church – Saint
Francis of Assisi and Saint Dominic. He embarks on a song of praise for the
remarkable founder of the Franciscan order and his followers, all of whom renounced
their material possessions to embrace a life of poverty. For Dante, Saint Francis
embodies the new spirit of Christ on Earth.*

O Thou insensate care of mortal men,
  How inconclusive are the syllogisms
  That make thee beat thy wings in downward flight!

One after laws and one to aphorisms
  Was going, and one following the priesthood,
  And one to reign by force or sophistry,

And one in theft, and one in state affairs,
  One in the pleasures of the flesh involved
  Wearied himself, one gave himself to ease;

When I, from all these things emancipate,
  With Beatrice above there in the Heavens
  With such exceeding glory was received!

When each one had returned unto that point
  Within the circle where it was before,
  It stood as in a candlestick a candle;

And from within the effulgence which at first
  Had spoken unto me, I heard begin
  Smiling while it more luminous became:

"Even as I am kindled in its ray,
  So, looking into the Eternal Light,
  The occasion of thy thoughts I apprehend.

Thou doubtest, and wouldst have me to resift
  In language so extended and so open
  My speech, that to thy sense it may be plain,

Where just before I said, 'where well one fattens,'
  And where I said, 'there never rose a second;'
  And here 'tis needful we distinguish well.

The Providence, which governeth the world
  With counsel, wherein all created vision
  Is vanquished ere it reach unto the bottom,

(So that towards her own Beloved might go
  The bride of Him who, uttering a loud cry,
  Espoused her with his consecrated blood,

Self-confident and unto Him more faithful,)
  Two Princes did ordain in her behoof,
  Which on this side and that might be her guide.

The one was all seraphical in ardour;
  The other by his wisdom upon Earth
  A splendour was of light cherubical.

One will I speak of, for of both is spoken
  In praising one, whichever may be taken,
  Because unto one end their labours were.

Between Tupino and the stream that falls
  Down from the hill elect of blessed Ubald,
  A fertile slope of lofty mountain hangs,

From which Perugia feels the cold and heat
  Through Porta Sole, and behind it weep
  Gualdo and Nocera their grievous yoke.

From out that slope, there where it breaketh most
  Its steepness, rose upon the world a sun
  As this one does sometimes from out the Ganges;

Therefore let him who speaketh of that place,
  Say not Ascesi, for he would say little,
  But Orient, if he properly would speak.

He was not yet far distant from his rising
  Before he had begun to make the earth
  Some comfort from his mighty virtue feel.

For he in youth his father's wrath incurred
  For certain Dame, to whom, as unto death,
  The gate of pleasure no one doth unlock;

And was before his spiritual court
  '*Et coram patre*' unto her united;
  Then day by day more fervently he loved her.

She, reft of her first husband, scorned, obscure,
  One thousand and one hundred years and more,
  Waited without a suitor till he came.

Naught it availed to hear, that with Amyclas
  Found her unmoved at sounding of his voice
  He who struck terror into all the world;

Naught it availed being constant and undaunted,
  So that, when Mary still remained below,
  She mounted up with Christ upon the cross.

But that too darkly I may not proceed,
  Francis and Poverty for these two lovers
  Take thou henceforward in my speech diffuse.

Their concord and their joyous semblances,
  The love, the wonder, and the sweet regard,
  They made to be the cause of holy thoughts;

So much so that the venerable Bernard
  First bared his feet, and after so great peace
  Ran, and, in running, thought himself too slow.

O wealth unknown! O veritable good!
  Giles bares his feet, and bares his feet Sylvester
  Behind the bridegroom, so doth please the bride!

Then goes his way that father and that master,
  He and his Lady and that family
  Which now was girding on the humble cord;

Nor cowardice of heart weighed down his brow
  At being son of Peter Bernardone,
  Nor for appearing marvellously scorned;

But regally his hard determination
  To Innocent he opened, and from him
  Received the primal seal upon his Order.

After the people mendicant increased
  Behind this man, whose admirable life
  Better in glory of the heavens were sung,

Incoronated with a second crown
  Was through Honorius by the Eternal Spirit
  The holy purpose of this Archimandrite.

And when he had, through thirst of martyrdom,
  In the proud presence of the Sultan preached
  Christ and the others who came after him,

And, finding for conversion too unripe
  The folk, and not to tarry there in vain,
  Returned to fruit of the Italic grass,

On the rude rock 'twixt Tiber and the Arno
  From Christ did he receive the final seal,
  Which during two whole years his members bore.

When He, who chose him unto so much good,
  Was pleased to draw him up to the reward
  That he had merited by being lowly,

Unto his friars, as to the rightful heirs,
  His most dear Lady did he recommend,
  And bade that they should love her faithfully;

And from her bosom the illustrious soul
  Wished to depart, returning to its realm,
  And for its body wished no other bier.

Think now what man was he, who was a fit
  Companion over the high seas to keep
  The bark of Peter to its proper bearings.

And this man was our Patriarch; hence whoever
  Doth follow him as he commands can see
  That he is laden with good merchandise.

But for new pasturage his flock has grown
  So greedy, that it is impossible
  They be not scattered over fields diverse;

And in proportion as his sheep remote
  And vagabond go farther off from him,
  More void of milk return they to the fold.

Verily some there are that fear a hurt,
  And keep close to the shepherd; but so few,
  That little cloth doth furnish forth their hoods.

Now if my utterance be not indistinct,
  If thine own hearing hath attentive been,
  If thou recall to mind what I have said,

In part contented shall thy wishes be;
  For thou shalt see the plant that's chipped away,
  And the rebuke that lieth in the words,

'Where well one fattens, if he strayeth not.'"

Canto XII

*After Saint Thomas' speech, the lights are encircled by a fainter circle – the
followers of Saint Francis – as they resume their motion. The twin circles symbolize
the interdependence of Love and learning and the unity between orders. Just as the
Dominican eulogized Francis of Assisi back in Canto XI, the Franciscan
Bonaventure now extols the life and works of Dominic de Guzman, founder of the
Dominicans, who removed false doctrine using zeal and true wisdom. Introducing
himself, he names Illuminato da Rieti, Fra Agostino, Hugh of St Victor, Peter
Mangiador, Peter of Spain, Nathan, Chrysostom, Anselm, Donatus, Rabanus and
Joachim of Flora.*

Soon as the blessed flame had taken up
  The final word to give it utterance,
  Began the holy millstone to revolve,

And in its gyre had not turned wholly round,
  Before another in a ring enclosed it,
  And motion joined to motion, song to song;

Song that as greatly doth transcend our Muses,
  Our Sirens, in those dulcet clarions,
  As primal splendour that which is reflected.

And as are spanned athwart a tender cloud
  Two rainbows parallel and like in colour,
  When Juno to her handmaid gives command,

(The one without born of the one within,
  Like to the speaking of that vagrant one
  Whom love consumed as doth the sun the vapours,)

And make the people here, through covenant
  God set with Noah, presageful of the world
  That shall no more be covered with a flood,

In such wise of those sempiternal roses
  The garlands twain encompassed us about,
  And thus the outer to the inner answered.

After the dance, and other grand rejoicings,
  Both of the singing, and the flaming forth
  Effulgence with effulgence blithe and tender,

Together, at once, with one accord had stopped,
  (Even as the eyes, that, as volition moves them,
  Must needs together shut and lift themselves,)

Out of the heart of one of the new lights
  There came a voice, that needle to the star
  Made me appear in turning thitherward.

And it began: "The love that makes me fair
  Draws me to speak about the other leader,
  By whom so well is spoken here of mine.

'Tis right, where one is, to bring in the other,
  That, as they were united in their warfare,
  Together likewise may their glory shine.

In such wise of those sempiternal roses / The garlands twain encompassed us about, /
And thus the outer to the inner answered.

Par. XII, lines 19–21

The soldiery of Christ, which it had cost
  So dear to arm again, behind the standard
  Moved slow and doubtful and in numbers few,

When the Emperor who reigneth evermore
  Provided for the host that was in peril,
  Through grace alone and not that it was worthy;

And, as was said, he to his Bride brought succour
  With champions twain, at whose deed, at whose word
  The straggling people were together drawn.

Within that region where the sweet west wind
  Rises to open the new leaves, wherewith
  Europe is seen to clothe herself afresh,

Not far off from the beating of the waves,
  Behind which in his long career the sun
  Sometimes conceals himself from every man,

Is situate the fortunate Calahorra,
  Under protection of the mighty shield
  In which the Lion subject is and sovereign.

Therein was born the amorous paramour
  Of Christian Faith, the athlete consecrate,
  Kind to his own and cruel to his foes;

And when it was created was his mind
  Replete with such a living energy,
  That in his mother her it made prophetic.

As soon as the espousals were complete
  Between him and the Faith at holy font,
  Where they with mutual safety dowered each other,

The woman, who for him had given assent,
  Saw in a dream the admirable fruit
  That issue would from him and from his heirs;

And that he might be construed as he was,
  A spirit from this place went forth to name him
  With His possessive whose he wholly was.

Dominic was he called; and him I speak of
  Even as of the husbandman whom Christ
  Elected to his garden to assist him.

Envoy and servant sooth he seemed of Christ,
  For the first love made manifest in him
  Was the first counsel that was given by Christ.

Silent and wakeful many a time was he
  Discovered by his nurse upon the ground,
  As if he would have said, 'For this I came.'

O thou his father, Felix verily!
  O thou his mother, verily Joanna,
  If this, interpreted, means as is said!

Not for the world which people toil for now
  In following Ostiense and Taddeo,
  But through his longing after the true manna,

He in short time became so great a teacher,
  That he began to go about the vineyard,
  Which fadeth soon, if faithless be the dresser;

And of the See, (that once was more benignant
  Unto the righteous poor, not through itself,
  But him who sits there and degenerates,)

Not to dispense or two or three for six,
  Not any fortune of first vacancy,
  'Non decimas quae sunt pauperum Dei,'

He asked for, but against the errant world
  Permission to do battle for the seed,
  Of which these four and twenty plants surround thee.

Then with the doctrine and the will together,
  With office apostolical he moved,
  Like torrent which some lofty vein out-presses;

And in among the shoots heretical
  His impetus with greater fury smote,
  Wherever the resistance was the greatest.

Of him were made thereafter divers runnels,
  Whereby the garden catholic is watered,
  So that more living its plantations stand.

If such the one wheel of the Biga was,
  In which the Holy Church itself defended
  And in the field its civic battle won,

Truly full manifest should be to thee
  The excellence of the other, unto whom
  Thomas so courteous was before my coming.

But still the orbit, which the highest part
  Of its circumference made, is derelict,
  So that the mould is where was once the crust.

His family, that had straight forward moved
  With feet upon his footprints, are turned round
  So that they set the point upon the heel.

And soon aware they will be of the harvest
  Of this bad husbandry, when shall the tares
  Complain the granary is taken from them.

Yet say I, he who searcheth leaf by leaf
  Our volume through, would still some page discover
  Where he could read, 'I am as I am wont.'

'Twill not be from Casal nor Acquasparta,
  From whence come such unto the written word
  That one avoids it, and the other narrows.

Bonaventura of Bagnoregio's life
  Am I, who always in great offices
  Postponed considerations sinister.

Here are Illuminato and Agostino,
  Who of the first barefooted beggars were
  That with the cord the friends of God became.

Hugh of Saint Victor is among them here,
  And Peter Mangiador, and Peter of Spain,
  Who down below in volumes twelve is shining;

Nathan the seer, and metropolitan
  Chrysostom, and Anselmus, and Donatus
  Who deigned to lay his hand to the first art;

Here is Rabanus, and beside me here
  Shines the Calabrian Abbot Joachim,
  He with the spirit of prophecy endowed.

To celebrate so great a paladin
  Have moved me the impassioned courtesy
  And the discreet discourses of Friar Thomas,

And with me they have moved this company."

Canto XIII

*The twin circles of lights whirl around Dante and Beatrice while praising the Trinity
and Christ's divine and human status. Dante tries to describe this phenomenon by
comparing it with the heavenly constellations. Saint Thomas Aquinas speaks about
Solomon's kingly wisdom and then warns Dante against making hasty moral
judgements. He gives another warning about predicting the actions of God. A mortal
cannot automatically suppose that if one person steals and another makes offerings the
first one will be damned and the second one saved. God may see things differently.*

Let him imagine, who would well conceive
  What now I saw, and let him while I speak
  Retain the image as a steadfast rock,

The fifteen stars, that in their divers regions
  The sky enliven with a light so great
  That it transcends all clusters of the air;

Let him the Wain imagine unto which
  Our vault of heaven sufficeth night and day,
  So that in turning of its pole it fails not;

Let him the mouth imagine of the horn
  That in the point beginneth of the axis
  Round about which the primal wheel revolves,—

To have fashioned of themselves two signs in heaven,
　Like unto that which Minos' daughter made,
　The moment when she felt the frost of death;

And one to have its rays within the other,
　And both to whirl themselves in such a manner
　That one should forward go, the other backward;

And he will have some shadowing forth of that
　True constellation and the double dance
　That circled round the point at which I was;

Because it is as much beyond our wont,
　As swifter than the motion of the Chiana
　Moveth the heaven that all the rest outspeeds.

There sang they neither Bacchus, nor Apollo,
　But in the divine nature Persons three,
　And in one person the divine and human.

The singing and the dance fulfilled their measure,
　And unto us those holy lights gave need,
　Growing in happiness from care to care.

Then broke the silence of those saints concordant
　The light in which the admirable life
　Of God's own mendicant was told to me,

And said: "Now that one straw is trodden out
　Now that its seed is garnered up already,
　Sweet love invites me to thresh out the other.

Into that bosom, thou believest, whence
　Was drawn the rib to form the beauteous cheek
　Whose taste to all the world is costing dear,

And into that which, by the lance transfixed,
　Before and since, such satisfaction made
　That it weighs down the balance of all sin,

Whate'er of light it has to human nature
　Been lawful to possess was all infused
　By the same power that both of them created;

And hence at what I said above dost wonder,
　When I narrated that no second had
　The good which in the fifth light is enclosed.

Now ope thine eyes to what I answer thee,
　And thou shalt see thy creed and my discourse
　Fit in the truth as centre in a circle.

That which can die, and that which dieth not,
　Are nothing but the splendour of the idea
　Which by his love our Lord brings into being;

Because that living Light, which from its fount
　Effulgent flows, so that it disunites not
　From Him nor from the Love in them intrined,

Through its own goodness reunites its rays
　In nine subsistences, as in a mirror,
　Itself eternally remaining One.

Thence it descends to the last potencies,
　Downward from act to act becoming such
　That only brief contingencies it makes;

And these contingencies I hold to be
　Things generated, which the heaven produces
　By its own motion, with seed and without.

Neither their wax, nor that which tempers it,
　Remains immutable, and hence beneath
　The ideal signet more and less shines through;

Therefore it happens, that the selfsame tree
　After its kind bears worse and better fruit,
　And ye are born with characters diverse.

If in perfection tempered were the wax,
　And were the heaven in its supremest virtue,
　The brilliance of the seal would all appear;

But nature gives it evermore deficient,
　In the like manner working as the artist,
　Who has the skill of art and hand that trembles.

If then the fervent Love, the Vision clear,
　Of primal Virtue do dispose and seal,
　Perfection absolute is there acquired.

Thus was of old the Earth created worthy
　Of all and every animal perfection;
　And thus the Virgin was impregnate made;

So that thine own opinion I commend,
　That human nature never yet has been,
　Nor will be, what it was in those two persons.

Now if no farther forth I should proceed,
　'Then in what way was he without a peer?'
　Would be the first beginning of thy words.

But, that may well appear what now appears not,
  Think who he was, and what occasion moved him
  To make request, when it was told him, 'Ask.'

I've not so spoken that thou canst not see
  Clearly he was a king who asked for wisdom,
  That he might be sufficiently a king;

'Twas not to know the number in which are
  The motors here above, or if 'necesse'
  With a contingent e'er 'necesse' make,

'*Non si est dare primum motum esse,*'
  Or if in semicircle can be made
  Triangle so that it have no right angle.

Whence, if thou notest this and what I said,
  A regal prudence is that peerless seeing
  In which the shaft of my intention strikes.

And if on 'rose' thou turnest thy clear eyes,
  Thou'lt see that it has reference alone
  To kings who're many, and the good are rare.

With this distinction take thou what I said,
  And thus it can consist with thy belief
  Of the first father and of our Delight.

And lead shall this be always to thy feet,
  To make thee, like a weary man, move slowly
  Both to the Yes and No thou seest not;

For very low among the fools is he
  Who affirms without distinction, or denies,
  As well in one as in the other case;

Because it happens that full often bends
  Current opinion in the false direction,
  And then the feelings bind the intellect.

Far more than uselessly he leaves the shore,
  (Since he returneth not the same he went,)
  Who fishes for the truth, and has no skill;

And in the world proofs manifest thereof
  Parmenides, Melissus, Brissus are,
  And many who went on and knew not whither;

Thus did Sabellius, Arius, and those fools
  Who have been even as swords unto the Scriptures
  In rendering distorted their straight faces.

Nor yet shall people be too confident
  In judging, even as he is who doth count
  The corn in field or ever it be ripe.

For I have seen all winter long the thorn
  First show itself intractable and fierce,
  And after bear the rose upon its top;

And I have seen a ship direct and swift
  Run o'er the sea throughout its course entire,
  To perish at the harbour's mouth at last.

Let not Dame Bertha nor Ser Martin think,
  Seeing one steal, another offering make,
  To see them in the arbitrament divine;

For one may rise, and fall the other may."

Canto XIV

As Thomas Aquinas finishes speaking, he instructs Beatrice to ask the Doctors of the Church about the state of the blessed after the flesh is resurrected. King Solomon replies with a discourse on grace, love, vision and radiance. Dante makes out a third circle of light whose radiance bursts upon him and Beatrice as they are lifted into the sphere of Mars, the Fifth Heaven. They behold a vision of the victorious celestial Cross: two intersecting bands of light pricked by myriads of glowing rubies (each one a soldier who fought in Christ's name and now sings its praises to him).

From centre unto rim, from rim to centre,
  In a round vase the water moves itself,
  As from without 'tis struck or from within.

Into my mind upon a sudden dropped
  What I am saying, at the moment when
  Silent became the glorious life of Thomas,

Because of the resemblance that was born
  Of his discourse and that of Beatrice,
  Whom, after him, it pleased thus to begin:

"This man has need (and does not tell you so,
  Nor with the voice, nor even in his thought)
  Of going to the root of one truth more.

Declare unto him if the light wherewith
  Blossoms your substance shall remain with you
  Eternally the same that it is now;

And if it do remain, say in what manner,
  After ye are again made visible,
  It can be that it injure not your sight."

As by a greater gladness urged and drawn
  They who are dancing in a ring sometimes
  Uplift their voices and their motions quicken;

So, at that orison devout and prompt,
  The holy circles a new joy displayed
  In their revolving and their wondrous song.

Whoso lamenteth him that here we die
  That we may live above, has never there
  Seen the refreshment of the eternal rain.

The One and Two and Three who ever liveth,
  And reigneth ever in Three and Two and One,
  Not circumscribed and all things circumscribing,

Three several times was chanted by each one
  Among those spirits, with such melody
  That for all merit it were just reward;

And, in the lustre most divine of all
  The lesser ring, I heard a modest voice,
  Such as perhaps the Angel's was to Mary,

Answer: "As long as the festivity
  Of Paradise shall be, so long our love
  Shall radiate round about us such a vesture.

Its brightness is proportioned to the ardour,
  The ardour to the vision; and the vision
  Equals what grace it has above its worth.

When, glorious and sanctified, our flesh
  Is reassumed, then shall our persons be
  More pleasing by their being all complete;

For will increase whate'er bestows on us
  Of light gratuitous the Good Supreme,
  Light which enables us to look on Him;

Therefore the vision must perforce increase,
  Increase the ardour which from that is kindled,
  Increase the radiance which from this proceeds.

But even as a coal that sends forth flame,
  And by its vivid whiteness overpowers it
  So that its own appearance it maintains,

Thus the effulgence that surrounds us now
  Shall be o'erpowered in aspect by the flesh,
  Which still to-day the earth doth cover up;

Nor can so great a splendour weary us,
  For strong will be the organs of the body
  To everything which hath the power to please us."

So sudden and alert appeared to me
  Both one and the other choir to say Amen,
  That well they showed desire for their dead bodies;

Nor sole for them perhaps, but for the mothers,
  The fathers, and the rest who had been dear
  Or ever they became eternal flames.

And lo! all round about of equal brightness
  Arose a lustre over what was there,
  Like an horizon that is clearing up.

And as at rise of early eve begin
  Along the welkin new appearances,
  So that the sight seems real and unreal,

It seemed to me that new subsistences
  Began there to be seen, and make a circle
  Outside the other two circumferences.

O very sparkling of the Holy Spirit,
  How sudden and incandescent it became
  Unto mine eyes, that vanquished bore it not!

But Beatrice so beautiful and smiling
  Appeared to me, that with the other sights
  That followed not my memory I must leave her.

Then to uplift themselves mine eyes resumed
  The power, and I beheld myself translated
  To higher salvation with my Lady only.

Well was I ware that I was more uplifted
  By the enkindled smiling of the star,
  That seemed to me more ruddy than its wont.

With all my heart, and in that dialect
  Which is the same in all, such holocaust
  To God I made as the new grace beseemed;

And not yet from my bosom was exhausted
  The ardour of sacrifice, before I knew
  This offering was accepted and auspicious;

For with so great a lustre and so red
  Splendours appeared to me in twofold rays,
  I said: "O Helios who dost so adorn them!"

Even as distinct with less and greater lights
  Glimmers between the two poles of the world
  The Galaxy that maketh wise men doubt,

Thus constellated in the depths of Mars,
  Those rays described the venerable sign
  That quadrants joining in a circle make.

Here doth my memory overcome my genius;
  For on that cross as levin gleamed forth Christ,
  So that I cannot find ensample worthy;

But he who takes his cross and follows Christ
  Again will pardon me what I omit,
  Seeing in that aurora lighten Christ.

From horn to horn, and 'twixt the top and base,
  Lights were in motion, brightly scintillating
  As they together met and passed each other;

Thus level and aslant and swift and slow
  We here behold, renewing still the sight,
  The particles of bodies long and short,

Across the sunbeam move, wherewith is listed
  Sometimes the shade, which for their own defence
  People with cunning and with art contrive.

And as a lute and harp, accordant strung
  With many strings, a dulcet tinkling make
  To him by whom the notes are not distinguished,

So from the lights that there to me appeared
  Upgathered through the cross a melody,
  Which rapt me, not distinguishing the hymn.

Well was I ware it was of lofty laud,
  Because there came to me, "Arise and conquer!"
  As unto him who hears and comprehends not.

So much enamoured I became therewith,
  That until then there was not anything
  That e'er had fettered me with such sweet bonds.

Perhaps my word appears somewhat too bold,
  Postponing the delight of those fair eyes,
  Into which gazing my desire has rest;

Well was I ware that I was more uplifted / By the enkindled smiling of the star, /
That seemed to me more ruddy than its wont.

Par. XIV, lines 85–87

Here doth my memory overcome my genius; / For on that cross as levin gleamed forth Christ, /
So that I cannot find ensample worthy;

Par. XIV, lines 103–105

But who bethinks him that the living seals
  Of every beauty grow in power ascending,
    And that I there had not turned round to those,

Can me excuse, if I myself accuse
  To excuse myself, and see that I speak truly:
    For here the holy joy is not disclosed,

Because ascending it becomes more pure.

Canto XV

*In the Fifth Heaven, the souls of God's warriors, who are moving along the
horizontal arms of the Cross, as well as from its tip down to its base, stop their
singing so that one light may engage in conversation with Dante. The canto takes
an intimate and poignant tone as this soul turns out to be Cacciaguida, his
great-great-grandfather, who speaks to him about lineage, family history and the
shock of imminent exile from Florence. Dante's ancestor looks back on the virtuous
character of twelfth-century Florentines with nostalgia and laments their current
moral decline.*

A will benign, in which reveals itself
  Ever the love that righteously inspires,
    As in the iniquitous, cupidity,

Silence imposed upon that dulcet lyre,
  And quieted the consecrated chords,
    That Heaven's right hand doth tighten and relax.

How unto just entreaties shall be deaf
  Those substances, which, to give me desire
    Of praying them, with one accord grew silent?

'Tis well that without end he should lament,
  Who for the love of thing that doth not last
    Eternally despoils him of that love!

As through the pure and tranquil evening air
  There shoots from time to time a sudden fire,
    Moving the eyes that steadfast were before,

And seems to be a star that changeth place,
  Except that in the part where it is kindled
    Nothing is missed, and this endureth little;

So from the horn that to the right extends
  Unto that cross's foot there ran a star
    Out of the constellation shining there;

Nor was the gem dissevered from its ribbon,
  But down the radiant fillet ran along,
    So that fire seemed it behind alabaster.

Thus piteous did Anchises' shade reach forward,
  If any faith our greatest Muse deserve,
    When in Elysium he his son perceived.

"*O sanguis meus, O superinfusa
  Gratia Dei, sicut tibi, cui
    Bis unquam Coeli janua reclusa?*"

Thus that effulgence; whence I gave it heed;
  Then round unto my Lady turned my sight,
    And on this side and that was stupefied;

For in her eyes was burning such a smile
  That with mine own methought I touched the bottom
    Both of my grace and of my Paradise!

Then, pleasant to the hearing and the sight,
  The spirit joined to its beginning things
  I understood not, so profound it spake;

Nor did it hide itself from me by choice,
  But by necessity; for its conception
  Above the mark of mortals set itself.

And when the bow of burning sympathy
  Was so far slackened, that its speech descended
  Towards the mark of our intelligence,

The first thing that was understood by me
  Was "Benedight be Thou, O Trine and One,
  Who hast unto my seed so courteous been!"

And it continued: "Hunger long and grateful,
  Drawn from the reading of the mighty volume
  Wherein is never changed the white nor dark,

Thou hast appeased, my son, within this light
  In which I speak to thee, by grace of her
  Who to this lofty flight with plumage clothed thee.

Thou thinkest that to me thy thought doth pass
  From Him who is the first, as from the unit,
  If that be known, ray out the five and six;

And therefore who I am thou askest not,
  And why I seem more joyous unto thee
  Than any other of this gladsome crowd.

Thou think'st the truth; because the small and great
  Of this existence look into the mirror
  Wherein, before thou think'st, thy thought thou
                           showest.

But that the sacred love, in which I watch
  With sight perpetual, and which makes me thirst
  With sweet desire, may better be fulfilled,

Now let thy voice secure and frank and glad
  Proclaim the wishes, the desire proclaim,
  To which my answer is decreed already."

To Beatrice I turned me, and she heard
  Before I spake, and smiled to me a sign,
  That made the wings of my desire increase;

Then in this wise began I: "Love and knowledge,
  When on you dawned the first Equality,
  Of the same weight for each of you became;

For in the Sun, which lighted you and burned
  With heat and radiance, they so equal are,
  That all similitudes are insufficient.

But among mortals will and argument,
  For reason that to you is manifest,
  Diversely feathered in their pinions are.

Whence I, who mortal am, feel in myself
  This inequality; so give not thanks,
  Save in my heart, for this paternal welcome.

Truly do I entreat thee, living topaz!
  Set in this precious jewel as a gem,
  That thou wilt satisfy me with thy name."

"O leaf of mine, in whom I pleasure took
  E'en while awaiting, I was thine own root!"
  Such a beginning he in answer made me.

Then said to me: "That one from whom is named
  Thy race, and who a hundred years and more
  Has circled round the mount on the first cornice,

A son of mine and thy great-grandsire was;
  Well it behoves thee that the long fatigue
  Thou shouldst for him make shorter with thy works.

Florence, within the ancient boundary
  From which she taketh still her tierce and nones,
  Abode in quiet, temperate and chaste.

No golden chain she had, nor coronal,
  Nor ladies shod with sandal shoon, nor girdle
  That caught the eye more than the person did.

Not yet the daughter at her birth struck fear
  Into the father, for the time and dower
  Did not o'errun this side or that the measure.

No houses had she void of families,
  Not yet had thither come Sardanapalus
  To show what in a chamber can be done;

Not yet surpassed had Montemalo been
  By your Uccellatojo, which surpassed
  Shall in its downfall be as in its rise.

Bellincion Berti saw I go begirt
  With leather and with bone, and from the mirror
  His dame depart without a painted face;

And him of Nerli saw, and him of Vecchio,
  Contented with their simple suits of buff
  And with the spindle and the flax their dames.

O fortunate women! and each one was certain
  Of her own burial-place, and none as yet
  For sake of France was in her bed deserted.

One o'er the cradle kept her studious watch,
  And in her lullaby the language used
  That first delights the fathers and the mothers;

Another, drawing tresses from her distaff,
  Told o'er among her family the tales
  Of Trojans and of Fesole and Rome.

As great a marvel then would have been held
  A Lapo Salterello, a Cianghella,
  As Cincinnatus or Cornelia now.

To such a quiet, such a beautiful
  Life of the citizen, to such a safe
  Community, and to so sweet an inn,

Did Mary give me, with loud cries invoked,
  And in your ancient Baptistery at once
  Christian and Cacciaguida I became.

Moronto was my brother, and Eliseo;
  From Val di Pado came to me my wife,
  And from that place thy surname was derived.

I followed afterward the Emperor Conrad,
  And he begirt me of his chivalry,
  So much I pleased him with my noble deeds.

I followed in his train against that law's
  Iniquity, whose people doth usurp
  Your just possession, through your Pastor's fault.

There by that execrable race was I
  Released from bonds of the fallacious world,
  The love of which defileth many souls,

And came from martyrdom unto this peace."

Canto XVI

Proud of his descent and with his dignity gratified, Dante wants to hear more about twelfth-century Florence in her heyday as in his day the once-prominent families who boasted Roman lineage were dying out, many of the grand houses were being demolished and the city's once-solid moral fibre polluted as greedy newcomers from neighbouring boroughs flocked to her. Cacciaguida laments the expansion of his city's boundaries and the feud between the Amidei and Buondelmonte which ignited the conflict between Guelfs and Ghibellines. He also stresses that succeeding generations have an obligation to reinforce the noble actions of their ancestors.

O thou our poor nobility of blood,
  If thou dost make the people glory in thee
  Down here where our affection languishes,

A marvellous thing it ne'er will be to me;
  For there where appetite is not perverted,
  I say in Heaven, of thee I made a boast!

Truly thou art a cloak that quickly shortens,
  So that unless we piece thee day by day
  Time goeth round about thee with his shears!

With 'You,' which Rome was first to tolerate,
  (Wherein her family less perseveres,)
  Yet once again my words beginning made;

Whence Beatrice, who stood somewhat apart,
  Smiling, appeared like unto her who coughed
  At the first failing writ of Guenever.

And I began: "You are my ancestor,
  You give to me all hardihood to speak,
  You lift me so that I am more than I.

So many rivulets with gladness fill
  My mind, that of itself it makes a joy
  Because it can endure this and not burst.

Then tell me, my beloved root ancestral,
  Who were your ancestors, and what the years
  That in your boyhood chronicled themselves?

Tell me about the sheepfold of Saint John,
  How large it was, and who the people were
  Within it worthy of the highest seats."

As at the blowing of the winds a coal
  Quickens to flame, so I beheld that light
  Become resplendent at my blandishments.

And as unto mine eyes it grew more fair,
  With voice more sweet and tender, but not in
  This modern dialect, it said to me:

"From uttering of the '*Ave*,' till the birth
  In which my mother, who is now a saint,
  Of me was lightened who had been her burden,

Unto its Lion had this fire returned
  Five hundred fifty times and thirty more,
  To reinflame itself beneath his paw.

My ancestors and I our birthplace had
  Where first is found the last ward of the city
  By him who runneth in your annual game.

Suffice it of my elders to hear this;
  But who they were, and whence they thither came,
  Silence is more considerate than speech.

All those who at that time were there between
  Mars and the Baptist, fit for bearing arms,
  Were a fifth part of those who now are living;

But the community, that now is mixed
  With Campi and Certaldo and Figghine,
  Pure in the lowest artisan was seen.

O how much better 'twere to have as neighbours
  The folk of whom I speak, and at Galluzzo
  And at Trespiano have your boundary,

Than have them in the town, and bear the stench
  Of Aguglione's churl, and him of Signa
  Who has sharp eyes for trickery already.

Had not the folk, which most of all the world
  Degenerates, been a step-dame unto Caesar,
  But as a mother to her son benignant,

Some who turn Florentines, and trade and discount,
  Would have gone back again to Simifonte
  There where their grandsires went about as
                                beggars.

At Montemurlo still would be the Counts,
  The Cerchi in the parish of Acone,
  Perhaps in Valdigrieve the Buondelmonti.

Ever the intermingling of the people
  Has been the source of malady in cities,
  As in the body food it surfeits on;

And a blind bull more headlong plunges down
  Than a blind lamb; and very often cuts
  Better and more a single sword than five.

If Luni thou regard, and Urbisaglia,
  How they have passed away, and how are passing
  Chiusi and Sinigaglia after them,

To hear how races waste themselves away,
  Will seem to thee no novel thing nor hard,
  Seeing that even cities have an end.

All things of yours have their mortality,
  Even as yourselves; but it is hidden in some
  That a long while endure, and lives are short;

And as the turning of the lunar heaven
  Covers and bares the shores without a pause,
  In the like manner fortune does with Florence.

Therefore should not appear a marvellous thing
  What I shall say of the great Florentines
  Of whom the fame is hidden in the Past.

I saw the Ughi, saw the Catellini,
  Filippi, Greci, Ormanni, and Alberichi,
  Even in their fall illustrious citizens;

"You are my ancestor, / You give to me all hardihood to speak, /
You lift me so that I am more than I."

Par. XVI, lines 16–18

And saw, as mighty as they ancient were,
  With him of La Sannella him of Arca,
  And Soldanier, Ardinghi, and Bostichi.

Near to the gate that is at present laden
  With a new felony of so much weight
  That soon it shall be jetsam from the bark,

The Ravignani were, from whom descended
  The County Guido, and whoe'er the name
  Of the great Bellincione since hath taken.

He of La Pressa knew the art of ruling
  Already, and already Galigajo
  Had hilt and pommel gilded in his house.

Mighty already was the Column Vair,
  Sacchetti, Giuochi, Fifant, and Barucci,
  And Galli, and they who for the bushel blush.

The stock from which were the Calfucci born
  Was great already, and already chosen
  To curule chairs the Sizii and Arrigucci.

O how beheld I those who are undone
  By their own pride! and how the Balls of Gold
  Florence enflowered in all their mighty deeds!

So likewise did the ancestors of those
  Who evermore, when vacant is your church,
  Fatten by staying in consistory.

The insolent race, that like a dragon follows
  Whoever flees, and unto him that shows
  His teeth or purse is gentle as a lamb,

Already rising was, but from low people;
  So that it pleased not Ubertin Donato
  That his wife's father should make him their kin.

Already had Caponsacco to the Market
  From Fesole descended, and already
  Giuda and Infangato were good burghers.

I'll tell a thing incredible, but true;
  One entered the small circuit by a gate
  Which from the Della Pera took its name!

Each one that bears the beautiful escutcheon
  Of the great baron whose renown and name
  The festival of Thomas keepeth fresh,

Knighthood and privilege from him received;
  Though with the populace unites himself
  To-day the man who binds it with a border.

Already were Gualterotti and Importuni;
  And still more quiet would the Borgo be
  If with new neighbours it remained unfed.

The house from which is born your lamentation,
  Through just disdain that death among you brought
  And put an end unto your joyous life,

Was honoured in itself and its companions.
  O Buondelmonte, how in evil hour
  Thou fled'st the bridal at another's promptings!

Many would be rejoicing who are sad,
  If God had thee surrendered to the Ema
  The first time that thou camest to the city.

But it behoved the mutilated stone
  Which guards the bridge, that Florence should
                                    provide
  A victim in her latest hour of peace.

With all these families, and others with them,
  Florence beheld I in so great repose,
  That no occasion had she whence to weep;

With all these families beheld so just
  And glorious her people, that the lily
  Never upon the spear was placed reversed,

Nor by division was vermilion made."

Canto XVII

Beatrice tells Dante of the importance of conveying clearly to others the things he is learning. Dante is worried about what he has heard regarding his fate and Beatrice encourages him to ask Cacciaguida, his ancestor. He is told that he will be banished from Florence on false fraud charges but that the Della Scala family and Can Grande, Lord of Verona, will give him refuge. He is advised not to envy his neighbours because his future life will continue long after theirs. Dante is told not to be concerned about publishing his Divine Comedy. *He has been shown the fate of the famous in order that mankind can learn from his account.*

As came to Clymene, to be made certain
  Of that which he had heard against himself,
  He who makes fathers chary still to children,

Even such was I, and such was I perceived
  By Beatrice and by the holy light
  That first on my account had changed its place.

Therefore my Lady said to me: "Send forth
  The flame of thy desire, so that it issue
  Imprinted well with the internal stamp;

Not that our knowledge may be greater made
  By speech of thine, but to accustom thee
  To tell thy thirst, that we may give thee drink."

"O my beloved tree, (that so dost lift thee,
  That even as minds terrestrial perceive
  No triangle containeth two obtuse,

So thou beholdest the contingent things
  Ere in themselves they are, fixing thine eyes
  Upon the point in which all times are present,)

While I was with Virgilius conjoined
  Upon the mountain that the souls doth heal,
  And when descending into the dead world,

Were spoken to me of my future life
  Some grievous words; although I feel myself
  In sooth foursquare against the blows of chance.

On this account my wish would be content
  To hear what fortune is approaching me,
  Because foreseen an arrow comes more slowly."

Thus did I say unto that selfsame light
  That unto me had spoken before; and even
  As Beatrice willed was my own will confessed.

Not in vague phrase, in which the foolish folk
  Ensnared themselves of old, ere yet was slain
  The Lamb of God who taketh sins away,

But with clear words and unambiguous
  Language responded that paternal love,
  Hid and revealed by its own proper smile:

"Contingency, that outside of the volume
  Of your materiality extends not,
  Is all depicted in the eternal aspect.

Necessity however thence it takes not,
  Except as from the eye, in which 'tis mirrored,
  A ship that with the current down descends.

From thence, e'en as there cometh to the ear
  Sweet harmony from an organ, comes in sight
  To me the time that is preparing for thee.

As forth from Athens went Hippolytus,
  By reason of his step-dame false and cruel,
  So thou from Florence must perforce depart.

Already this is willed, and this is sought for;
  And soon it shall be done by him who thinks it,
  Where every day the Christ is bought and sold.

The blame shall follow the offended party
  In outcry as is usual; but the vengeance
  Shall witness to the truth that doth dispense it.

Thou shalt abandon everything beloved
  Most tenderly, and this the arrow is
  Which first the bow of banishment shoots forth.

Thou shalt have proof how savoureth of salt
  The bread of others, and how hard a road
  The going down and up another's stairs.

And that which most shall weigh upon thy
                                        shoulders
  Will be the bad and foolish company
  With which into this valley thou shalt fall;

For all ingrate, all mad and impious
  Will they become against thee; but soon after
  They, and not thou, shall have the forehead scarlet.

Of their bestiality their own proceedings
  Shall furnish proof; so 'twill be well for thee
  A party to have made thee by thyself.

Thine earliest refuge and thine earliest inn
  Shall be the mighty Lombard's courtesy,
  Who on the Ladder bears the holy bird,

Who such benign regard shall have for thee
  That 'twixt you twain, in doing and in asking,
  That shall be first which is with others last.

With him shalt thou see one who at his birth
  Has by this star of strength been so impressed,
  That notable shall his achievements be.

Not yet the people are aware of him
  Through his young age, since only nine years yet
  Around about him have these wheels revolved.

But ere the Gascon cheat the noble Henry,
  Some sparkles of his virtue shall appear
  In caring not for silver nor for toil.

So recognized shall his magnificence
  Become hereafter, that his enemies
  Will not have power to keep mute tongues about it.

On him rely, and on his benefits;
  By him shall many people be transformed,
  Changing condition rich and mendicant;

And written in thy mind thou hence shalt bear
  Of him, but shalt not say it"—and things said he
  Incredible to those who shall be present.

Then added: "Son, these are the commentaries
  On what was said to thee; behold the snares
  That are concealed behind few revolutions;

Yet would I not thy neighbours thou shouldst envy,
  Because thy life into the future reaches
  Beyond the punishment of their perfidies."

When by its silence showed that sainted soul
  That it had finished putting in the woof
  Into that web which I had given it warped,

Began I, even as he who yearneth after,
  Being in doubt, some counsel from a person
  Who seeth, and uprightly wills, and loves:

"Well see I, father mine, how spurreth on
  The time towards me such a blow to deal me
  As heaviest is to him who most gives way.

Therefore with foresight it is well I arm me,
  That, if the dearest place be taken from me,
  I may not lose the others by my songs.

Down through the world of infinite bitterness,
  And o'er the mountain, from whose beauteous
                                        summit
  The eyes of my own Lady lifted me,

And afterward through heaven from light to light,
  I have learned that which, if I tell again,
  Will be a savour of strong herbs to many.

And if I am a timid friend to truth,
  I fear lest I may lose my life with those
  Who will hereafter call this time the olden."

The light in which was smiling my own treasure
  Which there I had discovered, flashed at first
  As in the sunshine doth a golden mirror;

Then made reply: "A conscience overcast
  Or with its own or with another's shame,
  Will taste forsooth the tartness of thy word;

But ne'ertheless, all falsehood laid aside,
  Make manifest thy vision utterly,
  And let them scratch wherever is the itch;

For if thine utterance shall offensive be
  At the first taste, a vital nutriment
  'Twill leave thereafter, when it is digested.

This cry of thine shall do as doth the wind,
  Which smiteth most the most exalted summits,
  And that is no slight argument of honour.

Therefore are shown to thee within these wheels,
  Upon the mount and in the dolorous valley,
  Only the souls that unto fame are known;

Because the spirit of the hearer rests not,
  Nor doth confirm its faith by an example
  Which has the root of it unknown and hidden,

Or other reason that is not apparent."

Canto XVIII

As Beatrice consoles Dante, Cacciaguida calls out the names of eight warrior saints and joins them as they flash along the pattern of the Cross. Dante, and the ever-more-beautiful Beatrice, ascend to Jupiter, the Sixth Heaven. As the planet's silvery sheen replaces the ruddy glow of Mars, Dante beholds a spectacular display of lit-up letters (the souls of the Just) spelling out "Diligite justitiam qui judicatis terram" (Love justice, ye that judge on Earth). The final 'm' reconfigures into the imperial eagle, symbol of justice. Dante accuses the Pope of abusing his holy office.

Now was alone rejoicing in its word
  That soul beatified, and I was tasting
  My own, the bitter tempering with the sweet,

And the Lady who to God was leading me
  Said: "Change thy thought; consider that I am
  Near unto Him who every wrong disburdens."

Unto the loving accents of my comfort
  I turned me round, and then what love I saw
  Within those holy eyes I here relinquish;

Not only that my language I distrust,
  But that my mind cannot return so far
  Above itself, unless another guide it.

Thus much upon that point can I repeat,
  That, her again beholding, my affection
  From every other longing was released.

While the eternal pleasure, which direct
  Rayed upon Beatrice, from her fair face
  Contented me with its reflected aspect,

Conquering me with the radiance of a smile,
  She said to me, "Turn thee about and listen;
  Not in mine eyes alone is Paradise."

Even as sometimes here do we behold
  The affection in the look, if it be such
  That all the soul is wrapt away by it,

So, by the flaming of the effulgence holy
  To which I turned, I recognized therein
  The wish of speaking to me somewhat farther.

And it began: "In this fifth resting-place
  Upon the tree that liveth by its summit,
  And aye bears fruit, and never loses leaf,

Are blessed spirits that below, ere yet
  They came to Heaven, were of such great renown
  That every Muse therewith would affluent be.

Therefore look thou upon the cross's horns;
  He whom I now shall name will there enact
  What doth within a cloud its own swift fire."

I saw athwart the Cross a splendour drawn
  By naming Joshua, (even as he did it,)
  Nor noted I the word before the deed;

And at the name of the great Maccabee
  I saw another move itself revolving,
  And gladness was the whip unto that top.

Likewise for Charlemagne and for Orlando,
  Two of them my regard attentive followed
  As followeth the eye its falcon flying.

William thereafterward, and Renouard,
  And the Duke Godfrey, did attract my sight
  Along upon that Cross, and Robert Guiscard.

Then, moved and mingled with the other lights,
  The soul that had addressed me showed how great
  An artist 'twas among the heavenly singers.

To my right side I turned myself around,
  My duty to behold in Beatrice
  Either by words or gesture signified;

And so translucent I beheld her eyes,
  So full of pleasure, that her countenance
  Surpassed its other and its latest wont.

And as, by feeling greater delectation,
  A man in doing good from day to day
  Becomes aware his virtue is increasing,

So I became aware that my gyration
  With heaven together had increased its arc,
  That miracle beholding more adorned.

And such as is the change, in little lapse
  Of time, in a pale woman, when her face
  Is from the load of bashfulness unladen,

Such was it in mine eyes, when I had turned,
  Caused by the whiteness of the temperate star,
  The sixth, which to itself had gathered me.

Within that Jovial torch did I behold
  The sparkling of the love which was therein
  Delineate our language to mine eyes.

And even as birds uprisen from the shore,
  As in congratulation o'er their food,
  Make squadrons of themselves, now round, now long,

So from within those lights the holy creatures
  Sang flying to and fro, and in their figures
  Made of themselves now D, now I, now L.

First singing they to their own music moved;
  Then one becoming of these characters,
  A little while they rested and were silent.

O divine Pegasea, thou who genius
  Dost glorious make, and render it long-lived,
  And this through thee the cities and the kingdoms,

Illume me with thyself, that I may bring
  Their figures out as I have them conceived!
  Apparent be thy power in these brief verses!

Themselves then they displayed in five times seven
  Vowels and consonants; and I observed
  The parts as they seemed spoken unto me.

'*Diligite justitiam*,' these were
  First verb and noun of all that was depicted;
  '*Qui judicatis terram*' were the last.

Thereafter in the M of the fifth word
  Remained they so arranged, that Jupiter
  Seemed to be silver there with gold inlaid.

And other lights I saw descend where was
  The summit of the M, and pause there singing
  The good, I think, that draws them to itself.

Then, as in striking upon burning logs
  Upward there fly innumerable sparks,
  Whence fools are wont to look for auguries,

More than a thousand lights seemed thence to rise,
  And to ascend, some more, and others less,
  Even as the Sun that lights them had allotted;

And, each one being quiet in its place,
  The head and neck beheld I of an eagle
  Delineated by that inlaid fire.

He who there paints has none to be his guide;
  But Himself guides; and is from Him remembered
  That virtue which is form unto the nest.

The other beatitude, that contented seemed
  At first to bloom a lily on the M,
  By a slight motion followed out the imprint.

The holy creatures / Sang flying to and fro,

Par. XVIII, lines 76–77

O gentle star! what and how many gems
  Did demonstrate to me, that all our justice
  Effect is of that heaven which thou ingemmest!

Wherefore I pray the Mind, in which begin
  Thy motion and thy virtue, to regard
  Whence comes the smoke that vitiates thy rays;

So that a second time it now be wroth
  With buying and with selling in the temple
  Whose walls were built with signs and martyrdoms!

O soldiery of heaven, whom I contemplate,
  Implore for those who are upon the Earth
  All gone astray after the bad example!

Once 'twas the custom to make war with swords;
  But now 'tis made by taking here and there
  The bread the pitying Father shuts from none.

Yet thou, who writest but to cancel, think
  That Peter and that Paul, who for this vineyard
  Which thou art spoiling died, are still alive!

Well canst thou say: "So steadfast my desire
  Is unto him who willed to live alone,
  And for a dance was led to martyrdom,

That I know not the Fisherman nor Paul."

Canto XIX

An eagle appears. Its image is made up of many rubies each representing a soul. Its voice speaks for all the souls within it, who had left examples of justice on Earth that were not followed. Dante asks whether the souls of virtuous heathens are excluded from heavenly bliss. The eagle replies that mankind cannot expect to understand the workings of divine justice and should only question whether God's judgements conform to His will – not whether they are fair – because our concept of justice is but a poor reflection of God's infallible standard. Evil, contemporary monarchs, such as Albert of Austria and Philip IV of France, are openly condemned.

Appeared before me with its wings outspread
  The beautiful image that in sweet fruition
  Made jubilant the interwoven souls;

Appeared a little ruby each, wherein
  Ray of the sun was burning so enkindled
  That each into mine eyes refracted it.

And what it now behoves me to retrace
  Nor voice has e'er reported, nor ink written,
  Nor was by fantasy e'er comprehended;

For speak I saw, and likewise heard, the beak,
  And utter with its voice both 'I' and 'My,'
  When in conception it was 'We' and 'Our.'

And it began: "Being just and merciful
  Am I exalted here unto that glory
  Which cannot be exceeded by desire;

And upon Earth I left my memory
  Such, that the evil-minded people there
  Commend it, but continue not the story."

So doth a single heat from many embers
  Make itself felt, even as from many loves
  Issued a single sound from out that image.

Whence I thereafter: "O perpetual flowers
  Of the eternal joy, that only one
  Make me perceive your odours manifold,

O soldiery of heaven, whom I contemplate, / Implore for those who are upon the Earth /
All gone astray after the bad example!

Par. XVIII, lines 124–126

Appeared before me with its wings outspread / The beautiful image that in sweet fruition /
Made jubilant the interwoven souls;

Par. XIX, lines 1–3

Exhaling, break within me the great fast
   Which a long season has in hunger held me,
   Not finding for it any food on Earth.

Well do I know, that if in heaven its mirror
   Justice Divine another realm doth make,
   Yours apprehends it not through any veil.

You know how I attentively address me
   To listen; and you know what is the doubt
   That is in me so very old a fast."

Even as a falcon, issuing from his hood,
   Doth move his head, and with his wings applaud him,
   Showing desire, and making himself fine,

Saw I become that standard, which of lauds
   Was interwoven of the grace divine,
   With such songs as he knows who there rejoices.

Then it began: "He who a compass turned
   On the world's outer verge, and who within it
   Devised so much occult and manifest,

Could not the impress of his power so make
   On all the universe, as that his Word
   Should not remain in infinite excess.

And this makes certain that the first proud being,
   Who was the paragon of every creature,
   By not awaiting light fell immature.

And hence appears it, that each minor nature
   Is scant receptacle unto that good
   Which has no end, and by itself is measured.

In consequence our vision, which perforce
   Must be some ray of that intelligence
   With which all things whatever are replete,

Cannot in its own nature be so potent,
   That it shall not its origin discern
   Far beyond that which is apparent to it.

Therefore into the justice sempiternal
   The power of vision that your world receives,
   As eye into the ocean, penetrates;

Which, though it see the bottom near the shore,
   Upon the deep perceives it not, and yet
   'Tis there, but it is hidden by the depth.

There is no light but comes from the serene
   That never is o'ercast, nay, it is darkness
   Or shadow of the flesh, or else its poison.

Amply to thee is opened now the cavern
   Which has concealed from thee the living justice
   Of which thou mad'st such frequent questioning.

For saidst thou: 'Born a man is on the shore
   Of Indus, and is none who there can speak
   Of Christ, nor who can read, nor who can write;

And all his inclinations and his actions
   Are good, so far as human reason sees,
   Without a sin in life or in discourse:

He dieth unbaptised and without faith;
   Where is this justice that condemneth him?
   Where is his fault, if he do not believe?'

Now who art thou, that on the bench wouldst sit
   In judgment at a thousand miles away,
   With the short vision of a single span?

Truly to him who with me subtilizes,
   If so the Scripture were not over you,
   For doubting there were marvellous occasion.

O animals terrene, O stolid minds,
   The primal will, that in itself is good,
   Ne'er from itself, the Good Supreme, has moved.

So much is just as is accordant with it;
   No good created draws it to itself,
   But it, by raying forth, occasions that."

Even as above her nest goes circling round
   The stork when she has fed her little ones,
   And he who has been fed looks up at her,

So lifted I my brows, and even such
   Became the blessed image, which its wings
   Was moving, by so many counsels urged.

Circling around it sang, and said: "As are
   My notes to thee, who dost not comprehend them,
   Such is the eternal judgment to you mortals."

Those lucent splendours of the Holy Spirit
   Grew quiet then, but still within the standard
   That made the Romans reverend to the world.

It recommenced: "Unto this kingdom never
  Ascended one who had not faith in Christ,
  Before or since he to the tree was nailed.

But look thou, many crying are, 'Christ, Christ!'
  Who at the judgment shall be far less near
  To him than some shall be who knew not Christ.

Such Christians shall the Ethiop condemn,
  When the two companies shall be divided,
  The one for ever rich, the other poor.

What to your kings may not the Persians say,
  When they that volume opened shall behold
  In which are written down all their dispraises?

There shall be seen, among the deeds of Albert,
  That which ere long shall set the pen in motion,
  For which the realm of Prague shall be deserted.

There shall be seen the woe that on the Seine
  He brings by falsifying of the coin,
  Who by the blow of a wild boar shall die.

There shall be seen the pride that causes thirst,
  Which makes the Scot and Englishman so mad
  That they within their boundaries cannot rest;

Be seen the luxury and effeminate life
  Of him of Spain, and the Bohemian,
  Who valour never knew and never wished;

Be seen the Cripple of Jerusalem,
  His goodness represented by an I,
  While the reverse an M shall represent;

Be seen the avarice and poltroonery
  Of him who guards the Island of the Fire,
  Wherein Anchises finished his long life;

And to declare how pitiful he is
  Shall be his record in contracted letters
  Which shall make note of much in little space.

And shall appear to each one the foul deeds
  Of uncle and of brother who a nation
  So famous have dishonoured, and two crowns.

And he of Portugal and he of Norway
  Shall there be known, and he of Rascia too,
  Who saw in evil hour the coin of Venice.

O happy Hungary, if she let herself
  Be wronged no farther! and Navarre the happy,
  If with the hills that gird her she be armed!

And each one may believe that now, as hansel
  Thereof, do Nicosia and Famagosta
  Lament and rage because of their own beast,

Who from the others' flank departeth not."

Canto XX

As the eagle falls silent, its multiple voices rise up in an angelic chorus. A murmuring from deep inside the bird's neck becomes a single, clear utterance asking Dante to observe how the pupil and the upper curve of its eye socket are composed of six lights. These are the souls of the world's greatest justiciaries: King David (the eye), Trajan, Hezekiah, Constantine, William II of Sicily and Ripheus (the arch above). Dante is surprised to see Trajan and Ripheus among such exalted company but the eagle assures him that, though pagan, they died in true faith.

When he who all the world illuminates
  Out of our hemisphere so far descends
  That on all sides the daylight is consumed,

The heaven, that erst by him alone was kindled,
  Doth suddenly reveal itself again
  By many lights, wherein is one resplendent.

And came into my mind this act of heaven,
  When the ensign of the world and of its leaders
  Had silent in the blessed beak become;

Because those living luminaries all,
  By far more luminous, did songs begin
  Lapsing and falling from my memory.

O gentle Love, that with a smile dost cloak thee,
  How ardent in those sparks didst thou appear,
  That had the breath alone of holy thoughts!

After the precious and pellucid crystals,
  With which begemmed the sixth light I beheld,
  Silence imposed on the angelic bells,

I seemed to hear the murmuring of a river
  That clear descendeth down from rock to rock,
  Showing the affluence of its mountain-top.

And as the sound upon the cithern's neck
  Taketh its form, and as upon the vent
  Of rustic pipe the wind that enters it,

Even thus, relieved from the delay of waiting,
  That murmuring of the eagle mounted up
  Along its neck, as if it had been hollow.

There it became a voice, and issued thence
  From out its beak, in such a form of words
  As the heart waited for wherein I wrote them.

"The part in me which sees and bears the sun
  In mortal eagles," it began to me,
  "Now fixedly must needs be looked upon;

For of the fires of which I make my figure,
  Those whence the eye doth sparkle in my head
  Of all their orders the supremest are.

He who is shining in the midst as pupil
  Was once the singer of the Holy Spirit,
  Who bore the ark from city unto city;

Now knoweth he the merit of his song,
  In so far as effect of his own counsel,
  By the reward which is commensurate.

Of five, that make a circle for my brow,
  He that approacheth nearest to my beak
  Did the poor widow for her son console;

Now knoweth he how dearly it doth cost
  Not following Christ, by the experience
  Of this sweet life and of its opposite.

He who comes next in the circumference
  Of which I speak, upon its highest arc,
  Did death postpone by penitence sincere;

Now knoweth he that the eternal judgment
  Suffers no change, albeit worthy prayer
  Maketh below to-morrow of to-day.

Because those living luminaries all, / By far more luminous, did songs begin /
Lapsing and falling from my memory.

Par. XX, lines 10–12

The next who follows, with the laws and me,
  Under the good intent that bore bad fruit
  Became a Greek by ceding to the pastor;

Now knoweth he how all the ill deduced
  From his good action is not harmful to him,
  Although the world thereby may be destroyed.

And he, whom in the downward arc thou seest,
  Guglielmo was, whom the same land deplores
  That weepeth Charles and Frederick yet alive;

Now knoweth he how heaven enamoured is
  With a just king; and in the outward show
  Of his effulgence he reveals it still.

Who would believe, down in the errant world,
  That e'er the Trojan Ripheus in this round
  Could be the fifth one of the holy lights?

Now knoweth he enough of what the world
  Has not the power to see of grace divine,
  Although his sight may not discern the bottom."

Like as a lark that in the air expatiates,
  First singing and then silent with content
  Of the last sweetness that doth satisfy her,

Such seemed to me the image of the imprint
  Of the eternal pleasure, by whose will
  Doth everything become the thing it is.

And notwithstanding to my doubt I was
  As glass is to the colour that invests it,
  To wait the time in silence it endured not,

But forth from out my mouth, "What things are
                                            these?"
  Extorted with the force of its own weight;
  Whereat I saw great joy of coruscation.

Thereafterward with eye still more enkindled
  The blessed standard made to me reply,
  To keep me not in wonderment suspended:

"I see that thou believest in these things
  Because I say them, but thou seest not how;
  So that, although believed in, they are hidden.

Thou doest as he doth who a thing by name
  Well apprehendeth, but its quiddity
  Cannot perceive, unless another show it.

'Regnum coelorum' suffereth violence
  From fervent love, and from that living hope
  That overcometh the Divine volition;

Not in the guise that man o'ercometh man,
  But conquers it because it will be conquered,
  And conquered conquers by benignity.

The first life of the eyebrow and the fifth
  Cause thee astonishment, because with them
  Thou seest the region of the angels painted.

They passed not from their bodies, as thou thinkest,
  Gentiles, but Christians in the steadfast faith
  Of feet that were to suffer and had suffered.

For one from Hell, where no one e'er turns back
  Unto good will, returned unto his bones,
  And that of living hope was the reward,—

Of living hope, that placed its efficacy
  In prayers to God made to resuscitate him,
  So that 'twere possible to move his will.

The glorious soul concerning which I speak,
  Returning to the flesh, where brief its stay,
  Believed in Him who had the power to aid it;

And, in believing, kindled to such fire
  Of genuine love, that at the second death
  Worthy it was to come unto this joy.

The other one, through grace, that from so deep
  A fountain wells that never hath the eye
  Of any creature reached its primal wave,

Set all his love below on righteousness;
  Wherefore from grace to grace did God unclose
  His eye to our redemption yet to be,

Whence he believed therein, and suffered not
  From that day forth the stench of paganism,
  And he reproved therefor the folk perverse.

Those Maidens three, whom at the right-hand
                                          wheel
  Thou didst behold, were unto him for baptism
  More than a thousand years before baptizing.

O thou predestination, how remote
  Thy root is from the aspect of all those
  Who the First Cause do not behold entire!

And you, O mortals! hold yourselves restrained
  In judging; for ourselves, who look on God,
  We do not know as yet all the elect;

And sweet to us is such a deprivation,
  Because our good in this good is made perfect,
  That whatsoe'er God wills, we also will."

After this manner by that shape divine,
  To make clear in me my short-sightedness,
  Was given to me a pleasant medicine;

And as good singer a good lutanist
  Accompanies with vibrations of the chords,
  Whereby more pleasantness the song acquires,

So, while it spake, do I remember me
  That I beheld both of those blessed lights,
  Even as the winking of the eyes concords,

Moving unto the words their little flames.

Canto XXI

*On entering Saturn, the last of the planets, Beatrice avoids smiling because at this
level Dante's mortal senses would not be able to cope with her radiance. Dante beholds
a golden ladder on which countless splendours, the souls of the Contemplatives, ascend
and descend like birds in flight. Saint Peter Damiano, renowned doctor of the Church
and severe Benedictine ascetic, draws near. He indicates the unfathomable depths of the
mystery of predestination and denounces the indulgent lifestyle of prelates. The other
souls gather around him before sending forth a mighty cry of anger to express Heaven's
indignation at such laxity.*

Already on my Lady's face mine eyes
  Again were fastened, and with these my mind,
  And from all other purpose was withdrawn;

And she smiled not; but "If I were to smile,"
  She unto me began, "thou wouldst become
  Like Semele, when she was turned to ashes.

Because my beauty, that along the stairs
  Of the eternal palace more enkindles,
  As thou hast seen, the farther we ascend,

If it were tempered not, is so resplendent
  That all thy mortal power in its effulgence
  Would seem a leaflet that the thunder crushes.

We are uplifted to the seventh splendour,
  That underneath the burning Lion's breast
  Now radiates downward mingled with his power.

Fix in direction of thine eyes the mind,
  And make of them a mirror for the figure
  That in this mirror shall appear to thee."

He who could know what was the pasturage
  My sight had in that blessed countenance,
  When I transferred me to another care,

Would recognize how grateful was to me
  Obedience unto my celestial escort,
  By counterpoising one side with the other.

Within the crystal which, around the world
  Revolving, bears the name of its dear leader,
  Under whom every wickedness lay dead,

Coloured like gold, on which the sunshine gleams,
  A stairway I beheld to such a height
  Uplifted, that mine eye pursued it not.

Already on my Lady's face mine eyes / Again were fastened,

Par. XXI, lines 1–2

A stairway I beheld to such a height / Uplifted, that mine eye pursued it not.

Par. XXI, lines 29–30

Likewise beheld I down the steps descending
　So many splendours, that I thought each light
　That in the heaven appears was there diffused.

And as accordant with their natural custom
　The rooks together at the break of day
　Bestir themselves to warm their feathers cold;

Then some of them fly off without return,
　Others come back to where they started from,
　And others, wheeling round, still keep at home;

Such fashion it appeared to me was there
　Within the sparkling that together came,
　As soon as on a certain step it struck,

And that which nearest unto us remained
　Became so clear, that in my thought I said,
　"Well I perceive the love thou showest me;

But she, from whom I wait the how and when
　Of speech and silence, standeth still; whence I
　Against desire do well if I ask not."

She thereupon, who saw my silentness
　In the sight of Him who seeth everything,
　Said unto me, "Let loose thy warm desire."

And I began: "No merit of my own
　Renders me worthy of response from thee;
　But for her sake who granteth me the asking,

Thou blessed life that dost remain concealed
　In thy beatitude, make known to me
　The cause which draweth thee so near my side;

And tell me why is silent in this wheel
　The dulcet symphony of Paradise,
　That through the rest below sounds so devoutly."

"Thou hast thy hearing mortal as thy sight,"
　It answer made to me; "they sing not here,
　For the same cause that Beatrice has not smiled.

Thus far adown the holy stairway's steps
　Have I descended but to give thee welcome
　With words, and with the light that mantles me;

Nor did more love cause me to be more ready,
　For love as much and more up there is burning,
　As doth the flaming manifest to thee.

But the high charity, that makes us servants
　Prompt to the counsel which controls the world,
　Allotteth here, even as thou dost observe."

"I see full well," said I, "O sacred lamp!
　How love unfettered in this court sufficeth
　To follow the eternal Providence;

But this is what seems hard for me to see,
　Wherefore predestinate wast thou alone
　Unto this office from among thy consorts."

No sooner had I come to the last word,
　Than of its middle made the light a centre,
　Whirling itself about like a swift millstone.

When answer made the love that was therein:
　"On me directed is a light divine,
　Piercing through this in which I am embosomed,

Of which the virtue with my sight conjoined
　Lifts me above myself so far, I see
　The supreme essence from which this is drawn.

Hence comes the joyfulness with which I flame,
　For to my sight, as far as it is clear,
　The clearness of the flame I equal make.

But that soul in the heaven which is most pure,
　That seraph which his eye on God most fixes,
　Could this demand of thine not satisfy;

Because so deeply sinks in the abyss
　Of the eternal statute what thou askest,
　From all created sight it is cut off.

And to the mortal world, when thou returnest,
　This carry back, that it may not presume
　Longer tow'rd such a goal to move its feet.

The mind, that shineth here, on Earth doth smoke;
　From this observe how can it do below
　That which it cannot though the heaven assume it?"

Such limit did its words prescribe to me,
　The question I relinquished, and restricted
　Myself to ask it humbly who it was.

"Between two shores of Italy rise cliffs,
　And not far distant from thy native place,
　So high, the thunders far below them sound,

And form a ridge that Catria is called,
  'Neath which is consecrate a hermitage
  Wont to be dedicate to worship only."

Thus unto me the third speech recommenced,
  And then, continuing, it said: "Therein
  Unto God's service I became so steadfast,

That feeding only on the juice of olives
  Lightly I passed away the heats and frosts,
  Contented in my thoughts contemplative.

That cloister used to render to these heavens
  Abundantly, and now is empty grown,
  So that perforce it soon must be revealed.

I in that place was Peter Damiano;
  And Peter the Sinner was I in the house
  Of Our Lady on the Adriatic shore.

Little of mortal life remained to me,
  When I was called and dragged forth to the hat
  Which shifteth evermore from bad to worse.

Came Cephas, and the mighty Vessel came
  Of the Holy Spirit, meagre and barefooted,
  Taking the food of any hostelry.

Now some one to support them on each side
  The modern shepherds need, and some to lead them,
  So heavy are they, and to hold their trains.

They cover up their palfreys with their cloaks,
  So that two beasts go underneath one skin;
  O Patience, that dost tolerate so much!"

At this voice saw I many little flames
  From step to step descending and revolving,
  And every revolution made them fairer.

Round about this one came they and stood still,
  And a cry uttered of so loud a sound,
  It here could find no parallel, nor I

Distinguished it, the thunder so o'ercame me.

Canto XXII

Beatrice prophesies that Dante will live to see God's vengeance rain down on the
Church's corrupters. Looking up, he sees one hundred radiant orbs. The soul of Saint
Benedict, founder of the Monte Cassino monastery, draws near to lament the scarcity of
Benedictine monks committed to going up the golden ladder which, like the
contemplative life, leads to the summit of God's glory. He presages change before being
swept up into the choir of lights. Dante and Beatrice follow him to the Eighth Heaven:
the Fixed Stars. Dante looks down through the preceding seven Heavens and smiles at
the insignificance of the Earth.

Oppressed with stupor, I unto my guide
  Turned like a little child who always runs
  For refuge there where he confideth most;

And she, even as a mother who straightway
  Gives comfort to her pale and breathless boy
  With voice whose wont it is to reassure him,

Said to me: "Knowest thou not thou art in heaven,
  And knowest thou not that heaven is holy all
  And what is done here cometh from good zeal?

After what wise the singing would have changed thee
  And I by smiling, thou canst now imagine,
  Since that the cry has startled thee so much,

In which if thou hadst understood its prayers
  Already would be known to thee the vengeance
  Which thou shalt look upon before thou diest.

The sword above here smiteth not in haste
  Nor tardily, howe'er it seem to him
  Who fearing or desiring waits for it.

But turn thee round towards the others now,
  For very illustrious spirits shalt thou see,
  If thou thy sight directest as I say."

As it seemed good to her mine eyes I turned,
  And saw a hundred spherules that together
  With mutual rays each other more embellished.

I stood as one who in himself represses
  The point of his desire, and ventures not
  To question, he so feareth the too much.

And now the largest and most luculent
  Among those pearls came forward, that it might
  Make my desire concerning it content.

Within it then I heard: "If thou couldst see
  Even as myself the charity that burns
  Among us, thy conceits would be expressed;

But, that by waiting thou mayst not come late
  To the high end, I will make answer even
  Unto the thought of which thou art so chary.

That mountain on whose slope Cassino stands
  Was frequented of old upon its summit
  By a deluded folk and ill-disposed;

And I am he who first up thither bore
  The name of Him who brought upon the Earth
  The truth that so much sublimateth us.

And such abundant grace upon me shone
  That all the neighbouring towns I drew away
  From the impious worship that seduced the world.

These other fires, each one of them, were men
  Contemplative, enkindled by that heat
  Which maketh holy flowers and fruits spring up.

Here is Macarius, here is Romualdus,
  Here are my brethren, who within the cloisters
  Their footsteps stayed and kept a steadfast heart."

And I to him: "The affection which thou showest
  Speaking with me, and the good countenance
  Which I behold and note in all your ardours,

In me have so my confidence dilated
  As the sun doth the rose, when it becomes
  As far unfolded as it hath the power.

Therefore I pray, and thou assure me, father,
  If I may so much grace receive, that I
  May thee behold with countenance unveiled."

He thereupon: "Brother, thy high desire
  In the remotest sphere shall be fulfilled,
  Where are fulfilled all others and my own.

There perfect is, and ripened, and complete,
  Every desire; within that one alone
  Is every part where it has always been;

For it is not in space, nor turns on poles,
  And unto it our stairway reaches up,
  Whence thus from out thy sight it steals away.

Up to that height the Patriarch Jacob saw it
  Extending its supernal part, what time
  So thronged with angels it appeared to him.

But to ascend it now no one uplifts
  His feet from off the earth, and now my Rule
  Below remaineth for mere waste of paper.

The walls that used of old to be an Abbey
  Are changed to dens of robbers, and the cowls
  Are sacks filled full of miserable flour.

But heavy usury is not taken up
  So much against God's pleasure as that fruit
  Which maketh so insane the heart of monks;

For whatsoever hath the Church in keeping
  Is for the folk that ask it in God's name,
  Not for one's kindred or for something worse.

The flesh of mortals is so very soft,
  That good beginnings down below suffice not
  From springing of the oak to bearing acorns.

Peter began with neither gold nor silver,
  And I with orison and abstinence,
  And Francis with humility his convent.

And if thou lookest at each one's beginning,
  And then regardest whither he has run,
  Thou shalt behold the white changed into brown.

In verity the Jordan backward turned,
  And the sea's fleeing, when God willed were more
  A wonder to behold, than succour here."

Thus unto me he said; and then withdrew
  To his own band, and the band closed together;
  Then like a whirlwind all was upward rapt.

The gentle Lady urged me on behind them
  Up o'er that stairway by a single sign,
  So did her virtue overcome my nature;

Nor here below, where one goes up and down
  By natural law, was motion e'er so swift
  That it could be compared unto my wing.

Reader, as I may unto that devout
  Triumph return, on whose account I often
  For my transgressions weep and beat my breast,—

Thou hadst not thrust thy finger in the fire
  And drawn it out again, before I saw
  The sign that follows Taurus, and was in it.

O glorious stars, O light impregnated
  With mighty virtue, from which I acknowledge
  All of my genius, whatsoe'er it be,

With you was born, and hid himself with you,
  He who is father of all mortal life,
  When first I tasted of the Tuscan air;

And then when grace was freely given to me
  To enter the high wheel which turns you round,
  Your region was allotted unto me.

To you devoutly at this hour my soul
  Is sighing, that it virtue may acquire
  For the stern pass that draws it to itself.

"Thou art so near unto the last salvation,"
  Thus Beatrice began, "thou oughtest now
  To have thine eyes unclouded and acute;

And therefore, ere thou enter farther in,
  Look down once more, and see how vast a world
  Thou hast already put beneath thy feet;

So that thy heart, as jocund as it may,
  Present itself to the triumphant throng
  That comes rejoicing through this rounded ether."

I with my sight returned through one and all
  The sevenfold spheres, and I beheld this globe
  Such that I smiled at its ignoble semblance;

And that opinion I approve as best
  Which doth account it least; and he who thinks
  Of something else may truly be called just.

I saw the daughter of Latona shining
  Without that shadow, which to me was cause
  That once I had believed her rare and dense.

The aspect of thy son, Hyperion,
  Here I sustained, and saw how move themselves
  Around and near him Maia and Dione.

Thence there appeared the temperateness of Jove
  'Twixt son and father, and to me was clear
  The change that of their whereabout they make;

And all the seven made manifest to me
  How great they are, and eke how swift they are,
  And how they are in distant habitations.

The threshing-floor that maketh us so proud,
  To me revolving with the eternal Twins,
  Was all apparent made from hill to harbour!

Then to the beauteous eyes mine eyes I turned.

Canto XXIII

Beatrice and Dante look up expectantly at the sky's zenith. The vision of Christ, flanked by the Saints of the Church Triumphant, descends and shines its rays over the Garden of Triumph, the mystic rose of the Virgin Mary and the lilies of the Apostles. Christ shows mercy on Dante's feeble senses by withdrawing from direct view and casting his light from above: Dante can now sustain Beatrice's smile of bliss and is able to fix his eyes on the Virgin before the Archangel Gabriel whisks her back to the Empyrean.

Even as a bird, 'mid the beloved leaves,
  Quiet upon the nest of her sweet brood
  Throughout the night, that hideth all things from us,

Who, that she may behold their longed-for looks
  And find the food wherewith to nourish them,
  In which, to her, grave labours grateful are,

Anticipates the time on open spray
  And with an ardent longing waits the sun,
  Gazing intent as soon as breaks the dawn:

Even thus my Lady standing was, erect
  And vigilant, turned round towards the zone
  Underneath which the sun displays less haste;

So that beholding her distraught and wistful,
  Such I became as he is who desiring
  For something yearns, and hoping is appeased.

But brief the space from one When to the other;
  Of my awaiting, say I, and the seeing
  The welkin grow resplendent more and more.

And Beatrice exclaimed: "Behold the hosts
  Of Christ's triumphal march, and all the fruit
  Harvested by the rolling of these spheres!"

It seemed to me her face was all aflame;
  And eyes she had so full of ecstasy
  That I must needs pass on without describing.

As when in nights serene of the full moon
  Smiles Trivia among the nymphs eternal
  Who paint the firmament through all its gulfs,

Saw I, above the myriads of lamps,
  A Sun that one and all of them enkindled,
  E'en as our own doth the supernal sights,

And through the living light transparent shone
  The lucent substance so intensely clear
  Into my sight, that I sustained it not.

O Beatrice, thou gentle guide and dear!
  To me she said: "What overmasters thee
  A virtue is from which naught shields itself.

There are the wisdom and the omnipotence
  That oped the thoroughfares 'twixt heaven and Earth,
  For which there erst had been so long a yearning."

As fire from out a cloud unlocks itself,
  Dilating so it finds not room therein,
  And down, against its nature, falls to Earth,

So did my mind, among those aliments
  Becoming larger, issue from itself,
  And that which it became cannot remember.

"Open thine eyes, and look at what I am:
  Thou hast beheld such things, that strong enough
  Hast thou become to tolerate my smile."

I was as one who still retains the feeling
  Of a forgotten vision, and endeavours
  In vain to bring it back into his mind,

When I this invitation heard, deserving
  Of so much gratitude, it never fades
  Out of the book that chronicles the past.

If at this moment sounded all the tongues
  That Polyhymnia and her sisters made
  Most lubrical with their delicious milk,

To aid me, to a thousandth of the truth
  It would not reach, singing the holy smile
  And how the holy aspect it illumed.

And therefore, representing Paradise,
  The sacred poem must perforce leap over,
  Even as a man who finds his way cut off;

But whoso thinketh of the ponderous theme,
  And of the mortal shoulder laden with it,
  Should blame it not, if under this it tremble.

It is no passage for a little boat
  This which goes cleaving the audacious prow,
  Nor for a pilot who would spare himself.

"Why doth my face so much enamour thee,
  That to the garden fair thou turnest not,
  Which under the rays of Christ is blossoming?

There is the Rose in which the Word Divine
  Became incarnate; there the lilies are
  By whose perfume the good way was discovered."

Thus Beatrice; and I, who to her counsels
  Was wholly ready, once again betook me
  Unto the battle of the feeble brows.

As in the sunshine, that unsullied streams
  Through fractured cloud, ere now a meadow of flowers
  Mine eyes with shadow covered o'er have seen,

So troops of splendours manifold I saw
  Illumined from above with burning rays,
  Beholding not the source of the effulgence.

O power benignant that dost so imprint them!
  Thou didst exalt thyself to give more scope
  There to mine eyes, that were not strong enough.

The name of that fair flower I e'er invoke
  Morning and evening utterly enthralled
  My soul to gaze upon the greater fire.

And when in both mine eyes depicted were
  The glory and greatness of the living star
  Which there excelleth, as it here excelled,

Athwart the heavens a little torch descended
  Formed in a circle like a coronal,
  And cinctured it, and whirled itself about it.

Whatever melody most sweetly soundeth
  On Earth, and to itself most draws the soul,
  Would seem a cloud that, rent asunder, thunders,

Compared unto the sounding of that lyre
  Wherewith was crowned the sapphire beautiful,
  Which gives the clearest heaven its sapphire hue.

"I am Angelic Love, that circle round
  The joy sublime which breathes from out the womb
  That was the hostelry of our Desire;

And I shall circle, Lady of Heaven, while
  Thou followest thy Son, and mak'st diviner
  The sphere supreme, because thou enterest there."

Thus did the circulated melody
  Seal itself up; and all the other lights
  Were making to resound the name of Mary.

The regal mantle of the volumes all
  Of that world, which most fervid is and living
  With breath of God and with his works and ways,

Extended over us its inner border,
  So very distant, that the semblance of it
  There where I was not yet appeared to me.

Therefore mine eyes did not possess the power
  Of following the incoronated flame,
  Which mounted upward near to its own seed.

And as a little child, that towards its mother
  Stretches its arms, when it the milk has taken,
  Through impulse kindled into outward flame,

Each of those gleams of whiteness upward reached
  So with its summit, that the deep affection
  They had for Mary was revealed to me.

Thereafter they remained there in my sight,
  'Regina coeli' singing with such sweetness,
  That ne'er from me has the delight departed.

O, what exuberance is garnered up
  Within those richest coffers, which had been
  Good husbandmen for sowing here below!

There they enjoy and live upon the treasure
  Which was acquired while weeping in the exile
  Of Babylon, wherein the gold was left.

There triumpheth, beneath the exalted Son
  Of God and Mary, in his victory,
  Both with the ancient council and the new,

He who doth keep the keys of such a glory.

Canto XXIV

*Now that Christ and Mary have departed for the Empyrean, it is Saint Peter
the Apostle who guides the souls of the saints. Beatrice addresses the assembly of
lights within the Fixed Stars and asks them to allow Dante to share in their
bliss. They put on a dazzling display by forming into a spinning wheel. Beatrice
entreats Saint Peter to conduct an exploration of Faith, the first theological
virtue: its nature, presence, source, truth and content. Dante's answers proclaim
him to be a true believer and the soul of Saint Peter spins around the pilgrim
three times in jubilation.*

"O company elect to the great supper
  Of the Lamb benedight, who feedeth you
  So that for ever full is your desire,

If by the grace of God this man foretaste
  Something of that which falleth from your table,
  Or ever death prescribe to him the time,

Direct your mind to his immense desire,
  And him somewhat bedew; ye drinking are
  For ever at the fount whence comes his thought."

Thus Beatrice; and those souls beatified
  Transformed themselves to spheres on steadfast poles,
  Flaming intensely in the guise of comets.

And as the wheels in works of horologes
  Revolve so that the first to the beholder
  Motionless seems, and the last one to fly,

So in like manner did those carols, dancing
  In different measure, of their affluence
  Give me the gauge, as they were swift or slow.

From that one which I noted of most beauty
  Beheld I issue forth a fire so happy
  That none it left there of a greater brightness;

And around Beatrice three several times
  It whirled itself with so divine a song,
  My fantasy repeats it not to me;

Therefore the pen skips, and I write it not,
  Since our imagination for such folds,
  Much more our speech, is of a tint too glaring.

"O holy sister mine, who us implorest
  With such devotion, by thine ardent love
  Thou dost unbind me from that beautiful sphere!"

Thereafter, having stopped, the blessed fire
  Unto my Lady did direct its breath,
  Which spake in fashion as I here have said.

And she: "O light eterne of the great man
  To whom our Lord delivered up the keys
  He carried down of this miraculous joy,

This one examine on points light and grave,
  As good beseemeth thee, about the Faith
  By means of which thou on the sea didst walk.

If he love well, and hope well, and believe,
  From thee 'tis hid not; for thou hast thy sight
  There where depicted everything is seen.

But since this kingdom has made citizens
  By means of the true Faith, to glorify it
  'Tis well he have the chance to speak thereof."

As baccalaureate arms himself, and speaks not
  Until the master doth propose the question,
  To argue it, and not to terminate it,

So did I arm myself with every reason,
  While she was speaking, that I might be ready
  For such a questioner and such profession.

"Say, thou good Christian; manifest thyself;
  What is the Faith?" Whereat I raised my brow
  Unto that light wherefrom was this breathed forth.

Then turned I round to Beatrice, and she
  Prompt signals made to me that I should pour
  The water forth from my internal fountain.

"May grace, that suffers me to make confession,"
  Began I, "to the great centurion,
  Cause my conceptions all to be explicit!"

And I continued: "As the truthful pen,
  Father, of thy dear brother wrote of it,
  Who put with thee Rome into the good way,

Faith is the substance of the things we hope for,
  And evidence of those that are not seen;
  And this appears to me its quiddity."

Then heard I: "Very rightly thou perceivest,
  If well thou understandest why he placed it
  With substances and then with evidences."

And I thereafterward: "The things profound,
  That here vouchsafe to me their apparition,
  Unto all eyes below are so concealed,

That they exist there only in belief,
  Upon the which is founded the high hope,
  And hence it takes the nature of a substance.

And it behoveth us from this belief
  To reason without having other sight,
  And hence it has the nature of evidence."

Then heard I: "If whatever is acquired
  Below by doctrine were thus understood,
  No sophist's subtlety would there find place."

Thus was breathed forth from that enkindled love;
  Then added: "Very well has been gone over
  Already of this coin the alloy and weight;

But tell me if thou hast it in thy purse?"
  And I: "Yes, both so shining and so round
  That in its stamp there is no peradventure."

Thereafter issued from the light profound
  That there resplendent was: "This precious jewel,
  Upon the which is every virtue founded,

Whence hadst thou it?" And I: "The large outpouring
  Of Holy Spirit, which has been diffused
  Upon the ancient parchments and the new,

A syllogism is, which proved it to me
  With such acuteness, that, compared therewith,
  All demonstration seems to me obtuse."

And then I heard: "The ancient and the new
  Postulates, that to thee are so conclusive,
  Why dost thou take them for the word divine?"

And I: "The proofs, which show the truth to me,
  Are the works subsequent, whereunto Nature
  Ne'er heated iron yet, nor anvil beat."

'Twas answered me: "Say, who assureth thee
  That those works ever were? the thing itself
  That must be proved, nought else to thee affirms it."

"Were the world to Christianity converted,"
  I said, "withouten miracles, this one
  Is such, the rest are not its hundredth part;

Because that poor and fasting thou didst enter
  Into the field to sow there the good plant,
  Which was a vine and has become a thorn!"

This being finished, the high, holy Court
  Resounded through the spheres, "One God we praise!"
  In melody that there above is chanted.

And then that Baron, who from branch to branch,
  Examining, had thus conducted me,
  Till the extremest leaves we were approaching,

Again began: "The Grace that dallying
  Plays with thine intellect thy mouth has opened,
  Up to this point, as it should opened be,

So that I do approve what forth emerged;
  But now thou must express what thou believest,
  And whence to thy belief it was presented."

"O holy father, spirit who beholdest
  What thou believedst so that thou o'ercamest,
  Towards the sepulchre, more youthful feet,"

Began I, "thou dost wish me in this place
  The form to manifest of my prompt belief,
  And likewise thou the cause thereof demandest.

And I respond: In one God I believe,
  Sole and eterne, who moveth all the heavens
  With love and with desire, himself unmoved;

And of such faith not only have I proofs
  Physical and metaphysical, but gives them
  Likewise the truth that from this place rains down

Through Moses, through the Prophets and the Psalms,
  Through the Evangel, and through you, who wrote
  After the fiery Spirit sanctified you;

In Persons three eterne believe, and these
  One essence I believe, so one and trine
  They bear conjunction both with '*sunt*' and '*est*.'

With the profound condition and divine
  Which now I touch upon, doth stamp my mind
  Ofttimes the doctrine evangelical.

This the beginning is, this is the spark
  Which afterwards dilates to vivid flame,
  And, like a star in heaven, is sparkling in me."

Even as a lord who hears what pleaseth him
  His servant straight embraces, gratulating
  For the good news as soon as he is silent;

So, giving me its benediction, singing,
  Three times encircled me, when I was silent,
  The apostolic light, at whose command

I spoken had, in speaking I so pleased him.

Canto XXV

Saint James arrives to conduct Dante's examination on Hope, the second theological virtue. Having been chosen to witness the joy of God's elect, Beatrice argues that her ward possesses this virtue in abundance. Dante's replies on the nature, content and source of Hope conclude the examination in triumph. All the souls praise the grace of God as Saint John appears. Dante peers into the depths of his soul's fiery brilliance, hoping to glimpse the outline of a mortal body, but is warned that what he seeks is not there. Looking away, he discovers that he has been blinded by Love's radiance.

If e'er it happen that the Poem Sacred,
  To which both heaven and Earth have set their hand,
  So that it many a year hath made me lean,

O'ercome the cruelty that bars me out
  From the fair sheepfold, where a lamb I slumbered,
  An enemy to the wolves that war upon it,

With other voice forthwith, with other fleece
  Poet will I return, and at my font
  Baptismal will I take the laurel crown;

Because into the Faith that maketh known
  All souls to God there entered I, and then
  Peter for her sake thus my brow encircled.

Thereafterward towards us moved a light
  Out of that band whence issued the first-fruits
  Which of his vicars Christ behind him left,

And then my Lady, full of ecstasy,
  Said unto me: "Look, look! behold the Baron
  For whom below Galicia is frequented."

In the same way as, when a dove alights
  Near his companion, both of them pour forth,
  Circling about and murmuring, their affection,

So one beheld I by the other grand
  Prince glorified to be with welcome greeted,
  Lauding the food that there above is eaten.

But when their gratulations were complete,
  Silently 'coram me' each one stood still,
  So incandescent it o'ercame my sight.

Smiling thereafterwards, said Beatrice:
  "Illustrious life, by whom the benefactions
  Of our Basilica have been described,

Make Hope resound within this altitude;
  Thou knowest as oft thou dost personify it
  As Jesus to the three gave greater clearness."—

"Lift up thy head, and make thyself assured;
  For what comes hither from the mortal world
  Must needs be ripened in our radiance."

This comfort came to me from the second fire;
  Wherefore mine eyes I lifted to the hills,
  Which bent them down before with too great weight.

"Since, through his grace, our Emperor wills that thou
  Shouldst find thee face to face, before thy death,
  In the most secret chamber, with his Counts,

So that, the truth beholden of this court,
  Hope, which below there rightfully enamours,
  Thereby thou strengthen in thyself and others,

Say what it is, and how is flowering with it
  Thy mind, and say from whence it came to thee."
  Thus did the second light again continue.

And the Compassionate, who piloted
  The plumage of my wings in such high flight,
  Did in reply anticipate me thus:

"No child whatever the Church Militant
  Of greater hope possesses, as is written
  In that Sun which irradiates all our band;

Therefore it is conceded him from Egypt
  To come into Jerusalem to see,
  Or ever yet his warfare be completed.

The two remaining points, that not for knowledge
  Have been demanded, but that he report
  How much this virtue unto thee is pleasing,

To him I leave; for hard he will not find them,
  Nor of self-praise; and let him answer them;
  And may the grace of God in this assist him!"

As a disciple, who his teacher follows,
  Ready and willing, where he is expert,
  That his proficiency may be displayed,

"Hope," said I, "is the certain expectation
  Of future glory, which is the effect
  Of grace divine and merit precedent.

From many stars this light comes unto me;
  But he instilled it first into my heart
  Who was chief singer unto the chief captain.

'Sperent in te,' in the high Theody
  He sayeth, 'those who know thy name;' and who
  Knoweth it not, if he my faith possess?

Thou didst instil me, then, with his instilling
  In the Epistle, so that I am full,
  And upon others rain again your rain."

While I was speaking, in the living bosom
  Of that combustion quivered an effulgence,
  Sudden and frequent, in the guise of lightning;

Then breathed: "The love wherewith I am inflamed
  Towards the virtue still which followed me
  Unto the palm and issue of the field,

Wills that I breathe to thee that thou delight
  In her; and grateful to me is thy telling
  Whatever things Hope promises to thee."

And I: "The ancient Scriptures and the new
  The mark establish, and this shows it me,
  Of all the souls whom God hath made his friends.

Isaiah saith, that each one garmented
  In his own land shall be with twofold garments,
  And his own land is this delightful life.

Thy brother, too, far more explicitly,
  There where he treateth of the robes of white,
  This revelation manifests to us."

And first, and near the ending of these words,
  "Sperent in te" from over us was heard,
  To which responsive answered all the carols.

Thereafterward a light among them brightened,
  So that, if Cancer one such crystal had,
  Winter would have a month of one sole day.

And as uprises, goes, and enters the dance
  A winsome maiden, only to do honour
  To the new bride, and not from any failing,

Even thus did I behold the brightened splendour
  Approach the two, who in a wheel revolved
  As was beseeming to their ardent love.

Into the song and music there it entered;
  And fixed on them my Lady kept her look,
  Even as a bride silent and motionless.

"This is the one who lay upon the breast
  Of him our Pelican; and this is he
  To the great office from the cross elected."

My Lady thus; but therefore none the more
  Did move her sight from its attentive gaze
  Before or afterward these words of hers.

Even as a man who gazes, and endeavours
  To see the eclipsing of the sun a little,
  And who, by seeing, sightless doth become,

So I became before that latest fire,
  While it was said, "Why dost thou daze thyself
  To see a thing which here hath no existence?

Earth in the earth my body is, and shall be
  With all the others there, until our number
  With the eternal proposition tallies.

With the two garments in the blessed cloister
  Are the two lights alone that have ascended:
  And this shalt thou take back into your world."

And at this utterance the flaming circle
  Grew quiet, with the dulcet intermingling
  Of sound that by the trinal breath was made,

As to escape from danger or fatigue
  The oars that erst were in the water beaten
  Are all suspended at a whistle's sound.

Ah, how much in my mind was I disturbed,
  When I turned round to look on Beatrice,
  That her I could not see, although I was

Close at her side and in the Happy World!

Canto XXVI

*Having reassured Dante the Pilgrim that Beatrice's loving gaze will heal his blindness,
Saint John begins his examination on the object and nature of Love, the third theological
virtue. Dante the Poet describes its intensity, which begins and ends in God, and traces the
sources from which he obtained the knowledge that God is the ultimate good. When Dante
has given this answer Beatrice and the others sing "Holy, holy, holy!" and his vision is
restored. He sees that the soul of Adam has joined those of the three Apostles. In reply to
Dante, Adam proceeds to reveal the nature of the Fall, the date of his creation, the language
he spoke whilst on Earth and the length of his stay in Eden.*

While I was doubting for my vision quenched,
  Out of the flame refulgent that had quenched it
  Issued a breathing, that attentive made me,

Saying: "While thou recoverest the sense
  Of seeing which in me thou hast consumed,
  'Tis well that speaking thou shouldst compensate it.

Begin then, and declare to what thy soul
  Is aimed, and count it for a certainty,
  Sight is in thee bewildered and not dead;

Because the Lady, who through this divine
  Region conducteth thee, has in her look
  The power the hand of Ananias had."

I said: "As pleaseth her, or soon or late
  Let the cure come to eyes that portals were
  When she with fire I ever burn with entered.

The Good, that gives contentment to this Court,
  The Alpha and Omega is of all
  The writing that love reads me low or loud."

The selfsame voice, that taken had from me
  The terror of the sudden dazzlement,
  To speak still farther put it in my thought;

And said: "In verity with finer sieve
  Behoveth thee to sift; thee it behoveth
  To say who aimed thy bow at such a target."

And I: "By philosophic arguments,
  And by authority that hence descends,
  Such love must needs imprint itself in me;

For Good, so far as good, when comprehended
  Doth straight enkindle love, and so much greater
  As more of goodness in itself it holds;

Then to that Essence (whose is such advantage
  That every good which out of it is found
  Is nothing but a ray of its own light)

More than elsewhither must the mind be moved
  Of every one, in loving, who discerns
  The truth in which this evidence is founded.

"Begin then, and declare to what thy soul / Is aimed, and count it for a certainty, /
Sight is in thee bewildered and not dead;"

Par. XXVI, lines 7–9

Such truth he to my intellect reveals
  Who demonstrates to me the primal love
  Of all the sempiternal substances.

The voice reveals it of the truthful Author,
  Who says to Moses, speaking of Himself,
  'I will make all my goodness pass before thee.'

Thou too revealest it to me, beginning
  The loud Evangel, that proclaims the secret
  Of heaven to Earth above all other edict."

And I heard say: "By human intellect
  And by authority concordant with it,
  Of all thy loves reserve for God the highest.

But say again if other cords thou feelest,
  Draw thee towards Him, that thou mayst proclaim
  With how many teeth this love is biting thee."

The holy purpose of the Eagle of Christ
  Not latent was, nay, rather I perceived
  Whither he fain would my profession lead.

Therefore I recommenced: "All of those bites
  Which have the power to turn the heart to God
  Unto my charity have been concurrent.

The being of the world, and my own being,
  The death which He endured that I may live,
  And that which all the faithful hope, as I do,

With the forementioned vivid consciousness
  Have drawn me from the sea of love perverse,
  And of the right have placed me on the shore.

The leaves, wherewith embowered is all the garden
  Of the Eternal Gardener, do I love
  As much as he has granted them of good."

As soon as I had ceased, a song most sweet
  Throughout the heaven resounded, and my Lady
  Said with the others, "Holy, holy, holy!"

And as at some keen light one wakes from sleep
  By reason of the visual spirit that runs
  Unto the splendour passed from coat to coat,

And he who wakes abhorreth what he sees,
  So all unconscious is his sudden waking,
  Until the judgment cometh to his aid,

So from before mine eyes did Beatrice
  Chase every mote with radiance of her own,
  That cast its light a thousand miles and more.

Whence better after than before I saw,
  And in a kind of wonderment I asked
  About a fourth light that I saw with us.

And said my Lady: "There within those rays
  Gazes upon its Maker the first soul
  That ever the first virtue did create."

Even as the bough that downward bends its top
  At transit of the wind, and then is lifted
  By its own virtue, which inclines it upward,

Likewise did I, the while that she was speaking,
  Being amazed, and then I was made bold
  By a desire to speak wherewith I burned.

And I began: "O apple, that mature
  Alone hast been produced, O ancient father,
  To whom each wife is daughter and daughter-in-law,

Devoutly as I can I supplicate thee
  That thou wouldst speak to me; thou seest my wish;
  And I, to hear thee quickly, speak it not."

Sometimes an animal, when covered, struggles
  So that his impulse needs must be apparent,
  By reason of the wrappage following it;

And in like manner the primeval soul
  Made clear to me athwart its covering
  How jubilant it was to give me pleasure.

Then breathed: "Without thy uttering it to me,
  Thine inclination better I discern
  Than thou whatever thing is surest to thee;

For I behold it in the truthful mirror,
  That of Himself all things parhelion makes,
  And none makes Him parhelion of itself.

Thou fain wouldst hear how long ago God placed me
  Within the lofty garden, where this Lady
  Unto so long a stairway thee disposed.

And how long to mine eyes it was a pleasure,
  And of the great disdain the proper cause,
  And the language that I used and that I made.

Now, son of mine, the tasting of the tree
  Not in itself was cause of so great exile,
  But solely the o'erstepping of the bounds.

There, whence thy Lady moved Virgilius,
  Four thousand and three hundred and two circuits
  Made by the sun, this Council I desired;

And him I saw return to all the lights
  Of his highway nine hundred times and thirty,
  Whilst I upon the earth was tarrying.

The language that I spake was quite extinct
  Before that in the work interminable
  The people under Nimrod were employed;

For nevermore result of reasoning
  (Because of human pleasure that doth change,
  Obedient to the heavens) was durable.

A natural action is it that man speaks;
  But whether thus or thus, doth nature leave
  To your own art, as seemeth best to you.

Ere I descended to the infernal anguish,
  '*El*' was on Earth the name of the Chief Good,
  From whom comes all the joy that wraps me round

'*Eli*' he then was called, and that is proper,
  Because the use of men is like a leaf
  On bough, which goeth and another cometh.

Upon the mount that highest o'er the wave
  Rises was I, in life or pure or sinful,
  From the first hour to that which is the second,

As the sun changes quadrant, to the sixth."

Canto XXVII

*The assembly of the Church Triumphant congratulates Dante on his progress. Saint
Peter flushes with anger as he denounces all the evil popes, declaring the papal see
'vacant'. Heaven blushes in sympathy. The Apostle asks the pilgrim to repeat what he
has just heard to his fellow men. As the gathering whirls out of sight, Dante realizes
that he is standing above the point between Jerusalem and Spain. As Beatrice takes
him up through the Primum Mobile, the crystalline Ninth Heaven, she discusses the
origin of Time and foresees order being restored both in the Church and in the world.*

"Glory be to the Father, to the Son,
  And Holy Ghost!" all Paradise began,
  So that the melody inebriate made me.

What I beheld seemed unto me a smile
  Of the universe; for my inebriation
  Found entrance through the hearing and the sight.

O joy! O gladness inexpressible!
  O perfect life of love and peacefulness!
  O riches without hankering secure!

Before mine eyes were standing the four torches
  Enkindled, and the one that first had come
  Began to make itself more luminous;

And even such in semblance it became
  As Jupiter would become, if he and Mars
  Were birds, and they should interchange their feathers.

That Providence, which here distributeth
  Season and service, in the blessed choir
  Had silence upon every side imposed.

"Glory be to the Father, to the Son, / And Holy Ghost!" all Paradise began, /
So that the melody inebriate made me.

Par. XXVII, lines 1–3

When I heard say: "If I my colour change,
  Marvel not at it; for while I am speaking
  Thou shalt behold all these their colour change.

He who usurps upon the Earth my place,
  My place, my place, which vacant has become
  Before the presence of the Son of God,

Has of my cemetery made a sewer
  Of blood and stench, whereby the Perverse One,
  Who fell from here, below there is appeased!"

With the same colour which, through sun adverse,
  Painteth the clouds at evening or at morn,
  Beheld I then the whole of heaven suffused.

And as a modest woman, who abides
  Sure of herself, and at another's failing,
  From listening only, timorous becomes,

Even thus did Beatrice change countenance;
  And I believe in heaven was such eclipse,
  When suffered the supreme Omnipotence;

Thereafterward proceeded forth his words
  With voice so much transmuted from itself,
  The very countenance was not more changed.

"The spouse of Christ has never nurtured been
  On blood of mine, of Linus and of Cletus,
  To be made use of in acquest of gold;

But in acquest of this delightful life
  Sixtus and Pius, Urban and Calixtus,
  After much lamentation, shed their blood.

Our purpose was not, that on the right hand
  Of our successors should in part be seated
  The Christian folk, in part upon the other;

Nor that the keys which were to me confided
  Should e'er become the escutcheon on a banner,
  That should wage war on those who are baptized;

Nor I be made the figure of a seal
  To privileges venal and mendacious,
  Whereat I often redden and flash with fire.

In garb of shepherds the rapacious wolves
  Are seen from here above o'er all the pastures!
  O wrath of God, why dost thou slumber still?

To drink our blood the Caorsines and Gascons
  Are making ready. O thou good beginning,
  Unto how vile an end must thou needs fall!

But the high Providence, that with Scipio
  At Rome the glory of the world defended,
  Will speedily bring aid, as I conceive;

And thou, my son, who by thy mortal weight
  Shalt down return again, open thy mouth;
  What I conceal not, do not thou conceal."

As with its frozen vapours downward falls
  In flakes our atmosphere, what time the horn
  Of the celestial Goat doth touch the sun,

Upward in such array saw I the ether
  Become, and flaked with the triumphant vapours,
  Which there together with us had remained.

My sight was following up their semblances,
  And followed till the medium, by excess,
  The passing farther onward took from it;

Whereat the Lady, who beheld me freed
  From gazing upward, said to me: "Cast down
  Thy sight, and see how far thou art turned round."

Since the first time that I had downward looked,
  I saw that I had moved through the whole arc
  Which the first climate makes from midst to end;

So that I saw the mad track of Ulysses
  Past Gades, and this side, well nigh the shore
  Whereon became Europa a sweet burden.

And of this threshing-floor the site to me
  Were more unveiled, but the sun was proceeding
  Under my feet, a sign and more removed.

My mind enamoured, which is dallying
  At all times with my Lady, to bring back
  To her mine eyes was more than ever ardent.

And if or Art or Nature has made bait
  To catch the eyes and so possess the mind,
  In human flesh or in its portraiture,

All joined together would appear as nought
  To the divine delight which shone upon me
  When to her smiling face I turned me round.

The virtue that her look endowed me with
　From the fair nest of Leda tore me forth,
　And up into the swiftest heaven impelled me.

Its parts exceeding full of life and lofty
　Are all so uniform, I cannot say
　Which Beatrice selected for my place.

But she, who was aware of my desire,
　Began, the while she smiled so joyously
　That God seemed in her countenance to rejoice:

"The nature of that motion, which keeps quiet
　The centre and all the rest about it moves,
　From hence begins as from its starting point.

And in this heaven there is no other Where
　Than in the Mind Divine, wherein is kindled
　The love that turns it, and the power it rains.

Within a circle light and love embrace it,
　Even as this doth the others, and that precinct
　He who encircles it alone controls.

Its motion is not by another meted,
　But all the others measured are by this,
　As ten is by the half and by the fifth.

And in what manner time in such a pot
　May have its roots, and in the rest its leaves,
　Now unto thee can manifest be made.

O Covetousness, that mortals dost ingulf
　Beneath thee so, that no one hath the power
　Of drawing back his eyes from out thy waves!

Full fairly blossoms in mankind the will;
　But the uninterrupted rain converts
　Into abortive wildings the true plums.

Fidelity and innocence are found
　Only in children; afterwards they both
　Take flight or e'er the cheeks with down are covered.

One, while he prattles still, observes the fasts,
　Who, when his tongue is loosed, forthwith devours
　Whatever food under whatever moon;

Another, while he prattles, loves and listens
　Unto his mother, who when speech is perfect
　Forthwith desires to see her in her grave.

Even thus is swarthy made the skin so white
　In its first aspect of the daughter fair
　Of him who brings the morn, and leaves the night.

Thou, that it may not be a marvel to thee,
　Think that on Earth there is no one who governs;
　Whence goes astray the human family.

Ere January be unwintered wholly
　By the centesimal on Earth neglected,
　Shall these supernal circles roar so loud

The tempest that has been so long awaited
　Shall whirl the poops about where are the prows;
　So that the fleet shall run its course direct,

And the true fruit shall follow on the flower."

Canto XXVIII

Dante sees the reflection of a bright object in Beatrice's eyes and, turning around, beholds God as a small but extremely brilliant ball of light that is surrounded by nine glowing, concentric rings. These are the angelic ranks that co-ordinate the movement of the Heavens. Dante is puzzled because the highest-ranking celestial beings are represented by the smallest circles, which does not conform to the universe as he knows it. Beatrice explains that there virtue is not related to size as it is on Earth. She goes on to name the orders of the angels: Seraphim, Cherubim, Thrones, Dominions, Virtues, Powers, Principalities, Archangels and Angels.

After the truth against the present life
  Of miserable mortals was unfolded
  By her who doth imparadise my mind,

As in a looking-glass a taper's flame
  He sees who from behind is lighted by it,
  Before he has it in his sight or thought,

And turns him round to see if so the glass
  Tell him the truth, and sees that it accords
  Therewith as doth a music with its metre,

In similar wise my memory recollecteth
  That I did, looking into those fair eyes,
  Of which Love made the springes to ensnare me.

And as I turned me round, and mine were touched
  By that which is apparent in that volume,
  Whenever on its gyre we gaze intent,

A point beheld I, that was raying out
  Light so acute, the sight which it enkindles
  Must close perforce before such great acuteness.

And whatsoever star seems smallest here
  Would seem to be a moon, if placed beside it.
  As one star with another star is placed.

Perhaps at such a distance as appears
  A halo cincturing the light that paints it,
  When densest is the vapour that sustains it,

Thus distant round the point a circle of fire
  So swiftly whirled, that it would have surpassed
  Whatever motion soonest girds the world;

And this was by another circumcinct,
  That by a third, the third then by a fourth,
  By a fifth the fourth, and then by a sixth the fifth;

The seventh followed thereupon in width
  So ample now, that Juno's messenger
  Entire would be too narrow to contain it.

Even so the eighth and ninth; and every one
  More slowly moved, according as it was
  In number distant farther from the first.

And that one had its flame most crystalline
  From which less distant was the stainless spark,
  I think because more with its truth imbued.

My Lady, who in my anxiety
  Beheld me much perplexed, said: "From that point
  Dependent is the heaven and nature all.

Behold that circle most conjoined to it,
  And know thou, that its motion is so swift
  Through burning love whereby it is spurred on."

And I to her: "If the world were arranged
  In the order which I see in yonder wheels,
  What's set before me would have satisfied me;

But in the world of sense we can perceive
  That evermore the circles are diviner
  As they are from the centre more remote

Wherefore if my desire is to be ended
  In this miraculous and angelic temple,
  That has for confines only love and light,

To hear behoves me still how the example
  And the exemplar go not in one fashion,
  Since for myself in vain I contemplate it."

"If thine own fingers unto such a knot
  Be insufficient, it is no great wonder,
  So hard hath it become for want of trying."

My Lady thus; then said she: "Do thou take
  What I shall tell thee, if thou wouldst be sated,
  And exercise on that thy subtlety.

The circles corporal are wide and narrow
  According to the more or less of virtue
  Which is distributed through all their parts.

The greater goodness works the greater weal,
  The greater weal the greater body holds,
  If perfect equally are all its parts.

Therefore this one which sweeps along with it
  The universe sublime, doth correspond
  Unto the circle which most loves and knows.

On which account, if thou unto the virtue
  Apply thy measure, not to the appearance
  Of substances that unto thee seem round,

Thou wilt behold a marvellous agreement,
  Of more to greater, and of less to smaller,
  In every heaven, with its Intelligence."

Even as remaineth splendid and serene
  The hemisphere of air, when Boreas
  Is blowing from that cheek where he is mildest,

Because is purified and resolved the rack
  That erst disturbed it, till the welkin laughs
  With all the beauties of its pageantry;

Thus did I likewise, after that my Lady
  Had me provided with her clear response,
  And like a star in heaven the truth was seen.

And soon as to a stop her words had come,
  Not otherwise does iron scintillate
  When molten, than those circles scintillated.

Their coruscation all the sparks repeated,
  And they so many were, their number makes
  More millions than the doubling of the chess.

I heard them sing *hosanna* choir by choir
  To the fixed point which holds them at the '*Ubi*,'
  And ever will, where they have ever been.

And she, who saw the dubious meditations
  Within my mind, "The primal circles," said,
  "Have shown thee Seraphim and Cherubim.

Thus rapidly they follow their own bonds,
  To be as like the point as most they can,
  And can as far as they are high in vision.

Those other Loves, that round about them go,
  Thrones of the countenance divine are called,
  Because they terminate the primal Triad.

And thou shouldst know that they all have delight
  As much as their own vision penetrates
  The Truth, in which all intellect finds rest.

From this it may be seen how blessedness
  Is founded in the faculty which sees,
  And not in that which loves, and follows next;

And of this seeing merit is the measure,
  Which is brought forth by grace, and by good will;
  Thus on from grade to grade doth it proceed.

The second Triad, which is germinating
  In such wise in this sempiternal spring,
  That no nocturnal Aries despoils,

Perpetually hosanna warbles forth
  With threefold melody, that sounds in three
  Orders of joy, with which it is intrined.

The three Divine are in this hierarchy,
  First the Dominions, and the Virtues next;
  And the third order is that of the Powers.

Then in the dances twain penultimate
  The Principalities and Archangels wheel;
  The last is wholly of angelic sports.

These orders upward all of them are gazing,
  And downward so prevail, that unto God
  They all attracted are and all attract.

And Dionysius with so great desire
  To contemplate these Orders set himself,
  He named them and distinguished them as I do.

Not otherwise does iron scintillate / When molten, than those circles scintillated.

Par. XXVIII, lines 89–90

But Gregory afterwards dissented from him;
  Wherefore, as soon as he unclosed his eyes
  Within this heaven, he at himself did smile.

And if so much of secret truth a mortal
  Proffered on Earth, I would not have thee marvel,
  For he who saw it here revealed it to him,

With much more of the truth about these circles."

Canto XXIX

*Gazing at the Primum Mobile, the infinitesimal, spaceless point that is God, Beatrice
reads Dante's questions in it and proceeds to lay bare the mystery of Creation, the fall of
Lucifer and the relationship of angelic beings to each other, the order of the universe
and God since the time of the revolt. She corrects some earthly confusion about angels –
they do not possess memory, for instance, because they see everything within God. After
blasting the false teachings of presumptuous preachers, Beatrice asks Dante to reflect on
the infinite, indivisible nature of God and the pure, distinctive form of each angelic
nature. She explains that there are more angels than humans can comprehend.*

At what time both the children of Latona,
  Surmounted by the Ram and by the Scales,
  Together make a zone of the horizon,

As long as from the time the zenith holds them
  In equipoise, till from that girdle both
  Changing their hemisphere disturb the balance,

So long, her face depicted with a smile,
  Did Beatrice keep silence while she gazed
  Fixedly at the point which had o'ercome me.

Then she began: "I say, and I ask not
  What thou dost wish to hear, for I have seen it
  Where centres every When and every 'Ubi.'

Not to acquire some good unto himself,
  Which is impossible, but that his splendour
  In its resplendency may say, 'Subsisto,'

In his eternity outside of time,
  Outside all other limits, as it pleased him,
  Into new Loves the Eternal Love unfolded.

Nor as if torpid did he lie before;
  For neither after nor before proceeded
  The going forth of God upon these waters.

Matter and Form unmingled and conjoined
  Came into being that had no defect,
  E'en as three arrows from a three-stringed bow.

And as in glass, in amber, or in crystal
  A sunbeam flashes so, that from its coming
  To its full being is no interval,

So from its Lord did the triform effect
  Ray forth into its being all together,
  Without discrimination of beginning.

Order was con-created and constructed
  In substances, and summit of the world
  Were those wherein the pure act was produced.

Pure potentiality held the lowest part;
  Midway bound potentiality with act
  Such bond that it shall never be unbound.

Jerome has written unto you of angels
  Created a long lapse of centuries
  Or ever yet the other world was made;

But written is this truth in many places
  By writers of the Holy Ghost, and thou
  Shalt see it, if thou lookest well thereat.

And even reason seeth it somewhat,
  For it would not concede that for so long
  Could be the motors without their perfection.

Now dost thou know both where and when these Loves
  Created were, and how; so that extinct
  In thy desire already are three fires.

Nor could one reach, in counting, unto twenty
  So swiftly, as a portion of these angels
  Disturbed the subject of your elements.

The rest remained, and they began this art
  Which thou discernest, with so great delight
  That never from their circling do they cease.

The occasion of the fall was the accursed
  Presumption of that One, whom thou hast seen
  By all the burden of the world constrained.

Those whom thou here beholdest modest were
  To recognise themselves as of that goodness
  Which made them apt for so much understanding;

On which account their vision was exalted
  By the enlightening grace and their own merit,
  So that they have a full and steadfast will.

I would not have thee doubt, but certain be,
  'Tis meritorious to receive this grace,
  According as the affection opens to it.

Now round about in this consistory
  Much mayst thou contemplate, if these my words
  Be gathered up, without all further aid.

But since upon the Earth, throughout your schools,
  They teach that such is the angelic nature
  That it doth hear, and recollect and will,

More will I say, that thou mayst see unmixed
  The truth that is confounded there below,
  Equivocating in such like prelections.

These substances, since in God's countenance
  They jocund were, turned not away their sight
  From that wherefrom not anything is hidden;

Hence they have not their vision intercepted
  By object new, and hence they do not need
  To recollect, through interrupted thought.

So that below, not sleeping, people dream,
  Believing they speak truth, and not believing;
  And in the last is greater sin and shame.

Below you do not journey by one path
  Philosophising; so transporteth you
  Love of appearance and the thought thereof.

And even this above here is endured
  With less disdain, than when is set aside
  The Holy Writ, or when it is distorted.

They think not there how much of blood it costs
  To sow it in the world, and how he pleases
  Who in humility keeps close to it.

Each striveth for appearance, and doth make
  His own inventions; and these treated are
  By preachers, and the Evangel holds its peace.

One sayeth that the moon did backward turn,
  In the Passion of Christ, and interpose herself
  So that the sunlight reached not down below;

And lies; for of its own accord the light
  Hid itself; whence to Spaniards and to Indians,
  As to the Jews, did such eclipse respond.

Florence has not so many Lapi and Bindi
  As fables such as these, that every year
  Are shouted from the pulpit back and forth,

In such wise that the lambs, who do not know,
  Come back from pasture fed upon the wind,
  And not to see the harm doth not excuse them.

Christ did not to his first disciples say,
  'Go forth, and to the world preach idle tales,'
  But unto them a true foundation gave;

And this so loudly sounded from their lips,
  That, in the warfare to enkindle Faith,
  They made of the Evangel shields and lances.

Now men go forth with jests and drolleries
  To preach, and if but well the people laugh,
  The hood puffs out, and nothing more is asked.

But in the cowl there nestles such a bird,
  That, if the common people were to see it,
  They would perceive what pardons they confide in,

For which so great on Earth has grown the folly,
  That, without proof of any testimony,
  To each indulgence they would flock together.

By this Saint Anthony his pig doth fatten,
  And many others, who are worse than pigs,
  Paying in money without mark of coinage.

But since we have digressed abundantly,
  Turn back thine eyes forthwith to the right path,
  So that the way be shortened with the time.

This nature doth so multiply itself
  In numbers, that there never yet was speech
  Nor mortal fancy that can go so far.

And if thou notest that which is revealed
  By Daniel, thou wilt see that in his thousands
  Number determinate is kept concealed.

The primal light, that all irradiates it,
  By modes as many is received therein,
  As are the splendours wherewith it is mated.

Hence, inasmuch as on the act conceptive
  The affection followeth, of love the sweetness
  Therein diversely fervid is or tepid.

The height behold now and the amplitude
  Of the eternal power, since it hath made
  Itself so many mirrors, where 'tis broken,

One in itself remaining as before."

Canto XXX

*The angelic circles fade from sight. Beatrice's beauty is now transcendental because the
pair have entered the Empyrean, where Dante will behold God, the angels, the saints
and the souls of the blessed in the flesh (a vision of the two courts of Heaven). Dante's
eyesight is dazzled then rekindled after drinking from the River of Light. This image
changes into the White Rose of Paradise, symbol of divine Love. Its yellow centre is the
light of God's glory whilst the petals rise up in tiers on which the saints are seated on
thrones. An empty seat awaits Emperor Henry VII.*

Perchance six thousand miles remote from us
  Is glowing the sixth hour, and now this world
  Inclines its shadow almost to a level,

When the mid-heaven begins to make itself
  So deep to us, that here and there a star
  Ceases to shine so far down as this depth,

And as advances bright exceedingly
  The handmaid of the sun, the heaven is closed
  Light after light to the most beautiful;

Not otherwise the Triumph, which for ever
  Plays round about the point that vanquished me,
  Seeming enclosed by what itself encloses,

Little by little from my vision faded;
  Whereat to turn mine eyes on Beatrice
  My seeing nothing and my love constrained me.

If what has hitherto been said of her
  Were all concluded in a single praise,
  Scant would it be to serve the present turn.

Not only does the beauty I beheld
  Transcend ourselves, but truly I believe
  Its Maker only may enjoy it all.

Vanquished do I confess me by this passage
  More than by problem of his theme was ever
  O'ercome the comic or the tragic poet;

For as the sun the sight that trembles most,
  Even so the memory of that sweet smile
  My mind depriveth of its very self.

From the first day that I beheld her face
  In this life, to the moment of this look,
  The sequence of my song has ne'er been severed;

But now perforce this sequence must desist
  From following her beauty with my verse,
  As every artist at his uttermost.

Such as I leave her to a greater fame
  Than any of my trumpet, which is bringing
  Its arduous matter to a final close,

With voice and gesture of a perfect leader
  She recommenced: "We from the greatest body
  Have issued to the heaven that is pure light;

Light intellectual replete with love,
  Love of true good replete with ecstasy,
  Ecstasy that transcendeth every sweetness.

Here shalt thou see the one host and the other
  Of Paradise, and one in the same aspects
  Which at the final judgment thou shalt see."

Even as a sudden lightning that disperses
  The visual spirits, so that it deprives
  The eye of impress from the strongest objects,

Thus round about me flashed a living light,
  And left me swathed around with such a veil
  Of its effulgence, that I nothing saw.

"Ever the Love which quieteth this heaven
  Welcomes into itself with such salute,
  To make the candle ready for its flame."

No sooner had within me these brief words
  An entrance found, than I perceived myself
  To be uplifted over my own power,

And I with vision new rekindled me,
  Such that no light whatever is so pure
  But that mine eyes were fortified against it.

And light I saw in fashion of a river
  Fulvid with its effulgence, 'twixt two banks
  Depicted with an admirable Spring.

Out of this river issued living sparks,
  And on all sides sank down into the flowers,
  Like unto rubies that are set in gold;

And then, as if inebriate with the odours,
  They plunged again into the wondrous torrent,
  And as one entered issued forth another.

"The high desire, that now inflames and moves thee
  To have intelligence of what thou seest,
  Pleaseth me all the more, the more it swells.

But of this water it behoves thee drink
  Before so great a thirst in thee be slaked."
  Thus said to me the sunshine of mine eyes;

And added: "The river and the topazes
  Going in and out, and the laughing of the
                                        herbage,
  Are of their truth foreshadowing prefaces;

Not that these things are difficult in themselves,
  But the deficiency is on thy side,
  For yet thou hast not vision so exalted."

There is no babe that leaps so suddenly
  With face towards the milk, if he awake
  Much later than his usual custom is,

As I did, that I might make better mirrors
  Still of mine eyes, down stooping to the wave
  Which flows that we therein be better made.

And even as the penthouse of mine eyelids
  Drank of it, it forthwith appeared to me
  Out of its length to be transformed to round.

Then as a folk who have been under masks
  Seem other than before, if they divest
  The semblance not their own they disappeared in,

Thus into greater pomp were changed for me
  The flowerets and the sparks, so that I saw
  Both of the Courts of Heaven made manifest.

O splendour of God! by means of which I saw
  The lofty triumph of the realm veracious,
  Give me the power to say how it I saw!

There is a light above, which visible
  Makes the Creator unto every creature,
  Who only in beholding Him has peace,

And it expands itself in circular form
  To such extent, that its circumference
  Would be too large a girdle for the sun.

The semblance of it is all made of rays
  Reflected from the top of Primal Motion,
  Which takes therefrom vitality and power.

And as a hill in water at its base
  Mirrors itself, as if to see its beauty
  When affluent most in verdure and in flowers,

So, ranged aloft all round about the light,
  Mirrored I saw in more ranks than a thousand
  All who above there have from us returned.

And if the lowest row collect within it
  So great a light, how vast the amplitude
  Is of this Rose in its extremest leaves!

My vision in the vastness and the height
  Lost not itself, but comprehended all
  The quantity and quality of that gladness.

There near and far nor add nor take away;
  For there where God immediately doth govern,
  The natural law in naught is relevant.

Into the yellow of the Rose Eternal
  That spreads, and multiplies, and breathes an
                           odour
  Of praise unto the ever-vernal Sun,

As one who silent is and fain would speak,
  Me Beatrice drew on, and said: "Behold
  Of the white stoles how vast the convent is!

Behold how vast the circuit of our city!
  Behold our seats so filled to overflowing,
  That here henceforward are few people wanting!

On that great throne whereon thine eyes are fixed
  For the crown's sake already placed upon it,
  Before thou suppest at this wedding feast

Shall sit the soul (that is to be Augustus
  On Earth) of noble Henry, who shall come
  To redress Italy ere she be ready.

Blind covetousness, that casts its spell upon you,
  Has made you like unto the little child,
  Who dies of hunger and drives off the nurse.

And in the sacred forum then shall be
  A Prefect such, that openly or covert
  On the same road he will not walk with him.

But long of God he will not be endured
  In holy office; he shall be thrust down
  Where Simon Magus is for his deserts,

And make him of Alagna lower go!"

Canto XXXI

*Dante contemplates the White Rose of Paradise and beholds the two-fold Host of
Heaven: tier upon tier of blessed souls being tended to by angels flying like bees between
them and God. It is time for Beatrice to bid Dante farewell. As she takes her place
among the redeemed, the pilgrim sends her his prayer of gratitude. She smiles at him
before reverting her gaze to God. His new guide is Saint Bernard who informs Dante
that his ultimate vision of God is made possible through the Virgin's intercession.
Raising his eyes, he sees the Queen of Heaven in her enthroned splendour.*

In fashion then as of a snow-white rose
  Displayed itself to me the saintly host,
  Whom Christ in his own blood had made his bride,

But the other host, that flying sees and sings
  The glory of Him who doth enamour it,
  And the goodness that created it so noble,

Even as a swarm of bees, that sinks in flowers
  One moment, and the next returns again
  To where its labour is to sweetness turned,

Sank into the great flower, that is adorned
  With leaves so many, and thence reascended
  To where its love abideth evermore.

Their faces had they all of living flame,
  And wings of gold, and all the rest so white
  No snow unto that limit doth attain.

From bench to bench, into the flower descending,
  They carried something of the peace and ardour
  Which by the fanning of their flanks they won.

Nor did the interposing 'twixt the flower
  And what was o'er it of such plenitude
  Of flying shapes impede the sight and splendour;

Because the light divine so penetrates
  The universe, according to its merit,
  That naught can be an obstacle against it.

This realm secure and full of gladsomeness,
  Crowded with ancient people and with modern,
  Unto one mark had all its look and love.

O Trinal Light, that in a single star
  Sparkling upon their sight so satisfies them,
  Look down upon our tempest here below!

If the barbarians, coming from some region
  That every day by Helice is covered,
  Revolving with her son whom she delights in,

Beholding Rome and all her noble works,
  Were wonder-struck, what time the Lateran
  Above all mortal things was eminent,—

I who to the divine had from the human,
  From time unto eternity, had come,
  From Florence to a people just and sane,

With what amazement must I have been filled!
  Truly between this and the joy, it was
  My pleasure not to hear, and to be mute.

And as a pilgrim who delighteth him
  In gazing round the temple of his vow,
  And hopes some day to retell how it was,

So through the living light my way pursuing
  Directed I mine eyes o'er all the ranks,
  Now up, now down, and now all round about.

Faces I saw of charity persuasive,
  Embellished by His light and their own smile,
  And attitudes adorned with every grace.

The general form of Paradise already
  My glance had comprehended as a whole,
  In no part hitherto remaining fixed,

374

In fashion then as of a snow-white rose / Displayed itself to me the saintly host,

Par. XXXI, lines 1–2

And round I turned me with rekindled wish
  My Lady to interrogate of things
  Concerning which my mind was in suspense.

One thing I meant, another answered me;
  I thought I should see Beatrice, and saw
  An Old Man habited like the glorious people.

O'erflowing was he in his eyes and cheeks
  With joy benign, in attitude of pity
  As to a tender father is becoming.

And "She, where is she?" instantly I said;
  Whence he: "To put an end to thy desire,
  Me Beatrice hath sent from mine own place.

And if thou lookest up to the third round
  Of the first rank, again shalt thou behold her
  Upon the throne her merits have assigned her."

Without reply I lifted up mine eyes,
  And saw her, as she made herself a crown
  Reflecting from herself the eternal rays.

Not from that region which the highest thunders
  Is any mortal eye so far removed,
  In whatsoever sea it deepest sinks,

As there from Beatrice my sight; but this
  Was nothing unto me; because her image
  Descended not to me by medium blurred.

"O Lady, thou in whom my hope is strong,
  And who for my salvation didst endure
  In Hell to leave the imprint of thy feet,

Of whatsoever things I have beheld,
  As coming from thy power and from thy goodness
  I recognise the virtue and the grace.

Thou from a slave hast brought me unto freedom,
  By all those ways, by all the expedients,
  Whereby thou hadst the power of doing it.

Preserve towards me thy magnificence,
  So that this soul of mine, which thou hast healed,
  Pleasing to thee be loosened from the body."

Thus I implored; and she, so far away,
  Smiled, as it seemed, and looked once more at me;
  Then unto the eternal fountain turned.

And said the Old Man holy: "That thou mayst
  Accomplish perfectly thy journeying,
  Whereunto prayer and holy love have sent me,

Fly with thine eyes all round about this garden;
  For seeing it will discipline thy sight
  Farther to mount along the ray divine.

And she, the Queen of Heaven, for whom I burn
  Wholly with love, will grant us every grace,
  Because that I her faithful Bernard am."

As he who peradventure from Croatia
  Cometh to gaze at our Veronica,
  Who through its ancient fame is never sated,

But says in thought, the while it is displayed,
  "My Lord, Christ Jesus, God of very God,
  Now was your semblance made like unto this?"

Even such was I while gazing at the living
  Charity of the man, who in this world
  By contemplation tasted of that peace.

"Thou son of grace, this jocund life," began he,
  "Will not be known to thee by keeping ever
  Thine eyes below here on the lowest place;

But mark the circles to the most remote,
  Until thou shalt behold enthroned the Queen
  To whom this realm is subject and devoted."

I lifted up mine eyes, and as at morn
  The oriental part of the horizon
  Surpasses that wherein the sun goes down,

Thus, as if going with mine eyes from vale
  To mount, I saw a part in the remoteness
  Surpass in splendour all the other front.

And even as there where we await the pole
  That Phaeton drove badly, blazes more
  The light, and is on either side diminished,

So likewise that pacific oriflamme
  Gleamed brightest in the centre, and each side
  In equal measure did the flame abate.

And at that centre, with their wings expanded,
  More than a thousand jubilant Angels saw I,
  Each differing in effulgence and in kind.

Until thou shalt behold enthroned the Queen / To whom this realm is subject and devoted."

Par. XXXI, lines 116–117

I saw there at their sports and at their songs
  A beauty smiling, which the gladness was
  Within the eyes of all the other saints;

And if I had in speaking as much wealth
  As in imagining, I should not dare
  To attempt the smallest part of its delight.

Bernard, as soon as he beheld mine eyes
  Fixed and intent upon its fervid fervour,
  His own with such affection turned to her

That it made mine more ardent to behold.

Canto XXXII

*Saint Bernard guides Dante's gaze across the Rose's symmetry. A line of saintly
women, then men, extends from the throne of the Virgin, between Peter and Adam,
to that of John the Baptist, between Lucy and Saint Anne. On the left are the thrones
of the New Covenant saints (who believe in the coming of Christ) and the children
saved by baptism. On the right are the thrones of the Old Covenant saints (who
believed Christ had already come) and the pre-Christian children saved by Love. Saint
Bernard calls on Dante to join him in a prayer to the Virgin.*

Absorbed in his delight, that contemplator
  Assumed the willing office of a teacher,
  And gave beginning to these holy words:

"The wound that Mary closed up and anointed,
  She at her feet who is so beautiful,
  She is the one who opened it and pierced it.

Within that order which the third seats make
  Is seated Rachel, lower than the other,
  With Beatrice, in manner as thou seest.

Sarah, Rebecca, Judith, and her who was
  Ancestress of the Singer, who for dole
  Of the misdeed said, '*Miserere mei*,'

Canst thou behold from seat to seat descending
  Down in gradation, as with each one's name
  I through the Rose go down from leaf to leaf.

And downward from the seventh row, even as
  Above the same, succeed the Hebrew women,
  Dividing all the tresses of the flower;

Because, according to the view which Faith
  In Christ had taken, these are the partition
  By which the sacred stairways are divided.

Upon this side, where perfect is the flower
  With each one of its petals, seated are
  Those who believed in Christ who was to come.

Upon the other side, where intersected
  With vacant spaces are the semicircles,
  Are those who looked to Christ already come.

And as, upon this side, the glorious seat
  Of the Lady of Heaven, and the other seats
  Below it, such a great division make,

So opposite doth that of the great John,
  Who, ever holy, desert and martyrdom
  Endured, and afterwards two years in Hell.

And under him thus to divide were chosen
  Francis, and Benedict, and Augustine,
  And down to us the rest from round to round.

Behold now the high providence divine;
  For one and other aspect of the Faith
  In equal measure shall this garden fill.

And know that downward from that rank which cleaves
  Midway the sequence of the two divisions,
  Not by their proper merit are they seated;

But by another's under fixed conditions;
  For these are spirits one and all assoiled
  Before they any true election had.

Well canst thou recognise it in their faces,
  And also in their voices puerile,
  If thou regard them well and hearken to them.

Now doubtest thou, and doubting thou art silent;
  But I will loosen for thee the strong bond
  In which thy subtile fancies hold thee fast.

Within the amplitude of this domain
  No casual point can possibly find place,
  No more than sadness can, or thirst, or hunger;

For by eternal law has been established
  Whatever thou beholdest, so that closely
  The ring is fitted to the finger here.

And therefore are these people, festinate
  Unto true life, not 'sine causa' here
  More and less excellent among themselves.

The King, by means of whom this realm reposes
  In so great love and in so great delight
  That no will ventureth to ask for more,

In his own joyous aspect every mind
  Creating, at his pleasure dowers with grace
  Diversely; and let here the effect suffice.

And this is clearly and expressly noted
  For you in Holy Scripture, in those twins
  Who in their mother had their anger roused.

According to the colour of the hair,
  Therefore, with such a grace the light supreme
  Consenteth that they worthily be crowned.

Without, then, any merit of their deeds,
  Stationed are they in different gradations,
  Differing only in their first acuteness.

'Tis true that in the early centuries,
  With innocence, to work out their salvation
  Sufficient was the faith of parents only.

After the earlier ages were completed,
  Behoved it that the males by circumcision
  Unto their innocent wings should virtue add;

But after that the time of grace had come
  Without the baptism absolute of Christ,
  Such innocence below there was retained.

Look now into the face that unto Christ
  Hath most resemblance; for its brightness only
  Is able to prepare thee to see Christ."

On her did I behold so great a gladness
  Rain down, borne onward in the holy minds
  Created through that altitude to fly,

That whatsoever I had seen before
  Did not suspend me in such admiration,
  Nor show me such similitude of God.

And the same Love that first descended there,
  "Ave Maria, gratia plena," singing,
  In front of her his wings expanded wide.

Unto the canticle divine responded
  From every part the court beatified,
  So that each sight became serener for it.

"O holy father, who for me endurest
  To be below here, leaving the sweet place
  In which thou sittest by eternal lot,

Who is the Angel that with so much joy
  Into the eyes is looking of our Queen,
  Enamoured so that he seems made of fire?"

Thus I again recourse had to the teaching
  Of that one who delighted him in Mary
  As doth the star of morning in the sun.

And he to me: "Such gallantry and grace
  As there can be in Angel and in soul,
  All is in him; and thus we fain would have it;

Because he is the one who bore the palm
  Down unto Mary, when the Son of God
  To take our burden on himself decreed.

But now come onward with thine eyes, as I
  Speaking shall go, and note the great patricians
  Of this most just and merciful of empires.

Those two that sit above there most enrapture
  As being very near unto Augusta,
  Are as it were the two roots of this Rose.

He who upon the left is near her placed
  The father is, by whose audacious taste
  The human species so much bitter tastes.

Upon the right thou seest that ancient father
  Of Holy Church, into whose keeping Christ
  The keys committed of this lovely flower.

And he who all the evil days beheld,
  Before his death, of her the beauteous bride
  Who with the spear and with the nails was won,

Beside him sits, and by the other rests
  That leader under whom on manna lived
  The people ingrate, fickle, and stiff-necked.

Opposite Peter seest thou Anna seated,
  So well content to look upon her daughter,
  Her eyes she moves not while she sings Hosanna.

And opposite the eldest household father
  Lucia sits, she who thy Lady moved
  When to rush downward thou didst bend thy brows.

But since the moments of thy vision fly,
  Here will we make full stop, as a good tailor
  Who makes the gown according to his cloth,

And unto the first Love will turn our eyes,
  That looking upon Him thou penetrate
  As far as possible through his effulgence.

Truly, lest peradventure thou recede,
  Moving thy wings believing to advance,
  By prayer behoves it that grace be obtained;

Grace from that one who has the power to aid thee;
  And thou shalt follow me with thy affection
  That from my words thy heart turn not aside."

And he began this holy orison.

Canto XXXIII

*Saint Bernard implores the Virgin's intercession so that the pilgrim may be granted
the grace to contemplate God's divine majesty. Dante prays to be able to convey in his
writings some of the celestial glory he has witnessed. His soul grows calm with rapture
as his eyes penetrate the Divine Light. In it he sees the unity of Time, Creation, the
Three Persons in the One Essence (expressed as three interlocking circles) and the
fusion of Christ with the Godhead. Although Dante cannot describe the truth of what
he sees, his soul bears the stamp of Truth in God's Love.*

"Thou Virgin Mother, daughter of thy Son,
  Humble and high beyond all other creature,
  The limit fixed of the eternal counsel,

Thou art the one who such nobility
  To human nature gave, that its Creator
  Did not disdain to make himself its creature.

Within thy womb rekindled was the love,
  By heat of which in the eternal peace
  After such wise this flower has germinated.

Here unto us thou art a noonday torch
  Of charity, and below there among mortals
  Thou art the living fountain-head of hope.

Lady, thou art so great, and so prevailing,
  That he who wishes grace, nor runs to thee,
  His aspirations without wings would fly.

Not only thy benignity gives succour
  To him who asketh it, but oftentimes
  Forerunneth of its own accord the asking.

In thee compassion is, in thee is pity,
  In thee magnificence; in thee unites
  Whate'er of goodness is in any creature.

Now doth this man, who from the lowest depth
  Of the universe as far as here has seen
  One after one the spiritual lives,

Supplicate thee through grace for so much power
  That with his eyes he may uplift himself
  Higher towards the uttermost salvation.

And I, who never burned for my own seeing
  More than I do for his, all of my prayers
  Proffer to thee, and pray they come not short,

That thou wouldst scatter from him every cloud
  Of his mortality so with thy prayers,
  That the Chief Pleasure be to him displayed.

Still farther do I pray thee, Queen, who canst
  Whate'er thou wilt, that sound thou mayst preserve
  After so great a vision his affections.

Let thy protection conquer human movements;
  See Beatrice and all the blessed ones
  My prayers to second clasp their hands to thee!"

The eyes beloved and revered of God,
  Fastened upon the speaker, showed to us
  How grateful unto her are prayers devout;

Then unto the Eternal Light they turned,
  On which it is not credible could be
  By any creature bent an eye so clear.

And I, who to the end of all desires
  Was now approaching, even as I ought
  The ardour of desire within me ended.

Bernard was beckoning unto me, and smiling,
  That I should upward look; but I already
  Was of my own accord such as he wished;

Because my sight, becoming purified,
  Was entering more and more into the ray
  Of the High Light which of itself is true.

From that time forward what I saw was greater
  Than our discourse, that to such vision yields,
  And yields the memory unto such excess.

Even as he is who seeth in a dream,
  And after dreaming the imprinted passion
  Remains, and to his mind the rest returns not,

Even such am I, for almost utterly
  Ceases my vision, and distilleth yet
  Within my heart the sweetness born of it;

Even thus the snow is in the sun unsealed,
  Even thus upon the wind in the light leaves
  Were the soothsayings of the Sibyl lost.

O Light Supreme, that dost so far uplift thee
  From the conceits of mortals, to my mind
  Of what thou didst appear re-lend a little,

And make my tongue of so great puissance,
  That but a single sparkle of thy glory
  It may bequeath unto the future people;

For by returning to my memory somewhat,
  And by a little sounding in these verses,
  More of thy victory shall be conceived!

I think the keenness of the living ray
  Which I endured would have bewildered me,
  If but mine eyes had been averted from it;

And I remember that I was more bold
  On this account to bear, so that I joined
  My aspect with the Glory Infinite.

O grace abundant, by which I presumed
  To fix my sight upon the Light Eternal,
  So that the seeing I consumed therein!

I saw that in its depth far down is lying
  Bound up with love together in one volume,
  What through the universe in leaves is scattered;

Substance, and accident, and their operations,
  All interfused together in such wise
  That what I speak of is one simple light.

The universal fashion of this knot
  Methinks I saw, since more abundantly
  In saying this I feel that I rejoice.

One moment is more lethargy to me,
  Than five and twenty centuries to the emprise
  That startled Neptune with the shade of Argo!

My mind in this wise wholly in suspense,
  Steadfast, immovable, attentive gazed,
  And evermore with gazing grew enkindled.

In presence of that light one such becomes,
  That to withdraw therefrom for other prospect
  It is impossible he e'er consent;

Because the good, which object is of will,
  Is gathered all in this, and out of it
  That is defective which is perfect there.

Shorter henceforward will my language fall
  Of what I yet remember, than an infant's
  Who still his tongue doth moisten at the breast.

Not because more than one unmingled semblance
  Was in the living light on which I looked,
  For it is always what it was before;

But through the sight, that fortified itself
  In me by looking, one appearance only
  To me was ever changing as I changed.

Within the deep and luminous subsistence
  Of the High Light appeared to me three circles,
  Of threefold colour and of one dimension,

And by the second seemed the first reflected
  As Iris is by Iris, and the third
  Seemed fire that equally from both is breathed.

O how all speech is feeble and falls short
  Of my conceit, and this to what I saw
  Is such, 'tis not enough to call it little!

O Light Eterne, sole in thyself that dwellest,
  Sole knowest thyself, and, known unto thyself
  And knowing, lovest and smilest on thyself!

That circulation, which being thus conceived
  Appeared in thee as a reflected light,
  When somewhat contemplated by mine eyes,

Within itself, of its own very colour
  Seemed to me painted with our effigy,
  Wherefore my sight was all absorbed therein.

As the geometrician, who endeavours
  To square the circle, and discovers not,
  By taking thought, the principle he wants,

Even such was I at that new apparition;
  I wished to see how the image to the circle
  Conformed itself, and how it there finds place;

But my own wings were not enough for this,
  Had it not been that then my mind there smote
  A flash of lightning, wherein came its wish.

Here vigour failed the lofty fantasy:
  But now was turning my desire and will,
  Even as a wheel that equally is moved,

The Love which moves the sun and the other stars.